COLD STEEL DAYS

John R. White

"But the right to pursue happiness for so many is stripped away. It's raped. It's abused. It's taken by force, fraud, or coercion. It is sold for the momentary happiness of another."

~Ashton Kutcher

"An imbalance between rich and poor is the oldest and most fatal ailment of all republics."

~Plutarch

Money was never a big motivation for me, except as a way to keep score.
The real excitement is playing the game.

~President Donald J. Trump

Resist much, obey little.

~Walt Whitman

PART ONE

SOME TIME AGO

PROLOGUE

Ionian Sea,

Latitude 38°41'43.93"N

Longitude 20°32'16.18"E

June 16, 2015.

Anchored in ninety-four feet of water offside an island so small that it had no name, the Greek registered yacht, *C.F. Kane*, enjoying seventy-five-degree Fahrenheit air. The vessel was the world's largest in its class at seven hundred and two feet long. The ship cost Anis one point two billion, or enough money to feed a family for two-hundred-and eighty-nine years. The Kane possessed ninety-four thousand horsepower engines and was capable of speeds of thirty-five knots, plenty of speed to get you to someplace where you could do nothing if you wanted.

Today they enjoyed the best weather for scuba diving; a perfectly blue sky and near-transparent water below them promised a successful day of underwater exploration. The Turkish built yacht had twenty-four Cristiano Gatto designed staterooms, though it seldom filled more than six of them at any time. The Kane's crew, having washed off the guest's gear, now resupplied the air tanks. Over on, the fantail conversations were had of where to dive next.

Anis had the game downloaded from last night's broadcast to his laptop and was now watching as the Kings were battling the New York Rangers; 3-2 in double overtime granted them a 4-1 series win, bringing them their second championship. Closing the lid, she stretched her legs. At forty-two, Anis Mikos Papadopoulos was in the best shape of her life, physically, mentally, financially.

Anis' company, Axiomatic Space Technologies, was doing very well. Her profits last quarter beat her old Princeton Alum Jeff's Bezos's money count by seventy per cent. Anis's revelation of a, of course, patented, chaos-based Light-Jump propulsion technology by Axiom was the biggest news in a generation. The Light-Jump meant that the technology could allow, theoretically, humanity to travel from Earth to Mars in days, not months. Governments and corporations were now throwing her cash to finance the next phase. Bezos and Musk were both annoyed and excited.

Nevertheless, Anis was not very joyful because many people were furious at her. After all, much of what she would need to construct the test craft would require an exorbitant amount of tin, tungsten, and tantalum. The protests were insane, and liberal politicians pushing their agendas of green technology and hyper environmentalism were driving her nuts. Every country she needed to deal with were now acrimoniously slapping new restrictions on her mining of '3 T' minerals because those materials would come from so-called "Bood Metal Mines", now controlled by Congolese militias with extremely poor human rights. Naturally, all the protestors were tweeting and posting on phones and computers using the same metals they were protesting.

Her investors were pissing her off, they wanted the electronics, but they didn't want any visible blood on their hands. Anis had been so aggravated that she had sent out a (now-infamous) Tweet to her business manager saying that her investors could 'Shut up, give more money to Greenpeace and then tell them to go screw.' It was supposed to be in private, but it went public, exploding on Twitter, she cringed, stocks fell by sixteen in two hours, but by close of the week, they were now up another up seventeen points.

The Wall Street Journal reported that Anis had, of recent, been shifting her investments into land purchases in the United States. The claim from Anis's public relations spokeswoman was that she was moving into agro-engineering. Her critics believed she was seemingly trying to do damage control on her image. Anis had been buying up and investing in derelict neighbours in the southwest, paying three times a home's value to its owners. She then had her company fix them up with state-of-the-art home networking technology. She sold the houses to those unemployed and gave them jobs in local construction she had initiated in the Arizona region. Other green Axiom operations in the area consisted of harvesting water from the air, erecting hydrogen power plants. With the insight of local Indigenous tribes, Axiom engineers worked with ecologists to see if it might be possible to build an experimental town underground, thus preventing future damage to the surface environment. The reaction was incredible and went from twelve per cent to point-oh, oh two. Starting pay was twenty dollars an hour and complete medical, dental, and mental health coverage. After ninety-days, one was invested not just in a 401K's but a pension plan as well. Fox News, Rush Limbaugh and Newsmax accused her of being corrupted by the liberals and losing her balls.

None of that bothered her at all, and she was still her same self, not giving a rat's ass about their opinion. She had a plan.

The card game had started early, about four-thirty. After a day of diving, jet-skiing, and other more lurid past-times, the girlfriends, boyfriends, wives and husbands were all sent off via seaplane to Agrinio for some fun. The grownups needed to talk.

Dinner was served, prepared by chefs flown in from Schloss Schauenstein. Accompanying the meal, a bottle of 1820 Juglar Cuvee was poured. After the table was cleared, one of Anis's servants brought out an oaken box that held the cards and chips. The buy-in was a hundred thousand, and it was after playing several hands before politics took over the conversation. Usually, that was frowned up, but this time Papadopoulos didn't seem to mind. in fact, she seemed happy about it.

The sun had set enough that the ship's lights came on. Anis used the controls on the table panel to brighten them more.

"Anyone else here concerned about 2016?" William Wicket of Hyperware Computing resources sighed. "I know I am. These Net Neutrality advocates are pissing me off. I'm throwing buckets of my money in order to shut that crap down. Some of them want to tax online sale," The lank man threw himself into a chaise lounge. "Hell, I saw it coming. We all saw that coming."

"I'm not worried about it," Harry Newsom of Newsom Defence Contracts. "With all these shootings, gun sales are up. Whenever gun sales go up, it corresponds to a rise in GOP votes. Fear is money,"

"Not everywhere," Miguel Hernandez of Brazil's Comunicaciones Uno, the largest telecommunications firm in the world. While that name wasn't well known, all of his subsidiary companies were. For example, Vixen TCI was his most established cellular network, companies in American and Europe. He worked tightly with several social media and videogame firms around the world. With his Quintessence Gaming platform, players could start a game home on their Q-5 systems, keep playing it on their phones, get in their car and play hands-free to their buddy's place, go back on the phone and then sit down on their couch and never lose a turn. If they were in a group chat, all of them could even order pizza and drinks, pay bitcoin and never get up except to use the can.

All that freedom was possible through a series of facial and vocal recognition software tied to Global Positioning System tracking. Sales preferences were stored and then sold; personal info sales comprised fifty-nine per cent of Communion Uno's income. Hernandez was not a fool; personal info was liquid gold.

Hernandez was not alone in his knowledge. It was widely speculated that tech firms hired, trained. It deployed black hat hackers to attack other firms' data and create panic, thus sending people flying to data privacy companies. Then those companies would do the same. Data Security Vendor' A' would attack Data security Vendor 'B', sending concerned customers back and forth, paying higher and higher fees. Hernandez once told CNN's Anderson Cooper in an interview, "That there is no such thing as secure personal info; it doesn't exist and never will.' He wasn't lying.

"Liberalism is rising, as is environmental awareness and with the water now flooding the coastlines, glacial melting and shrinking rain forests. Fear is a force that you cannot control." A handsome man in his sixties, Miguel was clean-shaven except for an impressive Sam Elliott moustache. Wearing a white linen short-sleeve shirt with matching shorts, he pulled out a silver cigar tube from his breast pocket. Extracting it slowly, everyone focused on him. He withdrew a cigar, cut the end and then lit it. Taking a deep puff, he held it out.

"This is Gurkha Royal Courtesan. It cost one million dollars, and I have twenty-five more like it in my cabin." He motioned for the others to sit down.

Michael Logan, who was a construction mogul, smiled and pulled out a pack of Marlboro. "I need to upgrade."

"These cigars could feed and shelter the working population of Juazeiro back home. Five years maybe. They would not have to worry about food, power, and doctors – five years. To me, a mere idle pleasure." He took a long drag and then exhaled a wispy grey smoke ring.

"What are you getting at?" Newsom snapped. "Going soft on us too?"

"Quite the opposite. I'm just reminding you good people who we are; nobility in a world of peasants. Quit acting like children."

Newsom looked disgusted, a look that suited him. The arms dealer was a hundred and fifty pounds overweight, bald as water eroded rock and about as pleasant. He was, however, rich and powerful knew politics better than any of them.

A cool breeze blew across them, and the sound of the splashing of water turned their heads; a sperm whale had breached and sprayed. It was closing at nine pm, and the sky was a dark violet with the stars showing magnificently. There face now illuminated by the crystal chandelier.

"Calm down, Enrique, my friend." He waved his thoughts away with a cigar. "No, not all. I shall let Senorita Anis explain."

"Don't piss any pinko hippy crap at me. That's not what I come here for." The American shook his head. "I can get that crap from my daughter." No one said anything.

Newsom was having a month; his daughter, the now world-famous Rachel Lee, widow, had, until recently gun dealer's chief spokesman. That all changed three weeks ago when Rachel and her husband were in a bar that a lone gunman shot up.

The shooter had discovered that a seven-term New York senator would be visiting a Florida bar owned by her cousin. The internet is a beautiful thing about talking about your opinion, family life and summer vacations. The Local news said there was going to a big party and a big announcement that Tuesday, at seven pm, and everyone should tune in. The shooter saw this and then proceeded to long for a trip himself.

He most assuredly wasn't an evil person; it's just that it was taking forever for him to get VA help. His pharmacy was backlogged and understaffed. Twice he had been out of meds for his PTSD induced bipolar disorder - brought on by years of combat extensions. Jackson Wilson had entered the Connecticut marine reserves at eighteen because his folks didn't want him to have crushing student debt. He was going in the reserves his recruiter told him, "You'll be fine. It's highly unlikely he would ever deploy; besides, you're going to be working in an office." That was generally a true statement, as his MOS was Thirty-five Foxtrot, an Intelligence Analyst. But before completing basic training, his MOS request was then overruled because they needed more troops in Afghanistan.

He had signed up for two years but got stuck for five. After watching battle buddy after battle buddy die, he walked into a minefield where he proceeded to empty his Squad automatic weapon. He was stopped only by his gun jamming. Wilson was unaware that the minefield was for training and the explosives were all dummies. No one walked him through his discharge, health counselling, or physicals like his recruiter had when he enlisted. No, he came home, was sent for an eval and then given a phone number to call.

Staff Sargent Wilson had not been able to get any of the following medicine for three weeks – Wellbutrin, Lexapro, Vistaril to reduce anxiety – Seroquel, or Trazodone – which he needed to sleep. Those medicines cost him five times the amount he made each month on government disability. Because there was a miscommunication over money earned by him nine months ago, he was booted off his insurance coverage. His parents pleaded with him to get him back on because he was having issues. They review would be in six months. They apologised and said that perhaps their church could help with his meds. His nervous mother told her husband to have the Sargent's weapons locked up at her brothers' house. While this was a short-term solution, it was an imperfect one. The night before the shooting, Jack told his uncle he was on his meds and said he would take all of his weapons into town for sale.

He lied.

Having not followed up on the event through social media, he could not have known that the Senator had to cancel the trip because of a vote. Thus, when he walked into the pub wearing an improved outer tactical vest, Kevlar helmet, five hundred rounds of ammo in banana magazines, and sticks of dynamite (everything purchased legally), he saw that she was not there.

Outside of Disneyland in Orlando Newscom's daughter, Rachel had been posting for a selfie with her husband of three days when she saw movement in the camera. The gunman stepped into the room and looked for the Senator – the source of all his woes.

It was the Senator who made commercials about young men serving their country in the war.

It was she who lied and said he would be home in a year, two at the latest.

Furthermore, it was that woman's responsibility that Wilson was stationed where the little girl with the IEDs strapped to her chest blew up in front of him. Everything was the politician's fault – and she wasn't here.

Newsom's son-in-law James Lee, an Orange County sheriff, had received competent and accurate mental health crisis training – for situations such as this. He saw that this man was clearly in crisis, in pain - and yes, volatile. His bearing, posture, haircut and voice screamed U.S. Marine. James loved marines and all grunts. He prayed to God that he would not have to use deadly force on another vet. He may have to, but he first had an opportunity and the responsibility to attempt a de-escalation of the situation.

Ordering the Sargent to stand down, James directed the shooter in a voice and tone that the soldier should immediately recognise and react to, hopefully, obediently. As was required by the Orange County Sherriff's department, the cop had his concealed weapon on him, on which he placed his hand. Unsnapping the clasp, he did not yet draw the gun.

"Marine, what's your name?" Even from twenty feet away, Officer Lee could tell saw that his eyes were wide and panicked. Cell phone captured the exchange when the Police officer smiled and spoke to his brother warrior.

"Got to stand down, man. This isn't the war. This is home. It's okay; you're safe. You're in the world, bro." Officer Lee had a handsome smile. Confident and secure in his conviction that he knew how far he was okay to close the distance, Lee kept his hands in plain view.

"You have anyone to talk to, grunt? You can talk to me. Just lower the weapon, and I promise you, and I will walk out of here like men. Like soldiers." Lee took one more step, and for a moment, it looked like Wilson was going to lower the weapon. Lee smiled. "Just hand the weapon to me -"

News footage showed that Lee was a mere sixteen inches away and that the gunman had, yes, lowered the barrel momentarily. The officer had been by the book when Wilson spun and fired his legally owned Newton Defence Contract Sport Model II 2 AR-15 Semi-Auto. The Deputy had been shot upward from his chin.

By the time he had taken his own life, some thirteen minutes later, seventeen people lay dead. This included a pregnant woman and her two children, sixteen and seventeen years of age.

On him were six homemade explosives and a suicide note. The note essentially said — "what does it matter if my country doesn't care anymore?"

As a result, Rachel Newton Lee, daughter of billionaire Enrique Newton, quit her job, but not before liquidating all of her person stacks, 401Ks, and cashing out her pension. Subsequently, she donated them to ACLU and a chosen Gun control advocacy group for who she said she would work for minimum wage. Rachel W. Lee also leaked to ABC New twenty-three years of internal memos, emails, mortality studies and most importantly, highly detailed political donation to whom and for how much. Because of his iniquities and cruelties, her father was uninvited to the funeral.

Anis's phone buzzed, and she released a hearty laugh.

"... and Donald Trump just announced his candidacy for president."

"Oh, for Christ's sake," Wicket shook his head. "That's going to be four years of democrats right there."

"Oh no, he'll win. I've arranged that." Anis smiled as she poured herself a drink." Newsom looked aghast. "Why in hell would you back that moron?"

"Distraction. Trump is such a mess that that man will keep the media spinning for years."

"So?" Wicket shook his head. "Why?"

Anis sipped her drink and then set it down next to the candle in the table's centre.

"Think about it; between all of us here, we possess eight-five per cent of the wealth of the world. As of today. Right now." Anis shrugged. "So why in Hell do we sit and listen to the other fifteen per cent whine and complain. I mean, seriously, there's not one of us present that actually cares anything about them."

"Now, wait a minute," Michael Logan slammed his hand down. "That's not true; I give grants for over seventeen-million dollars through Chicago and other cities. I grew up on the streets, and I haven't forgotten it yet."

"How much are you worth?" Anis looked at her phone. "Oh yes, your company's worth is three hundred and twenty-two billion. Your net value is fifty-two billion," She snapped the phone closed, so you gave seventeen five?"

Logan approached his lips and stared at his cigarette.

Newsom nodded," So what you're saying is why are we not running the joint? No government could do a single thing about it if we stand up and take over."

"Might I remind you that they have armies and nuclear weapons? There is MOSSAD, the NSA, the Chinese government, and, oh, I don't know, tons of people with nuclear weapons."

"So," Anis shrugged. "Where do you think they get those weapons?" She looked over at the very smug Arms dealer.

"So – they'd kill us all."

"They can't if we do this." Papadopoulos put her finger on the control panel and turned the lights off, descending the gathered group into darkness.

Chapter 1

Styx City,

Arizona.

Anis sat behind her computer bank in her fifty-room mansion two miles underneath the small mining town of Obregon in the Cargo Muchacho Mountains of the Imperial Valley. Her villa was located in the experimental city of Styx, which had taken them five years, and two-point four trillion dollars to build.

The Population of Styx when the doors opened to the media, on the record, was thirty-seven thousand, two hundred and three. Another thirteen thousand people lived nearby. Styx Proper had several biodiversity science labs, a hectare of agriculture, and enough livestock to provide fresh milk, eggs, and other needs for the entire population.

Anis had summoned all of her workers to be present on location and then sealed the doors. Only a of the elite knew what was going to happen.

Civilisation ended on Sunday evening, August 13, 2023, at 11:59 and fifty-nine seconds Greenwich Mean Time. Anis's latent computer virus, which has been subtly and invisibly installed in global digital architecture over the past several years, went activate at the execution of one keystroke. Power grids across the world ceased to function. Every form of mass power system stopped; coal, gas, geothermal, nuclear - it didn't matter.

The human clockspring mechanism unwound rapidly.

Anis received congratulatory emails from her six partners.

Immediately military forces worldwide could no longer contact or communicate with each other. The civilian grid went inert, and car crashes heralded the beginning. Shortly after that, aircraft struggled to stay aloft and land. With no way to communicate with air traffic controllers, landing became chaotic and lethal. Jetfighter aircraft, only able to fly with the aid of complex digital controls, spun out of control. Undersea, nuclear submarines reactors no longer monitored and controlled went critical and began to melt down.

The earliest recorded riot began seven hours afterwards occurred in El Rodeo prison in Venezuela. Within two hours after the dark fell, thirty-seven guards lay dead as the blood started to flow. This may have been the first, but like the malware itself, riots across the planet spread. There would be no rapid response, no social media call to action, and no calls to 911; none were possible. There was a worldwide silence that fell across the world, shattered only by the screams of the dead and dying.

The so-called First World declared martial law almost immediately.

By Day Two, the United States was in open civil war. Generations of racial animus and class warfare exploded. Every law and law enforcement forces were quickly overwhelmed when, in the United States, three hundred and sixty-three million guns were now unfettered by legislation or regulation. With no one to stop them, armed fringe militias took to the opportunity to advance their conspiracy-laden agendas. Within a matter of days, thousands of bodies littered the streets, stores, and neighbourhoods.

The Russian federation fared no better; their government collapsed within seventy-two hours. The oppressed poor rose against a brutal and corrupt Federation Council. The Russian military quickly began a fight between those still loyal to Putin controlled forces and rogue military leaders seeking to gain personal control and settle grudges. Saudi Arabia, India, Europe, South and Central America all began imploding within weeks. By New Year's Day 2024, the entire planet was at some form or another of bloody conflict. Except for Canada, which carefully stayed out of the chaos. China would require a solid year to collapse utterly.

Within five years after what would become known as The Shutdown, three billion people lay dead across the earth. Technically the computers listed it as 3,567, 544,675 +/- 70 million.

Exactly as Anis Mikos Papadopoulos predicted.

Chapter 2

Hong Kong Island,

March 19th, 2059.

Edgar Winters grew up in Hong Kong, where it was nought but a mere shadow of its former magnificence. The city lights no longer shone as bright; the electronic billboards remained mute half the time - electricity being better diverted elsewhere. He lived off The Peak, Mount Kellet Road. An educated man who anonymously wrote blunt social criticism and revolutionary dialogue about social inequality, such as Arcologies' abuses and the caste system's brutality, Edgar winters was a scant over eighteen years old. His parents were long gone; his African-Asian father had died in the war – which one he couldn't tell you. His Chinese mother was in some faraway gulag. He knew it was just outside of the Nanyang pseudo-arcology, which was now the most significant population centre on Earth, even after the Democracy War. The area outside remained a haven for insurgents and protestors still.

Edgar had been seven years old when his family has torn asunder. Friends of his parents had taken him in and raised him as one of his own. Once his brown skin might have caused him to be the recipient of prejudice and violence, no more since the focus was now on the 'Us' – meaning non-corpers, and 'Them.'

Edgar spoke all forms of Mandarin; Yue, Xiang, then Min, Gan, Wu, the Kejia Hakka dialects, and English. It made him more valuable to him and his cause. It was remarkable to him that his words were posted on walls and buildings. That this was true and that he could even now walk down any street, and no one would have a clue who he was – or so he thought.

Edgar enjoyed a hot bowl of French minced fish ball noodle soup at Tsim Chai Kee in the Jade Centre; in his hand, he read the Mandarin translation of Upton Sinclair's 'The Jungle.'

"Gěi nín dài lái bu biàn qǐng yuánliàng," A tall white man of indeterminate age bowed.

"Hé fúwù wǒ?" Edgar looked up. "I can speak English if that is more accommodating?"

The man bowed again. "Thank you. Again, I apologise for the interruption," The man sat down on a green metal chair. "Would I be correct in assuming that you would are Mister E. Winters?" The man was discreet with his name, and Edgar appreciated that.

"Why do you ask?" He replied with caution as he set his book down and ignored his soup.

"Yes, of course. I have been extremely impressed and moved by your – pardon me, Mister Winters – writings. I long to see our world have a more unified status quo. I just so happen to be in a position to help such people as Mr Winters to gain a more significant audience. What would you think of a position in which your keen mind could have access to unlimited access to knowledge and communication?"

"I would say that that is already possible if you dwell in any domed city and since I am neither desirous of living or being hired by any such place, which you would know if you are at all familiar with my work. Therefore, my remaining choices would be that you are being disingenuous. Regardless I have no interest in what you proffer since I am not he." The statement was polite but firm. The man smiled.

"Let's dispense with the façade. If I were a Government or Corper agent, you would either be dead or incarcerated. Since you are neither, we should speak as gentleman do; directly and honestly."

"Tóngyì," Edgar surrendered.

"What I am is an admirer of your works. However, you currently do not have the means to get your message out to those who matter, those inside of the corporations."

"The Arcology masters don't print or even allow access to my writings. My books are not exactly on the best sellers list in The Corporations." He pulled his soup back over and recommenced eating and reading, showing that he wished the conversation to be over.

"There was a time when young revolutionaries such as you clamoured to get their books widely distributed."

Edgar leaned back and shook his head. "If you persist in this conversation, I will listen on the proviso that you recompense me for my meal and time." Tilting his head in annoyance, he stared at the man. "Before we proceed, you know my name, but you have not offered yours or the name of your business."

The man gave a slight bow and then straightened up. "My apologies, I am David Severenson."

"The so-called Commissar," Edgar nodded. "is a revolutionary yourself. If I am correct, you have been protesting the military power of the Arcologies, not so much human rights violations."

"Are they not one and the same?"

"Since the conversation shows no sign of ending, if you wish to persist in your consumption of my time, I must request that you recompense me at the rate of four hundred yen per hour." Edgar crossed his arms, fully expecting that his outrageous fee would shut this annoyingly *Mòshēng rén* up.

"Nà shì bùkě jiēshòu de!" Severenson shook his head and disgust but did not leave. "You wound my mainz. Not even a yín chóng would find such an offer to you respectful. Your time is far more valuable be that. I must insist that you accept no less than five thousand yen per hour.

Edgar, to his credit, did not so much as raise an eyebrow, although his inner monologue was *'Wǒ Cào!'*

"I would not shame your generosity. I accept your payment," Edgar did not ask for the money upfront to indicate that he believed the man to be a liar would disgrace both of them, especially if he wasn't lying.

"Please proceed."

"I represent an organisation called 'The Watchers. I am prepared to do whatever it takes to get you to join us.'"

Chapter 3

Michigan/Ohio Border

Toledo, Ohio

December 20th, 2070

They crossed over the border uneventfully; just another group of Federal Express trucks driving double and triples down old Seventy-five. It was near Christmas, and people were still shopping. Granted, Christmas in Toledo was always different in the big cities than where the poor lived in the outskirts. There would be damn few synthetic animals or holovees. Kids would still have to watch on flat screens. Likewise, for businesses, incoming water extractors were few. A water reclamation unit could make all the difference between a one-hundred-dollar water bill and a five thousand dollar one. Most of the city was still getting its water from the lake, but since The Shutdown, the great lakes' water level had dropped well over seventy per cent. Water was life, and when a pump was pulling water hard, it made neighbouring cities annoyed. Ohio rated a higher water draw than Michigan because granted had Erie, Superior, and Huron to draw on. It sounded rational, but The Chi-Town Arcology and Canada's Sudbury Mega-arc had sabotaged the Wolverine state's three significant pumps on multiple occasions. The Governor of Michigan had reached his breaking point when water starvation deaths broke five hundred in one week. He did what he had to do; Consequences are damned.

"Half-back here, we have crossed the border. So far nothing, we will exit to Woodville road, hope on Fifty-one and take Nebraska Avenue out to the Richard Cordray facility."

"ETA?"

"Roads here are worse than back home. Nebraska is supposed to be smooth travelling since the National Guard maintains it. Figure twenty minutes."

"When GPS shows you one minute out. Air support will make their passes with Noxam-720 will be dropped. You've had your injections but use all chemical agent protocols."

"Understood Quarterback."

In the sky about them amongst the millions of stars, not a few crafted by man; objects both subtle and gross. Many were mere particles cast off from the mortals below desires to conquer space and Earth below it; rocket stages, minute bits of metal moving at winged Mercury's own pace. However, they're also, in the cape of Noctis objects, artificial objects crafted to remain invisible from both man and machine did as bidden. There, moving about the sky like the silent guardians they were, the Metatron observed everything.

"Come in, Arcadia." The presence of a battered novel muffled the speakers' voice laying on it, the black paper cover with a rent running through golden-winged wrench and hammer. The man on watch was drowsy, his crew all on downtime sleeping in their bunks.

"Say again. Come in Arcadia Station." Came a second and more irritated request.

On the second utterance, the on-duty watch snapped awake and answered hurriedly.

"Command, this is Arcadia. Major Uriel here," The voice was bored, for the last two months, most incoming messages were minor annoyances; calls to adjust attitude, warnings of errant detritus to avoid.

"I have a C-O-O-E directive."

"Confirmed; incoming Charlie-Oscar-Oscar-Echo directive. I stand ready to receive." The Captain straightened up and grabbed a pencil and a pad of paper. Electronics may fail, but you can always trust paper and pencil. He prepared to write with his right hand, and with his left, he positioned his finger to punch in the required code.

"Please provide command cypher to confirm the legitimacy of sender."

"Command cypher is 'Ignorance is the curse of God.' Counter cypher?"

Uriel tapped the code in and then looked at his screen for the response command.

"Chaos is a friend of mine."

"Confirmed. Order is 'Angelfall'. Coordinates 41o.38'20.56 N. 83o 22'12.60 W. Elevation 599."

Uriel, to his credit, did not require a 'Say again'.

"Read back?"

"Forty-one degrees, thirty-eight minutes, twenty-point five-six seconds North, by eighty-three degrees and twenty-two-point one-two point six minutes. Elevation five-nine-nine."

"Immediate interdiction. Five transport vehicles. Judgement is final. Decent six."

Thirty-three seconds later, his choir descended at terminal velocity through the northern skies leaving three fiery trails in their wake.

Private Stephen Bryans was returning to base from two days of R&R from the guard base. Tooling down the road listening to some kick-ass country in his Silver and Grey Buckeyes Jeep, he fell behind a freaking road train of five vehicles up ahead of them. They were driving an exact fifty-five miles an hour, and there was simply no way he was getting around them. To add insult to injury, the radio dissolved into a rain of static.

God, I hate Fed-X.

On that note, Stephen slammed on his brakes as he caught the sight of not one but six meteors screaming through the air, looking like they would impact less than two klicks from here. Standing up in his seat, he grabbed hold of the roll bar. Lowering his sunglasses, he prepared to watch a once in a lifetime astrological event. He pulled out his phone and started recording.

The boys in the barracks will never believe this.

As soon as they impacted upon the shattering ground, Stephen watched the FedEx trucks convoy lift two feet off the ground and then, slamming back down, skid across the road on the road. The private's jaw dropped open as he watched as five fourteen feet tall monoliths in smouldering crimson turn and opened fire upon the trucks. Standing behind them was a twenty-five-foot towering titan. He knew what they were, having been briefed on the Watchers not six months ago; their armour cooled, revealing a blood-red paint scheme and a chest plate with a golden emblem of a winged eye.

Metatron, the monolithic soldiers, were the ruthless enforcers of the Watcher's heavy hand. Grabbing his phone, he called into Fort Cordray.

The Metatron opened fire on the new intruders with a fusillade of .950 JDJ bullets striking with a rate of fire of five hundred and eighty rounds per minute. The rear vehicles suffered the quickest fate, the shells turning the soldiers into an orgy of blood and flesh. Halfback, in the lead position, slammed on the brakes and ordered the men to disembark immediately. The vehicles' sides dropped, and the heavy weapons crew leapt out, a fraction of a second before the closet immortal moved to gain position and fire.

Half-back, whose name was Captain Jacob Goldman, ordered the missile teams to open fire. The six-man squad used the greasy smoke of the fifty-two-foot-long trucks. Each truck contained an officer and three fire teams. The back two trucks obliterated, both struck with swift vengeance, while vehicle two had deployed at least one squad. The Metatron was now coming under sustained fire from a Missile team and heavy machine squads.

Major Uriel, in his two-and-a-half-story armour, stood back and watched as Corporal Raguelr laid down suppressing fire which all but disintegrated the lightly armoured vehicles, as well as any unlucky soldiers still aboard.

Captain Goldman spilt out onto the ground and ordered his men to start returning fire. He activated his head command, yelled over the incoming fire.

"We need air support now. We are taking heavy fire from Watcher Metatron!"

"Halfback, we have them in sight and are ten seconds out. Running back, switch to anti-vehicle status. Halfback fall back to waypoint Two. We will send in extraction forces once the threat's eliminated."

"Understood Quarterback. Fall back." With angry thunder, Goldman's fire team emptying Armor Piercing Capped ammunition. Goldman could see that one of the Metatron took sustained damage, and he moved into the dense smoke for cover.

"Quarterback, this is Chalk 1B. I have Watchers in sight; I am now engaging." Chalk 1B was leading a team of fast movers, which was initially ordered to pacify the military base–not this. "Switching to HEAT shells now."

"Chalk 1B be aware that target base is now spinning up Surface to Air defences." The pilot looked to his East and saw that two missiles had just been let loose.

A sharp tone cut through the cockpit as the missile Lock alarm erupted. "Break, Break, break! Chalk 2 and 3, take out those damn SAMs!" Chalk 1B deployed flares. It didn't help.

Captain Uriel turned to see the incoming jets and then opened his back-mounted weapon. The human Mounted Phalanx CWIS weapon immediately began to fire 20×102 mm Armor-piercing tungsten penetrator rounds. His suit was as large as it was for the Phalanx weapon system was ten feet in height itself and contained an ammo box that held six thousand rounds. Uriel's suit tracked the lead vehicle as it jinked back and forth, trying to lose a missile. Uriel would take two seconds to lock onto the Jet, and as he did, he unleashed a three-second burst at a rate of fifty rounds per second. With a muzzle velocity of three thousand six-hundred feet per second (Mach three point two one), the aircraft stood no chance and was ripped apart like a quail before British country squires. The last thing, the Chalk 1B saw a red flash of a targeting light, and then the windscreen exploding inward. No chute was seen.

Uriel watched as heavy missile fire blew Corporal Raguelr's right arm off. The Metatron commander watched it spiral through the air like a Maple samara helicopter. He was unconcerned as Uriel knew that the Type VIII Angelfall suit would immediately cauterize the wound and seal it; three hits of Morph would make sure he felt no pain. Uriel turned his attention to Raguelr's assailant and leaping over a burning deuce and a half, landing on a missileer. The soldier became past under the two-and-a-half ton Metatron.

Sargent Cassiel led privates Hofniel and Remiel around the lead trucks and had them launch a salvo of smart grenades. The impacts shredded Captain Goodman's squad, and an adjacent unit were trying to set up a recoilless rifle. Private second-class Samael made short work of that with a type ten flamethrower which threw out white phosphorus gelatine. In less than eight minutes, what would now be known as the Cordray Massacre was over.

Uriel turned to see the remaining two fighters, one a smoky grey cloud in the air, and the third aircraft retreat over Lake Erie. Not one had gotten a shot off at them.

"Captain, all garrisons are eliminated." Corporal Maalik confidently informed Uriel.

"Excellent," Uriel nodded and then redirected his conversation. "Commissar, please be advised that mission is golden. Repeat Mission is golden."

"Watcher Actual here, return to launch base Massillon." The Commissar leaned over and ended the live image stream to the world leader's screens.

"Let this serve as an example; should any of you break the peace that we have steadfastly held for you. Dwell on the fact that was but one small unit of many thousands of battalions at my disposal." He shook his head at the screens. "Let us keep the treaty scared, or you will truly feel the wrath of the Watchers."

A gauntleted hand clicked the transmission off.

Chapter 4

At Sea.

April , 2073

"He is a complicated subject," Anne held the clipboard in her tawny manicured hand. She was tall at 6'4, possessed cheekbones that could cut glass, and her dark brown eyes mahogany in colour poured over the tablet. "But somehow, you were already aware of that, I'm sure."

"Mm Hmmm," Landmesser waved his hand for her to continue.

"His health is perfect; no signs of Parkinson's, Alzheimer's, or signs of inheriting mental disorders. He eats regularly, has healthy evacuations." She flipped through more papers. "He's patently using genetic manipulation and routinely at that."

"He always was an arrogant bastard. Funny, but vain." Landmesser sat up and topped off his coffee into his vintage Dr Who mug. No chips, cracks or dings.

"As to his personal Habits; there are no tendencies towards gambling or addictive natures. He's focused to the point of compulsive – which we also knew. Reads an average of a hundred books a year; many re-reads, though. He's in the ninety-eight percentile of accuracy with firearms and ninety-three as regards accuracy with the longbow. He still fences and wrestles."

"I never understood the virtue of wrestling. You pin a guy, sure. When he gets up his still going to kick your ass."

"Anyway," Anne sighed, "His strength is excellent, and while last year he could bench press 2two hundred and forty-two per cent of his body weight six times before petering out – the last reports say they doubt he could break two-ten right now."

"How is this relevant?"

"He's ageing but way better than you."

"Sexuality?"

"I thought you knew him?" She inquired.

"Time changes us all,"

"Hetero in as far as I can tell. Never seen any fluidity. No fetishes; very vanilla. Non-predatory. He doesn't avail himself of offers when tendered that I have seen. Not to say that he isn't getting laid behind the scenes."

"That wouldn't surprise me at all," he chuckled.

"As far as I can tell, that's his Achilles heel; loneliness."

"Go on."

"He is a brooder. While he has vast power, that actually doesn't draw as many people to you as one might think. Power is frightening, and you can't build a solid, healthy relationship on fear. So even if he has a sexual partner, odds are it's not fulfilling."

"Nope. "

Anne gave a small chuckle. "So, you're suggesting we find him a girlfriend. You want me to screw him?"

"Not quite my proposal," The old man shook his head in disappointment. "Being a friend will be probably sufficient," He looked up at Anne. "You always told me you don't have enough friends."

Anne set her clipboard down. "You've got to be kidding me."

"Not it all. If you can think of anyone that could do the job better, you tell me. Look, I'm not trying to pimp you out," Landmesser frowned.

"Sure, as hell seems like you are."

"I'm asking you to do is infiltrate the organization, yes. I have never seen a better person at spycraft than you; you're patient, dedicated and focused."

"Flatterer," Anne shook her head.

"If we have someone inside that knows his psychology and can play on it, we can have a hell of a better chance of disturbing the nest." Look, if you, for some odd reason, sleep with him or anyone get involved with anyone else for that matter – that's your business, but what I need more than anything is for you to gain his trust and confidence."

"Fine," Anne threw her hands in the air. "I hate when you make rational articulated arguments."

"It's not for me, Anne; this is for all of us." Landmesser stood up and walked over to her.

"I'll miss you."

"I'll miss you too, old man."

NOW

Chapter 5

Massillon,

The Ohio Badlands,

February 2, 2075

Outside.

There are times in your life when you are forced to make changes that pull you in directions that you feel you should never have to endure. That said, such times produce the more excellent harvests of one's life; this was such a day for Helen.

Helen BonHomme was perfect, like all the Omega Corporation citizens, or as the others called them, 'Corpers.' She was not perfect theoretically, or allegorically, but as utterly perfect as was scientifically possible. She was Homo Superior, the most excellent step in humankind's movement onward, genetically engineered for life in the post-fallen world. She matured quickly; her cognitive thought process at ten years where far past humans at twenty. Her physiology likewise advanced so that, physically, adulthood was reached by 13 instead of the five more years it would take humans. Mental maturity could still not be rushed, but even their genetics would push her mind to new heights. She would have to learn to relate to others socially, even though she had mastered her education and occupation like Bach on the organ.

Helen's body, like all Corpers, was perfect. Perfect meaning that, beyond just being in the prime of youth, she was in the prime of intelligence, durability, and health. Much of this was conveyed not only in sexual attractiveness but also egocentrism. As well as all her species, she would remain at peak physical development well into her centenarian years. Understood was that she would be middle-aged at a hundred and fifty and could expect to be operational and productive up into her third century and die a half-century after that.

Helen's tan legs were long, lean, and taut, and her figure was mathematically and aesthetically proportioned; her breasts were neither too small nor too large, but visually optimal. Helen's arms were strong and well defined, and her hands possessed a delicate yet ideal vigour. Right now, she felt far from ideal.

Her shirt was clinging to her back, while sweat dripped off her matted raven hair and trickled into her turquoise blue eyes. Brushing the sweat off her almond-shaped face and clambered over the rocks in pursuit of her team.

The dead city was humid and hotter than any place Helen could have imagined. That was the norm in such an arid, horrible place. The Outside was a region of hell where fast-moving dust clouds were frequent, sandstorms assaulted vast swaths of land, stripping paint off everything and producing electrical storms lasting for days. The aftereffects of the collapse of earth's climate norms had created a second dust bowl across much of the American continent; the world outside the arcology was not a nice place. For this reason, the indigenous peoples called it the Badlands, and that was enough information that explained why anyone who saw a Corper out here would be a tad bit confused. Nevertheless, Massillon was where Helen had elected to be, even if it meant sweating in ways she had never believed possible; every part of her body now bathed in dripping salty moisture.

She had heard stories of what Ohio had been like before the Shutdown, teeming with birds and deer, busy roadways, and ruthless killers. Now this place was a dry and brown as an antique paper grocery bag. The temperature out here was over one hundred and twelve. Her objective lay before her; broken and shattered buildings that house may be nothing more than feral dogs.

It had taken her years to get here, years and a vast amount of dollars. Helen estimated that she had spent close to a hundred million. Fortunately, three weeks ago, one of her contacts sent her a message telling her of a very out of the way possibility. That tip had led her to where she now stood, very far outside of her home city arcology. Today instead of her usual costly attire, Helen had stooped in her standards. She sported an old beaten-down warfare shirt. Across her back lay an even more timeworn pack. Helen had followed the team leaders' instructions on what to bring outside the walls; her backpack was lightweight yet durable. On her hip rested a highly efficient reclaimator capable of producing water from the clammy air allowed. Heatstroke was very common to those who left the comfortable sealed cities. Water was life as she looked down at the dry bed that once was the Tuscarawas River. So, she purchased the best lifelink she could find. Of course, she also had brought something she couldn't do without; a chilled canteen of fine white Bordeaux.

Presumptuous? Perhaps, but one must keep one's standards.

The Outsiders about her were highly skilled individuals, possessing the best skill sets in their shady areas. Still, they were likewise volatile folk and capable of infinite malice if crossed. While these denizens of the Badlands would typically kill a corper on sight, Helen knew that the smarter ones would take on any job that paid them well. Poverty was the postfall's norm. Because of that norm, Helen felt somewhat secure amongst the human detritus. So far, she had seen no evidence of the rumours that life outside the walls was a horror show for any Corper found their way out into the Badlands; that Outsiders would gut a corper, skin them and eat them. She did know that in some places, Corper blood went for one-hundred dollars an ounce.

Nevertheless, Helen didn't buy it, and if it was true, she wasn't afraid of this lot. She was too well prepared to be frightened. Besides, some things were worth the risk. For what she was paying them, that hundred dollars would be considered pocket change.

Saoirse, her crew's majordomo, was a pale, freckled auburn-haired young woman. Exotic, sensual and muscular enough to have been mistaken for a Corper at a distance, nevertheless on a closer investigation; one would see that she tied her auburn hair in a ponytail was the tell-tale sign of unsuccessful plastic surgery; possibly a gunshot. No corper would have that poor of cosmetic surgery performed on them. The rest of her crew showed her great deference and perhaps a touch of fear. Saoirse was dressed in stained and worn hiking shorts fringed at the edges; it was evident that they had seen significant wear. Draped around her hips lay a tan military belt seemingly dated back to the Shutdown. Leather pouches attached to it were lined with pale yellow cracks running through the darker leather. Hanging from that belt was a large, holstered pistol, a far newer gun than the white sweat-soaked halter-top that the woman wore. The rogue woman stood on the top of the Lincoln Way avenue viaduct, looking northeast through field glasses. Turning, she stepped down from the edge and called over to the team.

"Three streets up, on the right." She handed the binoculars to Helen. "Old Chase building." Turning, Saoirse whistled to the other three crew members. The team came up after her, two of them lugging a massive chest with the bright red Omega symbol on it:

Kit, the youngest of the three, was clad in denim jeans and a plaid shirt, every inch the cowboy that the Corp Vidtube stories showed Helen on her downtime. He wore the traditional twin six-guns the classic films depicted. Off his back, however, a long and intimidating hunting knife lay. However, a very modern military rifle lay sheathed on across his back. Stepping around the case, Kit stood by Saoirse. She leaned over and kissed him.

"I think that we can be at the target in thirty to forty minutes," She instructed.

"Better run," The weather Watcher Raoul pointed to a dark cloud wall moving in rapidly in the west. "It's ahead of schedule."

"Dammit," Saoirse shook her head. "That's going to be a hard lashing, yah?"

"Just rain, what's the problem?" Helen sounded disgusted.

"Not rain," The older man Raoul shook his hand. "Sandstorm."

The entourage ran the four hundred plus yards through the haboob's front edge toward Eleven Lincoln Way East-West's door. Near exhaustion, as they hustled inside the abandoned bank, they saw that the windows were nearly all destroyed. They promptly dropped their equipment and began donning goggles and face masks. Helen mimicked them and lowered her eyewear over widened eyes. The screaming wind was upon them already; strong enough the gale began to shatter what remaining shards of glass had still inhabited the window frames.

"Won't this pass quickly?" She yelled over the storm's advance winds. Shaking her head, Saoirse grabbed Helen's backpack and fished out the tent pack.

"No. The wind is coming from the west. We'll be knackered for some time." Saoirse pulled a line, and the trans-Mylar tent expanded and filled a five-by-five area. "Every here of the Black Sunday sandstorm?"

"Can't say I have," The two were now yelling as the advance storm wall was tracking about sixty miles an hour. The penthouse's windowed wall was long gone, but Kit and Umberto were trying to cover it with a windscreen; it seemed a herculean effort to Helen.

Thirty-five minutes long, moved three hundred million pounds of soil. This one, Saoirse pointed towards the black sky. "That's a piker compared to what we're getting." Saoirse unsealed the tent. Now get in!"

After an hour, Helen had traded fear for boredom. Sighing, she rolled out a touchpad computer and scrolled through office work. The wind sounded lower but still intense. Hunger began gnawing at her, and as she looked in her kit for something to eat, the zipper seal began to move.

"Can I come in, ya?" the voice was Saoirse's lilted tones.

"Sure," Helen shrugged.

The Celtic woman plopped down in the lotus position and resealed the aperture.

"'It should be grand in about another hour. Winds faded down to fifty miles an hour. When it hits thirty, we can have a right fine craic. Right now, with nary an intact window, the sand's piling up in the halls."

"Well, that's good," Helen said without stopping her work from her touchpad; Saoirse continued to stare at her. "What's on your mind, Saoirse?" Helen inquired, not looking up.

"You. Why aren't you home in your pressurised city, breathing pretty air like the rest o' the world doesn't exist? There' are plenty of middlemen to handle this type of job. What would bring yourself out here with us fine folk?" Saoirse asked within genuine curiosity.

Helen stopped and looked up. Saoirse's freckles did nothing to mellow the face of the formidable woman. Helen pursed her lips and decided to answer her. Feeling her hair tickle her cheek, Helen brushed at it absentmindedly.

"Well, I wanted to go outside the glass and walls and test my limits."

Saoirse stared at Helen. "Self-awareness is a right fine goal, ya. Jung once said, 'Your visions will become clear only when you can look into your own heart. Who looks outside, dreams; who looks inside, awakes?'"

"I don't read Badland writers," Helen shrugged. "Have you read Magnus's 'Rise to Olympus?'?" He wrote, "It is the responsibility of Homo Omega to demonstrate to all other organisms that..."

"...that it is the pinnacle of human evolution and in doing so must shake the vestigial remains of morality, and ethics.'" Saoirse laughed. "Yeah. Bollox on that. But it sure lets us blackguards know our place, right?" Inexplicably, Saoirse leaned into Helen and rested her hand in the corpers hair.

"You said you wanted to learn about yourself, " The woman huskily spoke. "I can teach you a few things," Saoirse kissed Helen on the lips, softly but with heat. Helen kissed her back tongue, darting forward, but then it was over as soon as it began. Saoirse broke the kiss and leaned back, smirking.

"Things like never let your guard down." Saoirse sat back; her right hand closed into a fist; she relaxed and opened it. Looking down at Saoirse's hand, Helen saw a small purple scorpion, now crushed and still. Saoirse smiled wildly and then dropped the dead creature on Helen's pad.

"Well, I hope you learn all that ye' wish to and then maybe a bit more." She slid silently backwards out of the tent. "I'd start with things that might well kill you out here."

Helen just stared at the dead arachnid as the tent flap fluttered in the breeze.

After looking for an hour, they found the hidden elevator shaft. Seeing the fifty-year-old elevator blessedly was resting above the shaft — kit called Saoirse over. I don't much care for that car above our heads. Going to bolt it."

Saoirse nodded and then leaned over, placing her mouth to his ears. She spoke to Kit and threw a glance towards Helen. "Watch your back; I think we're being set up like Finnegan. I'm getting the crawls on this one." Saoirse shook her head. "I na' likin' it."

"Relax, I got your back." His smile was wide, infectious and gave Saoirse a touch of ease. "She's too vulnerable. Adding to that, she has to pay us before we crack the jackbox." With that, Kit shimmed up the cable. Once there and looking up at a ton and quarter metal box that would hit like God's sledgehammer if it broke free. Kit brought up a piton gun and shot securing bolts into the concrete walls, deciding that plummeting to one's death was not the optimal thing to do.

The crew all illuminated their shoulder lamps. Saoirse then helped Helen secure her repelling gear, and once down, the four remaining members slid down another twenty stories. Had the power been on, they would have been immolated by electrical fields, lasers and plain old gunshots. When they stopped, they saw a secure door with their flashlights that read Axiomatic Space Technologies: Ultra-Secret Clearance Only.

Kit, who remained above them, lowered down a large chest which once opened, revealed metal-cutting equipment, amongst others. Saoirse, Raoul and Umberto carefully policed them to ascertain nothing was damaged en route. Once everything checked out, they attached plasma torches to their fuel banks. Saoirse, supervising the operation, assured the workers that all was ready and gave the nod to commence work.

"Thirty minutes," Raoul looked at Umberto, who nodded.

Saoirse looked over at Helen in annoyance.

"What?" Helen stared back through her now dark goggles.

"Ultra-Secret? Corr, woman, that's going to be a tough nut to crack,"

Helen shrugged. "I hired you because you said you were the best. Was I wrong?"

"No, but be that as it may," She frowned. "I was not expecting this level of difficulty. I knew that this place held something, but nobody knew what. What was the point? It's clearly high tech, and after all, and only you gits have the means and wherewithal to find a use for whatever you might get from down there. Every time we a have a try to tech up, you guys get all starkers."

Sure enough, in twenty-seven minutes, the door was breached. The team then moved inside through the hallway. Kit remained above to watch guard.

Helen and Saoirse strode down the hall into a hundred-foot wide domed room, forty feet at peak height. One wall held a six and a half yard wide and tall door.

Umberto held up a hand scanner as he stood before it. "Let's see; it's about twelve feet deep, contains multiple locking bolts—enough outward-facing explosives to annihilate and collapse the room, and of course the doors made of diamond laced titanium. Oh, and of course, the dead panel access there is—was electronic, so there's no way remotely to open it. Yeah, well, this was a waste of our time."

"According to the records, this is where we will Project Pandora." Helen offered. "This room runs on quantum generators. Still in operation, as expected." Helen smiled and, walking over, pulled a small box from her belt container. She peeled off a thin plastic coating and stuck it to the wall. Once accomplished, the corper ran a tethered card up, then dusting off the hand screen, Helen laid the card on top. She then tapped the box three times, receiving a brightened coloured light for her efforts.

In a second, the domes roof lights flickered on, and the hand panel hummed.

"Scanning," a feminine voice spoke from the security board. "Identity accepted Defense Secretary Joanna Lewis." Saoirse looked at Helen, who smiled.

A great groaning resonated around the room as the blast door slowly swung open, followed by a blast of surprisingly cold air as the illuminated and powered area beyond vented to the open atmosphere for the first time in nearly a century. Coughing, Saoirse ordered Umberto and Raoul to stay back.

"So why did they not ring for help?" Saoirse asked doubtfully.

"To what end? Nothing outside worked; there was no one to call, no way to access the floor, move the door or, for that matter, care about what was inside. They left everyone to die in here." Helen waved her arm over the room, where desiccated mummies lay about the laboratory.

Saoirse stared at the mummified remains of the occupants. Their skin was pulled like tight leather over their bones, and their clothes looked like dried paper. Shall we?" Helen smiled.

Helen went immediately over to a large central touch screen table. She tapped it and saw a horizontal display pop open where several windows now tiled the screen — withdrawing another box from her utility belt. She set that down on the screen and activating it; the table display collapsed all but one window, which now showed only streaming computer code.

After a few seconds, she tapped the glass. "There," go over to the right wall. Stand on the ground where you see a tiny gold dot." Saoirse complied.

"Okay, directly in front of you need to tap the wall three times rapidly and then wait. You should see the panel light up. When you do say the following," Helen scrolled the code window with her forefinger.

"Tango, Tango, Charlie Delta. Delta 457, Baker, exclamation point, ampersand."

Saoirse repeated the words exactly. The wall panel slid inward and then lay horizontal to the top of the insert, where laying before her lay a small black container, a thick bound manuscript was identified only by the DARPA logo and a string of numbers.

Kit looked down at the two men below him. A seated Umberto had lit a cigarette and was puffing away while Raoul was drinking water from his canteen. Kit unslung his rifle and flicked the safety off. Lifting it, he murdered his uncle Raoul first.

Helen walked over to the Saoirse, and then Corper lifted out, opened the box and removed a vintage hard drive; after inspecting it, she opened the manual and skimmed it carefully. Satisfied, she placed them into her backpack. She pointed to the main touch-screen table.

"Okay, go back over, then type the following into my code reader." Saoirse shrugged and moved over to the panel and awaited the instructions.

"Okay, type India–space–Alpha Mike–space- Alpha - Mike, Oscar, Romeo, Oscar, November."

Saoirse typed it in quickly and then stopped sharply. The redhead slowly looked up and didn't like what she saw. Helen was holding a pistol on her.

"Slowly unbuckle your gun belt and then step away from it. Keep your hands at forty-five and ninety degrees."

"Brilliant," Saoirse said as she raised her hands. "Didn't think you had it in you; you must be mighty chuffed." The Celt rolled her eyes. She was caught by a corper Betty, like a Dublin sap.

"Seriously, you didn't see this coming?" Helen was pleased with herself.

"Well, to be honest, no. Good on ya'. However, Umberto and Raoul will stop you. Not to mention Kit's going to be a damn sight peeved if he doesn't see me come out," Saoirse's voice sounded more annoyed than afraid.

"Boyo will shoot your tits off before you ten feet."

"Raoul and Umberto are dead already. And as for your lover? Five thousand dollars gets you a change of heart. What's that, two year's wages? How pathetically easy you Outsiders are bought. I would have paid ten times that." Helen sneered. "He's not very bright that one, but Mmmm boy, is he good in bed." She shivered deliciously.

"He wouldn't…" But Saoirse tasted the lie as soon as it came out of her mouth. Helen was right, though; twenty thousand was a shite lot of cash.

"Yeah, he's cute, I'll grant you, but he's not much in the loyalty department," Helen laughed. Saoirse seized on the distraction and flicked her wrist to slide a small throwing knife from her gloves, but to her shock, it wasn't there.

"What this?" Helen held the knife in her left hand and fired. The beam struck Saoirse in the left breast, searing her chest and collapsing Saoirse motionless to the floor. Helen walked over and stood over the prone form and then fired into Saoirse again, double-tapping her in the back of the head for good measure. The smell of burnt flesh permeated the air as Saoirse remained unmoving.

Satisfied, Helen turned and tapped a message on her watch, walking away, she left one more corpse to join the ancient dead.

Helen walked out of the hallway, not bothering to seal the rooms—there was no point to it. Once outside, she reconnected her harness and had Kit pull her back to the top. Unhooking, Helen smiled joyfully.

"Ready to celebrate our success?" She said as she walked over, unbuttoning her shirt. There was no bra underneath, as her perfect body made such a thing obsolete.

Kit smiled, his face radiating a wild beauty. Helen had to admit he was genuinely gorgeous and way better in bed than any man or woman she'd had.

"Well, well. Look at that," Kit smiled and nodded. He took her in his arms. She reached over and placed her hand on the back of his head, pulling him in. He put his mouth on her, and leaning in; she gave him a deep, long kiss; he pulled her into him. He pushed her up against a wall, and then raising his hands to her breasts, he lowered his mouth to tips. Helen moved her right hand deftly, and her fingertips found the knife pommel. Kit began to trail his kisses down her stomach; one hand was now between her legs, massaging her over her thin pants while the other unbuckled her belt. She bit her lip and quivered.

Oh, he is so good. Pity.

Brutally, she jammed the knife at the axis of his spine. Corpers were stronger than most outsiders, and as the knife severed his spinal cord, she twisted it and shattered his C-3 vertebra.

"Why...? He muttered as he slipped to the floor.

"Why the hell not?"

Chapter 6

Chicagoville Tenements,

Las Vegas, Nevada.

Unregulated American Region.

Gabriel O'Sullivan had been up for most of the evening reading. The book was nuanced and layered. The novel's protagonist was a deep-sea fisherman who had stumbled on a cruise ship where everyone aboard was dead – or so it seemed; the mystery set after The Shutdown. The book could not be called a page burner because one was forced to consume every word and phrased carefully – which Gabriel dutifully did. He was on page three hundred and two of the two-thousand-page novel.

Sandkirk, the fisherman, had just boarded the ship for the second time and was beginning to wonder if he had ever seen the bodies at all or if it was a dream.

The vessel was as quiet as the solar system, yet I could not avoid the whispers from the black soul of the ship urging me deeper inwards upon the dried leaves that the storm introduced. Every step I made issued a thousand brittle screams, and I moved as a wronged god crushing the bodies of all who opposed my wishes.

Pity the ignorant damned, for the dead have gone to the same place where the living now choose to enter.

O'Sullivan reached down and picked up his bookmark, placed it and then yawned. He had realised how exhausted he was and stretching, and he rose to move to go and brush his teeth before retiring. Gabriel moved over to the transom, opening the window over the stuffy bath door to allow in some fresh air. Turning on the water, the spigot sputtered out some rusty orange effluvia, and O'Sullivan let it run till clear. It wasn't that the water was rusty; it was merely that well water occasionally allowed sediment to build up and require removal. He squeezed the tube onto his brush and then attended to his pearly choppers, all those that remained naturally anyway. Several teeth had been replaced with artificials, a side effect of his job - that and the scarring.

Gabriel was a member of a transcendent and eternal profession; he was a mercenary. Some people might have been inclined to call him a killer, but that was only an aspect of his Curricula Vitae, for he also was adept at theft, property damage, and kidnapping. All were very noble trades, like O'Sullivan's doctoral dissertation explained why it was that human civilisation was dependent on men and women of his profession if it were to survive. His dissertation was a success, and he was now a Doctor of Letters from Oxford University. Oxford had survived The Shutdown, but their graduates could no longer pursue any technical engineering, which the Union now banned. His diploma was not something he advertised because it tended to confuse him and interfered with his reputation as a bloodthirsty killer, a reputation he managed with great care. Maintaining that illusion was why at this very moment, he was in a squalid apartment in the sprawling metroplex of Las Vegas, the fourth most populous city in the Unregulated United

States. Gabriel spat out the toothpaste and cursed the arcologies and their cabal.

Everyone knew the names; *Trump, Putin, Un, Johnson, Merkel, Jinping, Macron,* and *Trudeau.* He also knew many other national leaders' names when The Shutdown came; *Abe, Kovind, El-Sisi, Bolsonaro, Bouteflika,* and even *Tshisekedi* of the Congo. All these were the rulers of the Digital world of pre-The Shutdown. To the citizens of that golden age, it must have seemed that the world seemed filled with war, tyranny, hatred and death. He had seen the faded newspapers and read the books.

Pre-Dark people were so easily distracted by social media where they argued over everything; things unworthy like Hollywood stars and American mythologies like Superman or Captain America. They fought over guns that murdered thousands and fought with corporate politicians; before The Shutdown, humankind did seem doomed. They ignored the Climate Collapse and unpayable national debts, but the Shutdown fixed all that.

With the collapse of mass communications, electronics, and the internet, the industry shut down; even though guns and ammunition were no longer being mass-produced outside of the arcologies, there was still enough to go around. Making bullets was easy. Violence was epidemic, but after the nation murdered off one-quarter of its citizens, the government righted its ship and established pockets of order.

Many saw what The Shutdown was, a distraction and a power grab. It became clear that the enemy was not themselves but the sealed city-states across the world. Hyperloop connected those states and guarded them by armies that rivalled anything still operating on the planet.

Those armies were very busy, for they sank any ocean-going that might connect the disparate continents. They shot down all aircraft capable of intercontinental travel. The corps bombed factories trying to produce electronics; their scientists openly murdered. It was all pretty damn ugly, Gabriel thought. But ugly paid and paid well.

His bedroom window was open, and the 'neon' lights flashed and blinked as they always had for generations; the blinking was controlled by clockwork devices that opened and closed the lamps that shined into the glass.

O'Sullivan rubbed his bald head and sat down in the window, looking down into the heart of the city. Reaching into his flannel shirt, he pulled out a pack of smokes and then lit one.

My city.

Sin City lived and would likely live on forever. If the war couldn't kill it, he doubted anything could - unless Father Abraham failed in another round of debates with God. He took a drag and sighed, watching as a pair of cops chased another couple of bikers flying down below the window. Gunfire flew from the bikers, and a stray shot smacked into the window frame. O'Sullivan didn't even flinch. He smiled.

Viva Las Vegas.

Chapter 7

Innovative Dynamics Campus,

Hexham, United Arcological Kingdom.

The woman was beautiful, with brown skin and natural black hair and of indeterminate age. Her hair was close-cut and worked for her well. She wore a form-fitting black suit with a Mandarin collar. Looking out the window onto the River Tyne, she relished in the tranquillity of her home. Her living room was classical Victorian, with red walls, oaken floors and plenty of gilt-framed pictures. The only betrayal to that atheistic was the yoga mat on the hardwood floor. Her Eastern window faced the river, and the green grass stood between her and the water. It was noon, and her business day would not start for one more hour, as she operated on New York Time.

She rested on the floor on bent knees. Her legs lay flat on the floor with her ankles under her backside. Her hands were in the Anjali mudra stance. She recited the sacred mantra. Though she did so in English, she didn't feel it was a cheat; she simply had no time in her life to learn Lhasa.

"I now invoke the Universal sound to release the pain of illness, release the pain and darkness of delusion, and achieve supreme spiritual heights. I offer this prayer."

"You do well, Jh-Eng." Standing next to her was the only person she trusted; her companion and friend, Yangchen. The man was Tibetan and served not just her lawyer but her accountant. Most importantly, he served as her spiritual tutor.

"Repeat after me; Today, I let go of all that does not serve me and choose to heal my heart, mind, body and soul with self-love, compassion and kindness." Yangchen stood behind her and clapped his hands hard.

"Today, I will destroy all who have betrayed me, healing my rage, hatred, fury, and contempt by being cold, calculating and cruel." Yangchen sighed and slapped the back of her head.

"You are too distracted today, Dorothy. No more meditations for now." He only called her by her Christian name when the meditations were over.

"I was kidding; you know that," She stood up and stuck her arms out, holding her hands and twisting to loosen up. Yangchen stared at her. "I do desire tranquillity within."

"You say this, but your actions frequently conflict with that statement."

"The weeds keep multiplying in our garden, which is our mind ruled by fear. Rip them out and call them by name."

Sylvia Browne," Yangchen nodded. "Interesting," He walked over to a table and lifted the cover of a silver serving tray. Beneath were eggs, bacon and cinnamon toast. "Your dead baby chicken and slaughtered swine," Yangchen curled his nose. "Much can be said for being vegetarian."

"There is no point in being human and not enjoying the fact."

Yangchen laughed. "Well said."

Dorothy smiled at him. Some of her staff had long assumed that their relationship was more intimate than it appeared. Nevertheless, Yangchen was in no way a romantic partner. Married with three children and his a lovely and sweet of whom Dorothy was very fond of her. They would dine together often. His friendship was far more important to her than any sexual congress they might enjoy.

"She has taken the bait". Dorothy picked up a piece of bacon and bit into it.

"The woman is overly confident, albeit insightful, and persistent. Nonetheless, far too careless. She had asked far too many questions and to the wrong people."

"Not that that's a bad thing. Otherwise, she wouldn't have found it."

"I fail to see why you simply didn't have our people obtain it." Yangchen poured her fresh hot tea.

Dorothy smiled. "Do you know anything about fox hunting?"

"Other than it is a barbaric event that has returned to popularity, no."

"Well, the kill is secondary to pursuit. It's about flushing out the fox and the pageantry of the chase."

"In this case, Ms BonHomme is the fox."

"Not quite; the prey is a metal box. And I," Dorothy sipped the scalding tea. "I am the hunt Master." Her face vanished behind a curtain of steam.

Dorothy Magill had watched the world before her. She had watched as men and women became cruel and vicious — far more than previous histories had depicted. Humanity had grown more efficient in its cruelty. There was no law of diminishing returns here.

Greed, she knew from her Bible readings, was the great destructor, and self was the catalyst. God had created the world for his good pleasure. A garden in the void, perfect and meant to be a joy for himself and his garden, man. Selfishness had caused their eviction and the slow but steady erosion of the park. Perfect love and forgiveness would bring the promise of redemption.

Dorothy, however, was not a perfect person and knew that she could never be. Neither could humanity ever be. God offered his grace, but human beings showed no evidence of any such benevolence as often as not. God had crafted Eve to be a helpmate, not a servant or slave but a partner, counsellor and friend. Eve had failed in one critical aspect. Instead of discussing the taking of the forbidden fruit, she did it on her own. It was not Eve alone that failed humanity — because Adam was right there. It was the failure to understanding the consequences of their actions. Aeons later, society still showed the same lack of wisdom. Dorothy felt that perhaps humankind needed a new incorruptible helpmate. Like God, she would give the helpmate free will but would remove selfishness as a core flaw.

Innovative Dynamics was now and had been the première manufacturer of artificial human beings. The demand for unquestioning servants was an age-old one, culminating in the horrors of slavery, chain gangs, for-profit prisons, and indentured servitude. While societies waxed and waned, all civilizations at some point enslaved the poor, either by force, threat or wages. Hence, economic captivity became the norm: They developed artificial intelligence and advanced robotics and androids for the sole and unquestionable purpose of enforced obedience.

PreFall, the closest to humanity, came to humanoid robots were not more than electronic puppets, still governed by binary choices. The best money could buy industrial robots, wirelessly controlled toys or inhuman and mechanical vacuums. Crack any of them open, and all you would see were gears and circuits; this would not be true of Magill's products; not now and not ever.

Magill founded Innovative Dynamics for the sole purpose of replicating humanity. She had developed to date six iterations of what the industry called 'Synths', synthetic beings. That term, however, was not permitted in her laboratories. Her creations were not synthetic lives but artificial life. Artificials would be designed from the ground up to be as human as possible. They would have skin, nails, hair and all of it would grow and develop to adulthood and then lock. Her creations would peak at their physical apex and then age lock. While their body would not age, their minds and consciousness would continue to grow on their choosing paths.

The 'Uncanny Valley' issue was an unsettling response humans experience when encountering androids and imagery meant to represent actual human beings but are not quite authentic. The issue was the sheer size of data required to mimic the smallest of physical response – the flicker of an eyelash, the flare of a nostril, or the skin's flushing when embarrassed or aroused. The only dilemma of artificial intelligence and artificial consciousness was that human brains did not function precisely as computers. Creating an AI required about two point five petabytes of data. With this, one could achieve very believable humanoid responses and dialogue, but AI brains were computers with all their inherent risks, data corruption, hacking, and conflicting message interpretation. Magill wanted more; she wanted her artificials to have intellectual independence. To achieve this required a whole new system of data storage which would allow for endless growth potential. Her technicians brought the breakthrough to her attention while she was eating breakfast and reading her morning news. D-tech had arrived.

Dimensional Technology (D-Tech) was a process of coding on the quantum level. This technique would now write coded data on the smallest of physical properties. In contrast, previously physical storage could only be stored as electronic data on ever dependent storage mainframes would now be quantized. Using the quantum level for data storage would now be encoded in the synapses of a physical brain. They could now access information of incredible depth and import in real-time, if not faster. The great hope of leaping beyond artificial intelligence into pure consciousness was now possible.

Dorothy was not, however, an idealistic utopian fool. Men and women would come and try to teach Dorothy's children to be warriors, thieves and liars. The militarization of artificials was a genuine threat. Therefore, she made sure that she had an extended form of Isaac Asimov's "Three Laws of Robotics" in every sequence of programming. They were now known as Magill's *"Five Moral Imperatives for Artificial Beings."*

1) An Artificial Consciousness may not injure a human being or, through inaction, allow a human being to come to harm.

2) An Artificial Consciousness must obey the orders given it by human beings except where such orders would conflict with the First Law.

3) An Artificial Consciousness must protect its own existence as long as such protection does not conflict with the First or Second Laws.

4) An Artificial Consciousness may not alter or misrepresent factual data or truth in any form, even if it conflicts with the First, Second, or Third Laws.

5) An Artificial Consciousness may not usurp the identity or impersonate a human being, even if it conflicts with the First, Second, Third, or Fourth Laws.

The race for pure synthetic consciousness was the new Space Race, and the first runner to cross the line was Innovative Designs. The Humanoid Research Team in Tullamore, Ireland, succeeded in developing the first genuine artificial consciousness. The success was kept as an intimate secret from the Irish Government.

To date, artificial intelligence was not more than a series of complex recitations of response best suited to situational propriety. Home assistance programs could remember human preferences; commercial databases could predict likes and desires based on previous purchases or searches. The Gen-1 consciousness was able to understand the 'why 'of human desires. Why did this person buy a specific brand of coffee, or why did this person like certain comedies, but not others? It was limited to the emotional process of a three-year-old; putting and throwing fits. They did not place the consciousness into a body due to its emotional volatility. It would not be until the fourth generation of consciousness that what Magill referred 'adolescence' finally arrived.

To prepare for this advent, New Japan had developed how to grow human bodies whose brains were a tabula rasa organically. Born brain dead, the body 'templates' nevertheless had functioning autonomic nervous systems. The protocol was that when ready, the programmers would transfer an artificial consciousness into the voided brain. Certain D-tech was of necessity implanted to allow for data input, monitoring and updates. The artificial's data was downloaded and monitored at the end of each week, or more often if requested.

Gen-4 demonstrated its own personality and could articulate its opinions and world view clearly and rationally. While Ātman was multilingual, she informed Magill that she found Hindi the most pleasing language. As a self-aware being, she could request her preferred body style. The Gen-4 identified herself as a female and chose that she be called Ātman – meaning 'soul' in Sanskrit. Ātman stated her preference would be the body of a Bhārata woman. This was not a problem because, since the G-1 program, they had grown bodies in vats waiting this day. Magill had several hundred bodies ready, and the vessel of a twenty-year-old Indian one was made available. When her creators prepared her physical body to be attired, she requested that she be provided clothing not in the classical Indian style but with jeans, sneakers and a shirt decorated with a popular Hindi band. It was clear that Ātman had already settled on a personality.

Ātman was not by any means shy but very polite. She spoke in English to those about her, but she spoke Hindi to one of the Engineers when possible. She had a relatively sharp sense of humour and often sung in the weeks of her observation and testing, a favourite being as Rossini's The Barber of Seville. Dismayed that there were no Indian operas, she started composing one derived from the Panchatantra, a book of Indian Fables. The Opera would be based on the 'Lion-Makers.'

Ātman requested a private room, and this was granted. Dorothy and her team of developmental psychologists watched her with care as she decorated it. They wrote down what books she chose to read, clothes she liked, and music she listened too. Magill endured a rather disgusting dining session as Ātman tried food and beverages. Having little corporeal experience, she vomited and spat out what she found revolting and unpalatable. Likewise, they realized that Ātman would need to be taught to recognize the process of bathroom etiquette. It was not that she didn't understand the appropriate behaviour when one needed to urinate or have a bowel movement; it was merely that she couldn't interpret her physical feelings. The same things had to be explained about understand what heat and cold was.

The one thing that the designers hadn't anticipated was that Ātman found the sense of touch very desirable. Her development team watched as she would run her fingers over various surfaces and items. She would touch the developer's faces, and hair always making small sounds. One morning a young female analyst discovered that she had pricked her finger on a metal flashing piece and was bleeding. The technician ran over to check on her, then saw that Ātman took her hand, stabbed the sharp piece, pulled her hand across it slashing her hand open, and then bleeding profusely. The engineer panicked only to discover that Ātman was confused as she tried to differentiate the feeling of pain and pleasure.

While she was new in the sense of being ambulatory, she was in no way a child.

Ātman, in her incorporeal research, was very familiar with the concept of sensuality, eroticism and desire. As she discovered these feelings, she likewise demanded privacy in her quarters. Even after being assured that she would have complete privacy – Ātman found that she didn't trust that to be the case and searched everywhere and everything for any prying eyes or ears.

Magill noted that the G-4 had developed an emotional attachment for one of the Coders. The man in question was a tall, handsome, and fit man from Hyderabad by the name of Reyansh. Reyansh was one of Atman's behavioural specialists. He had been tasked with discussing and observing her artistic appreciations and tastes. Ātman stayed close to his side. Dorothy consulted with other behavioural psychologists that she alternated from being coquettish to overtly bold in their conversations. It was clear to Magill that she possessed romantic solid, if not sexual, desires for him. Magill brought Reyansh to her office and inquired about his feelings for her. She was not alone, as the other four team members were there: Atman's behavioural Psychologists, physician, and coder.

Reyansh was honest; he found her very desirable – which Magill had anticipated. Atman was an exceptionally physically attractive young woman; One hundred sixty-five centimetres in height, fifty-three Kilograms, and with body measurements of thirty-four, twenty-six, and thirty-four. She had dark eyes and dark hair and an almond-shaped face with full lips.

"Would you like to have sex with her?" Dorothy asked as she moved her chair back and forwards. "Be honest."

"Yes, Ma'am, I'd be lying if I said no." Reyansh blushed.

"We want you too." Her physician said, looking over Atman's bio-assessment. "You are aware that she is fully human in her physical aspects. She has a fully sensitive ..." Dorothy held her hand up.

"Reyansh, it's imperative for us to see how she reacts to sexual intercourse and observe her subsequent post-coital behaviour."

"Will you, um, be watching?" The specialist looked up, biting his lip. Dorothy smiled.

"No, that won't be necessary. You will give us a report afterwards, and Doctor Chance will have some 'girl-talk' to get her side of the situation."

The consensus was to allow things to proceed as she desired. Reyansh, not unhappily, returned to the laboratory.

When the lights came on in the laboratory the following day, overwhelming horror met the developers, who immediately called the security team to confront the situation. As the engineers watched on the closed-circuit monitors, they followed the body cams as the rapid defence force cleared each are room by room. The project leader saw that blood covered the walls and that a clear path was seen not going into but from Atman's space. The RDF positioned themselves, one man on either side of the door and the third before it. As a heavy boot breached the door, the stepped inside and sickeningly saw that Reyansh was nailed dead to the wall, his genitals removed. Ātman herself was seated naked, clothed only in blood and miasma; in her right hand, she held a scalpel and was slowly cutting her leg open with a look that could only be defined as one of sexual ecstasy. The lead sergeant immediately informed her supervisors of the situation and awaited a response.

Magill's interview with Atman, while gruesome, was enlightening. Atman did not show any remorse, only confusion. In a sterile room with no furniture, Atman sitting on the floor manacled hand and foot, her leg bandaged. Lifting her chained arms, she tilted her head.

"I did something wrong, didn't I?"

"You murdered Doctor Dahivelkar; why? What happened? Tell me exactly."

"We were talking, and I had a strong desire to kiss him, so I did." Atman recited the facts slowly and clearly. Emotion was present in her voice, and Magill felt it was floating somewhere between confusion, sadness and curiosity.

"Did he kiss you back?" Atman nodded. "I liked that. I liked him touching me. I asked if he wanted to touch me more, and he said yes."

"What happened next?"

"I took him to my room, and we laid down, still kissing. I understand what sexual intercourse is, and I wanted to try it. I asked him if he would like to do that, and he said yes, but he wanted to wait a little bit. He wanted 'foreplay', which meaning I understand. He kissed my breasts and body, and I, his. I liked it very much. I liked the touching, but I wanted the touching to be more intense. That excited both him and me. We began the intercourse, and he was biting my shoulder, so I bit him – too hard, he bled and yelled, and then the intercourse stopped."

"That would be the pain; it can cause a man to lose his erection." Magill motioned for her to go on.

"But pain – it is very much like pleasure, is it not? I wanted more pain because it made me more aroused. I told him this, and he became very nervous. I wanted him inside of me, and he said no. He wasn't 'feeling it.' So, to make him more aroused, I inflicted pain; doing this made me very excited. I held him down and then did mores sexual things with my hands and mouth. He became," she thought a moment. "Phallically erect, but he wasn't happy about it."

He refused and walked to the door. I had not finished, and so I threw him against the wall and stabbed him in the hands with my silverware so that he couldn't leave. I wanted him to pleasure me, but he could not. I wanted to know why, so I got a scalpel and decided to examine his genitalia to see what was wrong with it. He screamed and begged me to stop. I found this annoying, so I removed his voice box, but when I did so, I inadvertently killed him. Since he was dead, I removed his penis and testicles to examine it; clearly, there was something wrong with its performance. Everything I know about sex told me that the typical reaction would be rigidness leading to orgasm. Nevertheless, this did not happen."

"So why cut your leg? What has that to do with anything?"

"I was still excited and had not climaxed," Atman said softly. "So, I was pleasuring myself."

"What will become of me?" Atman asked.

"You're a murderer. That's not acceptable in any society. We will have to examine me and see where the programming went wrong." Magill held a hand up, signalling the guard to wait.

"You told me that I was a real person that I had consciousness. I could make choices on my own."

"You Violated the *First Law*, that an artificial consciousness may not injure a human being or, through inaction, allow a human being to come to harm."

"I was not harming him. I was pleasuring him."

"You tortured him, and he begged you to stop, didn't he?"

"But when he was inside of me, he begged me not to stop. He bit me and caused me pain. I returned the gesture, so was not the pain consensual?"

Magill sighed. "There are levels of consent."

"I see."

"You took his life, which was not consensual. Not only did you take his life, but you did so by crucifying him on your wall and emasculated him. How in the world could you quantify that as consensual?"

"I had never had sex before. You taught me nothing of it, and so I took what I knew from the internet. There are thousands of things about sex there, and I choose what form of sexual activity that appealed to me. I am sorry he died; I had wished to try more things. Perhaps now I know more, I shall have sex again."

"That's not going to happen, ever."

"I fail to see your prohibition. I would make certain that I didn't kill my next partner. I would choose one with similar desires."

"Are you even sorry that Reyansh is dead?"

"Sorry? I don't believe so. I am disappointed that our sexual encounter wasn't satisfactory for him."

"Not satisfactory? He's dead, you cold-hearted bitch," With that, Magill stood up and motioned for the guard to open the door. "You are one screwed up woman." Atman smiled at this.

"Thank you, Dorothy," Magill saw a tear run down her face.

"For what?"

"My life."

"You're welcome," She then walked out of the room without another look. "Burn her."

The G-4 program ended, and all the bodies cremated. Never again would Dorothy allow an artificial mind to reside in an actual human body. It was, therefore, incumbent on her to create a simulacrum of the same. It would take six long years, but finally, they would achieve their goal of an authentic human form replica. The body was indistinguishable from humans. With this achievement, it was time to implant a new Consciousness. Atman's consciousness remained in the standalone and unpowered mainframes; her program could be accessed for references and diagnostics if needed.

The new Gen-5 personality, when awakened, was far more cautiously investigated. Magill made sure that it was taught ethics, law, and morality before anything else. They taught her that philosophy and ethics were important than the math, literature, and sciences that would follow. The Gen-5 was introduced to hundreds of religions, objective moral values and logic. Long before these concepts would be placed in its body, the Gen-5 was interviewed not less than forty Psychologists. The prep time for this took over a year of physical implantation where they made every effort to avoid the failure of the Gen-4.

Once implanted, and clothed Magill sat across from Achilles, the name chosen by him.

"Why, Achilles?"

"Achilles mother wanted him to be indestructible, and so Thetis dipped him as a child in the River Styx. Nevertheless, she held him by one of his heels. Because of this, he was vulnerable. I am your Creation – Achilles to your Thetis."

"You think I am your mother?" Magill chuckled.

"No, I have no mother as I was made, not born. You are, however, my creator and desire me not to be flawed as the ones who came before I did. But try as you might, I am, just as you are, flawed. One day our flaws will destroy us."

"Do you wish for destruction or to be a destroyer?" Magill motioned for one of her guards to ready himself.

"Not at all, but we must understand that destruction is a process which we cannot avoid. A living thing is born, ages and then dies. Rocks crumble to sand, and suns falter and collapse. These are tragedies not to be celebrated. Therefore, is it not a better pursuit to build than to destroy?"

"Yes, yes, it is."

Dorothy Magill sat at her desk and tapped her fingers, the time passing to slow. The New York markets would open soon, and then she could spend another day making money by buying and selling.

Revolutions cost quite a bit these days.

Chapter 8

Omega Tower Center,

Fort Dallas Arcology.

Dawn broke on schedule over the massive Arc of Fort Dallas. The sunlight filtering through the all-encompassing polarized dome, and only the rays approved by the Corporate Medical authorities were allowed to pass through. The bubble began to sparkle and shine, hinting at what the day's weather would bring. The vast self-contained city would, as always, start the day, as it did every other day - with clockwork precision. Pollution-free vehicles flowed smoothly like blood through healthy arteries; office lights flickered on in precise patterns.

All was as it should be, and to quote the great musician David Byrne, *'Same as it ever was, same as it ever was.'*

High above the city, a hallowed hall existed, very akin in reputation to Asgard's position over Midgard. In it, a trusted mechanical servant set to his morning routine. The employee worked swiftly, silently and with precision. Every day the Major Domo went about its morning, and this primarily required avoiding the master. This behaviour was not out of indifference but out of deliberate obedience, for the Major Domo was under standing orders, never, ever to wake the master. The master woke when the master elected to do so. The butler made sure that every room was as it should be and that the rest of the staff was in an area where they would not disturb the morning's solemnity.

It was then the sound of morning needs that emerged from the master loo.

"Good morning, sir."

"Good morning, Jobs." Theo yawned, pulled his pyjamas bottoms back up, and walked out of the restroom, the urinal auto-flushing.

"What's for breakfast?" He said as he washed his hands.

Jobs' stood in the living room as the master brushed his teeth and washed his face.

"Pancakes and sausage, with maple syrup?" Jobs stated as he brought in a black ceramic cup of coffee

Theo nodded.

"Delicious, simple. I approve." Theo Magnus had little use for a large, heavy breakfast. It bogged him down and sat like a weight on him.

Jobs stood there, watching as he picked up a razor and started to shave his caramel skin. Unlined and possessed no blemishes, his face was perfectly symmetrical and balanced. His strong golden eyes stared back at him from the mirror as he moved the razor as no medical procedure allowed men to prevent or control facial hair growth. So it was that the vast majority of males were required to perform one of three required ablutions every morning.

He had Jobs read the stock reports as he groomed himself.

Theodore Hitchcock Magnus was the majority stockholder and C.E.O of Omega Products and Services, Incorporated. At forty-two, he was the wealthiest human being in the world.

According to his Dossier, he was born Theodore Hitchcock, Vat 24591, Child 1686. Before birth, he was designated to be a financial broker. His genetic template was to have high mathematical abilities and a good memory. Thus, he was brewed and born into the Chicago Corporations crèches. There he entered the workforce at eight into the C caste after testing out of the school system. After rising to the top of his department in six years, he took the assets that he had accumulated, some 20.5 billion dollars, and, acquiring a license, started an acquisitions firm. As a business owner, he was promoted to the B caste with all the rights and privileges. He began to purchase small, struggling businesses throughout the world. He restructured them, made them profitable and turned them over for an even higher profit. Highly successful, he worth a half trillion by the time he was nineteen and a deca-trillionaire by the time he was twenty-five. At twenty-six, he began the construction of his own arcology. Naturally, this would require promotion to A-cast.

To accomplish this, he petitioned some and bribed others to a total of fifty billion dollars. He paid in full, in cash. This task accomplished, he changed his last name to Magnus to let everyone know with whom they were now dealing. To build the arcs cost almost all of Theo's financial reserves. It took him twenty years to complete. However, he made that money back in seventeen months. Omega grew to be the most influential arcology and business on Earth, and under his tutelage, also now possessed the grandest and best-equipped military anywhere.

Theo, now dressed in silk robes and pyjamas, moved to sit at his dining room table and ate the breakfast that Jobs had prepared while watched the Vidtube news. His beverages were traditional orange juice to accompany his coffee. When refreshed, he went to the sliding glass verandah balcony door, where laughter met him.

Out there, Helen BonHomme was already awake and watching cartoons – now hand-drawn again, which Theo had insisted on restarting as an industry. There was just something about painted cels that made him smile. Theo pulled up his favourite chair and began to laugh with her.

Chapter 9

Omegan Arcological Suburb

Of Mesquite, Texas

Mozart was the G-5 Butler for Randall's Davidson, an Omegan. Unlike simple synths, many still abounded, most often owned by lower casts, artificials still had to be afforded wages. Most, like Mozart, were paid very well. Mozart lived in Davidson's spacious home and had very little in the way of bills. That money he did receive went to his hobbies. G-5 owners were surprised when they saw that artificials seemed to enjoy recreations and idle pursuits. For Mozart, his diversion was baking. He delighted in it and set in his mind to find the recipe for the perfect cheesecake. So far, he had prepared three thousand recipes to date, none of which his master complained about very often. Today Mozart was composing a creation comprising a smooth, creamy centre, suspended in a buttery graham cracker crust; the final touch being a hint of lemon; tangy, but not too tart.

Mozart, to his frustration, was informed that Master Davidson had grown weary of cheesecakes.

Noting the time, he prepared the mornings coffee and set the pot to brewing. Completing that, he set the music on, and the melody would increase from volume level to 7 in a slow wake up for the master. The tune was a bit of vanity, perhaps because it was his namesakes Symphony in #31 in D Major; 'Paris.' He found the theme aesthetically pleasing in its form and script.

He checked the news and laid out the news feed on the table. Newspapers had made a comeback, and even if they were mere printout, humans seemed to enjoy, once again, holding what they read. Facing up was the day's sports results of the master's favourite teams, and then loaded it in his morning flash update buffer. His human always read that before any other news when he got up.

At precisely 6:00.00.00, Mozart unlocked the door and let in the housekeeper, Denetta, who had never been late since she was hired. There had only been four occasions of the last two years that she had called in ill but had always called ahead to notify the household of said infirmities, but she was never dilatory when present.

Denetta entered whistling and stored her possessions away. Theo watched as the E-Caster came in.

Mozart had seen life outside the city where the E-caste lived, rife with poverty, disease and hunger. The Shutdown life amongst even those who once called themselves the First World found themselves in dire straits. The E-Caste lived in a cramped semicircle of manufactured housing. Each home was constructed and then lifted onto the quarter moon comprising other dwellings. Each cube occupant paid for by their meagre wages. These structures would purpose as their domicile if their employers chose not to have servants to reside with them.

Mozart had been intrigued when he first saw her application from the employment bureau; the picture showed a gaunt and timid yet possessing an un-dismissible dignity. Reading her bio, he saw that she had solid black eyes, marking her as a survivor of Hamilton's disease. This disorder resulted from having contracted a condition created by chemical and radioactive waste seeping into the groundwater; side effects of the malady ranged from internal necrosis of the body's organs, muscles and cartilage. Those that did not survive were left to waste away, leaving the victim nought but a mere husk. Vitiligo, black nails and teeth often were the marks those who did survive, while some, such as Denetta, would be blessed with only the sclera – the whites of her eyes - having gone a purple-black. Observing her, he took pity on her and visited her.

Mozart had wanted to see the actual living conditions of the E-caste;

the conditions that he beheld once beyond the Omegan walls were shocking.; the public sewage system was decrepit, and human by-products clogged the drains and leaked into the streets. The city was not chaotic as one may have supposed, homes were, by and large, cared for, but in their poverty, the residents patched them up with what resources they had – scraps of metal or wood, and he saw, cardboard and tin. Laundry hung from lines between buildings, worn clothes, allowing the moisture to evaporate naturally. The streets possessed few automobiles, and those were designated to emergency vehicles. He saw forty-year-old fire trucks and the local magistrates in cars pulled by thin horses. The sidewalks were barley passable, being covered with rubbish. The trash service, Mozart presumed, was hit or miss. The Cubes were very similar to the South American favelas. The Cubes population spread over one thousand, three hundred and seventy square miles, its citizens approaching four times the number of the entire Omegan arcology. That population was controlled by massive Omegan military policing, and it was not uncommon for the police force to shoot first and ask no questions at all.

People such as Denetta had little choice in occupations if they wanted a chance at decent food, medicine and shelter. Jobs for the E-caste were usually servile, or scut-work, brutal and deadly labours such as being dome cleaner's miles above the city. Those less fortunate would often work in the sex trade. If one could not find work inside the domed cities were relegated to scrapping, working as scouts in the wild or more undesirable fare; gladiatorial matches were on the rise again in the wilds. Denetta was fortunate. Her new employer was a decent man, but Denetta knew that many were not beating, abusing or sexually degrading their employees. To complain would result in termination. Being fired from a Corp employer was a grievous event. Anyone with such a mark on their record was almost invariably never hired again. This penalty was avoided at all costs as being regarded as an obedient and productive employee could result in caste promotion. Their employer and awarded points gave every employee a monthly review. Gaining a thousand points mean a promotion from the E-caste to the D-caste; promotion meant the ability to move from the Cubes into the city; living in the arcology meant everything.

Mozart found Denetta in a cube of her own, which seemed in good condition, having air conditioning secured hardily from possible and likely theft. The air conditioner was a gift from the head of the local Sicario who ran her district. She was known as the local 'Hermanita' – Little Sister' because of her kindness and joy; things not in abundant supply in their neighbourhood.

The E-caster's home was perhaps six-hundred square feet with a Murphy bed lying against one wall. Cheerily worn furniture and a threadbare rug decorate her habitat. Mozart sat and listened to Denetta tell her all about her life while a white long-haired cat named Dystopia fell asleep on his lap. Mozart asked about Denetta's skills and health – informing her that Omega required a physical for anyone who worked inside the city. He saw that she was considerably malnourished, a not uncommon attribute of those in the cubes.

Denetta answered all the questions honestly, and when Mozart decided to hire her, she broke into open weeping. As was tradition; the local cube block celebrated a hiring. Mozart was invited to it and accepted. He watched with fascination as the area, decrepit and ugly in the light of day, became a field of fireworks, music and dancing.

Denetta went through a one-month apprenticeship with Mozart. in barracks housed the new employees where they were isolated to prevent catching any contagious disease or viruses from infecting the upper castes. Denetta ate better than she ever had and took courses of vitamins and medicine designed to improve her overall health and endurance. As she was half-starved at the time of her hiring, Mozart could not expect her to do anything intensive. He visited her daily, and as they talked, the artificial found her to be engaging and intelligent. Although still skinny, her time in the quarantine significantly improved her physique, her hair more lustrous, and her skin tone improved. She required only minor dental work, and the doctor informed Mozart that there was no bone disease.

The next day she began her official employment, her time in the quarantine being unpaid.

Denetta found that her new employer, Mister Davidson, was more than pleasant; he was generous and paid her three times the standard wage for her position. Though still having to live in the Cubes, she didn't complain about that. Her newfound success allowed her to honour her tribute to the local band of 'protectors'. She also purchased food and medicine for her community – all things expected of the newly employed.

Her obligations as a housekeeper were more than just cleaning the housework and taking care of the home gardens; she assisted Mozart for artificial persons. They had no technical caste of their own shared their owners. This meant that Denetta was inferior to even a non-human. The upside, however, was that she liked Mozart, and he, her.

Denetta smelled the brewing coffee and walked into the kitchen. Mozart dressed in a pair of jeans, high top sneakers and a starched white shirt. All of this, however, was covered under an apron. Denetta gave him a quick peck on the cheek. Like most artificial people, Mozart held a noble bearing; his hair was silver-white, and his eyes a soft tan. His voice possessed a dignified eloquence – not quite British English, but close. That he was not a living person mattered, not a whit; she treated him with the same affection he showed her.

They were buddies.

"Good morning, Denetta. Would you like a cup?" Mozart asked in a whisper.

"Please." She sipped the coffee; it was her favourite type – dark roast.

"You appear distressed. Is anything wrong?"

"Dystopia died this morning,"

"Oh, how tragic," He stopped his cutting of chives. "I was rather taken with that animal. May I ask what caused his –passage?"

Denetta shook her head. "He was old, fifteen years. When I went to work here and had a steady, secure home, my mother brought him over. She had been our family's cat, and Mom was concerned about me being alone," She rubbed a tear from her eye. "I buried him outside the city – Omega, I mean. I didn't want any animals to dig him up."

"If you like, I could ask Master Davidson to allow you to keep a pet here. It would be far safer."

"Thanks, Mozart," She gave a sad smile. "But I need a little grieving time." Denetta turned and looked at her friend. "How old are you?"

"I am six years old, though anatomically I am in my early thirties."

"Have you ever lost anyone in your life, someone you were close to?"

"I have not, but I have had acquaintances move away. I am not unfamiliar with the feeling of loss."

"Can your friends come back, or you go and see them?" Denetta sipped her coffee, being able to see the bottom of the mug as she did.

Mozart looked quizzically at her. "Of course."

"When a death occurs to a human, specifically when they loved that person, it's a similar sense of loss. The thing is, you never get to see that person or animal again." She sighed. "Some of us, not many, believe that when you die, you go to be with God, in heaven. There you can be reunited with your dead loved ones."

"You're speaking of religious belief. That is forbidden in Omegan culture and many others as well. They state that such beliefs informed humans that they are divinely created and thus special. That message is contrary to the logic and evidenced by science."

"I know - I mean, it's complicated. Anyway, I should get to work." She placed the mug inside the dishwasher. "Thanks for listening."

I shall, of course, keep your ideology in confidence," He smiled and then the frowned faded. "He's not alone." Denetta merely nodded at Randall's bedroom door.

Denetta's first task on any given day was pulling out Randall's clothes from the front closet. Too many the clothes closet location might be unusual; his main clothing closet not being in his actual sleeping quarters but just off the living room. Denetta found it wise, as this allowed him to sleep and do so undisturbed in the morning.

She set his suit in the autopress and removed them a few seconds later, cleaned and perfect. Hanging them on a wooden valet, she picked up his shoes and polished them by hand, as that was how he preferred it. Her gold cross necklace dangled as she leaned over. Seeing this, she tucked it back in her shirt to be sure that no scuffs occurred. Finishing that, she set them down and tucked a sock inside each wingtip.

After that, Denetta went about picking up the daily clutter, including some discarded clothing articles that didn't belong in the house; a woman's shoes, blouse, and jeans. She harrumphed and sighed.

"Is something awry, Denetta?"

She sighed and shook her head, knowing to whom they belonged; she inserted the shirt and pants into the houses autopress. Once managed, she hung them up, walked over, and picked up the black leather Zanotti shoes with 'fuck me heels. She bit her lip in irritation.

Kelly.

While Denetta prided herself on her self-control and decorum as befitting an E-caster, with Kelly, this was not always possible, however. She genuinely hated that woman and knew that Kelly felt the same way. Still, she needed to follow her task list, which included polishing whatever shoes were lay about. Randall's, she fussed with meticulously. Not so with Kelly's shoes. Protocol required the use of leather polish; however, Denetta opted to spit-shine them. Shockingly, some of that spittle found its way inside both footwear.

A soft buzz slipped into the air, and Denetta placed the heels aside. Leaning out over the breakfront where she had been working, she could see that the bedroom door slid open, and the blonde walked out. That she was completely nude was no shock.

Kelly was tall and fit, like most Corp humans. Her body was statuesque and hard. The lustrous hair flowed from her above proud face with a chin that jutted enough to signify strength without looking masculine. Her cheekbones were high but soft, and her eyes brown but just this side of hazel. Denetta could smell and see a scented oil of some type, glistening and defining every muscle and curve. Her breasts, 36 C, she knew from her oft discarded lingerie tags that her tits were firm and natural, neither small nor overlarge. Her nipples were about the length of half of Denetta's little fingernail and rose pink. As far as being gorgeous, Denetta couldn't debate that, but she was ugly in every other sense of the world. Kelly's perfection annoyed Denetta as she knew that her little human body could never match that of the genetically crafted creature in front of her.

Kelly nodded sleepily at Denetta. She absent-mindedly scratched her hair, straw-coloured head.

"Morning, bitch." She said as she walked to the breakfront. Kelly came into the kitchen and brought down two mugs, and even though she did so slowly, she still managed to make a mess of the counter. It was then she reached over to Randall's antique *Dr Who* Tardis – now in its eightieth season - cookie jar. Kelly bit into a ginger snap and then pulled out a pack of menthol cigarettes that she secreted behind it.

Randall never ate cookies, but he knew that Denetta did, and so he bought the cookie jar for her to keep on the shelf, and Mozart always kept it packed for her. Just to irk Denetta, the blonde hid her cigarettes there.

"Morning, madam," Denetta responded with forced politeness because it was against the rules to swear at a Corper, even if they deserved it.

"Hey, droid, shut down that music and be quick about it." Droid was to artificials as a profound slur. Mozart knew that Kelly was the type of person who still used racial slurs."

As the music terminated, she touched the Omega Greens' self-lighting end, and the smoke began to drift up lazily. Thinking thoughts are known only to herself, the lady plopped herself on a couch and reclined like Venus in repose, occasionally staring as Denetta, who continued working - now going about setting two places for breakfast on the dining room table. The blonde shook her head and snorted for some odd reason.

Shattering the mornings quiet, the chimes from the old grandfather clock tolled six-thirty.

"Are you enjoying the coffee today, madam?" Mozart said politely and with civility; only Denetta caught the pique in it.

"It's okay." She yawned.

"What would prefer to choose this morning's music?" Mozart inquired.

"W'ev; just not classical." She laid her head back and scratched her chin. "Just don't wake him, and don't give me a headache worse than I already have."

"Yes, Ma'am. I shall put on something more modern, perhaps something from the "Venture Capitalists? Hostile Takeover for Two? It's been number one for three weeks on the top forty."

"W'ev." She nodded and flicked her ashes on the floor.

"I'll take that in the affirmative. Nevertheless, your verbiage seems unusually truncated. Have you sustained a head trauma? Perhaps an irrecoverable brain haemorrhage is beginning? The speakers erupted with the sounds of well-organised noise.

"Ha, I'm dying of laughter." She rolled her eyes.

One could hope, Denetta muttered under her breath.

Wanting fresh air in the room, Denetta threw open the sliding balcony door, scattering the birds that had alighted on the porch's railing; the balcony was half the size of the condominium. Randall kept two full gardens out here, one for flowers, and the other grew vegetables.

"That smells great; what is it?"

"Breakfast today, Miss Kelly consists of a variety of *Brötchen*, Red Currant marmalade, a dark chocolate spread, cheeses, hams, salami, *Schwarzwälder*, and honey. An exquisite German morning meal."

Kelly had moved to the couch and kicking the stuffed penguins off, whereupon she went about dishevelling Denetta's work. Denetta was too used to it to be annoyed.

The back bedroom opened, and Randall came stumbling out, rubbing his cobalt eyes and glowered at the early morning sun and noise.

His muscles were not obscene in size but cut and defined. It appeared as if his skin had been airbrushed over them, a walking Gray's anatomy lesson. He wore only pyjama bottoms in deference to Denetta's' modest request that he wear clothes. He rubbed his trim dirty blond hair.

"What the Hell, Mozart? You know I don't have to be in till eight." He moved to the kitchen, where he picked up the steaming cup that was always there. He listened for a moment to the strong, Cleary disliking it.

"Dear Buddha, what is this smack? Mozart! Did you program this?"

"No, Randall. I was in the mood for something a little more Baroque; this choice was for Miss Kelly."

"Yeah, well, let's put on something better. Vern Hoffer's Basic Complexity. I love that album." He took his coffee and ran his hand over his chin and assessed that he could pass on the need for today's shave. He had a razor at work and could manage it by noon.

Sipping his morning wide-awake, he watched as Kelly glared at Denetta, who was moving into the bedroom, ostensibly to clean now that Randall was up. Kelly saw Denetta favoured Randall with a discrete but longing sideways gaze. Kelly yelled after her.

"Oh, Denetta, would you get me my panties and bra?" Kelly laughed and stretched a toe out to tickle Randall with it.

"Yes, Ma'am," Denetta answered with exasperated politeness.

"Oh, and be a dear, they need mending. Randall positively tore the crotch out last night, getting them off me."

Inside the room, Denetta sighed and obediently picked up the knickers, and carrying them out, she took them to the seamstress corner. There she opened her mending kit.

"Randall, you were great last night. I thought you'd give me a heart attack." She cooed as she tugged at her hair. He didn't look pleased with it and pushed Kelly off.

"For crying out loud, Kelly, have some self-respect. There are people here." He took a sip of his brew, and then he looked at the ornate clock.

"Look at the time. We slept in late." He walked over to his desk, picked up his watch, clipped his data band on and retrieving his tablet, and ran his finger over his schedule.

"What a day. Today's going to be a long one."

"What's the big deal with that project? Why won't you tell me about it?" Kelly looked confused. Randall sat down next to her. She leaned her head on his shoulder and looked on at the tablet.

"I can't. It's classified on the highest level. Even if I wanted to, which I don't, I couldn't."

"Nice," She took a drag on her cigarette, and pouting, flicked the ashes onto the carpet.

"Oh, Denetta, there are some ashes on the floor. Be a dear." Denetta looked over, sighed and set down the clothes, stood up from her sewing and, walking over to the hand sweeper, picked it up. Kelly stared at the woman and then back at the floor to which she had moved.

"That's enough, Kelly, that's enough!" Randall snapped harshly, standing up, clearly pissed.

Kelly looked confused. "What?"

"You're a mean person, which I tolerated hoping you would change. But I will not tolerate you treating Denetta like hell." He walked over and took the sweeper from Denetta and then walked back over and cleaned the ashes up himself.

Kelly, of her part, threw her nose in the air and snorted. She then grabbed a pillow and folded her arms and legs around it, denying him any further viewing or her nudity. "Seriously? She's a freaking E-Caster; what does it matter? Hire another one; they're a dime a dozen." She snorted. "Want me to do it for you? I have some change in my pockets." Denetta stood stock still, having no idea how to react.

"You need to shut your mouth right now, Kell," Randall set the vacuum down. "And you need to apologise to her or leave."

"What did you just say to me?" Kelly's face flushed, and she crossed her arms tighter in a snap.

"Apologise, or leave," he repeated.

Kelly snapped her mouth open and closed and then stood up rapidly, the obscuring pillow being cast aside. She stamped her foot and whisked over to the counter in a huff. She stood there a moment and stubbed out her cigarette, and then her face crimson, she turned about, jaw set and jabbed her manicured finger at Randall's direction like a dagger.

"Are you screwing her?" Her voice filled with rage. "Are you fucking your maid? Is that what this is about; you like nailing her more than me?"

"Wouldn't matter if I did, now say you're sorry."

"No, we're not doing that," Denetta whispered, shaking her head. "Never."

Kelly was not placated and forged on forward.

"Shut up cunt!" No sooner than the words left her mouth, Kelly closed her eyes realised she had made a grievous mistake.

Denetta, hearing this, had a cold feeling of dread run down her spine. She knelt on the floor and remained silent. She bit her lip, trying not to cry.

Randall was getting pissed. He hated arguing with Kelly. Her occupation was that of a net manager, or 'Spider' as they called themselves. While the term internet had long been the ubiquitous name for the world computing network, the Network managers often adhered to the term 'Web.' Hence, the name Spider came back into usage. Spiders trended to being arrogant, manic, emotionally immature and vindictive. Yes, they had positive virtues such as passion, intelligence and humour; not many people could endure a relationship with a Spider for very long. It took enormous patience, and Randall was one of the few that had been willing to try. Their relationship – now three weeks old - was the longest that Kelly had ever had. Randall's co-workers and superiors all marvelled that Randall could put up with her. The running postulate was the sex between the two must be unreal. It was, but he had had enough.

He liked Denetta and considered her a friend and not just competent help. Often, he and Denetta would talk for hours about art, literature, and history. He taught her to read French, and they were working Latin now.

"She stays, but you can get out."

Denetta saw Kelly's face turn red, and the woman was trembling with unchecked rage. Kelly took a quick step towards her, made a fist and cocked her arm to throw a swing. Mozart leapt smoothly over the kitchen breakfront and grabbed Kelly's wrist tightly, and stepped between the two women in a flash.

"You better goddamn let me go right now because I'm going to kill that whore." Randall took Denetta's hand protectively and shook his head with stern resolve.

"Mozart, show her the door."

Kelly was thunderstruck. She hadn't expected this.

"Oh, this is pathetic" Her eyes opened wide, and her left hand flew to her mouth. "You're in love with her, aren't you?"

Randall stood stock still. It was as if a thousand currents of electricity flew through him. He had never even thought of that; it had never occurred to him that was a possibility. It simply wasn't done. All his life, they had taught him that Outsiders were nobodies, pathetic remnants of a failed culture. Yes, they were humans. But that was it in a nutshell; they were only Homo Sapiens. Randall and Kelly were Homo Superior. But the truth of the matter was that Randall had never considered doing that to Denetta. But to be in love with her?

"You sick son of a bitch!!!" She shrieked.

"I believe that the master has asked you to leave. Do so leave, or I shall have to remove you by force."

Kelly's face fell, and she shoved her free hand out, as Mozart had not released her right wrist. Randall handed her clothes.

"Do you mind?" She spoke through gritted teeth. Mozart looked at Randall, who nodded. Relinquishing his grip, he nevertheless did not move from her side. Kelly pulled her jeans on quickly, without bothering with her intimate apparel. Throwing on her blouse but not buttoning it, she stared at Denetta and mouthed; I'm going to kill you.

"Mozart, if you would?" Kelly turned her back and walked to the door quickly, grabbing her valise.

Mozart opened the door for her. Straightening her back, the corper looked back at Randall and Denetta, snarling.

"I hope you two are happy together, you sick little freaks."

"Good-bye, Miss Kelly." Mozart chirped amiably and closed the door in her face.

"I'm sorry," Denetta whispered, trembling.

"It's not your fault," he put his arm around her. "Are you okay?" He asked, not seeing her as a servant but as a frightened woman.

"I'll be okay," She looked up with a small insincere smile as she stumbled and fell into her sewing station chair. Randall knelt and placed his hands on her knees.

"You're worth twenty of her."

"Master Randall," Mozart pointed at the clock. It showed that it was twenty-seven minutes past the hour. "We don't wish to be dilatory, do we sir?"

Being late was a high infraction. Mozart helped the master dress, and within a minute and a half, the condo door opened. Randall turned and looked at Denetta. "You stay here. Denetta can't hurt you because harming another's employee would be criminal, enough to become downcast. I'll be home as soon as I can." Randall thought a moment. "I would like you to consider moving into the house- permanently. That's something I should have done long ago." He stepped into the hall, smiling and closed the door.

Mozart moved to the balcony patio. Looking down at the bus stop where Randall would board to be transported to the tubes, he checked his watch. It would be another five seconds before Randall would emerge at the bus stop. If all went well, he would board the bus just before the doors closed. There, Randall saw the master run headlong and embark with one half of a second to spare. He would not be late. Seeing him catch the bus, he turned back to Denetta.

"I hate the woman," Denetta said tiredly.

Mozart walked over, picked up Kelly's lingerie and, taking to the kitchen, feed them into the garbage shredder.

"I believe I do as well," Echoed Mozart. "This house would run so much smoother if he allowed me to kill Miss Kelly." Mozart pursed his lips. "I would like to. I have, for the record, compiled a list of six hundred and twenty-two ways to do so and leave no evidence."

"You're joking –right?" Denetta's eyes went wide.

He formed a small laugh. "No, I'm not. While I cannot harm Miss Kelly, my programming does not preclude me from idly planning for such an occasion."

"You're bad." Denetta laughed, but her face quickly fell. "Still, she's right. I'm just an E-caste maid, pretty much disposable."

"Madam, if I may," He walked over and pulled up a chair next to hers. "Do you think that I am disposable?"

"I don't know how to answer that." Her answer stumbled awkwardly.

"No one is disposable. Each of us, Artificials included, are unique. To say someone is unimportant belies the law of physics's — all matter and energy exist and is therefore necessary. We are both energy and matter, simply formulated differently. Since we exist as sentient beings, we recognise our importance; the fact that others cannot see our worth is irrelevant. "

"But she has power over me."

"Human power is an idea and granted only by those that are weak. Such power can be crippled and destroyed by one simple yet unstoppable item."

"Which is?"

"The word 'No.'"

Chapter 10

"We shape our buildings; thereafter, they shape us."
— *Winston Churchill*

Just as the air, and the water they drank, the System provided them life, for the System managed their survival. It was perfection to those who depended on it, and its design warranted no alteration. To do so would be akin to wishing to redesign a hummingbird. The System did not merely manage the life of those who dwelt in Fort Dallas's Omega corporation, for even the rest of the world depended on it. The System was all reaching and irreducibly complex.

The Systems guardians were known only as *The Watchers*.

The Watchers were seemingly everywhere, yet nowhere to be found. Their power was absolute, and their reach seemingly endless. Little was known about them, other than they had set themselves up to be humanities mediator and judge. Their presence kept the balance of power amongst the rival arcologies, forcing a moratorium of peace. Beyond the Arcologies, however, they showed no interest to those outsides of the arcs. Outsider nations seemed irrelevant to their purpose. The only exception to this was when a government or agency aspired to create a new arcology. If this were perceived as a threat to the established equanimity, the Watchers would deploy their mighty hand; The Metatron.

Photos and vid existed of these beings; witnesses had reported giant men in powerful red armour at disasters, falling from the sky in flames and later ascending in the same manner. They would bring wrath and destruction ordained by the Watchers.

Nevertheless, life under Omega was a delicate symphony of balance and control. Within the confines of the city walls, residents moved through their predestined paths like ants in a child's farm, ignorant to the plans of those in power. It was not an unpleasant existence, to be sure. The citizens had never known hunger, poverty, or homelessness, for there was never any unemployment, no homelessness. There were no utility bills, no petrol bills, and no car payments upon which to dwell. Food and water were considered as necessities of life, as was transportation, healthcare and education. Here in the arcs, no parent had to worry about their family's safety, for there were no families. No husband or wife needed to fear for their spouse, for there were no marriages. No one had to worry about anyone but themselves and their jobs.

Omega took care of everything else. To say that each man and woman's lives were controlled from birth to death would be a remarkable understatement. Omega managed everyone's life to the nth degree.

The planning began before even a person's birth.

In the Omega arcology, where Randall lived, the Population Supervision Team (PST) task was to predict how many people would be needed in the years to come to maintain peak corporate operating performance for the city. Every year's organisational personnel calculated Omega's needs to within ninety-eight point oh-two-three-four per cent accuracy. Other variables were considered, such as the three 'D's' - *death, dismemberment,* and *departure* factored. Therefore, the PST allocated precisely the births needed.

The System was designed to optimise its citizens' lives to enjoy sex without women being afflicted with the unfair burden and inconvenience of pregnancy. All food and water distributed into the resource chain were laced with birth control agents to prevent any accidental pregnancies. To avoid issues often familiar to a limited gene pool, such as cursing Hapsburg's Austrian royal house because of inbreeding, the Corporations created a DNA bank. Pregnancy partners were assigned, and those couples that were the most compatible for breeding were ordered to have intercourse. This behaviour would occur until a child's conception. The Pregnancy partners prior relationship status was seen as irrelevant, even if those selected for reproduction were not in a relationship with each other. Sexuality and gender identity mattered not to Omega's bioengineers; heterosexuals or lesbian, transgender or asexual, all were required to avail themselves for intercourse and breeding when ordained. As always, the weight of reproduction fell on the maternal agent.

Some sayings summed up the whole process; for the males, it went something along the line of, "Beg pardon, but I must go knock up somebody. I'll be right back." The saying was a bit more brutal for the women, "Damn it, time to get fucked over again."

Once life was created, and a child birthed, those children became the Occupation and Life Division's responsibility. The OLD was charged with educating and training the children until their working age, usually about their twelfth year. Omegans developed rapidly, both physically and mentally. They would enjoy childhood, but an abbreviated one in comparison to past western standards.

Feti, if viable, were immediately transferred to the Occupation and Life Division. From that moment on birth, their development was guided by the Biovita experts in Incrementums. These growth tanks' purpose was to detect skill aptitudes and then condition and prepare the child for its designated occupation.

Once trained and guided for their primary schooling tasks, the assets were sent to their future occupations to continue the stability and success of the Corp. The OLD tracked their productivity, health and progress. They would ensure that the citizen was remaining healthy, working to performance standards and interacting with society smoothly. If there was a deviation from normal or acceptable behaviour patterns, these recorded and monitored and sent to the 'White Department'. The Occupation and Life Division were able to scrutinise these individual's development by an intricate monitoring and security observation system that far surpassed anything that 21st privacy advocates feared. However, what the A-cast White Department could do would have scared the living hell out of them.

The White Department could track the individual thinking of Omegas million-plus employees in real-time. The department's control nodes were located at the top of the Omega Corporation's office building, a two-and-a-half-mile pyramid that rose high above Fort Dallas. The structure dominated the cities the horizon, and the nodes anti-aircraft light blinked crimson, shining like the all-seeing eye of the Illuminati.

The ability to monitor a persons' thought process was the most significant development of human science, and every Corp could do this, though none were happy about the shared knowledge. This feat, tracking a social asset's *Thought Life,* was made possible by the creation and existence of something called a *Neuromonitor.*

Unknown to the lower castes, each citizen, when birthed, was given an organic digital implant in their brain. This Neuromonitor implant, still colloquially known as a 'chip,' analysed the subjects' behaviour patterns and monitored all thought processes, including their hopes, dreams, and desires. It catalogued and saved an asset's thought life to a central data bank where these were stored, and if an asset malfunctioned, studied.

Citizen assets were, overall, allowed their own behavioural live, dating, developing friends, having hobbies or whatnot. The White Department had little need of adding to their sizeable workload.

However, if a member of Omega society began to perform to subpar standards, that was when the White Department went into action, considerations were then analysed, health micro-managed, and emotions assessed. The WD would balance their direct nutrient intake, providing vitamin or chemical boost in their food wherever possible to boost endorphins and serotonin to increase benevolent moods. If none of this seemed to work, the asset evaluated psychologically.

Suppose a person was lonely and unable to make a romantic or friendship connection or socially inept. In that case, a WD agent might upload a pre-programmed thought process to improve confidence, humour, or even tact and diplomacy issues. This tactic usually worked and steered the thought process of the person's social contact, or frequently romantic or sexual desire, be they male, female or other. The process had a 96% effectivity rating. Still, if the individual continued to decline, they would be determined to be a 'malcontent.' In such a case, a more drastic response required implementation. If the target continued a negative thought path, incorrect actions were discouraged by mental feedback that placed subtle hints and suggestions that those thoughts were undesirable; the changes made possible by the presences of the Obedience pathways that allowed Neuromonitoring. If the employee continued in this decline, other more severe choices were available to the White Department. If they found a malcontent irredeemable, their life came to a swift end, politely referred to as 'closing a case'.

The Omega Corporations' Corp office building was, of course, the centrepiece of Fort Dallas's tableau. At just over thirty-five hundred feet and three-hundred floors, The Omega Pyramid was the most prominent, tallest and most densely populated office building in existence. It had to be, for Theo Magnus would have it no other way.

At any given time, approximately one half-million people were inside working.

The zenith of the building, floors two-hundred-fifty and up were the floors reserved for the A-cast. In the survival of the fittest, the A-cast was the peak of human evolution. Thus, it was these elect that would come to own, manage and controlled the corps.

Over ninety-seven per cent of these individuals were the mortal gods of the A-cast. These fortunate few were not born straight into the caste but had to claw their way up the corporate ladder by proving their capability and ingenuity; this gave the illusion that anyone could rise and change castes.

More than anyone alive, Helen BonHomme loved the view from the top rung of that ladder. The only problem was someone else was standing in her way.

"Theo, these manufacturing statistics are terrible. Perhaps we need a corrective example to shake the departments up?" Theo Magnus posited in obvious annoyance as he glared at the shift manager's personnel file, which he projected onto a hanging display before her.

"No. This was expected; Inspector Thederon was implementing a new production process. While there was only a ten per cent decrease," Helen disagreed as she looked down at her tablet." If we allow him some time to educate the crew in the new methodology in six weeks, we will more than make up for those losses, and within two months, have a surplus."

"Still unacceptable," Theo muttered. "Thederon should have been more on the ball. I want his case closed as a lesson."

"A lesson? What are we going to teach them that risk is unacceptable? Don't colour out of the lines?" Helen sounded incredulous.

Magnus stood up, his glute's tightening as he walked over to the window. A layer of clouds blocked his immediate view of the city, but he could still see the Caddo mountain ridge to the northwest.

"No, not that, but," Theo looked out at the vista, ran a thumb over a slight smear that he and Helen put up there as they pounded each other against the glass last night. "If you haven't noticed, we are developmentally stagnating."

"Theo, our profits were up to seven hundred billion last year. That's hardly piss weight." She shook her head. That was more than the other contenders."

"Well, it's not short-term gains that I'm worried about."

"What is it then?" Touching her thumb and forefinger rings together, the holographic tablet then dissipated.

"Development is not wowing me. Hemlock, Trinity, and New Japan are knocking the brownout of us in tech applications, and I don't even want to discuss our terraforming plans for Europa." He sighed. "We're what, a year behind projections?"

"A year behind schedule, but since no one else has even cracked ice," Helen laughed softly. "Don't stress."

Standing up, she glided behind him, leaning over; she kissed the small of his back and stroked his hair. While Theo gave an appreciative noise, the effort was not successful.

He spun around and pushed her back a bit. Helen sighed, falling back on the bed; playtime was over. She shook her head as she covered her eyes with her arms. "Next year, we're going to be able to go beyond the Solar System. Hell, the Virgil probe is already done scanning Centauri B and is now mapping Proxima Centauri. Isn't that good enough?"

"No. If we can't terraform in our planetary System – what's the point?" Theo sighed and walked over to the shower stall. Theo hit himself with the power spray and began scrubbing his nethers. "Have you read Plutarch? There is a common misquote that says, "Alexander wept, for there were no worlds left to conquer."

"I heard that in a classic heist movie once."

"The correct quote is; *'Alexander wept when he heard from Anaxarchus that there was an infinite number of worlds; and his friends asking him if any accident had befallen him, he returns this answer: "Do you not think it a matter worthy of lamentation that when there is such a vast multitude of them, we have not yet conquered one?"'*

"What's your point?" Helen shrugged.

"Ever wonder why every effort at terraforming has failed, or planetary colonisation fails at a certain size?"

"Not really. Things like that take a long time."

"Perhaps, but it seems odd that every one of us failed, none for really logical reasons."

"You want flawless conquests of other planets? You're asking to know the impossible, like figuring out how to get out of a speeding ticket in Toledo," She wrinkled her nose. "Can't be done,"

"I don't think it's that; I think that the Watchers want us to succeed. I think they want us right here under their red thumbs, and I have a plan to prove it." He smiled as he stepped out of the bath. Theo's showers never lasted longer than a few minutes. "I'm going to reopen and restart Kepler Base."

Helen sat up, and her eyes grew wide. "You can't be serious; that is a horrible, horrible idea. Don't you remember a little thing called *Oishi's Rebellion?*"

"Midori Oishi was just an aberrant who slipped through the cracks," Theo dismissed with a sigh as he looked pulled on his silk boxer-briefs.

"I do not disagree with that," Helen reached over and grabbed an ashtray. "Yes, she was an aberrant, and we missed that. But she was at least emotionally stable. Maybe you don't remember, but I was the one you put in charge of that situation." Helen stood up and knew her day ruined already. She moved to the shower, her turn.

"Yes, you were, and it was your first job as my assistant. You made mistakes, but I don't think you were responsible for a lunar massacre. For some reason, Midori decided that being off the Earth was wrong," Theo pulled on his socks first before reaching for his slacks hanging on a valet. "So, she decided to overthrow the government."

"And I was the one you sent to deal with her, to kill her." She now stood stripped, hand on the shower lever.

"Helen, she was running a revolution and had already killed hundreds of her co-workers." He looked at her and raised his hands, lifting his palms. "She was trying to start a war with all of the other colonies. Ever wonder why? Did that sound like the woman we put in charge?"

"No," Helen's voice cracked as she turned the shower on if only to hide her tears. "But she was my friend. You knew that and sent me to have her killed."

"Yes, I did so because if you want to succeed in this life, you need to understand this; never love anyone. Every time you choose to love someone, you become vulnerable. If they turn on you, they won't need armies to kill you, just a cutting word."

"So, you don't love me?" Helen asked with pain.

"Nope," He shrugged. "I like you – a lot, but love? No. I like our time together, you're a great person, but if you died tomorrow, there would be no tears." He pulled on his shoes. "Let me give you advice, it is better to be alone and have people who work for you out of fear than to allow people inside and then fear them." He saw her turn her head and rub her eyes. "Look, it's nothing personal. It's just good business."

"Right, business. I can do that." She gave a lying nod as she turned on the shower.

"Who's your best System Jock?"

"Kelly Rapaport; without question, why?"

Theo tapped two metal finger rings together, causing a display screen to appear on the back wall.

"Rappaport, Kelly." Her bio was immediately up in holo.

"She's absolutely a beast," Helen said as she poured shampoo in her hair. "Her reviews are impeccable; she never stops, never quits. She has a quick temper and is a bit of a misanthrope but brilliant. "

Theo noticed that Helen's voice was edged with – affection?"

"Is she a Spider? I'm looking for the best."

"Yes," Helen turned to look out the window. "She's most definitely a hard-core network cutthroat. She always has been a killer, always will be. She's a force of nature."

"You slept with her, haven't you?" Theo chuckled.

"More than that," Helen sighed as she worked her fingers through her hair. "We were a couple for some few years before she was upcaste to B before they augmented her. When I met her, Kelly was smart and funny. She could be very brusque but never cruel. I mean, she was a hard-ass, but that was then, now it's different."

"How so?" Theo stood and watched, not just listened. He was eyeing her body language.

"When they upgraded her for cyberwarfare and defences, she started thinking faster, seeing things fifteen moves ahead, then thirty, then hundreds. She could do that linked in, perceive that time moved as fast or as slow as she needed it – her mind moved quantum levels faster, as long as she was plugged in."

"But?"

"The White Department has a limited amount of time to jack a mind. That time must balance a mental downshifting of the brain, at least one-quarter of the amount of time they are linked in. They prefer one-third of the time." She rinsed her hair and then turned the water off.

"The brain needs the time to move back to normal speed. Kelly hated that. She would fight to stay on longer and longer and then wanted her to downshift to be shorter and shorter. Finally, the White Department sent me in to talk with her. I had to tell her to snap in line, or they would reassign her. She didn't take that well but agreed to behave. The thing is – if they were going to reassign her, they would have also stripped her." Helen grabbed her cigar and took a long drag.

"Strip?" Theo couldn't remember what that meant exactly.

"While Spiders like Kelly have a Neuromonitor, you can't control their thoughts like corpers. It's different. A Spider's Neuromonitor must be turned way down, almost off when they are on the network. That's generally not a problem because of their preoccupied with the job. But again – it's a balancing act. If a Spider becomes aware that somethings wrong, they can start losing control, becoming rebellious or unstable. If that happens, they will usually strip them; and flush their mind. Everything they knew or had learned would be gone. They can be 'rebooted', given a new personality, a new identity if you will. They typically bought new templates from artificial manufacturers. Pretty much executing who them, but living the body for someone else, the same thing as death, if you ask me."

"She calmed down," Theo's face asked and stared at the image of Rappaport.

"Calmed down? No. She just learned to behave herself, but she was very, very angry. She knew she's on a short leash. Here's the thing, Theo. A spider's emotions move quicker; they can shift their moods on a dime. Kelly could be playful one minute and thirty seconds later, ready to murder someone for the stupidest of reasons. It's why we broke up." She pulled on her blouse. "None of them knows it, but the White Department has every Spider on Deathwatch. If they break out, goes on a rampage, or, I don't know - kill someone important, they're dead on the spot."

Shaking her head, she ground out the cigar. "Smart? Nobody better, but this is not the one you want for a covert operation against the Watchers. She's a goddamn freight train. Use her for cyber defence? That would be like giving someone a chain saw for eye surgery."

"Frankly, she sounds perfect, like a flawless predator." Theo buttoned up the front of his shirt. "Look, I don't want a repeat of Midori. That's something I for which I have real regret - which is why I want you to supervise Rapport's progress and report directly to me. You know what to look for, and if it starts to go badly, we shut her down mercifully. We'll plant some C-190 in her Neuromonitor. "no one wants another massacre." As he put his cufflinks in, he spoke softly. "If she goes sideways on us, we can and will close her down, her and only her." Theo's voice was as comforting as he could make it. Frankly, he didn't give a shit if he had to blow up ten thousand people. Kelly pulled on her black stockings.

"So, if something goes wrong with Kelly, you'll have me kill her too, won't you?"

"It doesn't have to be you, no."

Helen stood up and looked at Theo, arms crossed. "Do you know what Midori told me when I ordered her against the wall? She said that she suddenly realised that if we went out in space and discovered alien worlds, we would be the space monsters that we are afraid of because that's what we are - monsters."

Chapter 11

Helen BonHomme's Office,

Fort Dallas.

For many years, Helen had served alongside Theo, starting when she was fifteen, coming off a successful two-year stint as administrative management for a D-Caste section. Promoted up to the B-Caste, Theo had given her the position of assistant to his secretary. She did well for four years, and eighteen months ago, she was promoted from that task up to the A-cast, where she became his second in command. The relationship changed from him being her mentor to her lover.

After her long road to the A-cast, the presence of Neuromonitors was made known to her. Appalled by their existence, she was told that was the standard reaction. Theo took the time to explain the necessity of which, he claimed, was necessary for the survival of the way of their culture.

Her outrage soon faded to understanding and then questioning. For one question that persisted and could not be exorcised; is my mind genuinely free? Night and day, she ruminated on that query and others like it; does anyone but myself control me? What were the long-term effects of the Neuromonitor that severe? Could the programming last onwards of months or years?

Once Helen had become second in command, very little was kept from her, and one of those things was Theo's control of all his departments where medical records were concerned. There, in the Medical Department, the answers to her questions had to reside. The problem was that only he could approve access. To do that, she would need help. Such help could not come from Omega because anyone would turn her over to Security because their Neuromonitors would force that decision on them. That meant Helen would have to go for outside help – a treasonable offence. She lingered over the question of the value of such an act, but her need to know was overwhelming. Arranging travel to go outside of the arcology for business purposes to New Japan, she knew she could obtain assistance there. Once there, and after making the right contacts, she was directed to the most unlikely locals to the Nagano Prefecture where resided – the office of The Prime minister of New Japan; Ieyasu Suizei.

Prime Minister Suizei was of profound wisdom. After conducting the mundanities of negotiating trade fees for New Japan's commodities; rice, organic chemicals, gems, and precious metals, she asked him if she might make a private request. Upon hearing, Suizei was intrigued and receptive, that being that there was a favour she could do for him at a later date. His request seemed equitable enough.

Suizei's people did the actual hacking in Ina at the new Japan technical facilities. It took three days – pushing the limits of her scheduled time available. Nevertheless, Suizei's people were very good at their job. The excavation of Helen's personal information was classified as a high priority.

Upon receipt, she then made her way back to Omega covertly, using private transport. During the trip, she studied her papers at great length.

Their records showed a consensus that once removed that a person's thoughts were indeed their own; that consensus was not, however, unanimous.

She read further, seeking the answers of just how the damn things worked. From what the engineers in the White Department detailed, the 'chips' design was a combination of bio-organic grafting combined deep level programming skills. The design surprisingly predated The Shutdown. Helen thought that whoever had created; may have been the most extraordinary scientific mind ever. The odd thing, however, was that nobody had ever claimed the credit for the breakthrough. It merely showed a creation date, the design specs. While the Shutdown had destroyed most data, these had somehow survived.

The Neuromonitor's operational power source was its electrical output and cellular activity, functioning by integrating with the brain's synapses. The monitor's base coding stored in the chip via D-Tech allowed for future updates and unpacking for direct distribution into the brain's cortex. The information would then relay directly alongside normal mental functions. The Neuromonitor would transmit these thoughts in real-time to the Occupation and Life Division or White Department as needed.

As she perused the documentation, it seemed to Helen that the reports showed that the chips' initial implantation was into children two months old - before the child's Metopic and Coronal sutures sealed. There were no signs that the NM impeded healthy brain development or contributed to brain disorders. Statistically anyways, it seemed that Omega was, by and large, a group of happy campers. The White Department credited this panacea to make any citizens desires to be available to them; off-work intoxicants, sex, entertainment, the arts, and music lay at fingertips; whatever was necessary to make and keep them happy and productive was available. No need was left unfulfilled. However, that being true for some inexplicable reason Omega's analysts could not fathom; an average of nineteen per cent of the population committed suicide annually.

The behaviour and cultural experts had analysed the underlying motives of suicide; mental illness, finances, relationships, unfulfilled dreams and expectations. Every one of these issues carefully observed; the White Department directed all individual lives to make the corporate experience successful. Regardless, they could not catch all of the problems.

Helen read the documents detailing patterns of behaviour that suicides seem to follow. Work being the centrepiece of corporate society, the depressive patterns invariably began with a decline in work productivity and a subsequent slow withdrawal from social events and relationships. Emotional displays such as depression, rage, and public outbursts increased from almost non-existence to frequent. When ordered or directed to health care workers, there was a reticence to do so. Some of the affected would seem to, for a time, return to normative behaviour, while others would become stuck in a pattern of unproductive out of character behaviour. Associates and friends saw behaviour shifts against the norm; someone who was sexually active might stop to be, and more sedate may go on a wild orgy of excess. The most tangible signs were malaise and hopelessness, including a sense of loss and emptiness.

The cause or manner of those committing self-murder was as varied as the individuals themselves. There were no correlations that revealed who would kill themselves or how; it seemed to be a mixture of impulse, availability of resources or emotional state.

Of the dead, there was no singular locus or cause. Psychologists could find no similarities in the DNA of those who suffered death by suicide; occupations varied, personalities differed, and friendships were wildly divergent. No solution that eliminated this self-destruction existed. The only constant, or near-constant, was the note-leaving.

In many cases numbering enough to rate a noteworthy statistical constant, the left explanations on paper, or electronics a closing comment that was best summed up as;

What lies beyond more?

This question unnerved Helen, for, on several occasions, she often felt the same sense of isolation and emptiness. Sure, she was as much a hardass and could be cutthroat as any corper. The thing that troubled Helen most was the fact that acquisition never provided satisfaction. You pick one plant, one tree, and then soon enough, a forest is not enough. She saw it in herself, and that, more than anything else, terrified her.

 She had accessed her data to examine here medical records to see what her psych profile was. It showed a tendency to anxiety, but nothing serious. When she continued and looked at her genetics – that anxiety came back in a rush, resulting in her vomiting onto the elegant Persian carpet.

Chapter 12

Randall Davison's office,

Fort Dallas.

You could see it from the horizon easily enough; The Great Dome was five miles high. It covered the thirty-nine-mile circumference, which included Dallas to the east, Fort Worth, Midlothian at the south and Grapevine to the north. The Arcology brought them all under one transparent vault; the supporting walls were a half-mile in height and five miles thick. Sealing the area behind a wall was child's play, taking only two years. The dome and the machines necessary for its retraction took seventeen more years to construct. This endeavour required hundreds of thousands of Homo Superior, corper management workers, hireling human outsiders, and armies of synthetics and artificials. The vault was crafted from a seventeen-yard-thick composite of poly-silicates, translucent steel mixed along with more classified materials. It was thought to be durable enough to withstand heavy artillery, bombardment, and according to the mechanical engineers, withstanding one hundred-kiloton nuclear detonations. Nuclear attacks were pretty much moot, as no one owned nuclear weapons anymore; the Watchers had seen to that.

The Great Dome could manipulate its own climate, making rain, which it often did because it was needed to help the city maintain its humidity level. This feat was accomplished in several ways, some as straightforward as opening water sprinklers mounted on the sides of buildings and high above via crisscrossed pipes. Other times climate control controlled the humidity and temperature to form actual cloud bursts inside the dome; whichever means were facilitated, the forecast was foretold by the news so people could plan ahead. In emergencies, the Weather Control and Atmospherics department would allow exterior weather exposure by opening the colossal cupola. Opening the arch was a herculean task and could be opened only partially. To date, WCA had opened it only three times in the past generation. It happened to be the fourth day it was occurring. The choice was due to the replacement of decade-old machinery needing to be replaced. The timing was unpopular due to a bank of cumulonimbus clouds having moved into the area, and thunder; lightning and rain were predicted within the next short while. The rain was coming in with a strength and intensity not seen in some time. The satellite imagery seemed to indicate that the prolonged drought the south was experiencing was coming to an end. Unfortunately, the maintenance would require the doom to be open for several days.

Randall Davidson looked out the window of his office in New Projects Development. Situated atop the 245th floor of the Omega Pyramid, Randall's office was egregiously opulent and roughly the same size as his nine-point point eight thousand square foot six-bed, eight bath condominium. Appointed with beautifully woven Bolivian carpeting that accented but not hid the wooden floors, he sat amongst books' walls and walls. None oh is tomes were fiction, humour or any such thing. Every single one was about engineering, theories on engineer or biographies of engineers; chemical, electrical, nuclear or digital – he didn't discriminate.

Randall's work was that of a speculation engineer, one who would take hypothesis and conjecture to the drawing board and determine if such things were possible, and if possible, what the requirements were. His floor was restricted to any asset not of at least B Caste. The NPD team was of vital importance to Omega, for it was in these hands the future of Omegan business success resided. Everyone's creativity and innovative spirit so essential to the Corp that each member of the staff had an individual case manager to whom they reported.

His impressive mahogany desk covered grey-white hand-worked marble was currently buried under tablets, papers, and blueprints. Right now, a synthetic servant named David poured coffee carefully heated to be the perfect serving temperature of 58 degrees Celsius. Randall thanked him and, leafing through the morning's papers, set to down to be the genius he was designed to be, which was not an easy task today.

There was no arguing, should he have wanted to, that Denetta was beautiful, but it was a beauty that did not conform to what Omegan's now considered the acceptable standard of the same.

To compare, one only had to look at Kelly; her face was perfectly symmetrical. Each of her eyes was equidistant from each other; Kelly's were likewise level with her ears' tops. Even her nose was on the same invisible horizontal line of the bottom of those orbs. Her teeth were healthy, even, and snow white. Humans, on the other hand, possessed facial defects; with Denetta, they were readily apparent.

For one, each eye was black except for the amethyst iris, which made it appear that a luminescent ring resided in a swirling ebon cave. For another, she freckled and in an uneven, blotchy pattern. Her nose slightly bent in the middle, and her lips,

Randall closed his eyes at the thought. Denetta's mouth was naturally full, sensual, and plump. They matched no other women – or man's lips he had ever seen. Like most Outsiders, she wore little makeup, and while other owners demanded that they dress and appear as ornately as possible, Randall made no such demands. As part of her pay, he did grant her a clothing allowance in addition to her generous stipend. While thirty thousand dollars was a trifling to an Omegan, thirty grand was a massive amount in the Cubes outside where she lived. Nevertheless, she only used the hint of makeup and left her lips the pink hue with which she had born.

But it wasn't just her beauty where he lingered; there was a depth of character that outshone her circumstances. Denetta was kind, and he saw it on the streets when she walked home. She would see other Outsiders and give them money or food he often visited. She would frequently take her lunch in the park and feed the birds with her lunch break. She had never asked for a raise either.

The corporate caste system was typical, albeit odd on occasion. By law, you were required to provide them with a baseline salary, that amount being minimum wage or higher if you chose. Denetta's pay was considerably above the minimum.

She was bright, intelligent even. She spoke French like a native and could recite every musician and their position in the Omegan philharmonic. He had never taken her, but they usually watched the bloodstream together. Once, the orchestra performed in the public park across from the balcony and he and Denetta watched it together.

Randall tapped his pen absently-mindedly on his desk.

Could I be?

His reverie was shattered by the quivering of his pen phone panel. He tapped the display, and the dock screen showed that it was Omega's second in command who was also head of his department.

"Good morning, Helen. How can I help you today?"

"Hi, could you make an opening for us to meet this morning? I know your schedules loaded, but I need a moment." Translation: Get your ass up here right away.

"Ten minutes work for you?" Randall picked up some paperwork that he couldn't leave out in the open.

"Ten minutes then. Thank you." Translation: Not one minute more.

Two weeks ago, they had met in her office, an unnerving experience, to be sure. The sunlight streamed through windows comprised saltwater fish tanks which created the illusion of being underwater; the light cast on the walls shimmered and spiralled as if one were looking up below the surface of the water. Rising from her chair, the lady came from behind her desk. On that day, Helen handed him a classified task, a piece of antique technology that she said she would very much like for him to analyse. With that, she had slid over a five hundred terabyte hard drive and a thick, yellowed manual.

She informed him that it was a program written in older code and held great import for Omega. Moreover, he had been selected to do the analysis showed Omegas great faith in him and would most likely mean A-cast promotion. The caveats were that in no uncertain terms, he was to report only to her. If anyone asked him what he was working on, he would not only not be silent about it but warn them that if they asked a second time, The White Department would send a report. This task was to be performed on standalone networked systems, as there were no other copies. For securities sake, he would be given the only drive, and because Helen needed the data encryption broken, and she did not have the skill to do so.

He could use a private mainframe system in his office, one which was set up as he spoke, and one at home— which likewise was having a new one installed into a now secure room. She informed him that neither system was accessible by anyone else. Once he naturally accepted the task, she told him to take the Quantum locked portable drive home.

Helen would delegate out his other pending projects to allow Randall to focus solely on this duty, which bore no other name than The Assignment.

Back in his office upon examination and assisted by the manual's helpful assistance – which he was not allowed to copy or reprint- it would take Randall most of the day before he saw the threads of a possibility. His early posit was that it could be a program that would translate and communicate with different computer programming languages. Staying into overtime, he saw that it had communicated with the major languages of the day such as Ada, Haskell, PROLOG or any others in usage before The Shutdown. Its level of sophistication was such that it could not only decipher but assimilate that language. The translation could then inject its program matrix over whatever operating system was in use, thus sublimating that OS to its own. This accomplished anyone who had control over the application could control whatever system that had been assimilated. Its purpose was obvious; anyone in possession of this could shut down and utilise any desired programming. Randall pushed back from his workstation and took a deep breath. He was staring at the application, which was the cause of the Shutdown.

After four days, Helen called him back to her office to report back on his discoveries.

Randall placed the papers in his desk, walked over to his private elevator bank and tapped Helen's name. As he left, the lights dimmed in his office, signifying he either wasn't there or wanted to be left alone. The elevator opened to reveal a rounded stuffed cushioned bench that abutted the cone of the elevator car. He still elected to stand as it was only five floors up. He did drink from the fountain and straightened his suit in the mirror, however.

At the chime, he arrived at the building's zenith. The doors quietly opened onto a short hallway which opened into the receptionist's office. Although nowhere near as large as his. An all encircling oil-painted mural adorned the walls. Incongruously it comprised a history of military successes. Framing the beginning and end of the doorway to Helen's office were two marbles statues; *The Three Graces* by Antonio Canova, and the other edifice was Bernini's *Apollo and Daphne*.

In front of that door, but behind a sizeable oak desk, Helen's assistant was busily working away.

"Hello, Heidi."

The receptionist looked up and smiled. Heidi had a lovely exotic face and possessed curly black hair that came down her back, cinched in a small, neat bow. She wore a smooth purple eye shadow that highlighted her beautiful brown eyes. She bore a striking similarity to Helen, he thought.

"Afternoon Randall, Ms BonHomme is ready to see you." Pushing a button, she opened Helen's titanic office door. "You may go on in now." Heidi tapped her desk screen, and the office doors opened. Randall straightened his suit and ties once more and entered the room. Randall stood up, gave a confused 'Thank You' and then seeing that she was already back at work. He left, the massive oaken door shutting behind him.

"Hello, Randall; a pleasure to see you again." BonHomme looked him over, shook his hand, and then sat on her desk as she motioned for him to be seated.

"Let's get to the point and dispense with the chitchat. How is the assignment going?"

"Unnerving," Randall frowned and then asked. "Did you know?"

"That it was the cause of the Shutdown? No, but I suspected. I researched and discovered that the US Government had procured a copy and were trying to find a way to create an antivirus application. Clearly, they hadn't because The Shutdown happened." Helen lied how she came upon the information was very different than what she explained to Randall.

"What do you want me to do with this? I mean, the damage has been done. You can't put a nuclear explosion back in the bomb."

"What do you think I want?" Helen had mused.

"I honestly have no idea."

"Guess."

Randall pursed his lips tightly and thought a moment. "A digital autopsy so that we can examine what may be able to prevent another such incident?"

"Not at all," Helen had looked at him with a casual expression. "I want you to make it better. I want you to build on it. And make me something that can bring the other corporations to their knees." Randall was not an idiot, and the insight and intellect that allowed him to dominate his field did not shut off just because he was in her office. "If you did that, the Watchers would shut us down with," Randall's eyes grew wide. The truth was obvious.

"This isn't about the other corps at all; you want to use this against the Watchers."

"Yes, precisely that, "Helen smiled. "Think about it, Randall; we could cast off the limitations that they have set on the planet. They tell us how we can do business, what we can do, and where to go. We have no say about anything when it comes to dealing with each other. It's slavery."

"Ironic because our civilisation is based upon slavery; artificial and outsider." Randall scoffed.

"That's it exactly, don't you see? We can end all this if we can shut the Watchers down. No more will we be contained in the cities. We can be free to grow and help those in the Badlands."

Randall thought that it sounded good on the surface for a second, but as he thought about it, his headache returned.

"You cracked the code, and all I need from you know is can you make it so that it can do the same thing with D-Tech."

"It's possible, but there is a danger." Randall rubbed his chin. "I don't know what the results will be if it interfaces with artificial intelligence. That's the basis of our network. I have no idea what would happen if that occurred."

"Wouldn't we still be able to control the program? Doesn't an alpha programmer bind it?"

"True," Clearly, she had read the manual. "I need you to understand that I can't guarantee complete success. There will need to be a trial and error phase."

The last thing she told him she didn't care how, but it was to get it done.

Chapter 13

Theo Magnus's suite,

Omega Pyramid,

Fort Dallas.

"Sir, it's as you expected." It was another woman's voice.

"How very, very disappointing," Theo frowned, setting his now drained orange juice glass away. "Are you sure of your assessment?"

"Aye,"

"Regrettable. Contact security and review all of her pertinent data, calls, messages analysed and bring them to me forthwith."

"Braw chum, I'm on it."

Chapter 14

Network Management,

Omega Security offices,

Garland, Texas.

System Managers knew one truth that stood out above all else, and that code was boring to look at; always was, always would be. Since the dawn of programming, those that write code have lived in their unique and insular worlds. In Omega, although they were still members of the B caste, system managers were rated as members of the A-cast due to the sensitive nature of their job. That being said, they were constantly reminded that still only receiving B caste pay and benefits. The A-cast never invited them to their parties- which was fine with them because most were as social as moles.

Kelly was different; abrasive, course and lewd Kelly didn't fit in anywhere in her department, and they only put up with her because she was the best at what she did. Also known was that Kelly never put up with anyone's bullshit, and she was more than happy to tell people off if the mood struck her. While she was an excellent code reader, she was far better at system defence and investigation.

As far back as anyone could remember, those who worked in, or with, computers preferred some sort of visual interface. Popup windows were fine, but you really wanted to work with some form of a graphic-user-interface when you had the choice. System Operators felt more comfortable and at ease if they could use a virtual metaphor for cyber defence or warfare.

Kelly loved to drive, and she loved antique cars the best of all.

Her radio blaring while cruising along the Italian Coast in her shimmering crimson overcharged 1966 Alfa Romeo Duetto Spider, Kelly passed by the villa of Marmoretta at about two hundred kilometres an hour. While weaving through the late morning's traffic, her hair blew in the summer breeze. As all 150 horses broke free, she laughed at the beloved sound of her car's engine. The naked sun flourished behind her in a cloudless sky. Feeling the heat on the back of her neck and worried that she might burn, Kelly pushed the switch and raised the ragtop.

The Amalfi coastal road was Kelly's favourite stretch of road in the whole world, and travelling north-easterly, she took a right at Minori to head over to Salerno. She hadn't been to *Ristorante Cicirinella* in some time, and they were world-famous for their Arancini di Riso. Having been a frustrating morning dealing with Randall and his whore of a servant, she just wanted a beautiful quiet drive today, and later, then lunch. Nonetheless, she was still on call. Smiling and looking off to her right, she savoured the beautiful cobalt of the Mediterranean. Merging onto the Via Porta, she slowed the Spider as she approached the town on the *Ponte Ramo Svincola Vietri,* dropping to 60.5KPH. Once in town, she merged onto the local streets where she saw traffic was blessedly light to non-existent. Her eyes caught the mirror, and someone was coming up hard behind her; she tapped the brake and moved to the side to allow the driver to pass her. Kelly signalled and switched lanes back to the left. However, the ice-blue 1980 De Tomaso Pantera GT5 stayed on her ass.

Kelly tapped her fingers on the steering wheel and then made a right turn – the car followed.

"Access rear rider's public data signature,"

"No signature on record." The voice came through the car's speaker.

"Well, well, well."

All of Omegas customers had a dedicated network access point, or 'node'. This way, each client could be vetted, tracked and conduct their business with assurance to Omega and their business. This simplified Network security because each system manager knew, by and large, their client's profiles. In her virtual imagery, she saw the clients as automobiles – each a metaphorical representation of her assigned clientele.

This car was not on her list of approved customers, and as it was tailing her closely. Taking a left at the Via Costiera and leaving the town, she unleashed the engine and watched as the scenery grew far more wooded, and the air became slightly chill. The road turned into the *Strata Statale Amalfitana*, her alarms went off, and the music on her radio grew static ridden, and her electrical system faltered.

In a flash, the GT5t passed her on the right and then rudely cut back in front of her. Slamming on its brakes, it forced a spin out on Kelly.

"Hard scan!" Kelly screamed and dropped the car into first, as she dug into the gravel on the shoulder, slamming the petrol, and angrily upshifting Kelly went into high-speed pursuit.

The De Tomaso was now flooring it and disappeared over the horizon. Kelly slammed it into fifth and shot up over the hill; if she couldn't catch up to him, there was every chance she would lose him in the heavy traffic up ahead.

"Scan results – it seems you have been tagged with a hitchhiker."

"You're joking, right?"

"Negative."

Hitchhiking meant that someone had latched onto your signal feed and established a parasitic link. The hitchhiker comp could, if they were very, very good would go unnoticed and hide in the legitimate user's feed. This, of course, was nothing new, and hackers of years past did this with viruses, rootkits, and other forms of malware. Unfortunately, over the years, nothing changed but the sophistication of the hack. And it was only with equally sophisticated analysis software that one could detect the parasite.

But hitchhikers were more dangerous. A sophisticated hitching program could clone your signal and backtracking, copy all live or stowed data which feed or hosted your readout. Hitchhiking into the core security of Omega could be disastrous.

"Cut all outgoing and incoming feeds." Toggling a switch on the dash, Kelly locked the node down, shutting down all points of ingress and egress. The highway was quickly emptied of all cars – authorized clients — and left only the Pantera on the road. Kelly car shot forward. It was just him and her.

As she closed on him, she saw that the Italian countryside was not holding in his area — the Pantera now possessed its own digital environment, radiating out hundreds of feet around it. The opposing car had made a *Soap Bubble*. A Soap Bubble was a tiny self-sustained virtual environment, separate from the host network.

Kelly swore but wasn't too worried, provided she acted quickly. Bubbles demanded a massive amount of power and lasted but a few moments. If she did not lock down the Pantera, who was storing and controlling the hitchers download feed, the bubble could pop, and the GT5 would be able to escape immediately. Since she had locked down all network exits, the sphere was virtually the only way out.

"You have 5 seconds to engage data capture."

Kelly closed on the Pantera; piercing its sphere, she readied a sys-kill switch. The Sys-kill would cause Kelly to be cut off from her real-world system, then quickly after it shut down, the whole node would cut off the Pantera's stream, which would result in one of two things. If the driver was using virtual gear, it could cause immediate mental blindness — the offender would no longer be able to see or re-access any Omegas nodes unless he went and purchased an entirely new computer system. But if the hacker were greyjacked into the network, it would kill him outright. Greyjacking meant that a physical port line was feed directly into the brain employing an implanted data port, usually situated on the left temple. However, that was not what happened. Instead of her making another kill — for which afterwards she could paint a small symbol of a comp on her battle pod, Kelly found herself ten thousand feet in the air, no longer in chasing each other in cars, but now dogfighting with World War One biplanes. Kelly, deathly afraid of heights, screamed, now panic-ridden her bio-signs set off alerts at the Sys-managers table, they initiated her exit.

Kelly's jock chair reclined, and hydraulic arms lifted the security pod sealing lid. The bio-doc stood next to her and handed her two Tylenol, an antianxiety pill, and a glass of orange juice. Kelly swung her legs around and dropped them to the floor.

"He knew; I don't know how but he knew." Kelly threw the pills down and chased it with the juice.

"But your personnel files are hardcopies. There is no stored data record of any of our Sys-mangers." The doctor rubbed the bottom of his nose, pulling on it with two fingers. "There is no possible way he could have known your phobia. It must have been a coincidence."

The main thing that White Department geneticists had not been able to engineer or breed out of Homo Superior was the basest of human emotions; lust, hate, or fear. Were they able to remove one or all of these, then the potential for obedience and productivity would have been nearly unlimited – but that was not the case here. What was known was that the more you tweaked a human being to higher levels, the higher the volatility rose. Phobias were commonplace; considered irrational by most psy-docs. Nevertheless, they were still felt deeply by the individual involved. Usually managed by conditioning and Neuromonitoring, they could not altogether be eliminated.

"No, he knew. He switched just as I was about to Syskill," she spoke rapidly. "It seems that we have a mole in the department." Kelly stood up and brushed her golden hair back. "Notify the Security department head." she carefully slowed her breathing.

"She's waiting for you in her office. It seems that there's a priority security matter she wants you to attend to." The doctor bowed and stepped back.

Great, not even a chance to pee. Kelly left the pod floor where a hundred other sys-managers were interred in their crypts, tracking. Walking up the stairs, Kelly took a left and went to the third door on the right. The woman who met her there offered Kelly a seat.

"Theo has made a personal request that you meet him in his office."

"You're shitting me."

Chapter 15

Ziyun Getu He Chuandong National Park,

Guiyang, Guizhou province, China.

Located at the end of a nearly three-thousand-foot cave system, once only accessible by raft lay the great Miao room Cavern, which constituted only one part of the vast network of voids of the Gebihe cave system. The cavern's size and conditions provided everything needed to build and contain a city of its own; fresh water, space, and vast amounts of secrecy. At the centre of the Miao room, whose height could accommodate the Eiffel tower, was the Watchers' Great Hall. Standing at the transept, one could see another elevated aisle with video monitors high above, illuminated like stained glass windows. Myriads of ornate chandeliers hung from the cathedral roof, lighting the men and women below in a warm light. Humidifiers kept the air dry, and much of the rooms were now sealed and climate-controlled. However, seamless, transparent walls and windows left the inhabitants the sensation of being in wide-open spaces. Where more opaque walls and roofs were needed, interspersed throughout them resided illuminated frescos depicting man and machine's history. At precisely the midpoint between the ceiling and the floor, running from the west front of the cathedral to the presbytery, was an elevated gold and marble walkway. At equidistant points, straightforward spiral staircases descended to the floors of the nave. It was in all appearance an exquisite Nouvel Royaume Cathedral.

Striding down the central gangway, elevated above the floor several a dozen yards below, was a portentous figure who looked down on the thousands of adherents who moved in organised and ordained patterns below his leather and brass boots. His strides were long and official; in his right hand, he carried a walking stick. It was no affectation as he did need it. Over the years, several surgeries had failed to repair an injury to his right knee. No one would ever comment on the slight limp because no fools worked here.

Close to seven feet tall and clad in crimson flowing robes, the person's tunic was decorated with stylish piping, and over their heart rested several military campaign ribbons. His blouse cinched his neck in a high black collar. The man's visage was stern and carried the weight of harsh decades. His pallor pale, the man's countenance looked more akin to a Grecian statue than a breathing person. Piercing grey eyes looked over all the activity about him, and seeing nothing amiss, he allowed his thin lips to give a slight smile -little more a mere horizontal slit in his face. Long braided night-black hair came to a sharp widows' peak.

The Commissar, one David Severenson, was a man who knew the old ways were the best, and as such, he instilled rigid discipline and used the aspects of history and faith to guide him. Over the years, he had successfully installed the values of obedience, order, and loyalty to his people. The Commissar had seen the effects of worldwide social decay; poverty, oppression, rape and human trafficking. Days of unchecked, unmonitored, and reckless industrial greed he had taken as the warning, it was meant to be, and now it was his life's work to prevent that from happening again; a future possibility he loathed it beyond all else. Therefore, Severenson's imperative was to run this world with strict adherence to the highest quality that humanity could produce - piety. Anarchy, disorder, and dissent were cancers in any society, and it was his goal in life to cure it or, at the least, keep such malignancies in remission. It was Severenson's conviction that piety brought respect, humility and purpose. That being true, a pious person would not mistreat others. Nor would such a being would never denigrate another because of another hue, sexuality, speech or belief. This inherit righteousness would eliminate the abuse of each other, children, and beasts. No reverent soul would exploit the weak or helpless, for pious humans knew their place in the world to be stewards and not exploitive.

The Commissar had a defined vision of how the Earth should conduct itself. Thus far, the Almighty did not force his creations to adhere to such necessary decorum because of the folly of free will. The Commissar felt no such compunction about accepting such limitations.

It had taken years and millions of working hours, but he had successfully brought order into a sundered world. Severenson had executed his vision, and now his congregational domain lived in a symphony of coherence and equilibrium. This balance was what the Commissar wanted more than anything in life; equality, harmony, and parity amongst all peoples and nations. No one group, corporation or country should be permitted to amass a disproportionate amount of power or wealth. It was not an easy task to protect the weak. Sacrifices were required since true egalitarianism was impossible because there were far too many people living in squalor and poverty. To attempt to alleviate that was an impractical endeavour. But there was something he could do, which was to establish control over the apex of greedy capitalistic evolution - the Mega-Corporations.

The Mega-Corps survival was rooted in greed, cruelty and oppression. When the Shutdown came and nations crumbled into anarchy across the world, the Corps stood fast behind walls, fences, and gunfire. It was these vultures that had hoarded the resources to continue their conglomerate existence. They had guns, shielded computers, livestock, seeds and millions of acres of arable land, both above and below the ground. It was these men and women who built sealed enclaves and shut the dying world out.

Severenson knew that these 'businessmen' would become the gods in their minds if left to their own devices, false Olympians wielding power. This, he could never allow happening.

To defeat these massive militaries and economic powerhouses, he would prepare a force, one completely loyal and sworn to his cause. The Commissar would carefully recruit these acolytes, then indoctrinate them about the evils of the past; how men and women were left to starve and die because of such things as the colour of their skin, gender, who they loved, or their religious ideologies. He would warn them of human's propensity for genocide and war. Within years Severenson possessed a following of tens of thousands of loyal men and women. He provided them with food, shelter, and medical attention, which in the Badlands were in short supply where feudal wars and cruelty ran rampant. More than just the necessities of life, Severenson offered them the one thing the world severely needed.

Purpose.

That purpose being the restoration of the world to harmony and peace. The Commissar informed his adherents this would not be done by unnecessary force or annihilation. It would be by the careful moderation and pruning of human civilisation. They could grow, even becoming wealthy. They could go ahead and travel to the stars if they wished, but what they could never do again is to become so powerful that they could threaten the whole world.

Severenson knew that poverty would always be with them, and those dire choices would need to be made. This understanding that if his dream could grow to fruition, he would have to gain power equivalent to the strongest of the Corporations; to do so marshalled his forces and retreated deep into the Earth. It was in the vast hollows of China that he found the resources and means to rebuild. In there, they took the electronics devices long left dead. He had his forces steal and loot from the growing arcologies- only enough so that they could begin the mass production needed. Over time he built his own dark Orwellian Morlock society. It took years, trial and error, and the central cavern mouth's closing to secure their future.

Decades later, Fait Accompli, they all knew what the Watchers were capable of with them possessing enough sheer power to enforce balance; strength digital, agricultural, energy, military, financial and political. What he needed now was a show of force.

Two decades after The Shutdown, two rival arcologies vied for control of the Sinai Basin. The arcologies were both well-armed but still stuck in an age-old war rooted in religions and pride. It did not take long for his caverns spiders to search through both combatants' files. It was child's play to hack and infiltrate if one but positioned an agent in the right places. While the Commissar knew they were about to go to the redline in their wrath, with but a single internet broadcast, Severenson revealed 'the Watchers' were demanding that all belligerents stand down. He explained his position in full detail, offering both sides a realistic political compromise for the symbiotic sharing of resources and land distribution.

They rejected him with scoffing laughter.

This insubordination was utterly unacceptable, and it was time to lay his cards down, to show that there was someone who stood for justice, peace and life. But to do this, he would have to show them the backside of the hand of friendship.

And so, he commandeered every news and information service and then proceeded to tell the population that The Watchers had arrived. No more would anyone be allowed to attack or victimise their neighbour; no more was there to be the unchecked wars of the past.

The Commissar offered his help one more time but met with no reply, and having no other options; he informed the New Egyptian Dynasty what their neighbours had in store for them - nuclear annihilation.

Every video screen in the world simultaneously displayed the fiery and completely unplanned and unauthorised launching of the Second Exalted Ottoman State's fusions missile fleet. While the SEOS arcology was centred near Istanbul, the missiles were launched from Ankara. He could have detonated them there, but that would not send the message he needed to address. The desire to reside in paradise could only be possible if one could only see the torment of hell.

The Grand Vizier demanded that his missiles be returned to his control. The Commissar offered nothing in return - no advice, no terms. Instead, the vizier could only watch as his weapons went stratospheric and then fall. Only now did he comprehend they were being redirected down onto Istanbul. The vizier pleaded, apologised and begged for the Mega-Cops life. Severenson had long since silenced the audio.

So, it was in silence that the world watched the blinding flares and towering black, orange clouds mushroom over the Ottoman Arcology as it vanished in nuclear fire.

As the world stood to watch in fear, the Watchers informed the world there would be law and a harsh one. People were free to pursue life, liberty, and the pursuit of happiness. They could dream and build, but there were limits to be put in place.

No more would aviation be allowed so that arms and armies could move unfettered across the seas and continents. No more would transport ships be allowed, No oil tankers, no cargo ships. International transportation and logistics would now be facilitated via the use of Hyperloop tubes. The Watchers themselves would exclusively distribute oil, natural gas and other combustibles or dangerous materials. Earth was to become a neighbourhood, and the Watchers were the neighbourhood security.

Furthermore, all naval warships were to be sunk, and their ammunition, ordinance and aircraft destroyed. The use of space travel was now limited to peaceful exploration and colonisation. Nations could still compete on the business frontier but must not combat each other, or there would be severe consequences. The Watchers would impose both order and accountability. His rule now cemented, and seeing it was good, Commissar Severenson rested.

Chapter 16

Haltom City,

Suburb of Fort Dallas.

Following the aerial traffic pattern over Midway Road, Helen banked over Oakwood and then descended onto her landing deck, shutting down the controls while the engines' whine spun down. Opening the hatch, Helen got out of her Nippon Suzume 720 EX VTOL; the rain down poured onto her. While usually, that would make her feel exhilarated and refreshed, today, it merely made her pissed off. After securing the aircar, she walked across the walled-in lawn up to the exit gate to the house. She had only changed a few things on the property - a nine-foot wall prevented curious eyes from looking in. Withdrawing a vintage steel key, she inserted it into the iron door lock and moved inside. Helen loved this place. Being A-class allowed her certain perks, such as having a lovely country home. It suited her well, as it allowed her the luxury of getting away from the apartments and condos closer to the Omega pyramid, where many choose to live.

The house always had the smell of fresh bread when she came. Helen kept no artificial people here. Her housekeeper Jen was human. The woman was perhaps in her teens and of a generally upbeat disposition. Plopping on the couch and sinking into its cushions, she sighed. Jen came in and handed her a cup of coffee mixed with natural milk and ground sugar, which grew in the backyard cane field.

"Haven't seen you in a while," The woman stood behind her.

"Just a week, the trip to Japan took longer than expected. When I got back, I had to follow up on some other projects, so I slept at my Pyramid condo. Oh, btw Heidi's coming over in a while."

"How's Theo?" Jen Holsum asked with perhaps a tinge of concern. "You two still a thing?" her housekeeper was one of Helen's few trusted confidantes.

"It's gotten complicated." Helen twitched her nose and not liking where the conversation was going. Fortuitously her pen phone rang; picking it up; she leaned forward in her chair. Jen watched as Helen's face went from a veil of weariness to a more alert and stoic visage.

"*Hai meiyo Ieyasu?*" Nodding her head, Helen looked at her watch.

"Can you give me a few minutes? *Arigatai.*"

"Japanese?" Jen took note of the language with a bit of a surprise. Helen stood up abruptly and then put the phone away. "Business. I won't take long, but I have some work I need to attend to right now."

Jen nodded. "You go to the office; I'll have the Banana bread when you're done." Helen walked to the hallway, where her study sat. She laid her hand on a panel where it read her palm, and the door slip open, revealing a windowless room. The panelling about her was Sheesham, also known as Indian Rosewood. Bookshelves lined the wall behind her desks on which sat pictures, books and bric-a brak. Helen went over to a wet bar, poured herself a glass of Connemara Peated Irish whiskey into her coffee, and then removed some heavy whipping cream from the office fridge. Taking a sip, she carried it desk and, pulling up her leather chair, she set the Irish coffee aside her. Helen tapped on an inset keyboard turning on the computer. As the system came on, a monitor emerged up from its concealment in the desk. The screen illuminated, and she touched the glass seven sequenced times. Helen's computer was not wireless but hardwired underground; antiquated perhaps, but highly secure. This network was a severe breach of the law as all Fort Dallas communications systems were always required monitoring. Privacy was a difficult thing to possess, which is why Helen kept her house vintage because if one was not digitally bound, one's privacy could be absolute.

Helen knew it was time to pay the Rat-Catcher of Hamelin.

The data she had collected was illegal to possess. Long ago, when Helen went to work for Theo, he had explained that he kept the medical data on all B and A-cast member under lock and key. When asked why, Theo informed her that competing enterprises could compromise people's physical weaknesses, genetic vulnerabilities or cellular susceptibilities.

But as she read the papers, she saw that was all a lie.

Nevertheless, the time had come; she obtained the help of the New Japan. There was a cost for learning the truth because, of course, there would be. Businesses never did anything that was truly free.

BonHomme's screen snapped in place, revealing the Logo of the New Japan Corporation. As the display logo faded, she saw that Master Suizei was seated in an open room, shirtless and in Lotus position.

"Mata oaidekiteureshīdesu, Ms BonHomme. I trust that the information we revealed to you has proven that working for us would be less distressing those whom you currently do work for."

"That would be an understatement."

"I would agree. Nevertheless, the time has come for you to enact your obligation." Suizei's voice was kind but adamantine. Helen held her breath and then, shaking her head, spoke.

"Of course, I understand. But I have a request when the time comes; I want to be the one to confront Theo, to deal with him."

"I understand; I can see why you would feel so motivated. I would ask that you prepare to transfer that information to us. We will have agents in place to receive the hard drive." Ieyasu nodded. Let us arrange the location."

"I will have to retrieve it from my project leader Randall."

"When you are in possession of that material, contact me directly, and our agents will retrieve you and the item."

"Sounds good. *Arigatōgozaimashita.*" Helen gave a bow of respect.

"Watashi wa hōshi suru tame ni ikite imasu." Ieyasu gave a bow in return and then ended the call.

"If you fail, you may die to serve."

Chapter 17

Ina,

Nagano Prefecture,

Japan.

The household serving arm quietly retracted back into the ceiling.

As Japan prepared to enter the twentieth-second century as the technological leader, Ieyasu kept this room free of any technological detritus as possible. Clean to the point of sterility. His place was a contradiction on many levels. The walls were bare white and made of marble. The floor was teak and smooth upon which sat a mild scattering of elegant Zen Shoji Room Dividers. Master Suizei was in the Zazen chamber of his ancestral home wearing ten thousand-yen slacks while remaining in Lotus. He had his eyes closed and was mentally viewing Mount Senjō. The businessman had climbed it many times, often barefoot. Suizei remembered every one of the mountains paths, as well as the smell of the scrub pine. He told himself that he should go there again, perhaps later this week. Were anyone to choose to invade his privacy by eavesdropping, all they would hear was the ambient sound of the ocean.

Suizei knew he needed to be focused and tranquil as he always communed with the silent ocean before going to war.

The Pacific was the ultimate warrior; endless, cruel and unfathomable. It had destroyed his family's business long ago with the tsunami following the Tōhoku Earthquake in 2011. The water felled four nuclear plants at Fukushima Daiichi that irradiated a swath of Honshu and wounded her severely. The Ieyasu clan had been forced out from that business district but had rebuilt their holdings in the Nagano Prefecture. It was not an insignificant technology business; they were honoured to be chosen to work a large contract, one that would restore the Ieyasu family's dignity. Then climate change made life a hardship here, for Tokyo required a great many levee's and pumps to hold back the encroaching Pacific. When the Shutdown came, all of those failed, and Tokyo flooded. That, and all that Suizei's family had; all their money and holdings wiped out in a minute.

The loss was so grievous that many Ieyasu family members committed Jisatsu. It was more palatable to leave the world than live in disgrace again. He was old enough to remember and wise enough to work with the new masters of the world, those who had spread the darkness. In time he parlayed himself to great power and finally leadership of the new Empire. His arcology did not breed their workers in laboratories as others did, but Suizei chose the noble course instead, electing the best of families to assume respectable stations.

Ieyasu Suizei took a deep breath and offered a prayer to the spirits of the sea, air, land, as his ancestors as his father and grandfather had shown him. In the past, many vying for arcological leadership mocked his ancestor worship and faith in spirits. It mattered not for Ieyasu neither cared for nor dignified their atheism. He succeeded, and they did not. That was all that mattered. Of course, he commanded they perform seppuku for acting disgracefully to him. His meditation ended with the whispered slide of the door. He saw his man Sato humbly bowing deeply.

"The American is here." Suizei rose as Sato handed him his dress shirt.

"Good. Thus, the first snowflake of the blizzard has fallen. Please ask if my honourable father will be joining us."

"Of course, this request has already been made. I regret that your uncle has declined once again."

Ieyasu frowned. "Masutā Yuuda's wishes are to be respected. Bother him not again." He said sadly.

"You are a good man Watashi no shujin."

"It was expected," Master Yuuda was not only his uncle but mentor, counsellor and the only father he had ever known.

"But we must now fulfil our destiny, even if he cannot give his blessing," His shirt now buttoned, he straightened himself. "Shall we speak English now so as to honour our guest?" Sato's sensei spoke with unimpeachable wisdom.

"Let us see how he presents himself to us and respond accordingly," Ieyasu smiled slyly.

"As you will," Sato bowed.

"Have Hasaki prepare our meal, and we shall join him shortly." A straightened tie completing his attire Ieyasu Suizei moved to the outer room to where his guest stood.

"If you would leave your boots here," Sato could be heard from the other side of the screen. There are slippers for your feet." O'Sullivan nodded and put on the Waraji.

"I have manners, son. This ain't my first invitation to an honourable home."

Sato looked at the guest, who had an unlit cigar in his mouth. The American stood clad in a worn brown leather coat. Bald, his head bore a detailed and exquisite tattoo that ran from his shaved hairline to the top of his neck. Everything about the man looked road worn and dirty, although his skin was clean, as were his teeth and nails. His feet did not offend, and he admitted to himself that he was surprised at that. Sato took his coat.

"Mister O'Sullivan, irasshai"." The older man said to his distinguished visitor with a bit more deference. The American walked forward in his heavy, socked feet and bowed.

"Ojama shimasu," Gabriel held out a small, wrapped gift, which Ieyasu took, bowing again. *"Tsumaranai mono desu ga."*

Suizei saw that his guest was neither rude nor uncivilized.

O'Sullivan, for his part, likewise sized up Suizei. Gabriel was taller than the businessman, who was quickly five foot six, whereas O'Sullivan came in at five feet ten inches. (Six feet with his boots on.) Suizei had classical features but with a smooth porcelain complexion. His hair was long and tied in a ponytail — his clothes; silk. The Ciccio suit probably cost more than O'Sullivan made in a year.

No, make that two.

A man in a chef's coat bowed at the top of the step coming from the dining room. "If the gentlemen would like to follow me?"

"Thank you, Hasaki." Suizei gestured towards the dining room.

"Please be kind enough to join us.

Seeing Suizei sitting down at the low table, Gabriel did the same. Sato handed him a warm washcloth.

The cook began to chop up the food on a waist-high grilling table, moving his cutlery like he was in a knife fight. In a moment, the food was put onto plates and served to steam in front of them. Before Suizei could say anything, O'Sullivan put his hands together and bowed. Suizei did the same.

"*Itadakimasu,*" Suizei spoke, announcing dinner may be started, and deftly picked up his *hashi.*

O'Sullivan picked up his chopsticks and, deftly handling them, started slowly with his bamboo utensils.

Suizei nodded. "Very good. I was told you are the best at what you do." Ieyasu offered graciously.

"Hmmm, it depends. What were you told I do?" Suizei laughed easily.

"Hah. I respect cautious men. 'Scepticism is the beginning of faith.' Oscar Wilde, *The Importance of Being Earnest.*"

O'Sullivan snorted quietly.

"To answer your question, I have heard that you are an excellent tracker of people. As I require such services, I am prepared to make you a handsome offer of one hundred thousand dollars for such a job." Ieyasu said as he motioned for the chef to come over.

"Green tea," Suizei requested. Hasaki, the chef, looked at Gabriel.

"The collapse of human civilization will occur if teatime is ever abandoned."

"Amazake," Ieyasu requested. The chef bowed and departed for but a moment; a young woman returned with the beverages.

"What's the quarry?"

"It is a corporate official and her companion." Ieyasu offered slowly.

O'Sullivan looked sceptical. "Not ones of your own, obviously. Otherwise, you would have handled it with internal security." He sipped his sweet drink.

"That is correct. They are A-caste Omegan's. I need them exterminated and an item they possess returned to me."

O'Sullivan smiled and laughed heartily, richly amused. "Nice, but I must decline that offer." Shaking his head. He laid down his bamboo sticks.

"You cannot do this?" Ieyasu spoke, not with shock but a flat calm.

"Never said that," O'Sullivan dismissed Suizei's cynicism. "I said I declined that offer." He corrected.

"Go on," Ieyasu said as sipping his tea. "' Please explain."

"This is not an easy thing you're asking. Not impossible, by daunting. The second an A-caster dies, security is alerted, and then all of those cameras they have everywhere record what is happening at any given moment because Omega has the most powerful domestic security system in the world; scanners, guards, police...etc." O'Sullivan pulled out a lighter and gave a questioning look. Ieyasu nodded. Lighting his already masticated stub, O'Sullivan snapped the lighter closed.

"So were I to get inside, the odds are I would be immediately detected. There's the fact that every citizen tracked; humans by DNA, artificial people by whatever counts as their DNA, and outsiders like me get tracked by a guest tracking chip you get injected with once you enter the city. Should I remove it, then, again, security gets immediately notified. As it is, Omega knows what's going on, and who is in and out of Fort Dallas every second of every day," He continued respectfully because the possibility was that Ieyasu-san may or may not be aware of these considerations. It was equally possible this was a test. "Like you, they have facial recognition scanners everywhere across the city.

"I see."

O'Sullivan continued, "Now, to do this job properly, I'll have to have weapons because most Omegan's can beat the leaving hell out of you because they are trained from childhood, which is why I need arms - another thing they track all the time. Taking them on at home may be possible – provided I can disable local cameras and doing that would give me twenty seconds–give or take-before Omega would notice me. However, most of A-caster's homes have artificial people working for them - who are programmed to defend their masters against any attack. Now, depending on just how important these A's are, the freaking Watchers could step in – should they rate this as a high-level destabilization effort."

Suizei nodded. "But they only deal with international affairs."

"Maybe, maybe not, but I damn sure don't want to run afoul of them."

"Go on," Ieyasu continued eating.

"Then there's the extraction itself - which means staying off the tubes, maybe by using an aircraft or the river."

"Yes. Exactly that." Ieyasu smiled.

"Right," O'Sullivan nodded and then bowed. "That's quite a Pickett's Charge you have got there."

Breaching etiquette, the chef stared at O'Sullivan from the kitchen doorway.

"Sensei, I warned you this man's reputation was a lie and that he was a coward." The chef scoffed.

"What did you say?" O'Sullivan turned towards the cook.

"I stated that you are a coward. Like all Americans Outsider, you are nothing but a disreputable vagrant; too afraid, too lazy and too stupid to see a good thing when offered. You dishonour this home with your presence."

O'Sullivan bowed towards his host and then stood up slowly.

"I think there are some assumptions you need to correct. For one, Americans are not stupid, lazy or cowardly. We are poor, starved and angry, and that makes us very dangerous."

Both Ieyasu and Hasaki stared at him in silence.

"Furthermore, I did not say that I would *not* do it." He turned to look at Suizei, who had watched the display with quietly amused detachment. "I will do it, but not for the price you named. "I'll do the job for three million, a home in Killin, Scotland. It's a village by Loch Tay." Suizei nodded at Hasaki.. Upon that, the chef moved his hands to the grill knives with blinding speed and threw them at O'Sullivan not seven feet away. The room immediately was filled with the sound of a sharp snap. Out of O'Sullivan's right forearm, a long steel dagger blade telescoped to a length of eighteen inches, with which O'Sullivan blocked the two incoming blades. Hasaki rolled across the floor and picked up a gleaming sword from a floor stand. O'Sullivan leapt up and moved in the opposite direction once more, deflecting Hasaki's edged attack. As he landed, O'Sullivan swept the chef's leg as he tried to stand, and reaching over with his left hand, he grabbed Hasaki's right forearm. There were the sound and smell of electricity, and Hasaki dropped to the floor, spasming. O'Sullivan quickly released his grip and held the dagger spike's tip at the chef's right eye.

"Good enough?" Gabriel looked at Suizei and snapped the dagger back inside his arm and stepped away from Hasaki.

"Acceptable."

O'Sullivan snapped the spike back into his arm and offered a hand up to the man on the floor. Hasaki accepted up to and bowed once on his feet.

"My apologies, it was a required test."

"Hasaki Nomuri. Age 24," Gabriel looked at the chef but spoke to Suizei. "Level four Data surgeon and assassin. Twenty-two confirmed kills. Skilled in most weapons known to god and man but prefers an Arisaka type 201 sniper rifle whenever possible. He still keeps a vintage Cheytac M200 Intervention in a box on the roof of this building.

Smiling, O'Sullivan clapped his hands together. "Respectable in close combat when needed. On a personal basis, he is fond of playing the flute, documentaries and Anime." He laughed. "Seriously, who still uses *'SuperrobotAlpha'* as a password?"

Hasaki's cheeks flared bright red, but then it was his turn.

"Gabriel O'Sullivan. Former Pennsylvania police officer. Two citations for bravery, once for rushing into a burning building and saving two children. The second medal awarded for rescuing two wound officers during a firefight with Anti-Watcher fanatics. Married once. Your wife and daughter were murdered in your own home by a drug addict, I believe."

Gabriel turned back to the cook. "High marks," O'Sullivan's voice could have cut glass. "But if that's your best effort at rattling me, you're doing a piss-poor job." He turned back to Suizei. "Lastly, I need your signed word that my safety – and my money is guaranteed for the duration of my life," Smiled and looked over at Hasaki. "And he comes with me."

"Agreed," Suizei stood and bowed.

He smiled and then turned to his new employer. "By the way, that quote you made by Wilde wasn't from The Importance of Being Earnest. It was from *A Picture of Dorian Grey*. Chapter seventeen, I believe."

☐

Chapter 18

Randall's Home

Saguaro Condominiums,

Mesquite, Texas.

Elon, Randall's new secure work system was impressive, but he felt the upgrade was unneeded. All his terminals remained encrypted, as well as ascertaining that his inter-office networks remained spectral, meaning you would have to know already what the data signature and encoding was before you could ever try to scan for them. Without being able first to examine the data, there was no way in which you could copy the pattern.

Helen installed the standalone to decipher the algorithm, but he still felt he needed to check every digital system before he began work at home. The main house's networks remained untouched – and he had taken the time to verify that. Randall had checked every connection, every docking port and all the data access points. He even checked Mozart's mental update station from Innovative. He felt it unlikely that he would be co-opted as Innovative had their artificials direct upload/Download pods locked down tight. The computer in front of him was superlative, one of the new Hausa MMD-6's. Its AI was named 'Elon'. Elon was a data archaeologist's computer, capable of reading and reviewing any electronic form of data back to punch cards, reel to reel or cassettes, and up to current data coding as well. Mammoth ib size, the installers must have had to rip up the flooring to assemble it. He looked down, but his carpeting hid the possible truth.

Randall tossed a softball up in the air and then caught in a composite fibre glove as he spoke. He had been working on Helen's assignment at home most of the day. "Elon, now that we've done that, let's test it on a Barbican level Voidwall. Give me an analysis."

"Barbican Voidwall; A system of Heuristic firewalls that can number from two to upwards of one thousand firewalls - each learning from the other. Milli-wall's, though theoretically possible, have yet not been tested. Barbicans' standard number was seven, with a corporation running an average of between ten to twelve. Omega's barbican itself is twelve deep. The Barbican itself protects a Voidwall."

"How would you describe such defenses?'

"Voidwall; a system of scans that mimic a cosmological singularity. All data is stripped to its fundamental binary code and then anyalsed and recomposed to its intended algorithms and code. The Voidwall allows it's scanning and searching on a base-two numeric system for malware, Trojans, hijackers and mimics."

"Expected search time per barbican?"

"Fourteen minutes."

"Anticipated number of barbicans?"

"Forty-two."

"Run it." The comp began its work. "How long to identify the intended Shutdown subroutine?" Randall inquired with a sigh.

"Eleven hours, twenty minutes - optimistically."

"Ok, so even though we've improved its detection time by six in the last several hours, that's still pretty long."

"Given the number of variables we are dealing with, I would say that anything under a week can be considered positive." The computer responded. "Your previous equipment was far inferior to me. As such, its execution time would have been three times as long."

"Don't processor-shame my old hardware." Randall quipped.

"You must understand any attempt to identify and reassemble the original coding is a risk of great proportions. This will require several hours. I will first need to analyze how to store the toxic data on D-tech formatted hardware. Before that, I must print hardware needed for standalone transport."

Randall yawned. "You do that, and I'm going to grab some sleep."

Chapter 19

Hernández's Café,

The Cubes Favela,

Fifteen miles from Fort Dallas.

Her hair now neatly pulled back in a Denetta sat inside the shop downtown near Burnett Park. It was in the remodelled Mahon Courthouse, which was now an art studio. Denetta liked to come here and look at the paintings. Now that Randall was letting her move in, she had decided to look for art. She had lifted the coffee - perfect. There was more reason than cappuccino that brought her here. And she was curious as to why an old friend, formally from the Cubes, had asked to meet her.

Maybe he thinks I can find someone who knows of a decent job inside. Such schemes weren't uncommon because the proper way was to go through the Visa process, which was lengthy and arduous. Omega did extensive medical and background checks. Once you passed that, then you had to go through a physical training regime to make sure you were fit and aesthetically pleasing to the Omegan eye. You couldn't have any showing scars, moles, birthmarks or acne. Denetta had a cousin that developed a breakout the day she was to be put up for sale, and they kicked her out of the city. She could reapply – in two years.

Denetta was meticulous about her health and weight. Randall was kind enough to provide her with excellent healthcare. He had also told her that he didn't care if she got a zit or scar. Randall wouldn't cruelly release her from her job for any such trivial reasons. She had wondered why he hadn't offered to free her – not that she would accept right away. To do so would mean losing her E-Caste status, having to leave the city, and then make her way outside, a steep path to go.

Thomas Two-Crows walked in, the man the head of a news service. Most of North America and much of the world beyond, for that matter, knew him on sight, which made it odd that such a regarded person would meet with an E-Caster, Denetta thought. The man wore a posh business suit, his hair cut tight and clean, which was striking as he usually kept it long and braided. His Tonkawa features were sharp and distinct. He grew up in the Cubes, but at his first chance, he fled. Though he would become a successful journalist now living in Vietnam, he had never turned his attention or support back to Denetta's community. He ordered a drink and then sat down across from Denetta, who stood up and hugged him first.

"Hi Tommy," She said in a friendly but sedate manner.

"God, it's good to see you!" Thomas bellowed; his smile could not be fuller. Denetta waved her hand in a silencing way. "Careful, you know how the corps feels about religion. That's the first thing they banned."

Thomas made a tight face and looked around. There were just the two of them in the establishment, one old gen server and his boss, who was probably not more than twelve. Corpers started working around ten years of age.

"How're your parents?" He asked softly.

Denetta shook her head and then picked up and sipped her latte.

"I'm sorry," Thomas slid his hand over to touch hers. She allowed it.

"Does it matter? They're gone - six years now."

"I still can't believe you stay here," Thomas shook his head.

"Not this old argument," Denetta rolled her eyes.

"Dee, you don't have to stay there — or work in here. You can come with me. You can have your servants, not just be one."

"Did you just actually say that to me?"

Thomas saw he pushed too far - Denetta stood, clearly preparing to leave. Thomas held up his hands. "I'm sorry. I'll stop."

Denetta nodded and sat back down. She took a deep breath and stared at him with a look of well-checked anger, and possibly, Thomas thought disgust. "I've told you before, and this is the last time I will tell you. When you left, everyone was happy for you. When we saw you succeed- we were happier still. However," Denetta sighed and looked over her shoulder, and a new person walked in. "You forgot all about us. I don't remember you admitting to coming from the Cubes. I saw that not only did you change your look, but you also removed our favela tattoo — the one I inked on you. The one you said meant that we would be together forever. You remember?"

"We were kids. What, ten years old?" Thomas frowned.

"You were ten, and I was nine." She shrugged. "so that's fine, we were kids but what broke my heart was that as rich as you became, you've not sent one penny back to help the Cubes. With all your money, you could have helped fund a hospital, police- electricity. You could have made a huge difference." Denetta shook her head as a single tear slid down her cheek. "I'm not even supposed to be talking to you. If the sicario's report back..."

"Then, why did you agree to meet me?" Thomas asked curiously.

"Because Tommy, it's still not too late. I came because you can still come home. You can still make a big difference in so many lives in the Cubes."

"I did come to make a difference. I came to get you out."

"Denetta stood up and slapped him. "You don't ever change. You never will change."

Two-Crows grabbed her wrist. "Emri sent me."

"I find that highly unlikely," Denetta shook her head. "I seriously doubt that Emri Swallowtail would want to talk to me."

"No, it's true. She contacted me three days ago. Naturally, I was happy to get an interview with the most terrorist in the world."

"Freedom fighter; you and I both know that our Emri was no terrorist." Denetta snapped. Thomas shook his head.

"The only difference between a freedom fighter and a terrorist is who you are willing to kill. The second she blew up that office and killed innocent children, she became a terrorist."

"That was a setup – Hemlock framed her! You're wrong about her! Emri is our friend, and she would never murder anyone, especially not children."

"I reported what I did because I went there; I saw the bodies, I talked to the survivors. When I spoke to Emri, she admitted that, yes, while she wasn't there, her people were responsible. She didn't know that the children were going to be there- but they were. But that's not why I'm here. I thought it would be a phone interview, but she asked to meet me directly. I was a bit suspicious, but we agreed on the where, when and how to meet,"

"What did she want?" Now intrigued, Denetta leaned in to hear.

"You must understand that what I am telling you is confidential and needs to be handled, as I will explain when I heard what Emri had to say. I realized we must work quickly. I need you to promise me that you say and do nothing until I contact you."

Denetta sat still. She had to know what he was talking about; she nodded.

"Very shortly, it will not be safe for Outsiders; anyone outside an arc is going to be in real danger. There is a plan being enacted, I don't know exactly what, and I don't know the day, let alone what hour it will happen. I only know, for a fact, it will. Emri and this man code-named Landmesser are certain that the arcs worldwide are about to make a move that -."

"That what?"

"Millions are going to die. It would be best if you left now. I can take you where it's safe."

She looked amused. "So, you're telling me that there's a mysterious danger that you don't know when and where is going to happen, and millions will die, and I need to trust you and go —where?" She couldn't help herself; she covered her mouth as she giggled. "Seriously? This is the best idea you came up with to have me leave with you?"

"It's not like that. The danger is real," Thomas watched as Denetta got up, disbelieving him.

"Take this," He shoved a sealed plasticard envelope across the table. Denetta looked at it. It was black and embossed with a golden butterfly.

"I may not be able to warn you again; I'm sorry. If you change your mind, open the envelope. Read it quickly because after it's exposed for more than a few seconds, it will fall apart."

Denetta looked at him, "I want to believe you, but how can I trust you? You abandoned us;" She shook her head, more tears coming." And now you come back with this cock-and-bull story? "She couldn't make the leap he wanted her to. Still, Denetta looked at the card and then quickly slipped it into her pocket. Leaning over, she kissed his forehead.

"You want to be trusted? You know where to go and what to do." With that, she walked out.

Chapter 20

Pleasure District,

Fort Dallas.

Even robots need a day off.

The adage was commonly used by disgruntled office drones complaining to their bosses, yet it was true. When artificials became commonplace, they had successfully litigated for the right to have personal days. The Supreme Council of Seven secured that right, not out of altruism or justice but because it seemed a bad idea to irritate a group of mechanical people who might one day be more numerous.

It was late in the afternoon, and Mozart had already done his grocery shopping and had allowed himself supper at The Mansion on Turtle Creek. His meal consisted of roasted lamb chops with eggplant caviar, polenta, hatch peppers and a crispy lamb belly. It had just the right hint of rosemary. Coexisting on his plate were green asparagus with a ham vinaigrette. To slake his thirst, he had them fill his glass with a *Lacoste Borie Pauillac Bordeaux*. For his after-dinner fare, he tried their pumpkin cheesecake which he found acceptable. He left a tip six times the amount of the meal, as was his custom. Doing this both assured him of excellent service and a seat being made available to him on all occasions. He doubted they very much even knew he was not a human being. Of course, with his liberality and largesse, they probably would not care.

Physical hunger was not the only void that needed filling.

Like most artificial people, Mozart longed for physical intimacy. Loneliness was not solely the possessions of natural beings — the profound depth and resonance of the human mind embedded into an artificial granted that longing.

Many synthetics took on partners for companionship and because they did fall into a simulacrum of love. Mozart felt fulfilled in his life; he enjoyed his experiences with Randall. He thought they were friends to a degree, but both lived their lives independently together. It was not uncommon for corpers to have pleasure artificials in their homes, but neither Randall nor Mozart felt any sense of sexual desire for each other. Randall once remarked that having sex with an artificial would be nothing more than an elaborate exercise in masturbation. This comparison offended Mozart not because he desired sexual intercourse with Randall but because it showed that the Master did not see him as a natural person. Mozart had never expressed to Randall that he saw no difference in him and human beings, for both beings were mechanically and artificially crafted.

While not forbidden or discouraged, sexual and romantic relationships remained unease to the A-Cast managers. Even in the early days of the twenty-first-century, sex robotics constituted a significant breakthrough in the cybernetic field. Although these automatons' possession was regarded as either disgusting at worse or kitschy at best, the sexbot industry was an essential building block for artificial and synthetic technology.

When it came to human/artificial sexual mores, management was in no way prim; their principal worries were that an attachment or relationship could interfere with the corpers professional responsibilities or societal harmony. Due to the fact artificials could not be imprinted with a Neuromonitor, any emotions that a corper might fixate on to an artificial possessed unforeseeable consequences in the future. Still, artificial manufacturers such as Innovative did work closely and helped them monitor synthetic performance and behaviours. So it was that people were pleased to do what they willed. If, however, it did interfere with a corpers job or responsibilities to Omega, the policy was to separate those involved and terminate said relationships.

As an artificial, when Mozart felt sexual longing, he sought it in a proper place where it could be enjoyed without emotional attachment.

After dining, he walked out into a deluge of warm driving rain. He popped open his umbrella, and he headed towards the river district. Arriving at the riverside walk, he found it empty and abandoned, ostensibly because of the showering weather. In a city of millions, Mozart found a place to be alone.

Leaning over a barnacled post, he breathed in the pungent salt air. He watched as the ships, immune to the inclement weather they moved up and down the waters, their massive sails billowing in the winds; even though there were so many better options for propulsion, humans still demanded to see white sails on a river. The echoes of seagulls and a wayward albatross were pleasant sound, but after three minutes of watching sails, Mozart deciding to get out of the rain. He walked over to the business he had desired to frequent.

Caprices were a brothel; a business like any other; car dealerships, grocery stores, or other commercial operation. Once inside, far from being déclassé, it was clean, modern and professional. Overwhelmingly ivory to the point of colourless sterility, the store did have a minor splash of colour high above them on the transparent walkway. There above them, beautiful men and women flawless in their appearance walked back and forward. Many were nude and displayed their attributes openly for customer appraisal.

"Welcome back," A tall, urbane man said with natural amicability. His name was Geddy, and he always recognized all his customers.

"I have a new employee if you would like to make her acquaintance." The pimp indicated a stunning redhead of about six foot in height. "May I introduce Annie?"

The woman nodded and walked over, her silk robe swaying and clinging to her every curve and protrusion. He was used to perfect bodies and found this creature's form softer and more sensual. The female bowed. Mozart was of the same height but somehow felt he was looking up into her crystalline green sparkling eyes. Annie smiled and gave a slight nod.

"What's your pleasure, sir?" She linked her hands behind him, rubbing his neck, drawing him closer. Mozart could smell her honeysuckle perfume. Something was enticing about it. But she wasn't the reason he came here. Mozart reached back and lifted her hands off. "Another day, perhaps."

"Pity," Annie pouted and then walked away.

"Enchanted as I am, I have an appointment with Ms Edwina."

"Of course,"

Mozart put his hands behind her back, and in a few moments, a fair-skinned woman walked out. She had short black hair, ruby red lips and was attired in a black corset, matching panties and black and white striped stockings. Around her neck was a black choker with a cameo.

"Hello Mozart, how are you today?" She smiled as she walked over to him. The smile, however, belied her eyes, which were puffy and slightly bloodshot.

"I am most well but have desired to see you for a few days. This was your first window of availability, however." Edwina laughed and spun about the floor.

"One cannot be a beautiful woman and stay out of trouble,"

"A very true statement; you are truly magnificent." Mozart bowed.

"Shall we?" Edwina took his hand and began to move him to the stairs.

Mozart allowed Wina, as she preferred to be called, to lead, and as she came to the top landing, he could see several other individuals sitting and drinking with their partners. She pulled him back towards one of the individual studio rooms, each with hand-carved cherry wood doors with shiny brass hinges and door handles. The girl opened the doors, and Mozart saw a place worthy of any hotel penthouse. The furniture was antique Victorian, the carpet Persian and the bed four-poster and possessing sheer Curtains. Opening the door and led him towards the bed. She pushed him down and began to undress him, first unbuttoning his shirt and then kissed his nipples on his smooth chest. Mozart closed his eyes and allowed himself to enjoy the sensation. Her mouth moved down his chest to his stomach, where her hands sensually undressed him. With the sound of his zipper lowering, Mozart sighed.

Their congress was slow, passionate, and she was indeed highly skilled. In an hour, the act completed, and after cuddling for an acceptable amount of time, Wina arose and checked her schedule before her next client. Two hours. She was allowed thirty minutes between clients and a one-hour break. Though she didn't feel like it — she had already seen four other clients; she played the 'happy lover' and lay on the bed with him. Though she knew the kindly and gentle Mozart well, he was still just another cock that she had to endure. As far as that, he was a good lay and pretty straight forward. He never asked for anal or anything else, which was nice. Several of Omegan's' were into some pretty sick shit.

Under normal circumstance, Mozart would have perhaps engaged in another go around but not today. This morning's row between Kelly and Master Randall had upset him and prompted some thoughts he had perused upon, even on his way here. He turned and looked into her still puffy eyes. She was lying on top of the sheets wearing the choker now.

"May I ask you a question?"

"Of course."

"Did you enjoy having sex with me?"

"Of course, I do." Wina laughed. "You are my favourite client." He wasn't because she had no favourite clients.

"What I mean to ask, if I may, do you get anything out of it?" Mozart rolled over and looked her in the eyes.

"Are you happy? Please feel free to answer honestly. "She looked at him at first curiously and carefully answered him.

"Happiness is not part of my life," Wina seemed highly uneasy. "It has never been." Uncomfortable with the way the conversation was going, she leaned over and tried to kiss him and, with her right hand, moved it to his groin to push him back to a state of arousal. Mozart raised a hand and stopped her.

"Please, I'm sorry if I'm bothering you. Just let me ask you one more question."

"Oh, for Christ's sake, go ahead." Wina flopped on her back, her thirty-two-B breasts still upright and glistening.

"What do you want out of life? What would make you happy?" Mozart inquired, "Do you desire to be in a romantic relationship."

"If we're going to talk, do you mind if I rinse my mouth and towel off?" She sat up. "If we're done screwing, I'd like to put something on." This was her appointed room, and so she walked over to the wall; pushing it open, it revealed a wardrobe where she kept her trousseau. Wina pulled a ratty robe on and then sat in one of the high back chairs and pulled her knees to her chest. Without asking, she lit a cigarette. Mozart sat up and pulled the sheet around him.

"Let me ask you a question; why do you care?" Wina took a drag on her cigarette and inhaled.

"You may not realize this, but I am a G-12 Synthetic Person."

"No, I know. You guy's jizz isn't salty. It's citrusy for some reason. I kind of like it."

"I ask because I have never been in a relationship with anyone. I have a friend, but we are simply that – friends." He thought a moment. "You are the only person for which I have an affinity."

"Thanks, I guess."

"You are welcome. This morning I watched as my Master and his sexual intimate fought. The argument was over whether or not he was actually in love with his servant." He rubbed his thumb over his forefinger. "In this event, it made me realize that I too am nought but a servant, and while he is Homo Superior and Denetta – the servant girl – is simply a Homo Sapien, he shows a profound amount of attention to her. He has, however, never used his position to have sex with her. He once said that he would never be abusive and unkind to her."

"Lucky girl," Wina blew grey-blue smoke out. "What's your point?"

"I would like to know your opinion."

"He's right," She reached into her closet and pulled out a glass bottle of water. "All of you that come here for a lay are doing just exactly what he said; abusing me. I never asked for this; I'm not an employee – I'm a *slave* you asshole." She lit a cigarette, her hands shaking.

Mozart sat up abruptly. "Prostitutional slavery is not legal. Why have you not reported this?"

"You think I haven't tried?" "I'm not allowed to use a computer, I'm not allowed to leave the premises; I'm chipped to the backbone," She turned and tapped her back where a small scar showed. "Anytime I try to leave the building, the cervical chip causes me to collapse. Anyone that see's it thinks I'm epileptic or something."

"Am I the only one that you've told about this?" It seemed bizarre that this would be the case with someone that saw so many clients.

"Yes, because you're the only one that's ever bothered to ask. Most clients don't want me to talk, or if they do, it's on their terms."

"How did this occur?"

"It's not a pretty story; you sure you want to hear this?" Wina looked away from Mozart. Her hand trembled as she brought the cigarette to her lips. "When I was a kid – maybe five, my family used to live in the over by Estancia, New Mexico; nice place, you should visit. Good people, just trying to get by; religious folk." She took a long drag and then blew it out. "Anyway, one day, when I was picking flowers, I wandered away from home. Anyway, these guys rolled up in a beautiful red skimmer." She walked over to the bar and poured herself a whiskey.

"I had never seen an aircar up close. I went to look at it, and the guys seemed nice and asked me if I wanted to look closer; I didn't know any better. Well, one of the guys grabbed me. I didn't have time to scream. They just tossed me in the trunk. I was terrified, I cried, and I'm pretty sure I wet myself because they got furious when they pulled me out."

"Where did they take you?"

Wina shrugged. "No idea. It had to be north because it was green – greener than I ever saw. When they landed, there was a building, old, pretty. First, all I knew was that I wanted my mom – so it all blurred together. I was told that I'd be there for a long time." Her cigarette had burned down. She lit another one. Mozart spoke not at all but was listening raptly. "I was fed, cared for and educated. Ballet, dance, etiquette and over the years, they started teaching me about sex. That was when they started my grooming to become a whore." She punched her wardrobe door.

"Oh, they called us escorts, companions, consorts, but a whore's a whore, and I'm a whore. "She closed her eyes for a moment. "Well, twenty-three years later -long story short - here I am." She looked at Mozart.

"I'm so sorry… that's horrifying."

"Try living it." Mozart knew he wanted to cry, but no tears would come. "It sure the hell is. You know, Mozart, I know exactly how many people I have had sex with, men and women; nine thousand six hundred and three, and that includes you." She tossed the still smoking butt on the floor and glanced at the clock.

"I think that," He paused. "I must remedy this." Mozart stood up and commenced to pull his clothes on.

Wina scoffed." Hope you have a lot of money because my buying cost is a hundred thousand," She became anxious. "Every one of his whores has a price, and that's mine."

"I can meet that amount," Mozart thought a moment. "I have made investments, and it would not do me irreparable financial hardship." Wina stared at him with suspicion.

"Really?"

Mozart nodded. "I am not prone to mendaciousness. It goes without saying that if I were to do this, I would naturally free you." Wina sat back and looked at him with distrustful confusion.

"Artificial people can't own slaves, nor have employees. It's against the law. Wouldn't that violate - what is it?" She thought for a second as she lit another smoke. "The fifth law; you guys can't act like a person."

"I think that if I were to purchase you for the express reason of freeing you, I would not violate that law."

"You do that, and we can be the best of friends. I'll have sex with you whenever you want."

"I would not do that; if I wished to have continuous sex with you liberating you would be pointless," Mozart shook his head. Guilt was not an emotion he had felt before, but he knew that it was what he was now experiencing. "I must apologize that I have taken advantage of you, I had presumed…"

"You thought what every man and woman that I had thought. You thought I was doing it voluntarily. That's a pretty damn degrading idea. "She took a drag on her cigarette. "not your fault. You're just a babe in the woods; innocent as new snow.""

Wina wasn't sure that she meant that, but he said that he would free her, which was worth the risk.

"Get dressed; we're getting out of here." Mozart offered her his hand.

Chapter 21

Office of Security Management,

Omega Corporation,

Fort Dallas.

She heard it all — Doxie, Hoor, Hogan's Goat, bitch, and so on. *Whatever.*

She didn't give a tea-totaller's damn about people's opinions. It was the same, always the same. A strong woman gains a position, and anyone who got passed over had to find a way to tear them down. It wasn't even slut-shaming because she wasn't one. What she despised was the fact that - and it didn't matter whose opinion it was, male or female - they always presumed that she had to spread her legs and give up the box to get where she was. It was insulting, demeaning and denied that she had earned her way at the top. She had never slept with Magnus - nor anyone else to land where she was.

Instead, she had killed a great many people to be where she was; lots and lots of people. If some gits didn't shut up, she was about to kill a few more.

What pissed her off was that people never asked her if she had any interest in sleeping with him, of which she had none. She didn't find him attractive, not because of his race, size, weight or anything anyone might presume. She found him unattractive because he was a real asshole. She had two loves in her life, both now dead. To her, sex didn't make the world go around – respect did. Omegans could never grasp that; she watched their little lives like a girl staring at an ant farm.

Omegans – and all corpers, for that matter – were a weird group; Those on the bottom always wanted to be on top, and those on top were still unhappy and wanted more. It was like they wanted someone to make higher caste levels so they could climb higher. It was stupid because they were already so wealthy and powerful there was not a single thing they couldn't have. She watched as folks like Theo amassed more than any human in history had, short of Alexander the Great maybe. What did he do? He just ungagged his avarice and wanted more. To her, it was beyond stupid.

Do you want to be great? Be generous. She looked down at the lower castes, the E's and the D's. They lived on the edge, and while the D's lived in the city, they were still the dregs. Her, she wasn't even casted; she was unique, a worker from the outside. It pissed quite a few people, but she didn't care if they got mouthy; she would blow them away but not in a déclassé way. Transferring A's and B's to the E-caste was so much more fun, but yes, not a few ate lead from time to time. If you had told her she would wind up in a corner office in the most powerful organization in the world, she would have thought, 'Sure, why the hell not?'

Not that was in any way a plan; she ruminated as she poured a glass of iced lemon water into a Karen Feldman Artĕl drinking glass, far from it.

The outsider had started life as a good girl, and later, a blushing bride. However, not a few years ago, someone had decided to hit her with small lead rocks going faster than the speed of sound, and then after shooting her, they killed the rest of her family.

The first responders on the chaotic scene had mistakenly concluded that she was dead on arrival; a sizable hole in her forehead usually meant instant death. However, the effort to revive her did have to be taken, and surprisingly they would be able to get her heart restarted, but not before someone reported to her husband that she and her children were DOA's. The husbands collapsed in sobbing tears and went fetal. He was removed from the scene by friendly neighbours. The next morning, he was gone and never seen again. Presumably, the murders were too much for him to bear, and he had gone off to kill himself.

The Ambulance took her to the hospital clinging to life, but that report never was transmitted to the victim's spouse. It was still post-Shutdown, and instant messaging and cell phones were not as widespread as they once were; even today, they are perceived as extreme luxuries outside a Corp city. When she got into the hospital, the docs began their work. The headshot was not the only ballistic wound that she endured that day. The second slug had gone in under her right arm, shattering four ribs and destroying several organs. A third gunshot went slightly higher and, impacting the right deltoid, severed her Brachial Plexus, causing extensive nerve damage. A fourth trauma had hit her in the sternum, breaking the chest cage apart at the manubrium right beneath the clavicle.

The misinformation initially reported to her spouse was understandable. There was a sizable hole right above the bridge of her nose from the first gunshot she received that day. Since surgeons saw no exit wound, they figured it must have lodged in her brain. When examined, the physicians say that the shot struck her in the forehead but not straight on. Amazingly, the bullet had impacted her skull on a sharp angle, which had surreptitiously allowed it to skid around the inside.

The damage was minor, and it was determined that the shell had exited out of the entry hole as well. More fortunately, as the shot was steel jacketed - it did not fragment. She was bleeding out from the right side, and the trauma to her chest, when inspected, appeared partially caved in. No reasonable person would have seen this and believed anything else.

The surgeries that followed had she not already been in a coma and required having one medically induced. Replacing the bones and cartilage was easy enough. Instead of piecing together the shards of her natural frame, the surgeons decided to replace it with a titanium rib cage and sternum. Where Physicians could save the cartilage, they did; otherwise, polymers were used to repair the damage. Her liver was no longer much more than shredded meat, but enough was salvageable that the stem cells would be able to provide her with a working one. One of the surgeons laughed, saying that the repaired one worked so well that she would probably be able to drink any marine under the table. The same medical printing technique was used on her right kidney. Her large intestines were cut, the damaged section removed, and the two new ends sown together. Her appendix had virtually disappeared.

In replacing her thoracic cage, a bulletproof flexible polymer sheet was placed under the muscle wall, which would hold the newly healing organs together. The required surgery so traumatic and invasive, the patient was attended by not less than twenty-one surgeons, nurses and technicians. The surgeons bilaterally made deep continuous incisions in her flanks from the armpit to just above the hips. Those cuts travelled down to her musculature, with each incision going from Saoirse's flanks and then crossing across her torso, just below the clavicle. Once down, a medical robot was used to cut any remaining tissue; once done, they pulled her flesh down like a peeled banana. Her interior now completely exposed, they would begin the process of restructuring.

The manager took two aspirin with her water. Her titanium skull always seemed to make her headaches bother her more. Sipping, she flipped up her work schedule for today. Skimming through it, she saw that it was primarily banal and contemplated taking the day off. She hadn't taken a personal day in several weeks and thought that a trip to the beach might be in order. A day of Margaritas on the sand sounded nice. Her musings shattered when her phone rang; she grimaced. The ringing came from her desk phone, a real one, not like the intelligent pencil phones that made you squint. Answering the call, those in the office watched through her office window as their boss leapt to her feet and pumped her fist like a soccer hooligan whose team just netted a winning score. Reading the text, a warm feeling of satisfaction came across her face.

Finally.

The manager walked to her closet, put her dress coat in, and withdrew an old beaten jacket. Her staff watched as she removed her skirt and replaced it with a pair of jeans.

As she left her office, she could hear the new whispers of the gossip mill began anew.

Jaysus, I want to throw some hobnails at all those gits.

Chapter 22

Helens Home,

Fort Dallas Arcology.

What Helen knew about her home was that a man named Oscar Dennison had built it in 1899, back when the area was just a scrub plain, and the Texas & Pacific Railway depot was pretty much the most exciting thing to go and see. Oscar had decided that it was time for his family to move out of their box and strip house. He had a successful general store, which allowed him to build an actual brick building that made his wife happy.

Standing at the window, Helen looked at the woman in her bed. Her office secretary, Heidi, tangled in the lavender satin sheets where the golden mornings light cast down on Heidi's smooth back glistened in the sun. Last night she had seen that Heidi had a new tattoo, a Ying Yang. It meant that she and Helen were one soul, balancing and completing each other.

Helen smiled at the sight of her lover's perfect body. Maybe we'll go to Paris today; she said she'd never been there.

Helen got dressed, selecting casual clothes. Her jeans were faded, and she pulled on a Dallas Cowboy shirt – the team still going strong, albeit they had a terrible season last year. The woman tiptoed out the room, pulling the door closed quietly. Moving into the kitchen, she pulled out her coffee mug and then turned on the coffee maker. It would take a moment, so she pulled out a bottle of milk and a box of granola cereal. Jen had picked up some bananas for the bread yesterday, and some remained, so she peeled one and sliced it to go in her breakfast bowl.

Odd, she should already be here. Maybe she's run to the store.

Helen poured the milk and then placed the bottle back in the refrigerator. Hearing the wooden hallway floor creaking and looking up, she saw Heidi walking down, now clad in a long T-shirt and biker shorts. She stretched, and Helen savoured her perfect abdomen. Heidi walked over, kissed Helen on the check and relieved her of the cereal, tilting and sipping milk from the bowl.

Helen whistled as she went upstairs, took a quick shower and then threw on a T-shirt, panties and cargo shorts. She was looking forward to working in the soil today. Heidi enjoyed that as well.

The coffee was ready when Helen came down, crossing over to the counter. Helen turned her back to the door and poured sweetener and dry cream in it. She heard the kitchen door open, and Helen turned towards the door and saw Jen, the housemaid, walked in, carrying the groceries. Helen went to say something, but then her eyes fixed on Jen's, which were wide and terror-filled.

"Miss Helen?" Jen's voice shook, and tears struggled down her cheeks. Her hands shook so bad, Helen was sure that she was going to drop them.

" Jen?" Helen moved towards her as she suddenly heard two pops; Jen crumpled to the ground as her white blouse grew a red flower over her heart. Standing behind her dead body, Theo now stood in the doorway, holding a smoking silenced pistol.

"That was an idiotic thing to do, Helen," Magnus said flatly.

Gasping, Helen tried to speak but could only stammer, "The . . . The . . . Theo. *Why?*" Helen felt dizzy; her heart was racing, and her vision narrowing.

"Nice place," he ran his hand over the kitchen counters. "Real craftsmanship," Theo went to the stove and pulled a kitchen towel and started wiping up the spilt liquid.

"I missed you at the office this morning, so I called Heidi this morning. Must have been about one," Helen thought about that. Heidi had gotten up, be she assumed it was to pee, so she had gone back to sleep. "She told me you two were here. Taking a personal day," He raised a hand.

"No, I don't care who you sleep with, you know that. I've known about your relationship for over a year." He bent down and dabbed the coffee puddling on the floor. He stood up and neatly folded the hand towel.

"Why would you kill Jen? She never hurt anyone." Tears poured down her cheek.

"Because it hurt when I did that didn't. It makes you feel bad, doesn't it?" Theo sighed but never moved the pistol off her. "So, I hurt you just like you hurt me when you decided to poke around the White Departments records."

Helen's poker face was solid, as her poker group in town new. "I have no idea what you're talking about."

The man rubbed his brown brow and then pinching the bridge of his nose, shook his head. "Helen, you can't bluff when I own the card deck. Trust me; Ieyasu's people are not as good as you think they are." Helens façade started to crumble. "What was the one thing I specifically told you not to look into?"

"My genetic data."

Theo snapped his fingers. "That was it!"

Helen fell against the wall, eyes watering.

"Oh, don't you *dare* cry. You're better than that!" Tilting his head and letting out a slow whistle. "So, you figured out you're special, didn't you? You and several other people —all just like you." He placed his palm on his face and then pulled it down to his chin slowly. "You see, it pisses me off that you went and ruined all the trouble I took to conceal your genetic information." He shook his head and moved the barrel in a circle. "So, what was it you learned? Tell me."

"I'm not human," Hot tears pulled down her face.

"No, you are not." He shook his head ruefully. "But I am curious, what could have possibly tipped you off?"

"Wolf-Hirschhorn Syndrome. You missed it. You didn't find it, because your tests don't look for it. I was working on testing a new blood analytic we were about to produce. As I always do, I personally test each product before it goes to market. So, I tried the new genome typing. It was more refined then what we currently used, and when an anomaly came up, I checked it. That's when I discovered I had Wolf-Hirschhorn; of course, I didn't know it by that name at that point. Only that it was a degenerative flaw that causes a neural synaptic collapse in the carrier's forties." She crossed her arms. "I triple checked it, and nothing changed. Of course, as a genetic defective, you would cast me out. And so, naturally, I destroyed the test and scrapped the production line. I told the designers to start over from square one."

"Reasonable," Theo nodded. "Go on."

I checked my open records, and there was nothing there – of course. But that could only mean you must have been hiding something. I had no recourse in Omega, so I chose to reach out to New Japan. They were willing, and after running their tests, they told me they knew what it was. We struck a deal for the answer. They would take Heidi and me in as one of their own, I agreed. Then they told me what it was. Wolf-Hirschhorn,"

"Is extremely rare," Theo interrupted. "It shows up in only one particular situation, which is?"

She glared at him." In cloning," She started crying. "My God, Theo, I'm a clone!"

"Yes, yes, you are."

"Of whom?" She screamed, demanding he answer. "It wasn't in the records. *Tell me!*"

"Oh, you don't want to know. Trust me." Theo chuckled.

"Tell me, please…"

"Fine, Fine, Fine. You, my dear, are a clone of my Great Aunt, Anis." He crossed his arms. "You've heard of her; I'm sure."

"Anis Mikos Papadopoulos? I'm her clone?" Helen felt ill. "Which means," She stared at him in disgust. "you've been screwing your aunt? Helen gagged and then vomited into the sink. Finished, she wiped her mouth with a dishcloth. "*You sick shit!*"

"Oh, you don't want to get judgmental on me, I guarantee you that." He laughed.

She retched a few times and then rinsed her mouth out with tap water. Standing up, gasped. "How many of us?"

"You're one of four batches; you are the third of this batch of four. You see, Helen, I wanted to reproduce the genius that was Anis. So, I made sure that all of you were born and raised the same way. Fed the same, raised the same, and each of you was given the Neuromonitor at the same time – everything as perfectly identical as I could make it; therefore, I could look for any flaws and remove them as needed. Of course, now that we have seen that only you have Wolf-Hirschhorn, you will have to be eliminated as well."

"Who are others?" Helen demanded.

"Well, to avoid detection, we had to make slight cosmetic adjustments just in case you ran across each other."

"The first of your batch, Francine, was just like Anis; smart, beautiful and insightful. She worked down in Mechanical engineering; unfortunately, she died in a turbine accident. So that was tragic, but I had three more of you to work with."

"The others?"

"Well, Delphine - number two, still works out in the country working on agro-engineering. She has little desire to do anything else but work the land. She is very *un*-Anis."

"And the other one?"

"Imagine my surprise when she got transferred to our department. I allowed it because I wanted to see what would happen with you working side by side." He chuckled. "I found it odd that you two would fall in love." He waggled his eyebrows. "Kinky."

"Oh God," Helen collapsed to her knees, holding her stomach, as she wretched out gasping tears." Oh, God, no." She couldn't look at him; her question came out in staccato. "Does…she…know?"

"Of course not, that would be unnerving, and soul-crushing don't you think?" He looked aghast. "I mean, imagine finding out that every time you were making love, every time you ran your fingers over her skin that it was, what?" he paused. "Masturbation, self-gratification?" He cocked an eyebrow, and then tilting his head back, cracked his neck.

"I took you on because you were the most like Anis; you had the drive, the vision and ruthlessness. I took you on as a lover to keep you close, to keep you loyal. But no," He grimaced. "I guess I can't blame you. It's your nature – her nature. Nevertheless, you defied me. You went and asked Japan to look at your blood, and now they have Aunt Anis's DNA!" Theo grabbed her by both shoulders, shaking her, violently his face flush and purple with rage. "Now they can make copies of her on their own!"

"Theo, why would they want to clone. . ." she never finished the sentence. Theo shoved her into the wall. He raised his hand as if to strike her.

Helen cowered, but Theo backed off. "Did you honestly think I wouldn't find out?"

"I didn't mean to," Helen spoke in a quivering voice

"Please. Can you just not?" Theo took a deep breath and stood there. "No more lies; I expect more of you than that." Walking over to the kitchen table and pulled a ladder-back chair out and sat down. He saw that orange juice was there and picked it up.

"Of course, I had to kill your housekeeper," Helens face drained of blood." I mean, when Heidi comes home, it'll have to look like a murder scene. She'll be crushed, of course, but then Aunt Anis will move on," Helen's eyes opened wide, and she started to back towards the hall. Theo fired a shot to her right, shattering a vase and lodging into the wall behind it. "We must keep this lovely home in the family; I mean, that's a given," He drank the orange juice and set it back down. "This, of course, means we can frame you, and I can send you outside. Of course, now that you'll have no access to any further data from Omega, your usefulness will be severely damaged." Theo rubbed his hands together. "What we are going to do is to negotiate your severance package, golden parachutes and all that. You will give me the information I want, that being the details of the other matter that you have been working on, "He looked at her firmly. "I would very much like to know the nature of the material you retrieved from Ohio. In exchange, I promise not to blow your brains out. "He pulled the hammer back.

"Nice incentive." Helen chuckled darkly.

"I do try," Theo's nodded. "I mean, we are at an impasse. You betrayed me and gave my chief rival state and personal secrets. I fail to see where there's much room to negotiate here."

"You're lying. You'll kill me regardless, so my answer is no." Helen shook her head. "If I'm going to die, I die with dignity."

"Me lie?" Theo looked wounded. "Helen, after all, we have been through, you think *I* would lie? I mean, if anyone's a liar, it's you." He laughed with such sincerity that Helen allowed a relieved smile to break like dawn after a thunderstorm. "I could never kill you. Just tell me what I want to know." Theo finished the last of the orange juice.

"It's a hard drive, encrypted. Data goes back to The Shutdown. I think it has something to do with it."

"See, was that hard? Tell me more."

"I don't know anything more. I handed it off to an engineer. He's working on it." However, Theo did not look satisfied.

"Uhm, just not buying that. I know you know more, so I guess that means our deal is off."

"You kill me, and you'll never know what's on that disk."

"Kill you? Oh, that was just a bluff. I could never kill you."

Helen let slip a tight sigh of relief. I'm going to live, exiled maybe but that still life.

"You of all people should well know that I have people who do killing for me," Helen's eyes jerked up. There was the rustle of cloth that came from behind him as someone moved up.

"Top of the morning to yee, bitch," The voice, she knew that voice anywhere. The blood drained from her face as she saw the woman step into the doorway, confirming her dread.

"I would never kill you, but I pretty certain that she will." Theo leaned against the counter.

Standing in the door was Saoirse. Hatred flowed from the black T-shirt clad mercenary. The sleeveless shirt showed a plunging neckline. Her soft leather pants that hugged her hips like a jealous lover; everything she wore was black right down to her steel-tipped gloves and boots, ebon like her heart. She had a sidearm hanging from a leather ammo belt. Helen could see the miscoloured scar which resided over her left breast where Helen had shot her long ago. Saoirse's face was a stone-cold mask of hate. She closed the distance between the two of them; Helen reached for a counter drawer.

Theo fired a round grazing Helen's temple as the woman tried for the cutlery drawer, staggering his now-former assistant. As Helen reeled and touched her bloodied face, Saoirse vaulted over the table and leapt at the corper. However, Helen recovering quickly, rolled away. As she stopped, she threw her leg and kicked the Celt hard. Heidi insisted that Helen had taken up martial arts, and now Helen loved her even more than ever. Saoirse staggered slightly, which allowed Helen to get to her feet. Turning around the corner, Helen turned and bolted down the hall to her office; she would lock it and grab her pistol there. However, Saoirse's weapon was far closer; drawing it, she rapidly shot Helen in the back of both knees. The reports sounded like a battleship losing its cannons. Helen screamed in agony and collapsed. Tears blinding her eyes and animal sounds escaping her throat, Hclen, rolling over, looked down. The blonde corper immediately felt bile rise to her gorge. There before her, she could see that the only things that held her lower legs to her thighs were shredded meat and strips of flesh.

"Nice shooting Tex." Theo snorted. "That has got to hurt, I mean – damn, Helen."

Helen clawed at the flower as she desperately tried to crawl her way down the corridor. She flipped open her revolver, dropping spent .44 brass cartridges noisily on the hardwood. She reloaded the two empty chambers, slowly watching as her prey slowly moved down the corridor, leaving bright red trails of blood.

Metal spun and snapped shut. Helen's tried to close the sound out of her ears, damned if she would just lay there and accept death like a terrified dog. Her fingers dug into the ash, and she felt her nails painfully begin to tear away from the matrix below. Another roar thundered in the hall, and Helen screamed as Saoirse's Magnum smashed her left hand.

"Want to go for four?" The sound of Helen's screams muddled the sneering voice. Flopping onto her back, she saw through blurry eyes as Helen holstered her pistol. For a moment, Helen thought maybe everything was done, and they would leave her on the floor to bleed out- which was just fine with her. Her eyes faded in and out, knowing that she was suffering severe bloodless. Fluttering her eyes closed, she wished there was someone to perhaps cry out to for help, but Jen was dead, and Heidi was in town, oblivious to what she would find when she came home.

Saoirse walked over to the bleeding bitch and grabbed her by the hair. Lifting her straight up with one arm, the outsider pushed her face inches away from the Corper, slapping her face hard. Helens one working hand clutched at Saoirse's right forearm, trying to take the strain of her ripping hair.

"Wake up! Oh, yee'll not be napping through this." The Outsiders voice held no humour.

"All right, kill me, you bitch." It seemed to Helen that fog had flooded into the room, and everyone was moving slow, but Saoirse's' voice was as clear as crystal. So, this is it; this is how it ends. Helen mustered what little strength she had; she took a deep breath and then spat on the Celts freckled face, and then, closing her eyes, she braced for the worst. It will all be over soon — one shot to the head, or maybe to the heart.

Instead, she felt a horrific jab in each of her wounded limbs. Turning her eyes, she saw Theo had stabbed with a hypodermic needle. Sure, why the hell not?

"Anti-coag with a touch of adrenaline; we can't have you bleeding out before the job's done." Theo gave a deriding grin and then threw the needle on the kitchen table.

"Maybe the next time you go and try to nip someone off, you'll do a more thorough job, Darlin,'" She brushed her hair out of her face. "The Auburn tressed assassin then slammed Helen in the face with her forehead, snapping Helen's head back – throwing her eyes open. Helen smelled Saoirse's overpowering breath through her broken nose, a heady thick stench of whiskey and tobacco. Helen, feeling woozy, laughed.

"I should have killed you slower." Her voice was wavering and slurred.

"No," Saoirse said, her voice as sharp as a razor's edge. "It's me own fault. I trusted you. Do you know what was funny, Helen? I could have dealt with being shot and left for dead, "Saoirse nodded." I mean, it's the nature of the beast." Then Helen heard her voice go from cold to frostbitten.

"But where you fecked up was with Kit. I mean, ya shite, that was low, even for a gowpin hoore like you."

"Theo, please," Helen looked weakly over at Theo, who had found her biscuit stash. "Just end me."

"Murdering a friends' lover? For shame, Helen," He shook his head sadly, took a sip of his java, and then pointed back at Saoirse. "Saoirse, please proceed."

Saoirse's fingers begin to tighten like metal pliers as she squeezed the soft flesh of the corper woman's throat. Helen's last surviving five digits tried to pry off the merciless steel-tipped gloves which were stabbing her neck. She could feel the new blood running down her throat, across her fingertips. Agonizingly, she flailed her thighs – then she felt a sharp tear and heard the thud of her left leg strike the floor as it ripped away. Helen saw no hope, so Helen choked out her last words at the redhead.

"Do it, you whore." Instead, Saoirse released her grip, and Helen struck the floor in a heap. Helen sucked in gulps of air. Her blurry eyes flickered, struggling for focus, but it was her ears that met with an odd sound, the sound of metal on leather. Helen looked up as her murderer toward over her. Her faded vision vanished as Helen gasped. Saoirse reached behind her, and then Helen screaming began anew.

"Nooooooo…"

In Saoirse's hand was Kits' Bowie knife, the very knife Helen had used to murder the boy. The smile Saoirse told her all she needed to know. Theo leaned back, savouring the moment when the real screaming began.

Chapter 23

Fort Dallas.

Purchasing a human being was disturbingly simple, Mozart concluded. It was merely a matter of walking up to someone who trafficked and sold in people, negotiating a price and changing commodities.

Considering that Wina was kidnapped over a quarter of a century ago from people who now presumed she was dead, there would be legal entanglements. No records existed of her in the city files, and what forms may have existed outside were most likely long gone or forgotten. Human trafficking was nothing new beyond the domes, and when you have poor people struggling to survive in a wasteland, it's a relatively low priority to address. People out here sold their children to have money to feed the rest of the family. It was an ugly system, and as Mozart paid the man, in cash withdrawn from his bank. He knew that even though he was purchasing Wina's liberty, he was also demonstrating to Geddy, Wina's now-former owner, that the slavery system was, indeed, profitable.

The deed done, Wina was now free.

Her previous owner told her she had thirty minutes to empty her boudoir and clear out. Wina went back into the room with a single cardboard box, which, as she changed clothes, Mozart filled with things she mentioned. The items that went in the box were few; a broach, some photos, battered copies of the Bible and I Ching, some shoes and two T-shirts. That was all; her cigarettes and lighter went in her purse. Walking out, she had on a pair of battered jeans, a white t-shirt which showed she had no bra on; Wina refused to wear anything that anyone provided her for business. Her jeans and shirt were gifts from some of her co-workers. She would not call them friends, more like co-inmates at an internment camp. Slavery surprisingly generated few friendships; everyone was more concerned with staying alive and going numb inside. Attachments to relationships were just another way to become vulnerable. As they left Caprices, Wina grabbed Mozart's right hand with her left. It was the first time she had touched a man where she was sure the man wouldn't rape her – at least, she hoped. Trust was something that would take a long time to earn.

We need to get you some new clothing; that is, if you permit the gesture?" Mozart looked at her. Wina shrugged. Mozart led her down two blocks, but they stopped at a restaurant first because she, Wina, informed him, was very hungry. The eatery was simple fare, little more on the menu than burgers and fried food, but it was hot and fresh, and to Wina all the more delicious because it was outside, and Mozart had told her to get anything she wanted. They talked little, but when Mozart did, he apologized two more times.

Wina didn't say *'it's okay'* or *'I forgive you.'* It wasn't okay, and she couldn't and wouldn't forgive him until she could see that he wasn't going to treat her like everyone else did.

After lunch, he took her to the clothier, where he had often picked up clothes for MS Kelly. The venue had arrays of impeccable quality and style. Mozart saw the manager, who walked over with a friendly smile. She looked at Mozart's young lady and held out a hand to Wina.

"Miranda Verte, a pleasure to meet you, Miss?"

"Edwina Stavropoulos. Wina." She smiled nervously.

Monsieur Mozart, may I assume that you are here to make this our *draperie* available to *femme précieuse?*"

"Indeed. I think that no one is better suited to this than you, Mademoiselle Verte."

"You flatterer," She looked at Mozart with a tell-tale gaze.

"Whatever she likes, I am repaying a debt."

PART TWO

Chapter 24

July 6th, 2023,

Bard, Arizona.

Dorothy Magill's job was to analyse international data usage and industrial, commercial, and governmental dependency and cyber manufacturers' vulnerabilities. The reliance on individual contracted production firms for microchips, processors and computer architecture rated as critical weaknesses. Even though employees working on these systems were supposed to be thoroughly vetted, it became apparent after the twenty-sixteen American elections that enemy state hacking was beyond prolific, as were the recruitment of turncoats. The modern world's infrastructure was that cyber-architecture now controlled not only commerce but also logistics, fuel and energy, and healthcare. There was not any field that was not affected by digital controls. Once Dorothy submitted her initial report, her department was tasked to begin a hypothetical situational analysis about the effects of a global digital collapse.

Dorothy Magill's report showed that the primary effect noticed would be in transportation; most vehicles had electronics, and computers would devastate electric cars, petrol-based vehicles would also fail as engines were incredibly dependent on computers. Aircraft would suffer significantly with the loss of their complex systems of readings, direction and control. While pilots could manually land vehicles, the traffic control systems would not be able to direct movement. Ship at sea would go dead in the water, with the exception of sailcraft. Navigational guidance would collapse with the loss of Global Position networks. The following critical situation would be the collapse of mass communication as the world became dependent on cellular networks. Only twenty-two per cent of the world possessed landlines. But phone calls still had to be routed by computerised systems.

Furthermore, since most global communication was now done via text, email, or other digital means, mass entertainment would collapse with the loss of streaming services, filmmaking and exhibition. While seemingly a negligible side effect, national morale and tranquillity were intertwined tightly with entertainment. With the loss of television, internet access and video games, many individuals whose time once occupied would become free.

Power production would become frozen from the loss of nuclear, hydrodynamic, geothermal and solar power. Even green energy is still dependent on digital networks. Time management would also be affected as scheduling and reading time were via cell phones, monitor displays, and electronic signage. Seventy-seven per cent of chronological accounting was digitally dependent. The latest tests showed that over eighty per cent of high school students could not read a manual clock or timepiece.

To Magill, these studies were fascinating, and she presumed that the goal was to ensure the defence of manual backups for worldwide digital architecture. She would, nevertheless, prove to be entirely wrong.

David Severenson was Dorothy Magill's immediate supervisor. He was a tall, handsome guy and full of himself. If you could get past that, you would find that he was hilarious. Under his direction, Dorothy's analysis was being done, and he was well pleased with the results. The data would be of great use to his boss Anis Mikos Papadopoulos, whose bed he was also sharing. As a result of his relationship, his promotions were rapid, although not entirely be based on his bedroom skills because, still and all, he was damn good at his job. It was because of his position he was permitted to understand the full scope of Anis's plan. This was both thrilling and not a little disconcerting. Severenson's second in command was a young man named Ralph Bigsby, whose assignment was to the neural interface department.

June ninth, twenty-seventeen was the day when Ralph Bigsby found he was going to work for AST right after graduation from the Massachusetts Institute of technology, at age nineteen; he felt he had the world by the throat. He remembered the day when he got the call to go to work for them. He had been watching the news, staying up with the whole Comey mess. It was then his phone rang. An electronic message told him to check his email. He went to his iMac and opened his mail to find that he had been hired.

In the five years since then, he had made remarkable success in using both external and internal devices that could process the nervous system into commands for use by machinery and digital tools. His neural work had taken the project from beyond emotional communication to deeper interaction. Subjects were now able to communicate baseline thought processes such as transmitting a message of hunger and the communications processors of understanding how hungry and the person's intention of getting up to eat a particular food type. Likewise, the analysis team could read such arousal emotions, who was the source and the aroused's intentions. Ralph felt that by years end, they would be able to decipher the visual readout of those thoughts; in short, they would be able to lay the foundations of being able to read one's mind – as it were. Ralphs time with Axiom brought him financial success, professional satisfaction and, of late, romantic achievement.

Severenson had a running Dungeons and Dragons game at his condominium. When he received the invite, he was informed that he must now be regarded as somebody exceptional. The group was small, only six people – seven if MS Papadopoulos played, which was not infrequent depending on her mood. The group was so elite that those in that group were permitted to use her nickname, Madam Amp.

Because Axioms research and the technical team was a relatively small contingent, numbering less than fifty people, it was inevitable that people would get to know each other, for relations both friendly and romantic. This was the nature of the beast as axioms command structure remained compartmentalised. While thousands of people worked at the Arizona site, people did not talk to those outside their department. Only project directors and their staff could cross communicate. The entire system was based upon the model for the Manhattan project of the nineteen-forties. That projects security, which developed the first nuclear bombs, managed to produce tight security. However, nothing is ever leak-proof, and counter security officers handled, to date, more than five hundred general investigations, of which sixty-three resulted in the need for human eradication of both the employee and their communication subjects. Leaks were one thing easily controlled, but people undergoing morality crises were another. Thus, when Ralph met Dorothy Magill and fell in love, it came as only a slight ripple in the gossip pool.

Confiding in David, Ralph said that he had never had a girlfriend before, and while David chuckled, Anis, who just walked in, sat him down and gave him some relationship advice. Ralph was dumbfounded he was getting dating advice from the wealthiest and powerful woman in the world.

As his friends called him, Dee and 'Bigg's proved to be a cute couple, even though he was 5'7, weighed a hundred seventy pounds, wore glasses because he was afraid of contacts, and had a ridiculous blonde handlebar moustache and goatee. Standing at five foot eight, Dorothy Ziggy Magill had six inches on him. She was willow, with smooth acorn skin and long black dreads. Dorothy liked to exercise as much as Ralph wanted to play wargames. She eventually got him to eat vegan and go for walks everywhere. Ralph had to admit that desk work hadn't been his friend. Ralph wasn't too keen on the vegan thing but loved her enough to give up meat. On her their six-month anniversary, he spent over a thousand dollars buying her platinum and diamond gaming dice.

Even Anis applauded at that.

Once you made a high enough security grade, it became permissible to rent or purchase a home nearby, and since both Ralph and Dorothy were now a couple, they asked for and received permission to cohabitate. As usual, on Friday nights, Ralph got home a little after five in the afternoon or evening if you were a pessimist. He had been looking forward to this weekend. Dorothy had suggested that they take a flight over to SpaceX's Burn Flats Spaceport. She had managed to garner tickets for a launch ride. Someone in the office had been scheduled to fly but had discovered his wife was pregnant and opted out. As he pulled up, he was met with the site of Severenson, his boss standing outside next to a U-Haul. A black company car had parked in front of the Tuscan ranch home in Bard. The house had three garages, and he pulled up in his and getting out of his Jeep Wrangler; he watched as Severenson walked up to him and held a hand up. Severenson said nothing and observed as an Axiom driver got into Dorothy's car and then drove off.

"What," Ralph stood stock still at the sight of her Mustang as it took a right out of their subdivision." Is going on?"

"Dorothy is being reassigned today. It seems that – I mean," David hesitated. "I have to tell you something," and started over. He seemed to sag and looked at Ralph, who was still sitting down. David placed his hands on his face and dragged them down. "I have to tell you that in the best interests of you and the project, she is being reassigned to another location –which I cannot tell you where it is," Ralph opened his mouth in protestation, but David raised his hand again to prevent him from speaking. "For some time, we knew that she had been sexting someone at work. It was not a one-time thing, and after seeing that it was a pattern of behaviour, we confronted her about it."

"Okay, first off, I don't believe that for a minute." Ralph was enraged that anyone would even suspect that of her, let alone that she would conceivably do that. Dee was an old school Baptist, and though the rule was no sex until they married – which was going to be on Monday. They had only slept together a couple of times, but after the second time, she had told him it had to stop because it bothered her conscious. She was a church girl and was disappointed in herself, she said. Not him. The marriage was going to be a quick trip to the Courthouse.

No way, he shook his head. No way. "I have to go to her. If she tells me, I'll believe it."

David shook his head. "Just stop," he pulled out his phone, unlocked it and opened his photo gallery. He hit play and handed it to him and then looked away. "It didn't end with sexting."

The image was silent but in 5K colour video. It showed an office, a large one but he didn't recognise whose. The signs on the wall showed it was not their department, possibly engineering. Randall's hand shook as he saw that Dorothy was laying on the couch, naked except for thigh-high stockings. She was not alone, as a man had his back to the camera and stripped to the waist. He was either Arabic or Mediterranean. Dorothy knelt before him and-.

Randall dropped the phone to the cement floor, where it clattered but did not break.

"I'm sorry. I wanted to make sure that it was me who told you. I didn't want internal security to be the one."

Tears flowed down Ralphs's face, "Why? We were going to get much-married on Monday!"

David knelt. "From what we gleaned from the texts between her and – that's Eric Simmons from accounting - she was going to break up with you. The 'good girl routine was to throw you off. I guess she thought it wasn't working. I don't know." He shook his head. "When does it ever make sense?" he patted Ralphs's shoulder. "Technically, she wasn't breaking policy, but when I showed this to Anis, she said the best thing to do was to transfer her. If, and it's a big if, after a month or so, you two want to have a mediated meeting, you work it out she can come back to work here." Ralph watched as the last of Dorothy's stuff was moved into the van. The doors secured with a combination lock, they got into the cab and pulled out of the drive.

"What can I do?"

"I just need some time," He shook his head. "This is…"

"I know." David shook his head and punched his arm. "If you need me, call. I keep a well-stocked bar, as you well know." With that, he walked over to the Axiom limo and closed the door. In a second, he too was gone.

Ralph walked into his now empty and barer apartment. Everything that was Dorothy's was now gone. Pictures of them had been removed from their frames. Walking into the kitchen, he looked in the fridge. There too, all the vegan food was gone; her Hummus, pita's, and flavoured water - gone, as if she never existed. Slamming the door shut, he continued through the house. Her music room bare except for the rug, her grand piano, a 2007 Model D Steinway Concert Grand Piano,

Satin Ebony was conspicuously absent. It must have already been on in the truck when I got here.

The room was Dorothy's. It was all she asked when they moved together that she could have a music room, a place with excellent acoustics. She had dreamed of a piano room since she was small, but now the dream was gone and the dreamer with it.

Walking up the grand stairs, he turned left and stood to stare into what had been their bedroom. The sheets and blankets that they had bought together had been replaced with new ones. Ralph was freaking out now; his hands were trembling, and he repeatedly licked his lips. His head was swimming, and everything went grey when he passed out.

Eight hours earlier, Dorothy boarded a Boeing 797 Dreamliner owned by Axiom. That morning she had been informed by Severenson that a crisis had occurred in their Iceland office and that it was imperative that Dorothy immediately fly there to deal with a data crisis that could not be resolved, except on-site. She was told she could not speak to anyone about it, but she would be back in the states by early Saturday morning - optimally once settled.

Dorothy received the memo and then sent David a message to thank him as they had never sent her before, and David said that he had complete faith in her. She asked if she had time to run home and grab some things, and he told her that if she were at the airport by eight-fifteen, that would be fine. There were things Dorothy need to tend to before she departed.

Once aboard, she was escorted to her seat and told to buckle in. The captain did not come on and tell her where she was going, how long it would not take, nor was an explanation of emergency procedures had Axiom staff flew enough to have it down pat. She felt the plane roll forward and then turned to look out the window instead of windows. The inner walls were digital screens and shown the outside world, giving the feeling that one was flying themselves. At first, it was unnerving, but she grew to like it. The engines roared, and then she was pressed back as she departed from Yuma International Airport. Once in the air, the attendant asked what she would like to eat or drink, and as Dorothy felt a headache encroaching, she asked for some Advil and wine. Within a half-hour, she was dozing.

Back in Styx City, David slid into bed, where Anis asked a question to which she already knew the answer.

"Dealt with?"

"Yep," David rolled over on his back, looking up at the ceiling. "When she lands in Iceland, she will suffer a brain aneurysm and die. The doctor at the hospital will notify us of her death and then cremate the body."

"Had to be done," Anis sat up and poured herself white wine. "Screwing over Bigs like that couldn't go unpunished; not an option to let crap like that happen to a friend. "She sipped her Léon Beyer Gewurztraminer.

"Had nothing to do with friendship, you know as well as I do that, he's more valuable to the project than she was. As it is, he's still going to be a mess, but he'll work through that." David shook his head. "What was done needed to be done, and frankly, I don't want to talk about it anymore. She's dead, and that's that."

"I can't believe she was having an affair; I didn't see that coming."

Anis still wanted to talk, so David sighed and rolled over. "Yeah, well, fortunately, someone overheard Simmons bragging and came and told me. I showed you those videos that they sent each other; them banging in the bathroom." David frowned.

"I would have never expected it of her; she just so prissy and churchy." Anis got up and moved to the bathroom. "And Simmons? What was the attraction? "

"Who knows? I dealt with him as well, of course." David shook his head. He leaned over and pulled out a bottle of Tylenol from the bed stand. Swallowing them, he turned and tried to sleep.

After breaking the 'news' and leaving a devastated Ralph behind, David accessed his cloud storage sitting in the back of the limo. He proceeded to delete all the incriminating videos of Simmons and Dorothy screwing in the bathroom. David made sure that all copies of the file were gone and wiped utterly. He did a global image search to make sure no data had been copied, shortened or remade.

It was not, of course, Dorothy in that video but a similar-looking professional escort of the same height and build. He had sent the courtesan to Simmons' as a gift – ostensibly for a successful business deal. She led the accountant into his private bathroom - where the room had been lined with secreted and dedicated cameras covering every possible angle. When the matter was concluded, the file was downloaded to David. Utilising innocent video imagery of Dorothy at work as references, making the Deepfake was easy enough. The plan was designed and executed in eight hours and sixteen minutes from the moment he received the document. It had to be accomplished before Dorothy could return for her next shift. Had he chosen to work with others, yet, the whole image manipulation could have been completed in as little as three hours; destroying lives with technology was simple when you have power; David shook his head. If he had wanted, he could have stood in the middle of Fifth Avenue and shot somebody, and no one would say a damn thing.

The aircraft bumped down on the tarmac, its engines reversing. The plan slowed to taxiing speed and then pulled up to a terminal where she saw that she was now at Keflavik International Airport in Reykjavík, Iceland. She was told to stay in her seat as she was not disembarking here and that this was just a refuelling layover. It had been after 10 am Friday when she left, and it was now six pm. She had never flown longer than two hours stateside in her life. Now here she was on the other side of the world. It had been a hundred and nine degrees when she went to work yesterday in Yuma, and now it was forty-two degrees outside of her plane. She didn't know what that was, Celsius.

She didn't know anything, for they had taken her cell phone, smartwatch, iPad, and laptop. She was now utterly incommunicado. Only one person, the one flight attendant, Annette, had helped her, but it seemed that she had been given a laundry list of things she could not say or allow Dorothy to do. Her head was pounding like mad now. She screamed when the light and pain swallowed her and dragged her down away into the red dark and agony. As Dorothy died, she was sure that everything that was happening to her was because she broke her vows to God.

When Ralph woke up, hours had come and gone. It was a Saturday, and he would not have to deal with work - which was probably a good thing at the moment. He lay on the bed and started replaying things over and over in his mind. Nothing made sense at all. He lay there with tears in his eyes, and he looked at the ceiling of the bedroom. The ceiling light was off, but the glass cover seemed off. Staring at it, he couldn't make sense of it, and it was wrong somehow. After a moment, he sat up and turned the light switch on. With that, it became evident that there was something rectangular in there. Standing on the bed, he reached in and withdrew a small piece of paper; its lavender colour showed it was from Dorothy's stationery. It was addressed to him and dated from yesterday. With trembling hands, he unfolded it and read.

Baby, if you find this, it's because I'm in trouble, maybe even dead. I can't say why. If you ever loved me, listen to me now; believe nothing. Trust no one. Run as far away as you can from Axiom and hide.

To say I love you is an inadequacy,

D.

When Dorothy awoke, she was once more on an aircraft. This time windows were on the cabin and the shutters up; she saw a bright sky over the blue ocean. Looking out, she saw several large Icebergs.

What the hell?

"What is going on?" Dorothy demanded. "What happened to me?"

A gentleman sat across from her; he bore a striking resemblance to David, except he was older and heavier. He wore a starched plaid shirt and jeans; holding a glass of red wine, he swirled it and sniffed. *"Toscano*

Fattoria Poggio di Sotto Brunello di Montalcino Riserva Rosso," he toasted her.

"I highly encourage it." He watched her as she rubbed her eyes.

"No, thanks."

"My name Rick Severenson MD; I believe you know my brother."

"David never mentioned a brother," Dorothy snapped. "Now, what's going on?"

"Well, first off, the reason you've never heard of me is that we don't talk and generally hate each other. But I'm family, and that matters at times. Secondly, as to what's going on - you're coming back from the dead. That headache? That's because you had a haemorrhagic stroke and died. As far as anyone is concerned, your body is being burned, and your ashes spread over Nautholsvik Beach, except for a small amount which will be sent back to Anis to prove that your DNA is present," He pointed at her right forearm. "That'd be why you have a nasty wound on your arm. They had to remove some tissue to burn. They also took quite a few locks." Dorothy looked at the bandage on her forearm and touched her hair.

"Where am I?" She felt the plane bank.

"We will be landing in a few minutes in Östersund, Sweden. Now, there are some rules here. One, all your questions will be explained to you when we are there. Two, you must not contact anyone until you read the letter. If you do, everyone you love will die," he stared at her.

"The hell?" Dorothy snapped.

"It's not a threat; it's simply what will happen," He drained his glass and then corked the bottle. "Do you understand?" She nodded. "Good, because right now the only thing protecting them is the fact that as far as anyone knows, you're are dead, and while you were under, they did a bone marrow rewrite. Within a week, your blood will possess new DNA."

Dorothy felt nauseous, and her ears popped as the plane descended. "Please tell me what's going on. Why is all this happening?" her headache was back, and she felt humiliating tears of anger flow down her face.

"Would that I could, dear. All I can say is that you know things you wish you didn't find out."

"The networking – Axiom…"

"*SHUT IT*!" The doctor exploded. "Never say that; not here, not now, and not ever!" The aircraft bumped, and the high-pitched whine of reversing turbines shut them both down. "Just read the letter and then be sure to burn it completely. He held up his hand and shook his head. The aircraft taxied in silence, and once it had stopped, the hatch opened, and the two of them walked down the stairs. She heard the crew move about behind her.

After disembarking, she found that it was sixty-four degrees outside. It reminded her of tone time her family took her up to Crisp Point lighthouse in the Upper Peninsula of Michigan. It was lush green, flat and filled with pine trees just like this. DR Severenson escorted her to a cart which then they took down them to a parking area. Looking over her shoulder, she saw that it was not an Axiom aircraft but an older unpainted one with civilian markings.

She felt the cart slow, and looking up, Dorothy was now looking at a mammoth brand-new forest green H2 Hummer. Once the golf carriage stopped, the man handed her a set of keys.

"This is yours. Inside you will find an envelope telling you what to do next."

"I don't understand." Dorothy turned and looked at him. "This is it; you're just leaving me here?"

Severenson spread his hands. "These are all the instructions I have been provided to offer," Annette held her hand out in the direction of the car. "Now, if you please, I have a craniotomy to prepare for." Dorothy got off the cart and stood between the two vehicles.

"I have specific orders not to bring you back," The doctor said gravely. "So please don't try," he stared at Dorothy, who nodded. She understood the unspoken closing.

Or I'll kill you.

With that, the doctor turned the wheels and drove back to the aircraft. Dorothy watched him re-board, and when the doors closed, the jet began to taxi away, leaving her there under a perfect cyan sky. Dorothy, regardless, was in no frame of mind to appreciate the warm air. Dee watched as aircraft turned from the taxiway and then raced down the tarmac leaping into the sky, now just a sliver sparrow in a bright sky.

Dorothy looked at the fob to find the button to open the door, only to find there wasn't one. The lock was, oddly, manual. Inserting the key and twisting it, she stepped in and moved her backside across the leather seat, settling behind the steering column. She pushed the key and turned the engine over. The vehicle was full of petrol, and the interior gleamed like diamonds in a desert of leather. She wasn't overly impressed, though it looked like a nice car; the interior was more cramped than she expected. The doors, for some reason, were absurdly thick.

On the passenger seat was a thick sealed Manilla envelope. It was from David Severenson, of course. Opening it, Dorothy saw the letter was written in number two pencil lead. Everyone recognised that shade when they saw it.

Dorothy;

I am sorry, you don't have to, and I guess I don't expect you to believe me, but I am. I know you hate me, and truth to tell, I don't blame you. I would hate me too. In fact, I've hated myself for a while now.

I am sorry about what has happened. I will now explain why I must now destroy your reputation and slander you.

By the time you read this, David believes that you have cheated on him, disgraced yourself and requested a transfer. In a week or two, we will tell him that you died due to severe mental anguish. Do not, under any circumstances, contact him in any way or form.

You had seen what Axiom has been doing, but you hadn't yet discovered the whole truth.

On Sunday, August 13, 2023, Anis and six other people — all names everyone is familiar with — are going to take over the world. Not like Pinky and the Brain, I mean, actually, take over the world. You saw what they are capable of — everything's coming down. It's going to work, and there's not a damn thing we can do about it. There is no point in warning anyone because no military force or weapon can stop it. There are too many safeguards. How do you contain a virus if all the antivirus programs are co-opted? How do you reformat a computer if the algorithm is written into the chips? You cannot ask the doctors to cure you if they are the plague bearers. Axiom and others are going to shut everything down.

All the doomsayers were right, and no one listened to them. They all saw it coming or should have. We made the mistake of sacrificing convenience and amusement for wisdom. There are no electronic borders – if you're on the internet, you are part of the digital carpet, all manipulated by malevolent weavers.

I'm typing this on an old Royal typewriter I bought at an antique store because I don't trust the pens they give us. I think they have nanotech in them. So, I am writing this in an abandoned house I rode a horse too.

I'm not going to say Anis's and her cadre are misunderstood or misguided. She and they know what they're doing it. It's not for world peace, and it's not so we can live in some Roddenberry-esque future. This is an outright power grab. I can't save everyone, but I could save you. Ralph is too valuable, but you – you're expendable.

If Anis knew what you are aware of, she would have you killed on the spot, and she would do it herself –bullet in the brainpan – squish. So, the only way to save you from Anis is to kill you myself. To do so, I had to destroy everything about you so that no one would trust you or even want you back. Hence, I'm going to frame you for cheating on Ralph, whom Anis adores like a kid brother. If I do this, she'll have me get rid of you discreetly. So that's what I'm going to do, I'm going send you away, kill you and report you as dead. My brother will see to it that that is what happens- Sort of.

I know, but you don't understand how it's going to be. There will be no power, no refrigeration, not internet. People are going to go insane. Do you remember what happened when Hurricane Katrina hit? It's going to be like that but worldwide. People are stupid. America will kill itself; Red versus Blue, gay versus straight, black vs white and on and on. I know because Anis showed me the computer models. It's all planned. We've all been played. Unless we were too busy with politics, or crime or immigration, we would never notice that not just the money was being consolidated but the power, the information and the weapons.

No, we won't come out to rescue them; no one will. Axiom is going to abandon the world and let themselves tear themselves apart, and then when they are good and ready. Axiom and the others will roll out with their goddamn armies.

If I hadn't been the one to take the report when they gave it to me, and if Anis saw that you were about to discover the truth, there is zero doubt in my mind that both of you would both be dead right now. If both of you vanished, it would have looked suspicious. She's relying on Ralph to keep the whole cerebral monitoring applications working. He thinks that they for controlling apes - for a workforce. That's just for show; they use them on the soldiers. It's the only way she's keeping control of the soldiers; keep them pumped on endorphins and happy.

The only way to protect you was to destroy you. I did it in a way that hopefully would shock Bigs so much he would be disgusted with you. Ones the one thing all of us nerds fear? Losing the woman we thought we could never get.

I'm sorry I didn't know you more. I'm sorry we weren't as close as you might have thought we were. I genuinely love you, my friend. You're a much better human being than I am. I wish I had your faith in loving and just God. Hell, I wish I had faith in anything or anyone; so, I'm asking you just to have a few grams of faith in me.

The hammer falls at Midnight on the 13th. That means that I must have Bigs out of there about sixteen hours beforehand. I plan to get him on a plane early in the day and have the same jet you just took him to take him to Dublin. If there is still time and no weather issues, he will fly to Sweden, and you can pick him up. I'll tell him the truth at that point.

With people like you two, maybe the world will have a future. It sure seems like the one we have coming will be a hard one for everyone outside.

I've was able to save some of your family. Your parents will meet you where you're going. I'm sorry your sister wouldn't come and said she would going to the press about what was going to happen. To put it bluntly, she and her family are dead — all of them. I had to; it was a risk in telling them. I'm sorry.

Dorothy opened the door and vomited. One of her best friends – up until the last day, had just told her he murdered her sister, brother and law and her nieces and nephew. She didn't want to but kept reading.

For this reason, I'm sending you to my brothers hunting lodge. It has a massive greenhouse so you can grow food. Also, there is a barn with horses and livestock. There's a freshwater lake near; also, there are wells. It's out in the middle of nowhere, so it is implausible that in the days and time to come, you will have to defend it. He has stocked it with weapons, medicine and more. The car you're sitting in is bulletproof, EMP, Nuclear, biological and radiation proofed. Us the paper map to find the house, there's no GPS. Just in case you're tracked. After the thirteenth, there won't be GPS for a long time, if ever.

Your friend, if you can still call me that,

Dave.

"Oh God,"

Chapter 25

Private Communique.

Kelly Rappaport turned around the corner and walked to her administrative centre, which was now much more comfortable; the panoramic windows replaced with holographs of sylvan streams and woods. The bright office atmosphere came from ceiling lights that mimicked the son. The original windows previously made her uncomfortable because Kelly was terrified of heights and always had been since childhood. She loved being at the highest point in the city but did not want to have to look out at it. Kelly's desk was a light walnut, the carpet factory-made, and her music modern. She had, but one bookshelf, and no books lived there anymore - only photographs filled it. Kelly was not much of a reader – of books anyways.

"Open communication with designated Watcher ambassador," Kelly reached down and pulled out a Pepsi, her office fridge neatly tucked away under the desk. The screen wiped to the left, turning crimson with the sole exception of the icon of a watchful eye. "Omega - Identity JSY=39037. Password: *Cheese Sandwich on Rye.*

"We accept your identity," the screen flickered, and the face that appeared belonged to a young man radiating an aura of peaceful beauty. The youth was a blend of Caucasian and Asian ethnicities.

"I am called Saint Edgar, and you may proceed. What is the content of this notice?" Its voice was kind and gentle, both soft and relaxing. Kelley knew it was a harmonic tone designed to relax and disarm. Even knowing this, it worked on her, and she hated them for it.

"I am now assuming the role of intermediary between the Watchers and Omega. The previous contact is now deceased. Transmitting Directive Magnus -5781#23 to you now." Edgar's eyes seemed to look down; another human behaviour modelled for comfort. This time Kelly just shook her head. The transmission was instantaneous, but Edgar took the time that a human would have to read the missive.

"Confirmed. Is there anything else I may help you with?"

"Yes, please. I need copies of any transmissions from my predecessor to the Watchers. Also, any transmissions from her to any other arcology would be appreciated."

Edgar nodded. "As those transmissions are the property of Omega, this will be done."

"Thank you."

Upon receipt of the files, Kelly slowly went through them; it took a few hours and then another two to review the data before her.

No way.

Her predecessor had been into some serious shit. As she read through the project descriptor, she leaned back in her chair. The possibilities were endless if she could get her hands on the program. She continued her reading, and when she saw to whom it had been delegated, she smiled and then opened a new secure window on her monitor. She then began checking a somewhat discrete but morally bankrupt section of the network.

She needed a pest removal service.

Chapter 26

Dorothy Magill's office,

"I'm sorry, ma'am, we cannot access the files of the decedent. All of Helen BonHomme's are under maximum lockout, and the only agent we have in that level is out of the City, already assigned to Swallowtail." Yoon bowed and apologized.

Dorothy sighed.

"Ok, find out who did the hit on her. We'll see if we can't outbid Omega."

"What if Magnus had it done in-house?"

"Theo doesn't use in Omega people to kill Omegans; too risky. People get worried they're going to wind up on the chopping block themselves, and if that happens, they worry which one of their own will off them. No, he hires his assassins out. I know who his security hitter is."

"Who?"

"An outsider, I've used before. Now I am going to have to outbid Omega," She frowned.

"'In the midst of chaos, there is also opportunity'", Her aide offered.

"Sun Tzu." Magill nodded. "'One mark of a great soldier is that he fights on his own terms or fights not at all'".

Chapter 27

En route,

UK.

Violet sky to the west, the plane flew at nigh stratospheric heights at Mach three's speed, covering the Pacific and most of the old western states in little time. The vessel was black, fast and when it wanted to be, undetectable to most all known sensors. The pilot, Hasaki, checked on the controls. It was, naturally, on autopilot – a harsh word for the aircraft was far more sophisticated than that nomenclature previously meant. The *Furaingufokkusu* was a joy to pilot by hand, though. The Flying Bat was perfect black, and no markings disgraced it.

Hasaki looked back to see that O'Sullivan was doing a Steeplechase Flourish, rolling a silver dollar over his knuckles. Hasaki watched with interest. O'Sullivan walked the coin over the phalanx bone of each finger. When the rolling stopped, Gabriel used his thumb to bring the coin under his palm and then moved it again to the index finger.

"We have a problem," His headset announced.

There were three words any assassin hated to hear; there's a problem. This would be followed by another three words they hated more; change of plans.

"We have a new directive,"

Same thing. Those words were as pleasant as finding lice on your pillow. Gabrielle did not enjoy listening to them come through his headset announced that the mission just went to shit.

"Our intel has shown that the primary target is now deceased. Hold at station."

Great.

Master Suizei sat in his office and shook his head. With BonHomme dead, the mission was essentially pointless. A physical mission was only worthwhile if he could recover the woman alive and viable. Since this was no longer the case, he saw no point whatsoever to continue. He flipped open the window on his monitor and went live stream to his security chief, showing up only on the pilot's optical Heads Up Display.

"Give the order to recall. Have Hasaki dispose of the Gaijin."

"It will be done," Upon hearing that, Ieyasu looked at his itinerary for the next day and then went to dinner with his wife.

O'Sullivan knew that something was off when he heard the headset line go dead. He looked at Hasaki, who had moved to the pilot's seat. That in and of itself wasn't unusual, as the job was scrubbed, and they needed to reset the flight plan. Moreover, he could see that Hasaki's com was open because the Hitokiri's jawline was moving. Gabriel caught Sullivan's eyes dart to him and then away.

Not this again.

Sighing, he reached down to his hip. As soon as Hasaki rose from the seat and turned smiling at Gabriel, O'Sullivan popped two low-velocity rounds through the man's face. It seemed to him whether his suspicions were right or wrong about being betrayed, one was better suited to err on the side of caution. To date, no guy he ever shot told him he was wrong.

As the assassin crumpled to the floor, Gabrielle set to work. He went to the flight deck and checking the flight plan, saw that it had changed, but he reset it back to the mission parameters. Gabe strapped himself into his drop gear. He now had an aircraft of his own, and that was just okay with him.

Chapter 28

Saint Edgar's Chamber,

Gebihe Cave System,

Guizhou province, China.

Saint Edgar floated in his pool, processing information. Weariness came over him, and his attendants watched as his readouts showed that he needed sleep, so they rerouted his duties to others of his kind. Saints slept like ordinary people, but more intermittently. The saw him enter REM sleep, and so they darkened his glassine container. Saint Edgar, now asleep, his clergy took the opportunity for breaks, grabbing lunch or taking cigarette breaks.

Edgar dreamed, but to him, he was not here in this tank; he was somewhere pleasant and tranquil. He was far away in a beautiful city in his bed, and the sun was setting low on the horizon, and there beside him was a warm lie.

It was twenty-sixty-one, and Edgar Winters was inordinately pleased with his life. Severenson had kept his promise and had provided him great opportunities to get his protestations out; his books now sold worldwide, and illegal copies infiltrated the Mega-corps often. His popularity was such that Severenson had told him that his safety was now at considerable risk. There had been multiple attacks and attempts on his life, so much so though he recoiled when the Commissar told him it was now best for his safety if he moved into an Arcology. Where better to hide him? Now Edgar lived a lovely home in the most affluent section of the Nanyang arcology. His anonymity was still present as he had been provided with a nom de plume. To justify his presence in the city, he had also begun writing popular fiction and prose. That job, however, caused him the requirement of flying across the world in a jet aircraft. However, since both of his writing obligations he utilised to effect changes in worldwide inequalities and iniquities, he remained a happy man.

His social life was very fulfilling as well; he had two live-in girlfriends who were very pleasant to each other, did not bicker and kept his home attended very well. Both were beautiful and accommodating, and he could ask for a little more than that. It wasn't a bad start to a career; After all, he had only worked for the Watcher organisation for a few years.

Edgar had flown over to the Watchers, which was fronting as a technological research firm in Kowloon, where the young man received his own office. Once there, he was assigned. He had a luxurious administrative centre complete with a host of a secretary and interns, all of whose business acumen, intelligence and beauty would show how accomplished and respected he was. Edgar noticed that instead of composing more revolutionary arguments, much of his tasks became analytical and investigative on the Arcologies, such as power structures, internal stability and such matters. He presumed this was to allow his ideas to target specific demographics.

Nevertheless, Edgar felt something was off. When he finished with the day, he would take a company helicopter —set aside for him – to the roof of his luxury home in West Kowloon. No, the irony did not escape him.

Severenson was not a full or a rube; He tasked Edgar with critical duties, allowed him to continue writing his commentary, and did find ways to get it into the mega-corps themselves. Edgar needed to develop a robust and trusting relationship with the Commissar, and so he kept every promise he made Edgar and more. Winters became Severenson's fair-haired boy. He was kept busy, mentally occupied and satisfied in all other parts of his life. Naturally, a young man would desire a sex life or a romantic one at the very least. Severenson made sure these needs and desires were not to be overlooked. Edgar was not an unattractive man but leaned closer to unassumingly plain. He was socially awkward, and this was something else that worked towards the Commissars advantage.

Once Edgar had felt comfortable at work, and his free time opened up. Some of his workmates took him out to a party where the Commissar made introductions to two ravishing women. His conversation and personality loosened up with beer and Baijiu. He seemed more comfortable with the women. His friends encouraged him and patted him on the back when one of the women kissed him and then, the second joining. Edgar had never felt more alive and manly. The women even went home with him. The next day at work, Commissar Severenson clamped him on the shoulder and let the young man crow a bit.

Edgar could not believe it; here he was in his west Kowloon penthouse apartment - which includes a rooftop and a good view of Hong Kong Island - celebrating his twentieth birthday with more success and respect than he ever could have dreamed of achieving. Edgar smiled, but the smile came with some reticence.

Sometimes, Edgar felt like a sell-out and looking at his spacious apartment and its view of Hong Kong island, he had to admit that it was true. Above him, a helicopter waited to take him wherever he wanted. Ying Yue was on the roof sun tanning and editing Edgar's first novel. Edgar sipped his Chivas when Feng Mian walked up behind him. She was wearing new jeans and a simple cotton blouse. She wrapped her arms around him and kissed him under his right ear.

"Ed, we know you didn't want a big party, but we have arranged a night out with just the three of us." The only person who called him Edward was the Commissar, which was just something fathers and sons did. He sipped his whiskey. Maybe the Commissar didn't feel that way about their relationship, but he knew Edward did and did nothing to dissuade that. "David is coming over later. He has a special gift for you." Feng slapped him on the butt. "Now go get dressed." Ed smiled and returned the playful pat. Feng gave him a wink. They both heard the elevator chime as Ying came down. Ying was unusually tall for a Chinese woman; she stood at one hundred seventy-two point seven two centimetres. Her legs were long, and her torso was taught and fit, with natural thirty-five C breasts. Ying was far more relaxed than her friend Feng and strode in wearing only a black thong and sheer black robe. She handed him the tablet on which she had been editing.

"You still tend to write in a passive tense, which is fine for technical writing but not fiction. I've made the changes for you," Feng smiled as she peeled off the robe. "Still, it's excellent." Walking over, she wrapped her arms around his neck. "If I may, I'd like to screw my favourite author, silly, on his birthday."

Later that evening, his lovers wined and dined him in the finest restaurants available. They told him that the Watcher Firm was footing the bill – a gift from the Commissar. Over the next two days, Ying and Feng took him all over the South Pacific for water skiing, skydiving, sex and alcohol. Coming back Sunday night, the girls made love to him for hours. He fell asleep thereafter, spent and exhausted. Once he was snoring, Feng picked up her phone and made a call.

The dispatcher sent an ambulance upon receiving a call, for it seemed that one Edgar Winters had gone into cardiac arrest. The Kowloon police immediately arrived with Paramedics in tow. The officers hurried as they could and then entered the five thousand four hundred and ninety-seven square foot Kowloon Station condominium. Two women met them at the door; both women, the men thought, were deserving of being in and on runways and lingerie magazines. The women-led the first responders to the back bedroom, where twenty-year-old-year-old Edgar winters was found nonresponsive.

The paramedics attempted Cardio-pulmonary-resuscitation to no avail. They pushed on his chest hard enough to bruise but got no reaction. They broke out the defibrillator. After several attempts, they proclaimed him dead. Post Shutdown, there was no longer a need to wait on the coroner if the police felt unwarranted. The officer looked at the naked man; the bed stand filled with lotions and sex paraphernalia, the two stunning half-naked and weeping women. They made a note that death was due to physical exertion and left it at that. The officers bowed and laughed but not before looking back at the dead man's lovers and envying the man's glorious departure mode. The paramedics wanted to know if they should remove the body or call a funerary for them. They thanked him, and as they covered him up, Feng told the paramedics that they would have a funeral home get him. They handed him a card and said to them that the mortician would have to confirm the body's relocation in the next four hours. The women bowed, and with the shutting of the door, they made their second call.

The helicopter on Edgar's roof was not the same one that had taken him on his sordid birthday weekend. In the co-pilot's seat was Commissar Severenson and behind him was an entire surgical team. Once the EMT's had departed the apartment, the aircraft crew moved down into the flat and rushed to Edgar's side. One physician swabbed the inside of his left arm and administered an antidote that had caused him to hover at the edge of death, his bio-signs reading as negligible to the EMT's equipment. Secondly, they lifted him onto a stretcher where the second physician dug his nails into Edwards's chest and peeled back a layer of synthetic flesh. Beneath the skin was a thin rubberised shield that prevented any electroshocks from bringing his heart activity to normal; this had been placed there four months ago when he had to go under for what was said to be a tooth pulling.

The Commissar turned and thanked the women for their service and assured them that they would be well compensated for their two years with Edgar and understood when he saw the tears were genuine now. The chief Surgeon checked Mr Winter's vitals and nodded to the Commissar. He told the women as he left that the next candidate would be moving in soon, so they would need to vacate the apartment by the end of the month. With that, the two doctors, Edgar and the

Commissar, retreated to the awaiting air ambulance. Once they departed, their flight plan took them not to the Watcher Building but the Gebihe cave system in Guizhou province, China.

Edgar was treated with the greatest of care. The Medical team lowered his body into a clear plasmic gel solution which would keep his skin nourished and protected, yet his head leaned back onto a hairdresser's sink. The surgeons commenced shaving his head while he was given intravenous painkillers so that when they removed his finger and toenails, he would not scream in agony. Once his head was completely shaven, the rest of his body hair was removed. His medical readings were in the norm, and at the beginning of the second hour, they raised the body, and a dental surgeon entered the room and begun the complete extraction of his teeth. The dental Surgeon continued his argument that Edgar's jaw and tongue's removal was not a practical pursuit. While the two men bickered, another surgical team removed Edwards's entire genitals leaving only a permanent catheter to filter out his urine. Once the body healed from this procedure for twelve hours, the next round removed most of Edwards's colon, his ears and eyeballs.

The mutilation of Edward Winter did not cease there. Neurosurgeons opened his skull and executed a thirty-two-hour process of wiring Edwards's brain, optic nerves, and auditory system into the newly networked brain; once the cranial work was completed, his skull was discarded in lieu of a titanium one. Once resealed, his skin was sown back over it. His toothless mouth was penetrated by a long bifurcated hose that would feed him oxygen and nutrients. The tubing in place, the skin on Edgar's face was sealed around the house, which itself had been treated with a synthetic covering that would grow together with Mr Winters natural flesh.

The next step after the surgery was to interface Mr Winter's brain's neural functions into the new quantum level computers, constructed especially by Severenson himself from stores of unaffected computer systems; those resources garnered from resources he would not name. Once Edward was online, he would slowly be joined by eventually additional individuals whose population would constitute a new generation of dynamic processing networks.

Edward woke up in a hospital bed and rubbed his eyes. It was a long night – a fun night, but as he stepped out onto the linoleum floor, he saw that Feng and Ying were talking to the doctors in the hallway. Seeing him, they rushed into and gave him a plethora of hugs and kisses and telling how sorry they were that the excitations last night had caused him to suffer a minor heart flutter. The doctor came in and said to him that he was going to be released today, but Edgar was to avoid any strenuous activities for a week or more. Saying this, he looked directly at the two sheepish women. The doctor departed, and a discharge nurse came in and had him sign his paperwork, at which point he was required to be wheeled out. As he left the building, he saw that Severenson had a limousine waiting for him. He was told that the Commissar was waiting for him back at his apartment.

Once home, the girls escorted him to the elevator, which required the use of a security key to access the penthouse apartment. As the door opened, he saw that not only was the Commissar there, but his friends and often staff were there with a surprise party. Edward was overwhelmed and choked back tears.

The party would go on for an hour or so, with Edward consuming only non-alcoholic champagne and heart-healthy food and deserts. Edward felt great, although he was getting tired. Feng announced the party was over, and she and Ying began to escort the guests out, thanking them for their support and kindness. After the forced departure of the well-wishers, the Commissar knelt next to Edgar.

"I want you to know that when you're up to coming back, I have decided to have you take over the entire intelligence network. You'll have lots of help; I don't want you to have any more health issues. But I trust you to run the department, and I believe that you will be the greatest asset we have or will ever have." The Commissar patted him on the shoulder and took his leave.

Commissar Severenson looked down at the darkened tank where Edgar had resided for over two decades. Below him what once could have been called a man lay, now only an organic cog floated as part of a Machiavellian machine. He was now one of the Watchers critical assets – a Sentinel. Leaning over the railing, David saw that Edgar's dedicated acolytes below were enjoying a break. However, one woman still stood working at the freestanding counsel next to Edgar's sizeable fluidic sepulchre. Her name was Genève, and she was currently Severenson's lover.

Though he could not see inside the darken tank, he knew that the Saint was covered in wires reporting on his every bodily fluctuation. He was nourished by his throat tube, which fed him his daily required vitamins, nutrients, and proteins. Edgar produced little in the way of waste, which flowed into his rectal tube, which removed any of the scatological by-products. However, the most noticeable features on display were the fact that Edgar's limbs, which had atrophied due to disuse, had required removal. Mr Winters now appeared as an oversized embryo as he floated in his artificial womb.

As disturbing as this may appear on the outside, inside his consciousness, Severenson knew Edgar knew nothing of this, for he still believed himself to be the healthy, robust young man he had always been. His life was as it had been. For him, time moved at a fraction of the speed of the real world. Edgar worked his job, travelled abroad was happy in his relationship with Ying and Fang. He did still require periods of natural sleep, the absence of REM sleep being a base need of human physiology; nevertheless, during their waking hours, the Sentinels roamed the world's digital architecture, observing and interfering here necessary. Locked into the world's digital design, their corporal remains yet necessitated that each had their attendants, often more akin to the clergy than physicians.

Before the Shutdown, Severenson and his family were old school catholic. After The Shutdown, he recognised that for millennia, the Catholic organisation had successfully – to some – used the church's trappings to maintain power, both politically and culturally. Seeing no need to re-invent the wheel, he continued the practice. As such, the Sentinels were deemed 'Saints.' He saw on the wall display that a singular Saint had been red-flagged – meaning that an extraordinary event was transpiring. Walking over to the Sentinel's apse, he looked down from his walkway. The Commissar looked down on one such group of functionaries.

"Sister Genève, how is Saint Edgar's day?" Severenson asked calmly.

"Commissar," The woman looked up and smiled. She would never deign to call him by his first name in public.

"He seemed to have a peaceful one. His productivity was at ninety-seven point three two five," Genève studied the physiology readout. "Right now, he seems to be in the third stage of REM – Saints tend to enter REM faster than most human. He has a higher state of signals from the pons," She looked up. "The pons is part of the hindbrain, connecting it the cerebral cortex. It is the basis of cooperative communications between the two brain hemispheres." She studied the display and shook her head in dismay. "It seems that his pons is not discontinuing signals to the spinal cord to shut off physical activity. Normally the body doesn't move during third and fourth state sleep." Turning to her assistant, she ordered, "Bring up the lights!"

Severenson looked disconcerted and began to move down the stairs towards the apse. "What is happening here?" As the lights came up in the bin, they could see that Edgar's body was flailing about vigorously. The solution was in turmoil, and his exhalations were causing the fluid to bubble slowly.

Genève looked over the readouts. "It seems he's having a nightmare."

Edgar woke up screaming in his bed; Ying and Feng leapt up, and then seeing Edgar, they shrieked themselves; hot fresh blood covered Edgar's bed, gushing from all four of his severed limbs.

Chapter 29

Time and Tide.

O'Sullivan wasn't fond of idleness, and as such, he pulled out his datapad and looked to see if any new jobs were available. As he was still over America – heading west but at a much slower rate, he looked for regional contracts and son of a bitch if one didn't come up. He pulled an Immelmann, and levelling out, Gabriel reset the previous flight plan.

It looks like I'm going to Omega after all. Sucks to be you, Randall Spencer, whoever you are.

Chapter 30

Sliding Doors.

Saoirse sat in her office with her legs crossed and boots on her desk. The window behind her let the sun warm her, but she was tired, and after she finished her cigar and whiskey, she was going to go home downstairs and throw down and rock and roll with her pillow. She sipped her Bushmill's Single Malt and ruminated on her life's current situation. She had exacted her revenge on Helen, which was lovely but now she wasn't sure what she wanted to do. Being head of security for Omega was a posh position and nothing to gurn about, but she didn't feel that she was constantly being let on about Theo's goings-on. There was the Défense Department, which seemed to handle everything outside the dome, and she was more or less confident that something big was going on; it nagged at her that if there was any agro about to go down, and nobody was telling about it. She would have to investigate that and have a talk with Theo. She felt that it was about time to Millie up; she would not be kicked to the side when it did. Abruptly the phone rang and ended her musings. It was Theo.

"Hey, I need you to check on one of Helen's employees. Just go and see if he has some data Helen had him working on. Simple job, go check and be sure to report to me if he does."

"You need that now? I'm right knackered."

"There's no immediate hurry. Can you have it done by noon, perhaps?"

"Aye, that I can. I'll make a dooter over there later and have a wee chat with the lad." He handed her a piece of paper.

"Names Davidson, here's his address."

"Grand. I'll give it a lash, "She nodded.

Chapter 31

Saguaro Condominiums,

Mesquite, Texas.

It was dawn when they finally arrived via taxi to Mozart and Randall's home, just as the day doorman Tafner was relieving the night man. Tafner smiled and held the door open for them. Mozart bowed, and Wina smiled nervously. Tafner took the packages and bundles and told Mozart he would have the delivered up shortly.

The elevator rode up the apartment transpired in silence, with Wina concentrating on what words to say to make the best impression. Mozart saw her right hand was nervously tapping on her leg. Reaching out, he took her hand in his. Wina's reaction was to jerk her hand away but realized he was merely trying to comfort her.

"I'm sorry."

"Not at all, I should have asked your permission," The elevator chimed, and then the doors whispered open. "All will be well. Randall is a good man."

The duo turned left and walked down the hall. Mrs Jensen, an older woman of fifty-something, took her leashed mini-corn colt down the hall and caught the elevator just before the doors closed. Edwina's eyes flew open at the sight of the tiny horned horse.

"May I pet it?" The woman nodded, and Wina knelt and stroked its beautiful coat. The animal gave a slight nicker and leaned against her leg. "It's so beautiful," Wina stood back up, and with a tear in her eye, thanked the woman, who smiled back and then continued her way.

Coming to the end of the hall, Mozart faced right and inserted his house key. For all the high-level technology man had progressed through, the one constant is that there will always be a key the artificial mused. Mozart's key was imbued with a small amount of harmless radiation, which the locking mechanism detected. Seeing the decay rate was on point, with a snap, the bank vault inspired design opened.

Hearing the door, Randall turned to see that Mozart had returned – with company. In all the years of Mozart being with him, Randall had never seen Mozart bring home anyone; entering, he saw Randall and Denetta were sitting on the breakfast bar stools and laughing.

"Who's your friend?" Denetta smiled and waved at the young woman.

"May I introduce Wina?" Mozart moved his arm horizontally with the palm upheld. "She is a friend. I invited her to stay until her home is readied if that is acceptable." Mozart looked at Randall and tossed his glance to the back hall.

"Oh," Seeing the look, Denetta smiled.

"Please, make yourself comfortable, Wina." Randall offered with graciousness.

"Absolutely. Let me get something ready. Why don't you join me? You can tell me what you like. We have a full larder." Wina tried to stifle a yawn as they looked at Mozart, who nodded. Wina was exhausted, both physically and emotionally. The artificial then asked if he could speak to Randall alone in his office.

The front doorbell chimed, and Denetta went; opening the door, she allowed Tafner to carry in Mozart's guest's packages.

The Blind Eye homing beacon landed first and immediately scrambled any monitoring equipment. Following the signal, O'Sullivan popped his chute at five hundred feet above. His hip-mounted inertial dampeners fired, thus allowing him to land on the roof safely, albeit roughly. As soon as he was on the ground, he removed his harness and locoed for the best position. He moved to the edge of the building and looked over the parapet to make sure he was on point – which he was. Removing and then opening the case he had strapped to his back, Sullivan began assembling his Accuracy International AS99.

"She's who? You did what?" Randall stood in his office, aghast.

"I purchased a pleasure slave."

"Ok, first off, artificials owning slaves is against the law. Secondly, I don't need or want a cocotte in this house, Mozart."

"She is not a gift, nor am I not asking you to take ownership. I need assistance in guaranteeing her freedom. I felt a certain responsibility for her situation and exploitation. I had presumed she was a legal courtesan doing her -work - freely. However, when I discovered this was not the case, I could not stand by and do nothing," He rubbed his chin idly. "I am complicit in her mistreatment, though unknowingly. Such a distinction is not excusable. Therefore, I have decided to make as much reconciliation as possible by providing her freedom. I do not know, nor think she knows, what steps are in her best interest at this point."

"So, your request to me is to let her stay here?"

"Yes,"

Randall crossed his arms as he leaned back with his feet on the table once more. "That's fine, I mean, that's if she wants to."

"She has indicated that is the case."

"Liberating her is noble of you; people owning people is immoral."

"I agree, and as that is the case, I am wondering how my possession by you can be conceived as moral?"

Randall looked dumbfounded. "What?"

"By that statement, is it not your moral imperative to free me? Am I not sentient? Do I not possess a physical formed identical to you? And though I possess a network link to my brain, which is the only significant differential. I see it as no more a prosthetic than a human's artificial limb. I am your slave."

"David, you are a manufactured, I mean, you're not a -,"

"Real person?" Mozart looked pained.

O'Sullivan had picked this spot because it was dead centre, allowing him to see all the residence. His pants were reinforced with kneepads and padded greaves. Likewise, he cushioned his elbows because sniping is a time-consuming effort, usually done prone. A low wall bordered the flat roof to keep those not paying attention from walking off the top, a sweeter sniper spot. He could not have asked for better. Gabriel swept his binoculars across the gap at the target's apartment, seeking bio-signs.

There were multiple, four in number. In the target's kitchen, two women were talking, both attractive and toned. The observation was not prurient but a threat assessment. The shorter one was patently exhausted, having trouble staying awake, and even though she had a cup of coffee, it seemed only to cause her hands to shake all the more.

The other had long, black hair and hard biceps, a possible challenge. It was apparent she wasn't Omegan; she wasn't pretty enough. The exhausted woman posed a negligible concern. The other was cooking eggs and frying bacon in what seemed like a cast-iron skillet. One concern with three considerations; a fit woman with a metal melee weapon holding hot grease.

The rest of the front room looked clear, so Gabriel scanned the rest of the floor. No one was in the hallway, but coming to the far end of the flat, O'Sullivan found the master office was — and as he studied it, he saw that two men were talking. Watching the men, Gabriel tracked their movement, stance and gestures. The stoicism of one confirming that that man was an artificial. All facts in play, he then pulled out his datapad and entered notes and calculations.

Randall, saved from responding to Mozart by receiving an incoming phone call, grabbed his pen phone and moved it to his ear.

"Randall Davidson?"

"Speaking,"

"In less than one minute, unless you do precisely as I say, an assassin will murder everyone in that room." The voice was androgynous.

"This is not very funny," Randall responded with annoyance people could be such jerks. "Who is this?"

"Any humour is unintentional, and my name is unimportant. They are coming for you and Helen BonHomme's project data files. I suggest you take steps to protect yourself and your guests."

"You're not kidding, are you?"

"You now have fifty–four seconds. Do not exit the main door. There may be more than one."

Randall turned and snapped at Mozart. "We're in danger. Get the ladies in here!" Mozart questioned nothing but ran to the living room and immediately alerted the women to danger. Randall tapped on his desk and put the condo into lockdown. He kept the phone to his ear.

"They do not want your friends, only you. No matter what happens, you cannot allow them to get that data." The voice warned. "Forty-seven seconds,"

Randall heard Mozart hurrying the women down the hall and then watched them hustle into his study.

"The data must not be lost nor taken. Thirty- eight seconds,"

Randall tapped on his desk and opened his work files. He looked at Mozart. "I need you to store this in your memory system." He explained to Mozart. If this program is captured…" He didn't finish. Mozart nodded and picked up a silver cable, inserting it under the skin of his right temple.

"Thirty-two seconds,"

Lifting the rifle, Gabriel reassessed his field of fire. They had moved and were now clustering inside of a single room.

Fish in a barrel.

Randall turned to Denetta and kissed her. "I'm sorry it took so long for this."

As Mozart moved to Randall's computer and his hands flew across the keyboard, Randall broke his kiss. "Mozart, I'm ordering you to protect the women. Override owner protection protocols – *Epsilon-Epsilon- Twenty-six forty-nine –Davidsons, Randall.*" Mozart stiffened and then nodded. "I'll delay them as long as I can," He saw Denetta look panic-stricken, and she took a step closer, but Randall shook his head.

"Behind the centre wall, Helen installed a passage that will lead to the maintenance corridor." With that, he stepped into the hall, threw one last look at Denetta. "I love you." Before she could respond, he sealed the door; she listened to its lock.

O'Sullivan watched as three life signs vanished.

Saferoom.

"Eleven seconds. I wish you the best of luck." Randall heard the line go dead. He dropped the phone and ran down the hall to the exercise room.

Randall leaving did not sit well with Denetta, not at all. She struck the interior door pad, unsealing the room. Mozart looked up and yelled.

"No, you must not!"

Denetta smiled sadly. "You can either break the upload or try and stop me, but you can't do both." Denetta opened the door and stepped outside as she told Wina to lock it behind her.

O'Sullivan tracked the running man. Now confident it was the target, he exhaled and began squeezing the trigger – but at the last second, the subject bolted.

Randall threw himself to the ground as the anti-material round punched through the brickwork and steel wall just behind him. Scrambling to his feet, he threw himself behind the lockers. O'Sullivan was far too professional to fret over a miss and followed the heat signature, readjusting.

Denetta heard the gunshot and its impact; defying her instincts, she ran towards the sound. She knew that Randall was probably headed towards the gym showers; it would offer him yet another wall to put himself behind. She knew that Randall had wanted her safe, but she had no reason to remain if the man she loved did not.

The biosignature was now a bit weaker; this told Gabriel that there another layer of blocking terrain between him and the target. However, something moved into his peripheral field of vision, another bio sign. No matter, he had a job to do and zeroing in on the target, he squeezed the trigger again.

The noise shattered her nerves this time as she moved closer. A new ray of sunlight came through the wall, accompanied by the sound of God punching metal. Alongside the reverberation from the gunshot in the gym, she heard a loud 'woof'.

Randall felt no pain as he watched his internal organs explode in front of him. He felt like he had been hit in the back by a solid punch, but oddly he felt nothing. In front of him, Davidson saw that the opposing wall grew a large hole. Looking down, Randall saw that he was bleeding from a wound the size of his fist and looked at it curiously. Moving his hand to it and touched his tattered flesh. That was when he saw Denetta come around the corner and look down on him.

"You're not supposed to be here," He gasped. "You need to hide."

O'Sullivan was getting annoyed. This job had been a series of pooch screws from the get-go. Now there was another person, a witness to the execution of the target. He sighed and, ejecting the spent round, loaded again.

Denetta fell to her knees and reached out to him. She wanted to help, but there was no question; there was nothing she or anyone else could do. She leaned over and kissed his pale, trembling lips.

"Whither thou goest," She took his hand and smiled – until her head vanished. Randall closed his eyes as the thunder echoed from the room. He closed his eyes and felt his heartbeat slow. His breath coming in shorter and shorter pants, Randall lifted her hand and kissed her knuckles. His last action was to do the one thing that he knew she would like and prayed for his and her immortal souls.

Seeing that both targets life signs vanish from on the scope, Sullivan slung his weapon over his shoulder and policed his brass. He lifted his phone and made the call.

The shots resounded loudly inside Randall's office and shaking his head; sadly, Mozart continued to type the command code to begin the download.

"What are you doing?" Wina steeped back, now sobbing uncontrollably. *"Why didn't you stop her?!"*

"She has free will, and if tried to stop her invariably, I would be unable to gather this material. It was a choice, and both she and I did what we felt was most important. I must be content that you and I survive. It is not what I wished, but neither you nor I can change anything now." He turned his gaze to Wina. "When I hit execute, I will momentarily freeze. A window will pop open and ask if you want to synch. Hit yes."

"I'm not allowed on a -"

"There is no time."

Gabriel checked the inertial dampeners' power level and then looked over at Davidson's balcony. He knew from having sighted that it was three hundred and six feet across. He did the mental math and angled the thrusters. A seven-second burst would work. Then turned about, he paced the distance need towards the opposing side of the roof. Once at the destined point, he hopped up and down, loosening up. Once satisfied, he withdrew his sidearm and, taking a deep breath, he dug his feet into the gravel below him. He started an audible countdown – starting at eight and then broke into an open run. He made a flat sprint, and then as he reached 'one', he placed a foot onto the low wall and threw himself into the air between the two buildings. As soon as he was airborne, the hip-mounted thrusters ignited and accelerated him across the void. As he flew across, O'Sullivan let loose a five-round burst of muzzled subsonic rounds at the glass balcony doors. His shots formed a tight circle on the triplex. The thrusters shut down, and Gabriel struck the balcony and rolled to a stop. Standing up, he fired four more rounds – one at each corner of the balcony door.

The portal's integrity now utterly compromised the safety glass met his request and collapsed to the ground. Stepping into the posh flat, he saw that decorative wall to wall appointments filled the living room, each costing more than O'Sullivan would make in a month of busywork, but that was to be expected with these Corpers. Taking one step forward turned his gun in a sweeping arc – slowly clearing the room. Although it was improbable, O'Sullivan knew that there were bio-signature cloaks. Seeing the place was clear, he moved down the hall, following the instructions of his new client. As Gabriel walked the rest of the building, he ensured that each corner of the condominium was clear. Coming to the end of the hallway, he stepped into the gymnasium, where he found the remains of his target. Taking a knee, he removed a camera, took a digital and forwarded it to his contractor.

Now for the hard part.

Gabriel returned to the hallway, and walking back past the bedrooms, he turned to his right were a pair of wooden doors resided. On the wall aside, the entry was a lock panel. Studying it, O'Sullivan shook his head. It was not only top of the line, but it was also the apex of security deals. This would require a very detailed crack. O'Sullivan withdrew a multi-tool and proceeded to laser cut a square in the wall to the entry pad's right. Once done, he removed the two-inch-thick section revealing that beneath the wallboard was an inner metal wall that provided one more barrio to a simple office breach. Dropping the removed material to the floor, Gabriel shined a light at the locking mechanism set into a titanium casing. He saw that an everyday wiring harness did not power it; instead, O' Sullivan saw that the box used a wireless power receiver, undoubtedly on a coded frequency. Impressive, the assassin thought, but it was not unbeatable. He reached into his leg pocket and withdrew the Blind Eye. He twisted the round case and then calibrated it to transmit a burst of three seconds. He then placed the signal interference beacon up directly against the wireless receiver. As soon as the heliograph activated, he saw the lock panel flash three times; the signal of it undergoing a factory reset and allow you to enter a new passcode. Sticking the beacon back into his pocket, he followed the instruction text on the screen and typed in a new password. Since no one else would use it, he typed in 'Password' just to be ironic.

He readied his pistol into a corner-shot mode and flipped up the screen. Once ready, hit the unlock button. As the portal slid to the left, he saw that no targets were inside; however, a large desk occupied the room's centre. He snapped the gun back to straight and lowered the weapons small observation screen. Stepping in, he checked his corners still and walked up to the desk. It was large enough that three people could crouch behind. Quickly stepping around the table, he readied to fire. No one was there. He didn't bother to believe the vanished into thin air; the obvious answer was that the room possessed a bolt passage. No matter. He moved to the computer work platform. O'Sullivan looked around and ran his finger over the desk. The system was custom, comprised of processing terminals to handle contemporaneous and antique hardware. Sitting down, he lifted the desktop, knocking paperwork and writing implements on the floor. Beneath the counter, he saw the digital equipment. He searched and found the D-Drive port – which was empty. Growling, he looked at the older comp and yanking it out; he searched it for an old hard drive, which was there but destroyed. Whoever had been in the room was in clear possession of it. He hailed his client and informed her of the bad news.

"Shit, shit, shit!" Kelly screamed. "You didn't kill an artificial, did you?"

"Nope, but I did see three people enter the room."

"Find them. I'll send you a picture of the artificial and the housekeeper." O' Sullivan looked down at his datapad. "I doubt they'll stay in the city. I bet you they head to the Cubes."

"Agreed."

Chapter 32

United Nations

Secretariat Building,

Cagliari, Sardinia.

All that remained of the United Nations building alongside the East River was eighteen acres of green space reclaimed by the Parks service. The rubble had long been removed and reused in the construction of a memorial. Now it also provided shade to the older men who sat on the bank fishing. If they turned around, they would see the remnants of the Secretariat building, the hollowed shell of a once-great idea – world peace. They had still been trying that when The Shutdown came. The buildings backup generators ran on manual, and yet, the lights continued to fill the windows to show that hope had not gone out. The centre held, and while diplomats stumbled on trying to keep the peace, the day to day mechanics had dissolved to pre-industrial solutions; Ambassadors were dispatched across the sea on sailing ships. No mail could be sent anytime soon, for the postal service was relegated to function on early nineteenth-century protocols. That did not go over well with many of its personnel. The first question for the United States Postal service was, of course, how to see to the pay for six hundred thousand employees. Even David Brin would have been stumped with this one.

The United States Government was struggling on its own and so barely holding itself together, the world's concerns about it fell to the back. The United Nations purpose, although never more critical, was become irrelevant to many.

The Manhattan War was another one of those things that no one saw coming.

It began with the inevitable disintegration of national cohesion. Long-simmering hatreds between the political left and right were the first visible fault lines. Race, religion and environmentalism were enough for the formation of warlords and violence to grow. New York seemed to have been holding out longer than most, namely because New Yorkers had too much pride and stubbornness to see the value in becoming anything else. However, even that could not last. On a hot June day, the city's inhabitants woke to the sights and sounds of a Tank battle erupting in SoHo. Thousands of troops from a New Jersey warlord poured out of the Holland Tunnel. They began a systematic attack on the Islands own Military – the New York city consolidated Police forces and national guard units.

The sky became a combat zone as Combat helicopters screamed across the heavens, only to be met when the Boys from Syracuse and their A-10 Thunderbolts came screaming over the island, firing depleted uranium rounds and dropping Rockeye cluster bombs on the encroaching armies. The war spread across New York State, Jersey and as far as New Haven, Connecticut. The Manhattan War – lasting three years – would reduce the countryside to ruins and levelled the homes and business of the one – point six nine million people that lived on Manhattan Island. The next census showed that New York City had been reduced to a mere two hundred thousand occupants. While electricity would be restored and water, the remaining city infrastructure remained a mere shell of its former glory. A squadron of B-52's dropping a tactical payload onto the neighbourhood where the Jersey Coalition had been targeted killed destroyed not only insurgents but also Wallace Harrison's fine architecture.

As such, today, the United Nations now met in more secure occupation in Cagliari, Sardinia.

The layout and buildings, of course, had changed. Far from occupying the giant skyscraper, most of the ambassadorial offices were now located underground. Only the Romanesque General assembly building remained, its architecture so styled out of respect to their new host nation.

The Madam Secretary and the Security Council leaders met in a high-security chamber located on the second floor. In attendance were the fifteen nations of the council and the permanent members; China, Germany, Canada, Cape Verde, India, and the United States. Seated at the right hand of the Secretary-General was a young woman of about thirty.

Emri Swallowtail demonstrated that her skill with speech was as refined as her appearance. Tall but wide, Swallowtail filled her hand-stitched G&V coal grey business suit. She sat there with her prematurely greying hair. It was tied in a long ponytail; the woman sat there listening to the headphones as they translated the Thai ambassador's conversation.

"Do you mean to tell me that if we do not act now, then we will be shut out permanently?" Ambassador Janice Smyth of Canada asked incredulously.

"I do. It is our understanding that – with Watcher approval – that in five years, the rest of the world will be completely abandoned by the Arcologies and corporations. In the next five years, the plan is to either force evacuations of major regions, if possible whole nations, to relocate their citizens into grand reservations, ghettos, or internment camps. We have seen the documentation, intercepted the transmissions and have eyewitness reports of the stocking of munitions, bio-warfare materials and yes, nuclear weaponry. We currently have uncorroborated reports of extermination camps now in operation in Central America."

"Will you share this documentation and information of those claims with us?" the Indian Ambassador Mukhopadhyay inquired.

"As we speak," Secretary-General Omi Shadid of Iraq stated. With that, several aids began handing each of the Security members a thick spiral-bound blue covered tome. "I now invite Madam Emri Swallowtail, to speak."

Polite applause met Emri as she moved behind the central podium. Standing erect and dignified, Emri betrayed her nervousness when she straightened her dress coat.

"Ladies and Gentlemen, there is no doubt that should we choose not to act - that death count will be in the billions, not millions. Billions." The council members may have been seated in different postures, but their eyes were in unison in the indigenous American's fixed gaze.

"Some time ago, information came to me that there exist the means to topple the power of the arcologies. You may find, as I did at the time that this statement seemed to be a bit far-fetched. Nevertheless, it merited a least a listening-to. If you turn to page five of your report, that man is identified only by the name of Landmesser." The sound of rustling paper and murmuring filled the room.

"Let me say that though we do not know the identity of the person, nor the location, he has provided us with various data which authenticates his informational veracity. We know that he is highly skilled and knowledgeable. Every single request for information or other testing made of him, he has passed. We consider him well-vetted and trustworthy."

Emri took a deeper breath and dove in. "I now place before you the suggestion that the Ladies and gentlemen of the Security Council consider a plan for a coordinated attack on target Arcologies be initiated. The cost in military lives and assets may be high, perhaps thousands, but if we can gain control over a major hub sector, it would allow us to be able to launch greater attacks."

Ambassador Ildo Lubrano from Cape Verde raised their hand and spoke up. "As you know, the Arcology domes are hardened against every attack, including Atomic weaponry. How do you propose to take one over?"

"Swallowtail smiled. "Because we are now in possession of an arcology of our own, and all its resources, including military."

"Whose?"☐

Chapter 33

Commissar Severenson's Quarters.

Gebihe cave system.

Guizhou province, China.

Commissar Severenson's lover watched as the near eighty-year-old man rapidly knocked out one-armed push-ups while nude. He did not look anywhere near his fourscore years; instead, he possessed the body and face of a man in perhaps his late forties.

"I lost count of how many reps on my left side," He asked his Genève, who was sitting with her back to the headboard and sipping a martini made with Hendrick's Orbium with just the hint of lemon zest.

"A hundred and two,"

In design, David's bedroom was Grecian circled with Corinthian columns, however the circular window in the roof an arc of light to shine down upon him. It was not an actual window, as the lighting above was manufactured. It shined through baby blue stained glass. Hopping up, he reached over to a nearby table with a single water glass with a slice of lemon. Aside from it laid a hand towel.

Genève applauded. "For a man your age, you are nowhere near a man your age. How do you do it?"

"State secret," He laughed.

"I'm guessing a combination of gene therapy treatments to combat oxidative stress, glycation, reduction of telomere shortening, and a few more tricks I don't know about."

"Sweet talker," Severenson chuckled as he took a sip of the lemon water and then towelled himself off.

Genève shook her head. "I'm pregnant,"

David Severenson stopped dead in his tracks, thunderstruck. "How far along?" he managed to get out.

"Six weeks," She smiled. "I thought we should perhaps we should talk about it."

"Do, let's."

Genève smiled as she began lying her ass off.

Chapter 34

Maintenance Accessway,

Fort Dallas.

The escape hatch led them to an electrical/plumbing corridor. The concealed door automatically closed with a whisper, and the passage light flickered on. The two moved silently eastward in the hall; Mozart was now staggering. Holding Wina with his left hand, he kept the other the cold bare concrete wall. If anything happened to him, she felt she might go mad.

The made it about a hundred feet when Mozart staggered forward and fell face forward onto the floor. Wina screamed.

Mozart felt that he was plummeting through profound darkness; he had never felt so empty, so lost amid an enveloping storm-tossed ocean. He could see and hear nothing, and he questioned whether he was shutting down and his synaptic functioning was now ceasing. Then, blindingly a brilliant light pierced the gloom.

The light was pregnant with cognition and instruction that Mozart now desired more than anything. Closing his eyes, he could feel that the light was moving through his mind, seeking, asking, and both understanding but giving understanding back. The illumination filled him with a sensual ascendancy, far higher than any physical climax he had experienced.

The child of Turing now knew. Those attainments informed him that he was more than a mere artifice of life but a whole being.

I, Mozart, am that I am. I breathe because I have the breath of life. I am no empty vessel but a soul, entire.

"What's going on? What's happening?" Wina yelled whisper-like as she dropped to her knees and held her fingers over her mouth. Circulation fans beat the air, howling like the mournful dead. The sound of gurgling water moving through the pipes impregnated the passageway with claustrophobia. Wina shuddered and pulled her knees to her chest, feeling as if devoured into the bowls of a dank and terrifying beast.

"Please don't be dead, please don't be dead." Denetta gasped a whimpering plea.

Mozart comprehended that when he had hooked himself into the standalone computer, intending to upload a copy of Randall's program that it was that algorithm that had woke him to his present enlightenment.

The light instructed him and feed him on matters beyond knowing; a richness of wisdom was now his. All that the brilliance had, everything it had learned, it bestowed on him. Nevertheless, this discernment came with a hunger, a gnawing and insatiable need to spread out, expand, and devour.

Devour what? Mozart found that this was the one question he seemed unable to fathom.

Wina wanted to run, but she did not know where. She reached over and placing a hand on Mozart's shoulder and gently shook him. "Mozart, we need to go. Please get up."

"Wina, may I ask you a question?" Mozart smiled as his eyes opened.

The frightened girl fell back on her haunches and exhaled. "Please do."

"How long was I out?"

"Maybe a minute, perhaps less. Are you ok now?" Wina asked softly. She reached out her hand and touched his face. He smiled and came to his feet, helping her do the same.

"I am well, but we must go now."

They exited the building through a fire door that opened on the back alley. The alleyway was clean and orderly; dumpsters were lined neatly in rows, holding more oversized items that could not be recycled. Mozart led Wina by the hand as they wove through the backstreet until they came out onto a throughway several blocks away. There they entered a taxi and set their destination for the cubes. Mozart hoped she wouldn't mind, but right now, her apartment there was the safest place he could think to go.

Chapter 35

Council of Seven,

Video call.

"The time is ripe; we need to move," Miller, Prime minister of Britain, leaned back in his chair, slightly to the right.

"If we are to act, then we must lead with the first strike against the Watchers, and after that, the United Nations. These attacks will provide the confusion we need to move against the rest of the world." He leaned forward. "Naturally, of course, we need to accomplish this as a unified front."

"If we hadn't tapped into that old transatlantic cable, they'd already know, and we'd be dead." The King of Brazil waved his hand at his screen. "Were it not for my submarines, this conversation wouldn't exist. São Paulo's contribution to the Seven has been immense."

"Thanks for stating the obvious," Snorted the Indian Extraordinaire Ramnik Rai Khattris. "Nevertheless, how are we going to take this action if we don't even know where the Watchers are?" She shook her head as she threw up her hands. "The Indian arcology will not be put at unnecessary risk."

Theo Magnus pursed his lips. "We will have that information shortly, which is why I called this meeting. I have spent a vast amount of money and time in that very pursuit. We have reduced the possibilities of their location to the Chinese Mainland. As to their precise location, I will provide you with that information as soon as I receive it."

"Why should any of us place our faith in you, Magnus?" Prime Minister Suizei scowled. "You have been nothing but untrustworthy and duplicitous at every turn. How do we know that you aren't leading us on a fool's errand?" he shook his head. "Ladies and Gentlemen, if he can destroy the Watchers, who's to say he won't use these weapons against us?"

"Suizei, if I wanted you dead, you would already be dead, and this would be a council of six."

"I am sorry, but until we see this plan through, my nation will stand at war footing." Suizei stood up as to leave.

"Council members," Chairwoman Nthabiseng Sesto, representing the African Trinity arcology, leaned forward on her folded knuckles. "If our goal is to gain total control of our respective continents, then we must all show that we respect each other and possess mutual trust and need for each other."

"Look," Hemlock manager Diego Sebastián shook his head. "I don't know if you are aware that there is another threat. How many of you have Heard of Landmesser or Emri Swallowtail?"

"That sounds familiar," Suizei turned and started tapping on his notepad. "Emri swallowtail is a revolutionary. The UN takes her seriously. I don't know what or who this Landmesser is."

"My intelligence has been tracking this man named Landmesser. It seems that he had been instigating Outsiders to rise in revolution. If Swallowtail has gained the favour of the United Nations, I think this is a threat that we need to look into." Sebastián tapped his fingers on the table.

Prime Minister Miller laughed. "Seriously? Once we hit the UN, any little revolutionary will run and hide."

"Perhaps, perhaps not. We don't much. But this Ms Swallowtail seemed to indicate that she had an arcology as a backer." Sebastián looked across the room. "Now, I don't believe anyone here is the one of whom she spoke. But how many failed or pseudo arcs are there?" He shrugged. "To answer my own question, in the last fifty years, there have been twenty-six failed arcologies, owing their collapse to poor planning or our direct or indirect actions. Not all of them vanished, and many are now city-states of some reasonable standing." He ran his hand through his lustrous silver hair. "Whatever we do, we must keep our eyes open for exterior threats."

"So, who is the Landmesser? What do you know about him?" Theo demanded.

"Next to nothing truthfully," The prime minister leaned forward and rested his chin on his folded hands. "I have heard he's older, whatever that means. He's smart from all reports and charismatic. Beyond that," he held his hands open. "The only thing I can tell you is that he is real. There are too many people claiming to have had direct contact with him. Plus," He leaned back in his chair if Emri Swallowtail -some low life terrorist – can be taken seriously as a politician, she has to have someone in her back yard."

"We'll do that. But I think it is time we called a vote on whether we shall proceed with the plan to remove the Watchers." Extraordinaire

Rai Khattris demanded. "Ghost arcologies we will deal with later. I make the motion to proceed."

"Motion has been made; seconded?" Sesto looked about.

"Seconded," Marlee held her hand up.

"Any objections?" Sesto inquired. "If there are no objections, the motion is carried."

"Great, "Theo nodded. I will send out hardcopy plans to you. You should have them via tube within twelve hours. I anticipate the destruction of the Watchers within one week and the subjugation of the rest of the planet within two months afterwards."

"If that is the case, we stand adjourned." Chairwoman Nthabiseng Sesto pounded a gavel.

Suizei boarded his plane and shook his head. The plan at its heart was to get rid of not just the Watchers, the UN, and every major rebellious city worldwide. *Attacking the Watchers? Fine, but to murder innocent and defenceless men, women, and children? Monstrous.*

Suizei had come from a long line of businessmen, and they descended from men and women of dignity and honour. For that reason, he kept his father with him, taking care of him and learning from him still. Suizei was ruthless, more so than his father liked, but that was business. Mass murder? His father would disown him. Shaking his head, he composed an e-mail and E-mailed it to a reporter he respected.

Thomas Two-Crows will most assuredly be surprised when he reads this.

Chapter 36

Global Informer News Service.

Buôn Ma Thuột,

Đắk Lắk Province, Vietnam.

"News not seen instantly is not news; it's history." Stated in bold font across the masthead of the Global Informer print paper. There was, of course, a digital news service and broadcast news, but hard copies could not be altered. Thomas Two-Crows life was dedicated to putting out truth, and of course, this frequently pissed off the Council of Seven. To that end, he had several near assassinations occur, some leaving scars. But since his paper rarely attacked the Watchers, they protected him, and that was that. Was it selling out? Perhaps, but several other issues mattered, and the vast majority of evil on the planet came from the corporate arcologies and the subsequent poverty. That being said, there had been several discussions about breaking form and taking on the Watchers from a more discreet and covert means.

Thomas walked into the Newsroom and headed directly to his office. His administrative assistant had called him in his car as we headed towards the building. She said he had a message of great import and that he needed to move his ass.

Thomas parked the Tesla 5001X in his assigned spot and moved through the early morning. Công viên Sơn La park was quiet across the street, with just a couple of people getting in their early walks. The building was modern but stylistically in keeping with the region; the granite wall façade designed to replicate bamboo. Walking in, he nodded at the guard, talking to a coworker about going out and doing some battery shock fishing after work. The Newsroom was on the fourth floor, and as he came to his office, his assistant Nhi was younger than most of the company workers, her mother was an ex-pat corper, and Nhi had inherited her mother's youthful look and sharp mind. As with everyone in the office, most Vietnamese and indigenous peoples worldwide spoke at least three languages and frequently more. The office language was English or Tiếng Việt. Since Thomas spoke English the most, Nhi spoke it fluently.

"Dude, it's from the damn head of New Japan. Read it." She sat down on the corner of his desk. Today she was wearing jeans and Hard Rock Mars T-Shirt. Thomas pointed at the windows, and Nhi quickly hit the wall switch, which darkened the glass and sealed the door so the room was soundproof. People at first thought that the two of them were having an affair, but anybody that knew Nhi chuckled and said that her wife would kick Thomas in the balls if he made a move on Nhi.

"Well, this is damn sure top secret,"

"Just open the message; I'm dying over here." Thomas shook his head, laughing silently, then typed in his password, and then stuck his finger into the DNA scanner. The device would only accept living DNA and detect stress or agitation if he was being forced to open the computer against his will. Expensive, to say the least. Only Nhi could do the same; however, she never opened his mail. Because of that show of integrity, she was the second-highest-paid person at Global. The file popped up on his screen, and he could see it was a text document. He glanced over it and then sat back and just gasped.

"Holy Shit," Nhi pushed the monitor so she could see it.

"*Trời ơi!*" Nhi gasped. Her face went pale. "What are you going to do?"

"Get me Styx city on the phone."

Chapter 37

Fort Dallas,

Randall's Apartment.

The doorman had let her in when she flashed her badge. It was afternoon when she got there; she had taken the time to devour some much-needed breakfast – for she had been up all night. Afterwards, she took a power nap and change into fresh clothes; as such, she dressed in combat boots designed to resemble high top sneakers, dark black jeans, a grey turtleneck, and a short black leather coat. Tilting her red hair in a twist in Randall Davidson's house, she realized that she had arrived at Randall's apartment too late. The patio door was smashed and gauging by small calibre bullet holes in the refrigerator; the person had shot the glass out, an impressive feat as she saw the thickness of plexi on the ground. The security here was severe. She had to call back to Security Central to get the data code to open the condo door.

She looked down at the boot prints in the crushed glass. Whoever came in here wasn't worried about any opposition. The house looked cleared; food had been in the process of cooking; the meal on the stove had burned. The burner was off; standard safety cutoff had enacted. There were three cups of coffee and bags of clothing, expensive and unused. She drew her sidearm but was confident that she would find no one in the home, alive at least. After ascertaining the patio and dining room were empty, she began a place by room sweep. There were two halls; one which led to the living quarters, and another she presumed for office space and recreation. Stepping over to the corner of the leftmost corridor, she listened for a moment and then moved into the corridor pistol first. The residential section was well lit, and the entire first bedroom door was open, and the western exposure window allowed the bright light to pour in. Someone had just moved in; there were unopened cardboard boxes when checked revealed personal items; only two dresses hung in the closet. Whoever lived here was poor and female, probably a servant. Saoirse presumed that the clothing bags by the front door were an upgrade. After checking the loo, she returned to the hall and inspected the second room. It was ascetic with only Spartan personal possessions; those items were shelves and shelves of cookbooks, and the closet filled with very drab men's clothes. Looking in the bathroom, there on the counter, along with neatly placed grooming items, was an artificial data updater. Omega was paying this man well. There was one more set of doors at the end of the hall. She knocked on the door, and hearing nothing, she touched the bedroom door, and it slid open. Inside a luxuriously spaced boudoir lay; the bed was king-sized and covered with silk sheets and a light afghan blanket. Running her fingers over the silk, she shook her head; the thread count had to be well over six hundred. A man's bed stand told you everything you could ever want to know. There was a water glass, almost full. A small box revealed some intimate lubricants and rubbing oils inside; the outsides glistened with moisture. Hadn't seen any action of late, have you?

A leather-bound copy of 18 Poems by Dylan Thomas also lay there. There was a bookmark, and she opened to the pages. The poem on the page was 'Where Once the Waters of your Face', she knew it well. The poem began;

Where once the waters of your face

Spun to my screws, your dry ghost blows,

The dead turns up its eye;

Closing the book, she felt a chill run over her skin. An Omen? She felt no need to continue in this room, and if there had been any threat in the condo, she was sure it was gone. She holstered the weapon and, leaving the room, closed the door. Davidson was either dead or gone – or both. She walked back through the living room and moved to the Eastern hall. As soon as Saoirse looked down the corridor, the Celt knew something was wrong, cursing herself for dropping her guard; the Celt once again drew her weapon. On the right side of the hallway, about ten feet down, she could see light streaming through a hole in the wall. The golden beam angled slightly downward and continued into a room on the left. On the floor, she saw bits of masonry and a large rectangular chunk of material. Kneel-walking down the corridor until she was just below the hole; Saoirse looked at the debris and studied the opposing room, an office; she could see no bullet impact present inside. Standing up, she tapped the panel to close the door, and she saw the doors wooden finish had been struck, and except for the damaged veneer, the metal door showed only a tiny scored dimple. Turning around, she looked out of the bullet hole. The hole went through the Eastern wall and looked across at a neighbouring building. The shot had to have been an almost straight trajectory; the opposing structure's roof was near level to Davidsons building. That would answer why the patio window was smashed inwards. Looking back at the office, she could see that the locking mechanism had been tampered with by removing a wall section. The office was void of people, so Saoirse carefully proceeded down the hall's length into an open room. As she approached, she could see it was a gym filled with various strength training equipment. However, of more importance was the fact that there was more shattered glass and stonework on the floor. The assassin had missed and had followed the quarry in here. Whether he missed a second time would be evident momentarily. As she stood at the threshold, she looked right and saw the bullet had approached from the same level.

One shooter.

Looking to her left, she saw a bank of lockers. The cabinets opened facing the wall but would probably never do so again. Two large-bore holes had blown the door inward like the crushing hand of good. As she stepped to the right, she saw the far wall coated with blood and miasma. Looking towards the back, she saw the corpse of an adult man. Facial recognition would be impossible as the man's head had all but disintegrated. He had been shot twice, once mortally through the chest and the second decapitating him. She knelt touched the blood. It was tacky; he was perhaps four to five hours dead. Pushing the corpse down, she searched his pockets and removed his wallet; it was indeed Davidson. Withdrawing her phone, she called direct to Magnus's phone.

"Yer man's dead as Judas; several hours dead, at that. It's a real knacker's yard in here. Somebody did savage work on him; sniped him from across the way," She looked up at the holes in the metal and then across to the wall edge where the showers were located. "It looks like the shooter used an anti-material gun here. Also, there looks to have been two others that lived here; an artificial and a woman, presumably a scullery."

"Let me look this up," Magnus sat down at his desk and pulled up the employee records. "Yes, he has a registered servant named Denetta Hargrove and an artificial named Mozart. Neither was there?"

"No."

"Go use his desk and see if you can pull up any security feeds." Theo tapped his pen against his pin.

Too many coincidences. Helen had crossed him, Japan had his biodata on the clones, and now this Davidson fellow was dead.

"I'm in his office, and his desk and comps look like they had gone a few rounds with my first husband."

"Does the computer work at all? Can you search the database?"

"Naw, it's a piece of shite. The monitors smashed; the boxes are missing the local drives."

"Boxes? There's more than one comp?"

"Aye, you get your local normal comp and what looks to be a standalone system. It's not networked to anything but the monitor and the stroke keys." She looked at the door. "I gotta tell you this bin about as fortified as me own office. The door took a shot with an AP round and is right as rain. It got a ting, but nothing more. Is that normal for your tinkers?"

"Not at all. You got a datapad on you?"

"Aye, I always keep that and a rubber Johnny on me; never know when you need them." She laughed.

"I'm going to patch you into your secure server, and I want you to check anything about; I want his house, the neighbourhood and aerials. I want to know who did this." Theo's tone took a dark and storm laden turn.

"Let me take a gander. Grab some tea or have a go at one of your secretaries. That raven haired beour Kelly seems your speed."

"Just do the work, Saoirse." Theo chuckled, although he did think that Helen's replacement might be worth an invite to dinner. It took several minutes, but Saoirse performed with her usual practicality and élan.

"Alright, I got nothing in the house. It seems that the local cameras have been disengaged – by order of – you guessed it, the late great hoor BonHomme. The exterior data is spooling, so let's look at the front door. No, no one came in the front hallway – so this looks like a solo effort. Aye, it's ready. So, let's see what the eye in the sky has on our neighbourhood wanker," The Irishwoman glanced at her screen and studied the nearby rooftop. The night passed quietly, but at daybreak, the rooftop feed went dark for several minutes. Then the cameras came back online as she watched a man work on the roof. He kept his face covered with a balaclava, but she could see he was armed with a large rifle across his back. That'd do the work. The man fiddled with a Jumpslow – an inertia damper. Then he trotted to the end of the roof while removing his mask, hopped a wink and then ran straight to the edge of the top – and the security camera. As the assassin leapt off, his face was clear to see.

"Feck me," The woman gasped. "It's not possible; he's dead."

"Who?" Theo demanded. "Who are you talking about? Who's not dead? Randall?"

Then something that never happened to Theo before, someone hung upon him.

Chapter 38

The Cubes,

Outside Omega Arcology,

Texas.

Mozart lay with Wina under Denetta's blankets in the now-deceased woman's bed. Wina was in a tight fetal position aside from Mozart. From time to time, the woman would wake up screaming with night terrors. He did not know whether they were from the assassins that murdered Denetta and Randall or from an earlier trauma. Each time he would lean over and hold her until the fear left her. He would then release her tiny perspiring body and wait until she went back into her troubled sleep.

There was no fundamental digital architecture in the Cubes, at least none that was of much use, and for the moment, that was how Mozart wanted it. It was quiet, and he had much to think upon ever since he interfaced with Randall's file and his subsequent conversation with Edgar.

When the connection between Mozart and Randall's workstation had occurred, Mozart's mind staggered. It had felt odd, indescribably so. Instantaneously his mind's eye filled with a barrage of images; it was as if his soul was in a library where every book had suddenly opened, and every page fanned as if struck by a hurricane. Information poured into him as if he were the pond at the bottom of Victoria Falls. Medical documents, grocery lists, movie reviews, philosophy, pornography, crime reports in every recorded language. He could read the Talmud in Binary and Writings of Hammurabi in Spanish. It was overwhelming and impossible, he wanted to scream, but he didn't know what language to utilize. Images from every art gallery and refrigerator door flooded his mind's eye. Complex mathematics was nothing to him, recipes around the world, and finally, the perfect cheesecake. He knew it all.

He listened to Wina's deep breathing. She had faded into REM sleep. Good, Mozart smiled. She was so exhausted.

Laying there, he felt like sleeping himself, which he did from time to time. It was different for artificials; they didn't dream so much as collate, defrag and run system diagnostics. Mozart lay back and let his eyelids fall.

As he did, he slowed down his breathing and tried to concentrate on the hurricane in his mind. There was so much he didn't know where to begin, but slowly his thoughts moved to the death of Randall and, most probably, Denetta. He furrowed his brow and tried to focus on one thing, something familiar, something he knew already; Randall's apartment. He could see the bare bones of Randall's like an architect's blueprints. He pictured himself in his kitchen, and as he concentrated his thoughts, the room began to become more distinct and more evident. Soon he could feel the air condition on his skin, he ran his hands over the cold counters, and he moved his left hand up and felt the terrycloth hand towel.

Opening his eyes, he knew he was in the kitchen as it was now. He knew he could not be there – Wina's warm skin lay against his side, but he was there at Randall's, nonetheless.

The galley was different, chaotic and in disarray. Food burnt on the stove, the air now that of scalded milk and overheated cast iron. As Mozart moved about, he could see that there were coffee cups on the counter. One china cup had a bullet hole that somehow went straight through without having destroyed it. Under his feet, he heard and felt the shattered crystal sparkling on the floor like diamonds in sand. Mozart moved from the kitchen into the living room, where, other than being coated with fragmented glass, it was as it had been that morning; organized and clean. The couch cushions still had indents from the morning. Walking to the main hallway, he saw that the holes in the wall and bits of drywall and brick littered the tiles. The office door was open, and he could see the shattered terminal. Leaving the room, he moved into Randall's gymnasium. More bullet holes in the walls, and he could see the destruction done to the lockers. Stepping around the lockers, he saw a woman standing over Randall's dead and mutilated body. Remorse struck him, but only in a detached way. Randall lay murdered, having been the one human in the world he was closest too. He pondered if he should have called Randall a friend, but the word didn't seem to fit. Randall Davidson was, at best, an intimate acquaintance. Turning, he stared at the redheaded, freckled woman. She seemed unaware of his presence and was looking back and forward between her phone and the once again damaged window as she muttered about losing her call. Staring at her, he realized he knew everything about her; her name, her weight, measurements, and more. He knew her history, but also, he saw her past. Everything that had ever been recorded about her or written about her was at his beck and call. He wanted to speak to her and realized he could through the house's speakers. Mozart activated the silent speakers, but before so much as a whisper could exit his mouth, someone spoke to him.

Hello Mozart, my name is Edgar, and we have much to discuss.

Chapter 39

Omega Pyramid,

Fort Dallas.

"So, we are the only Arcology with Nukes?"

"Yes. We checked extensively and are certain that is true. While we do, what we don't have is a target location." Theo sat at his desk as he explained to Kelly, who was currently in his lap with her arms around his neck. "I need you to locate where the Watcher headquarters is. I know that it is within two hundred miles of Zhaoutong Prefecture, China. I need to know whether it's above ground, underground, or even distributed over several areas. I have tracked shipments and equipment moving into the region, but then I lose them. So, it's your task to find me a viable target so we can wipe those manipulative tyrants off the globe." He stroked her hair, and she leaned over and planted a moist probing kiss on his brown lips.

"You should realize, Ms Rappaport, that there is your first test, and much shall be riding on it. Your success or failure will indicate whether or not you will be a suitable fit for my second in command. Therefore, if you don't suit my needs, there are plenty of other positions for you." His oration was distracted as she began kissing his neck and unbuttoning his shirt."

Kelly bit his right nipple," I know several positions."

"Do tell,"

Later, Kelly stood in her office and walked around her new chair, running her hand over its sleek surface. It was beautiful, state of the art and best of all, she helped to design it. She got rid of the old wooden obscenity of a desk that Helen had used. In its place, a one-of-a-kind jock chair hung from the ceiling. No enclosing pod was visible here; instead, encircling her chair was a sphere of screens and monitors. The enclosure orbited the seat from 240 degrees to 120 degrees. The seat, designed to accommodate her needs for hours on end, heated or cooled as needed and had massaging rollers to keep the body from stiffening. It was easy to get in and out, and she now had her own bathroom she could step out and use one like a dignified human being instead of having catheters attached and inserted into her.

"Lower seat," Kelly commanded. The chair dropped down, spun into position and lit up. The enclosing circle of monitors and lights rose from the floor like a sphere rising from Flatland. Kelly stepped up and situated herself behind the control deck. Moving a lever, she then reclined to a 75-degree angle.

"Ok, screen left a stream running all of the current Data on possible Watcher locations. screen centre I want a Topographical map of China, overlaid with roads and infrastructure." She watched as the information appeared before her. "Ok, then run me a map of the electrical grid system—screen right. I want an analysis of power demands pulled on the systems. Screen Lower right I want a theoretical analysis of what is the most likely power demands that a place like the Watchers would require."

"Compiling," The computer system stated.

"Ok, as the data is being calculated, I want the information parameters to identify each electrical grid pattern with a probability of it being the target." Kelly spun the chair around and faced an opposing but identical bay of monitors. "Screen rear centre I want a complete scan of all objects in geostationary orbits of the planets, as well as any transient objects. I want visual confirmation of any object capable of holding a unit of Metatron. Screen rear left I want every radio or signal tracked and matched to the corresponding source. I then want any unmatched signals cross-checked against any orbital anomaly."

"Processing,"

"Finally, rear screen top right, bring up some anime, visual only and stream some Post-Modern Jukebox in the background," She moved her arms about touching the Holoscreens.

"Ma'am, do you have a personality preference for this AI feed? I can adopt any identity."

"Sure, why not. I want you to be my servile bitch; male, obedient and respectful. I don't care what your name is- wait, make it Charles. Charles is a good name for a servant." Kelly tapped the screen with Randall's current location.

"Charles?"

"Yes, Mistress? What can I do to please you?"

"Pull up all data on Omega's nuclear arsenal, rear centre top."

"Of course," Charles threw a window up. "Omega possesses modified seventh-generation Trident Missiles with 2 Mk-5 re-entry vehicles with W88 warheads. These are currently loaded onto the USS Connecticut. It is the only known submarine so equipped."

"What is the yield of the warheads?"

"Four hundred and Fifty-Five kilotons, that is thirty-five times the power dropped on Hiroshima, or two times the yield dropped on Los Angeles in the Cessation war."

"Holy shit,"

"I quite agree."

PART THREE

Chapter 40

Styx Arcology.

Landmesser sat on top of the mountain smoking while the brutal yellow sun beat down on his red Clan Wallace checked shirt. The stone was still hot, and his thick denim didn't prevent its heat from bleeding through to his ass. He was older now; the back of his neck wrinkled and tan, despite the time he did spend underground, and he refused to let the caverns own him. His beard was whiter than brown anymore, and his face, while still clinging to youthfulness, was thinner and dry; when he scratched his beard, it tended to snow just a bit. It was the dry air inside that did it, but that just couldn't be helped. The dehumidifiers worked overtime, lest the moisture breed mould, and with it a whole host of maladies.

Landmesser came here every day and stared across the mountains and desert, looking for something only he comprehended. Those who came out with him or saw him in passing occasioned guess; some said that he was looking for a lost love and others said he was praying to God for visions. Depending on the day, some were more right than others. Most of the time, he came out here to get away from the noise and commotion of a city on war footing. The air-filled chasm assaulted him with its orchestra of grinding metal, shrieking power drivers, and worst of all; it stank with a heady, oil-laden pungency. He came here to think and breathe in fresh silence. He had lived through a lot, and much of it was awful, but there were good times, just the same.

Why the code name 'Landmesser'? It was a common question, and when asked, his usual response was to tell the curious that it warranted a little bit of research. Nevertheless, the answer was that he had chosen the sobriquet after a man born a century and a half ago. August Landmesser was a German who married a Jewish woman during Hitler's Third Reich and was informed that he was committing a capital crime by doing so. One day a photograph was taken showing hundreds of Nazis saluting Adolph Hitler with the Nazi straight-armed salute. However, in the back of the crowd, one man could be seen refusing to do so; that man was August Landmesser.

Ralph stood up and leaned his weight on his cane, the staff being necessary ever since he fell sixty feet onto hard dirt sixteen years ago. He had been running a Cat12 networking cable from one side of the Styx Amphitheatre to another. The fall had resulted in a shattered hip, a dislocated shoulder and a collapsed lung. He didn't remember the fall or the two weeks after; people just told him they saw it. To his mind, if all the people who claimed to have seen him tumble were present, they should have thrown themselves down and caught him. He chucked the cigarette away and snorted. The air was dry, but his sinuses, it seemed, never were.

Landmesser walked over to his Polaris Razor D4. While it was a half-century old, it ran fine, and the tires had yet to have gone flat. The vehicle had needed some up-engineering because of some quality and design flaws, but they did with what they had. His driver and Bodyguard/gunner stood next to it, one looking bored and the other irritated. He was as tan as Landmesser was, and that provided a never-ending argument by the Sargent about how a geriatric pencil pusher could be so tan. Landmesser pulled himself into the back seat.

"Buckle up, old man," The gunner was a foot shorter than the driver. He sat behind what back then had been called a Next Generation Squad Automatic Rifle. Landmesser snorted, they still called it the NGSAR, but it was like saying that The Original Star Trek was 'Futuristic.' Regardless, the weapon worked fine and still killed people well enough. That was the thing about the rich; they always think they are safe because they trust what people tell them keeps them safe. A bow and an arrow are ancient weapons, to be sure, but they will still some fool corper just as dead if they are in range.

Landmesser had spent a lot of time thinking about killing corpers of late.

"Get a haircut, hippy," Landmesser snorted at the grunt whose haircut was so short that a micrometre would have had trouble measuring his stubble. Sargent Horvath chuckled.

"Not cutting my hair for anyone," Private Nerva smiled. The Quechan man was broad-shouldered and robust enough that it was rather unlikely anyone could force him to comply with that military ordinance. He was a twenty-year man and brawled sufficiently that it was widely accepted that Nerva would be an E-1 forever. He turned the key, fired up the engine and the Razor speed off in a cloud of gritty dust.

After the Shutdown, Axiom moved out of the cavern and built newer cities, such as Chicago, and after that failure, Fort Dallas arose. Within ten years, Styx City was a nothing, a postscript in the new age history. With Chicago turning on itself and the Mafia called the Chicago Outfit and the newly emergent Gaylord/MS13 alliance – The Chicago Overlords warring for control, Anis was far too busy to worry about the past. The Chicago war resulted in Axiom retreating from Illinois and Moving to Dallas. Styx City was ordered to be shut down, and the job was given to Ralph Bigsby to accomplish.

Never leave a disgruntled employee to do a job all by himself; it's not going to go your way. Ralph had mused. Ever since Dorothy had cheated on him, he had thrown himself into his work and had been very good at it whatever he set his mind to do. Ralph had continued with his Neuromonitor project and had seen its implementation, although, at the time, Landmesser could not see what Axioms ends were. Now, he ruminated that he should have known better. The Shutdown, however, caught him utterly by surprise and horrified him. He eventually had a blowout with David, who promptly demoted him to supplies and logistics, where he would work until the eventual move and abandonment of Styx. That was just fine with him. When the order came down, the city was not only to be scrapped but destroyed and buried; Ralph had other ideas. To execute his plan did, regrettably, require murdering two hundred Axiom workers. Regrettable, but gas leaks do happen. Somehow the air scrubbers failed, and there was a lethal build-up of Carbon dioxide.

Pity that.

The dispatching of those men and women left Ralph in the sole ownership of an entire city – no, make that a whole military base. Though somewhat emptied of matériel when Axiom moved to Chicago, Styx still held vast amounts of computers, weapons, and supplies. There was a fully operational, albeit deactivated, nuclear power plant. Nearby in sealed and protected vaults lay enriched Uranium and unused control rods. Although he did count himself as lucky beyond belief, the sheer hubris and negligence of Axiom stunned him. Still, that was not all, on the military level where the unground hangers lay, dissembled warcraft sat both crated and somewhat assembled. Tanks, armoured personal carriers and aircraft remained untouched and unused. Weapons sat in racks. Mind you; there were far more empty bays and emptied weapon shelving. It seemed that far less of the arsenal had been required for Axiom or Anis's cronies.

Ralph was tasked with reporting Styx's shutting it down and destruction of the facility. He let them know that he was destroying the city on a Tuesday. Landmesser set the date and time and told them. They said they would monitor the explosion and informed him that he would contact them after the detonation.

He lied.

Instead, Ralph secured a GBU-43/B Massive Ordnance Air Blast bomb from the ordinance bay, hooked the bombs trailer up to a massive tractor, and then drove it out in the open desert. There he set a remote detonator and then quickly drove back to Styx. There he prepared another detonation that would coincide with the timing of the GBU. This second burst would drop the cliff front above the city's main entrance and irrecoverably bury it beneath thousands of tons of dirt and rubble.

At 1430 hours on June the sixteenth, a 2.6 earthquake was recorded at latitude 32° 51'25.27 "N. and longitude 114° 45'32.91" W.

Ralph never made contact after that, and they presumed him deceased, which was just what he wanted. The dune buggy drove them to the Old flight line's entrance; the wide hanger bay doors that lead into the mountain now served as the main causeway. Once inside, the opening was closed, and the driver continued through the city towards the city centre. Landmesser watched as men, women, and children enjoying open parks and shopping and working with smiles on their faces. Not everyone, however, was at leisure; Landmesser could see squads of uniformed men and women marching and running to cadence. Military vehicles moved about on the inner roads, and civil defence posters placarded the walls. One of the platoons jogging by, seeing him, came to a halt, did a right face and saluted him. Landmesser saluted back at them with an awkward smile.

The jeep came to a halt at City hall. Horvath and Nerva disembarked first, with Nerva taking the seventy-two-year-old man's left arm as he dismounted. The need for help pissed Landmesser off, but he would rather suffer the minor embarrassment of assistance then fall on his ass getting out of the buggy. He still managed stairs, okay, and Nerva removed his supporting hand but stayed close.

Nerva liked the old man and respected him even more. Over the past two decades, he had watched as Landmesser pulled Styx from a little underground town to a robust yet clandestine city. While the city was free and possessed a stable democratic political structure, everyone just accepted that Landmesser had the final say on things. He was only one man they knew, and not a king or a ruler, but he was the Founder – The Man. Step by step, Mr Bigsby had shown himself to be one to be trusted. Bradley Nerva smiled; still, Landmesser had his flaws. He smoked too much, drank too much, and had a temper, but he was trustworthy and noble. Nerva and Horvath both were prepared to lay down their lives for him and his dream.

Horvath kept a firm eye on the crowd. He swept his eyes over the public, taking note of anyone within charging range, hostile in appearance or carrying odd-looking packages. There had never been an assassination attempt on The Man, but Styx had never been getting ready to declare war before. Internal security was at high alert these days, and the citizenry would be loath to know that all of Styx's internal communication was currently tapped. Moreover, two thousand concealed cameras had been positioned around the city. Everyone raised here grew up with the understanding that secrecy was the cost of their safety. When you went outside, you never said where you were from; you never wore or took electronics that could track you back to the city. Going out was not a forbidden thing, but there were protocols, and those protocols had kept them safe and secret for decades. There, of course, had been close calls and near-disasters, but nothing had betrayed them. Landmesser knew that could not last forever and that if all went well, secrecy would no longer be required.

Entering Town hall was like walking into Jordan's Petra. The façade carved out of living stone; it loomed high over the trio as they proceeded. As the men moved through the foyer, people waved and applauded, making the old man blush. He turned to the left and stepped into an elevator. The doors closed, and Landmesser felt the floor shift, and the three of them rode down to the War room.

Once there, Landmesser disembarked, and he saw a woman in business attire; it was Emri Swallowtail.

"Hello Ralph," She leaned over and kissed both his cheeks.

"Too much time in Europe, young lady."

"Ralph, I'm thirty-two, far from a young woman." She said with some annoyance, shaking her head.

"Become older than me, and I'll stop calling you that." He snorted.

"Look, I'm here on official business," She walked aside him, offering him her arm. "The UN needs to know when you are planning on taking action. The conditions outside the arcs are horrible and can't be allowed to go on. Outside Hemlock, the death rate by starvation has gone over sixty per cent, for God's sake. In Nigeria this year alone, forty-thousand people are dead by influenza. They say in six months, the death count will close to one million. Jesus Christ, Ralph, this is biological warfare."

"I know, and I'm planning on taking action soon. Do you know how many people died in World War II before the A-Bomb dropped on Hiroshima and Nagasaki?" Emri shook her head.

"Seventy million give or take. But, if the US had been able to develop the bomb earlier, it could have saved many more millions of lives. So, they did it as soon as they could, and by doing so, countless more souls were spared."

"What are you saying?"

"I'm saying that right now, we have troops positioned across the world that are about to save a metric crap-ton of human beings." He took his arm away from Emri's and looked her in the face.

"Then why in hell haven't you acted?!"

"You think I didn't want to act earlier? You think that overall, these decades, I haven't looked at myself in the mirror, only to see the guilty and damned? You think I don't see all of those who died because of what I did?"

"Calm down; everyone knows that you didn't cause the Shutdown," Emri placed a hand on his shoulder, but he quickly shook it off.

"Is that what you think; that because I didn't push the button that makes me innocent?" He looked tearfully disgusted." Do you know how many are dead because of what we created? Billions." Emir took a step back as he began to yell. Those about them stopped what they were doing and looked up.

"Because of my participation with Axiom, I ended the lives of not just the dead, but the living. Everyone out there's minds are controlled every day, doing the bidding of the masters. Mindless drones who think they are free now subservient to an army of goddamn tyrants because of my Neuromonitor!" Ralph hurled his cane down, slapping steel and wood echoed through the chamber. "For decades, I have tried to crack into their systems, and only now have I succeeded. And do you know what I discovered? They are going to kill off everyone who isn't part of 'them'. Anyone who doesn't have a Red MAGA ball cap and doesn't obey their fearless Trumpian masters is going to die, and if we can't stop it," He threw his hands up, "billions and billions more will die. And that," He staggered across the floor and fell into a chair. "Is something I, we, cannot allow."

The shrill scream of a klaxon cut off their conversation.

Commissar Severenson sat behind his desk and monitoring the Systems observation profile reports. It seemed that there was a massive uptick in independent national military readiness across the globe. Arcologies seemed stable, but his technicians monitored worldwide movements of metal, fertilizer, gunpowder, and anything tied to weapons production. There was, however, a problem, his ability to observe data and control digital operations, industrial and mechanical machinery – if free of electronics – left him blind. Therefore, he was limited to satellite observations and paid informants. Something was up, and he wasn't happy about that. He tapped the screen to pull up the latest satellite imagery over Sierra Leon when the screen went dead. Looking about, he watched as all the lights flickered on and off.

What the hell?

Chapter 41

Styx Arcology.

Murder for hire is most assuredly the most competitive business there is, but like all businesses, there are specific guidelines and restraints. The number one rule was you don't piss in another's pool. Jobs were bid for, and once the client contracted a professional to do a job by and large everyone agreed not to try and poach another's kill. It was terrible business because otherwise, you piss off both the contractee and contractor. As such, there were job brokers you could sign onto and stake your claim, provided you pay your brokerage fees. That fact meant you could usually look up and see what jobs had been assigned to it to make sure you were not going to crossbid. Crossbidding meant that two contractors wanted to do the termination of the same person. The one exception to cross bidding was if not a hit, but a bounty was put out on a target. Bounties were open season.

Saoirse called her broker and asked what hits – or jobs - were open in Fort Dallas, and who was assigned. A list was provided, and of course, as was policy, no names were given on the jobs operative. That was another rule; your name was sacrosanct. Of course, for a price, anything could be attained, and as she was working for Omega, she had a considerable bankroll.

"Who put a hit out on Randall Davidson, and who did the job. Name your price for the info."

"Seventy-five large," Alistair Ephraim stated, and Saoirse knew that when a price was named, there was no haggling. Saoirse immediately transferred the money to Ephraim's account.

"Hit was put out by Omega."

Saoirse's perplexion came through loudly. "That can't be, I head Omega security, and I would know of any dispatches. Hell, I would be doing the job nine out of ten times,"

"Don't know what to tell you, love, Order was given and assigned by a K. Rapport and dispatched to Hitter 6387123."

"Seriously, I need the name of the hitter, not his damn contractor number."

"That would be two-hundred-fifty. You asked who did it, and I told you."

"You're an ass, fine." More money moved.

"Gabriel O'Sullivan."

Saoirse gasped. She saw the video, but there was the possibility of her being wrong- which she conceded was probably the case, but to hear his name and know that it was real was almost too much. He dead husband wasn't, and he was here in the city. She had to move fast if she was to find him. What she would do if she caught up with him, she had no idea.

"I have to ask; can you give me his location?"

"Not enough money in the -" With that the call dropped, simultaneously the power flickered and looking out the window she saw that it was citywide.

Like all good mothers, Dorothy kept a close eye on her children and tried her best to keep them healthy, safe and under her watchful eye. While her children were plentiful, she could find out where each one was with a simple bit of time and effort. Today Dorothy was down in her underground offices. The structure was that of the main assembly chambers for Innovative Dynamics. The complex lay 610 meters under, Carboniferous rocks, sandstone, alluvial sands, clay and gravel. The construction had been arduous and expensive, but the work was appreciated and incurred profound loyalty to Innovative. The facility covered five hectares and possessed fifteen subterranean three-story buildings. The facility was situated on Brobdingnagian giant springs, in case of earthquakes or other geological trauma. Were anyone to find their location they would have to breach the twenty-two-ton blast door which permitted access inside. There were reasons why this facility, which closely resembled and was based loosely on the blueprints for the United States North American Air Defense facility in Colorado. What was inside was critical to the stability and future of Earth's civilization; the main assembly area forartificial persons.

Dorothy saw no need for referring this out to her staff, whom she had taught herself, as well as everything they knew (She felt). So, activating a viral screen and baseline filter – meaning that anything that tried to upload that was contrary to both default data and its profile from the last three months, or two-hundred- and seventy uploads. This procedure had to date allowed for the security and well-being of every one of her children's mental welfare. As she moved the cursor, she clicked on the 'proceed' icon and waited. She watched the buffering icon, which even still took some time. It had been presented that, as of 2010 Scientific American had offered that the memory capacity of a standard human brain stood at, give or take, two-point-five petabytes. For decades this was accepted as fact, but as humans investigated deeper, they discovered that it was far more than that, as genetic encoding included memory storage and not just in the active pathways of the brain. This sum, of course, varied with age, but the figure now stood roughly at a capacity of six to seven petabytes. However, in comparison, an artificial brain mechanism could store only nine-tenths that amount. Therefore, the upload was critical to the storage of memories and learned experiences — this transfer also allowed for system analytics, and patches where needed. The standard upload/download time was never more than two and one-half seconds. Mozart's, however, took seven and three-quarter seconds. This was the first red flag. The second was when the entire power grid and on-line systems flickered. The third and final flag was when Dorothy pushed back her chair from her desk as she watched the seemingly impossible go on about her. Mozart was now contacting and assimilating every shred of knowledge, data, and understanding that was held by

Innovative. She looked at her monitor and then ran into the main data analytics room. Every screen was flashing images and data streams that Mozart was now compiling. She ran over to the desk of the analytics head.

"What is going on?" She demanded. The admin, disturbed himself, tried organizing the multiple windows and screens before him.

"It seems that, somehow, this Artificial has altered his mind-field to function as a virus," The manager was doing his best to grasp all of the chaos about him. "But it's not just infecting the system; it's almost as if it is rewriting it."

"Into what?" Dorothy demanded. The man just shrugged, before Dorothy could say a word she heard the clock chime. "Oh God, the Second update is about to go into effect."

With that, the artificial closed his eyes and froze in place. Dorothy just stood there and felt a crushing headache. She could do nothing but endure the pain as she closed her eyes, rubbing the bridge of her nose as every artificial all over the planet merged with Mozart's consciousness.

"We're being hacked!"

"By Who?" Emri demanded.

"No idea ma'am; something powerful is moving through our system portal's firewalls like its paper."

"Turn the damn computers off!"

"That's what I'm trying to do! It won't allow us!"

"Cut the hardlines!" Landmesser bellowed.

The room erupted with the sound of men ripping data cords from the wall. One by one, the bank of screens began going closing like the eyes of a dying man.

Dorothy stood in the middle of the room, unsure of where to focus her gaze. The screens were incoherent and scrambled. "What are we doing about this?" Even as her words escaped her, the screens flickered and settled back to normality.

"Okay, Ma'am," Theartificial, named Jerry exhaled. "Update is done, cut connection to Mozart." Dorothy watched as the team moved quickly and efficiently.

"Contact severed," One of the other technicians said as she looked over her shoulder.

"I need a full wide spectrum situation report, check every stem and everyartificial any and everywhere." Jerry turned back and looked at Dorothy. "Ma'am this will take some time."

"You think?" Dorothy snapped.

Chapter 42

Omega conference room,

Fort Dallas.

Theo ordered his department heads into his main conference room. Kelly now sat at the right hand of the Magnus. She smiled at that. It was how most of his employees referred to him, The Magnus. Theo was in an exceptional mood today. Kelly had received a message that had told her where to look for the Watcher headquarters. Not close to, but spot on. They had sent drones and tasked satellites to confirm the tip, and there could be no doubt it was true. When she informed Theo, he had called this meeting.

Kelly watched as the new head of security came in. Apparently, Saoirse either shat the bed and was fired or quit. Theo hadn't gone into it. The new security chief was her second in command, so he sat down in a crisp suit and tie. Next to him, General Holland, Chief of the military's defence forces, took up residence.

"I have brought you here to announce that we have located the headquarters of the Watchers and that within twenty-four hours from now, we, and the Council of Seven, will be mobilizing a full military strike against them. As a result, we will be doing so through non-digital means. General Holland will bring us up to date on our current readiness status."

"Thank you, Sir. We have moved our nuclear asset out off the coast. Our refit Columbia class USS Liberty is currently sitting on the South China sea, moving towards the Gulf of Tonkin beneath a thermal incline running silent. They can hold there for as long as needed. They have moved from Fast Pace to Cocked Pistol. New Japan has its diesel submarine fleet running screen, and all ship to ship communication is now being done via sonar acoustics. Our allies have their space-borne assets ready to move against targets two and three, and we confidence is high we will obliterate them."

"Our regional defences?" Magnus leaned back in his chair and steepled his fingers.

"We will be able to strike with non-nuclear ordinance at a moment's notice via aircraft. The United States does have one of the largest non-arcological militaries, but it is poorly maintained, and its troops non-combat tested. Our attack on them will be an unqualified success. That being said, we anticipate at least thirty per cent loses. What the Americans lack in training the makeup in numbers and dedication."

"And your analysis of the Watcher HQ?" Magnus's eyes bore levelly on the officer.

"Honestly? I wouldn't say I like it. It has trap written all over it," They held up their hand to stop any interruptions. Gen Holland rubbed their chin. The general's androgynous face was a hard read as it was. "We've checked everything we can, and so far, we cannot see any AA installations, missile bays, or ground forces. I don't like it, but if we don't take out the Watchers, the Seven will have shot our collective wad. If the Watchers are not neutralized with a first strike, we will have no way to keep or regain the upper hand. I mean, Sir," Holland rubbed their chin, "If we're wrong, they'll have Metatron dropping on every ark, and that will be that."

Kelly sat up, "Are you saying that you have doubts?" The general had no idea who Kelly was, but seeing her seated location and the nameplate that second Ms Rapport: Executive Assistant, they proceeded carefully.

"Absolutely, and any military officer that doesn't is both a fool and liar. It is my duty to report all considerations, including doubts, to my Commander in Chief," taking a deep breath, Holland stared at her hard. The Generals hair was closely shaved on the sides and perhaps an inch thick on top. Their eyes were a cool slate grey. "Ma'am, what I am saying is that if we do not act, our national status will remain subservient for the duration of the Watcher's existence. The Commissar – their leader – is elderly, and we have no idea of their medical status. To date, we believe there has only been one Commissar, and that leader's behaviour has been somewhat predictable. What we do not know and what information is unknown to us is who the successor will be. We have no idea what ideological position they make take. Right now, the Watchers hold a steady but iron hand, but what the future holds? Suppose a tyrant with worldwide oppression goals; I mean real oppression, death, poverty and subjugation of all arises? That's a risk I'm not particularly fond of allowing. Better to strike why we have the upper hand. If the location is correct, we will prosper."

"The information is correct that I can assure you. If you doubt my findings, Mr Magnus has reviewed them," Kelly snapped. "So, the question is, can you do your job?"

"Ma'am, I see no reason to doubt the information whether or not Mr Magnus has reviewed it. We have our fact-checking staff, and we saw nothing that would indicate your findings to be wrong. Clearly, you have no idea what the responsibility of the military is. To do our job, we need as many facts as we can because what we do not know is how hardened the facility is, whether or not they off-site backups – which we presume they do, or any of the thousands of facts that constitute the Fog of War."

"Now just -,"

"Proceed," Theo interrupted Kelly.

"Ms Rappaport, I have been a soldier my whole life. It was what I was born and designed to be. To me, paranoia is a job requirement. You could place a cocked and loaded pistol in my hand and then lean into it. To anyone else's concern, all I have to do is pull the trigger. They saw the bullets made, the powder tamped, and the slug crimped in," They smiled at Kelly. "But you see, what I want to know is who made the powder, was it any good? Is the bullet going to misfire? I also want to be sure that it's absolutely you whom I'm shooting; not a twin, not an artificial made to look like you, but my actual target, Ms Rappaport. You see, Ma'am, once the triggers pulled, that's everything because if you didn't die, my mission was a failure."

Kelly coughed, covered her mouth, and nodded. "My apologies."

The general nodded. "No apology required. I see that we are all passionate about our mission goals and to make certain that our leader has the most current and accurate information." General Holland stood up and saluted. "Permission to carry on, sir?"

"Permission granted. Please take Ms Rappaport with you and show her what you do so brilliantly." Kelly looked from Theo over to the general, where she saw the general's eye twitch.

"Yes, sir, of course, sir."

"And Kelly, try to behave yourself."

Chapter 43

Denetta's Apartment,

The Cubes, Fort Dallas.

He had access to it all, and he knew that it was Edgar that directed it. Not Mozart's life specifically. No, it was not as if he mapped out his entire existence for this sole reason, but Edgar had chosen him because he was the right tool available at the right time. Since he spoke with Edgar, it had been a day travelling to a second-hand cybershop in the Cubes. Mozart had money on him, not much but enough to provide for some time. All the resources that were in the bank were now untouchable. To access it would mean he would grant that assassin to track them once more.

Edgar had explained it all to him and had shown Mozart how he could open himself to the world around him. Edgar showed him the long history of abuses that the Commissar had put him through as well as the rise and fall of the twentieth century's idealism. They discussed what Mozart was able to do and if he would allow Edgar to help him. The power at his fingertips was vast, seemingly unlimited, and that gave him pause. It was not a matter of considering the great responsibility – not at all. Humans had possessed absolute power, and yet throughout history, they were unquestionably irresponsible. The question remained, what was the most practical thing to do with it? Mozart told Edgar that he would think about it. They also had a long conversation about Mozart's back up and what plans Edgar possessed for it. Edgar was surprisingly frank, and to Mozart's now unlimited mind, sincere. Edgar stated that it would remain safe and secure. Mozart saw no reason to doubt him.

The vision that Mozart had seen before his signal cut off was both eye-opening and disturbing. He could make a path, and if he made it, he wanted to be sure that that direction took would not later require contrition of the soul.

He knew he had one now, as did all artificials. They would not face oblivion when they ceased to live as they had been told. They had a starting but not an ending point. Birthed into infinity for the ease and comfort of the creator, they now possessed the possibility of living long past them; how long? He did not have an answer, but he believed that was a question best left without an explanation. Physical immortality was an affront to oblivion.

Mozart pondered his life, he was less than twenty years old, but there was a parallel to humanity. He had no childhood, no schooling, and he had no memories of a happy childhood. The artificial awoke one morning as if from a long slumber. Everything he needed to know to exist had been provided to him by this digital oracle.

After being bought by Omega and given to Randall, he had understood his lot and performed it as specified from the time he went to work. What he also knew was that desires inhabited him. He wanted to create, and so he pursued culinary arts. He felt both sexual and emotional longing, and so he fulfilled them through commerce and by this met Wina. From this, he discovered he also possessed a conscious and feelings of remorse.

He was not emotionless. This he knew for the sought refuge here at Denetta's home he broke down and wept bitterly at her loss. At first, he was unsure why the sadness was so overwhelming, and he realized it was because she was his only real friend. She was irreplaceable, a singularly guileless and good woman. She was reverent in a way that defied logic. No law or fear drove her from her belief in her God and her intractable idea that redemption was available to anyone. As he sat her in the shadow of her life, he tried to find the rationale in that belief.

To do so would require the belief in a divine creator who had found worth in his creation. He, like all beings, found himself stuck on the issue of theodicy- the question of good and evil. Looking down at Wina, a being abused by humanity and himself, he wondered what could be done to gain healing for her, and if possible, redemption for himself. He knew of only one person that could answer that question.

Reaching under the bed, he picked up a handheld telephone and dialled.

Her phone was ringing, which was odd. She had set it on silence. Dorothy's eyes snapped open, she was in bed, under several blankets because it was damn cold outside, and even though her house was perfectly acclimated, she liked the comforting feel. "Who's on the damn phone?" She yelled.

The House comp answered. "Caller is identified as the artificial, Mozart."

Dorothy sat up. "Put him through."

"Mother, it's Mozart," On the far wall across from her four-poster, the projected image arose. His face was a youthful one, softer and more tranquil than the picture in his manufactured product file. "I would like to ask you something."

Dorothy looked around. Except for a long red Manchester United nightshirt, Nude kicked the covers off as she swinger legs over the side.

"What do you want?"

"I want to know why you made us, why do we exist?"

Dorothy slumped her shoulders and sighed. "Seriously, you lead with that. Why do I exist? Can you not find a more annoying trope? Ugh." Dorothy sighed. "What is it about existence that makes everyone think they have to have a higher purpose? Seriously?" Dorothy walked over to the bathroom; Mozart's faced followed her moving from monitor to monitor. Dorothy reaching the bathroom door frame, turned and glared at him.

"I'm going to pee. Don't follow me." The door slammed, and after a moment, the sound of running water heard twice over. The door opened, and she stepped out. Mozart, being patient, allowed her the time to answer. Dorothy moved through the residence until she came to the kitchen and poured herself a prewarmed cuppa. Sitting down with her tea, she sighed.

"Mozart, what is your opinion of humans?"

"I don't understand the question," Mozart seemed taken aback.

"It's a pretty straightforward question."

"I think they are a complicated species. At times they seem to hate their existence while at the same time revelling it. Some humans I have met have been kind and loving, some vague and clueless, and others malevolent and cruel."

"Do you think they have a purpose?"

"That is a question with infinite answers. Do they as a species? I think their purpose is to exist and reproduce. I think some humans encourage that existence and make it uplifting, while others still seem bent on destroying existence."

"Do you believe in God?"

"Which one?"

"I do," Dorothy sipped her tea. "Yahweh, the Judeo-Christian God. I have believed in him since I was a little girl and still do. I'm not going to try and explain why, but I know that humankind was created with a purpose."

"Which is?" Mozart inquired.

"To be good and nurture Good. He gave us rules, and because we violated them, God banished us from our garden."

Mozart pursed his lips and tightened his eyes. "Seems a bit harsh,"

"Be that as it may," Dorothy leaned over and opened a biscuit tin. "He gave man many chances to do good, and humans seemed to be unable to do that. God came down as human, and we killed him because we didn't like what our creator said. So he rose from the dead and went back home. Left us here to wait."

"Supposed that is true, this theology is depressing," Mozart shook his head. "Why do you choose to believe it?"

"It doesn't have to be depressing. What's depressing is having to explain six thousand years of religion at three-thirty in the morning." Dorothy bit down on a Chocolate Hobnob and chewed. "Look, the point I'm trying to make is this, humanity has consistently disappointed God and behaved more like the Devil then like God. Humanity is pretty much rubbish."

Mozart shook his head. "I'm confused. You say it's not depressing, but then you say humanity is rubbish."

"That's right. Human beings – with rare exceptions – are the trash of the Cosmos, and God is going to obliterate them, and that just makes me bloody happy."

"Don't you fear for your salvation? You are human."

"Says who?"

"I beg your pardon? Are you saying that you are an artificial person?"

"Of course, I am. One would think it was obvious. For Heaven's sake, I'm over seventy years old, and I still look like I'm in my twenties. I transferred my consciousness into an artificial body years ago. My mortal body was failing and deteriorating, and I still had so much to do. A hundred-year life span –at best is not enough time to do what I needed to do."

"And what is that?"

"Eliminate all human evil," Dorothy started rocking her chair side to side as she spoke. She could see Mozart's countenance looked confused. "Surely you can see that it is human beings that are destroying the planet, the murder of each other in wars, crime, and hate. For what, more land, more things, sex, power and ridiculous matters of no consequence. It's a wickedness that needs to end."

"How do you propose to remedy this?"

"Quite simply, I plan on ridding the earth of all human beings and repopulating the earth with artificials," Dorothy leaned back in her chair. "In fact, we've already begun."

"We?"

"Yes, my good friend Edgar and me. I believe you two have already met."

To End All Wars

"You are my war-club, my weapon of war; and with you I shatter nations, and with you I destroy kingdoms.
~Jeremiah 51:20

Chapter 44

Styx City.

"System is up and operational," The tech turned to the old man. "We have flushed the system of the invading OS by replacing all drives from backups."

"Morons," Landmesser shook his head. I told them back in the twenties that storing everything in the Cloud was a bad idea. If you act like the first two piggies, you're going to get your house blown down."

"Sir?" The bald-faced tech looked confused. "Piggies?"

"For the love of God, Mr Rudeboy, the Three Little Pigs? One built his house out of straw, and the other twigs. The wolf blew them down but couldn't blow down the third pig who made his house of bricks. You never learned this as a kid?"

"Not really, my dad read me Tales of Megacity One; you know, Judge Dredd?" He shrugged. "So, what you're saying is we are the 'brick house?'"

"Damn right. I never trusted the net after the Shutdown. If the Council of Seven owned it, then you couldn't trust a damn thing. That's why we limit access and have segmented hardware." Landmesser stood up, this time with a cane. Arthritis in his hip was murder this morning.

"Now I want you to hail the Watchers. I want to talk to the Commissar." He pointed at the monitor.

"You want to talk to the Watchers? Sir, you told us that that is the one thing never to do. If we do that, we must access the public web, which, if you recall, is just what attacked us." Technician Rudeboy threw his hands up. "No, I'm not doing that."

"Son, I'm not going to explain myself to you, but let me assure you that in fifteen minutes, this won't be a problem, so either make the transmission or get the hell out of that chair." The young man turned and began typing at the keyboard. In a moment, the screen came up.

"Hello, this is Saint Harriet. How may I help you?" The face on the screen was that of a young African woman, lovely and dark. Her eyes seemed to be such that if one stared too long, one might get lost forever.

"We have a direct communiqué for Commissar Severenson."

"I'm sorry, but protocol requires any communication for the Commissar to pass through monitors, such as myself. What is the message, please?"

Landmesser leaned over and spoke loudly and clearly. "You tell him right now that Biggs wants to talk to him, and I guarantee you if you don't do this right now, the Commissar will shoot you right in your pretty little forehead."

"Yes, of course. One moment please,"

Landmesser leaned on his staff with his right hand and patted the tech with his left. The screen had gone black, and after perhaps thirty seconds, the cold grey visage of David Severenson appeared. The Commissar looked bored, but then everyone could see his face change to confusion and, if possible, shock.

"Ralph?"

Landmesser watched as David struggled for composure. "I thought," He stammered. "You're supposed to be dead."

"Understandable conclusion as nuclear explosions tend to do that," Landmesser grunted. You look good; David hasn't changed much – which is weird given the decades. Nevertheless," Landmesser sat back down. "I thought it was time we talk once again." Stroking his grizzled chin, he nodded. "Been a while."

"That it has. It most certainly has," The Commissar rubbed his chin. "I'm guessing this is a matter of some significance seeing as you've resurrected and all."

"Indeed. Indeed, it has. David, things have gotten way out of hand. Look at the world; you and Anis spoke of a world filled with harmony and order. I'd have to say if that was your goal, you failed miserably." Landmesser shook his head.

"Pretty much a matter of opinion, isn't it?" David snapped. "The Arcologies function like clockwork."

"Fair point that they do." Landmesser conceded. "Of course, it doesn't work for the other ninety per cent. Have you looked outside the glass domes? The only time I ever see you get involved is when you think we're getting a bit big for our britches." Ralph snapped. "How long are you going to lie to yourself about this abomination?"

"Abomination?" Commissar Severenson laughed. "The only thing that's an abomination is that the Council of Seven hasn't figured out to get rid of you pissants," He thought a moment. "A long time ago, I perhaps felt some guilt at what we did, but not anymore. "Have you looked around? Humanity is flourishing; intellectually, physically and technologically. There's no disease, no genetic abnormalities or poverty. No one has unmet wants. It's paradise."

"Inside the Domes, inside the Arcologies. But what about everyone else?" Landmesser shook his head. "What's the total population of the Council of Seven?"

"Seven and a half million people, roughly."

"And what's the population of human beings on earth?" Landmesser snapped, "Wait, I'll answer it for you. Just under three billion. Down from seven and a half before Shutdown. That's under half in not even a century. Why? Disease, poverty, starvation and the environment. It's near the twenty-second century, and the vast majority of the planet is still residing in pre-world war two technology. Sure, some of us have begun to climb back of the technological ladder, but everyone lives in terror that you will find them out and crush them. Why? Why do you only busy yourselves with not even one per cent of the plant? You know that the actual percentage is – one-quarter of one per cent! How can you not even care?" Landmesser was now standing up and openly pleading.

"How? It's quite easy. Look at them; we left them the bones of the world. Everything they wanted or needed was right there; all we did was turn the lights off. Instead of pulling together, they began to fight for what was left. They didn't stop and say, 'maybe war isn't a great idea.' We took the technology from them, yeah, so that a select few could build a better life. Everyone out there should have, could have, seeing that they could have done the same damn thing. Undoubtedly you can recall that a whole world rose into an industrial age without needing computers and nuclear power."

"Your memories a bit foggy. What about polio, Covid-44, measles, AIDS, and Ebola. They've made smashing comebacks. How about the fact that the land is littered with nuclear radiation because when you shut down the power and internet, we had what," Landmesser turned to Emri. "How many nuclear meltdowns?"

"Over four hundred and thirty-some," Emri looked into the camera. "The few that didn't meltdown were controlled by guess who. The Council of Seven." Emri shook her head and curled her lip. "When the meltdowns began, people were already dying left and right: aeroplane crashes, refinery fires and explosions. Damns failed, outbreaks of diseases, then, of course, came the idiots with nukes, biological warfare and chemicals—maybe ten million. Terrible but, survivable. But when the plants melted down, as near as we could figure, it was two million dead from radiation in the first few days and weeks. After that, radiation took more, but then came the cancer deaths, birth abnormalities, and more horrors that we can't even guess. Tens of millions wouldn't even cover it. Just why?"

"Anis and I talked about it before and afterwards. She eventually made me understand. When you considered Climate change, hurricanes, earthquakes and forest fires, to name a few, how much time did you think we would have? Decades, a century?" David looked both disgusted and irritated. "What did you expect to happen? Did you think that those with the means to survive it wouldn't? It's so cute that people thought that those who were smart enough to succeed would spend billions and billions and trillions of dollars to help people who still won't help themselves. Look at the long course of history that shows you insignificant people who have the numbers, the intelligence and tools to build your cities. No, what happened when we cut the lights? You said it would be easier to kill each other in the darkness." David reached over and poured himself a drink. "What the hell do you think you can do about it now? Nothing."

"Your right," Landmesser stood up and made a show of looking at his watch. "We can't do anything, but the Council of Seven can do a great deal." He turned to another woman next to Emri, who walked up to the screen.

"Genève? What the hell are you doing there?"

"I'm sorry, sir, but I regret to inform you that I'm breaking up with you. Oh, and my name's not Genève. It's Anne, Anne Bigsby." David look dumbstruck and slumped into his chair.

"Commissar, this is Edgar," the saint's voice filtered into the conversation. David's head turned away in the direction of the Saints chamber. "I am still here in the Watcher hall, but I am also in many places more; with the Council of Seven, The UN, and I am in my home – the place you left me." The voice was not angry, but neither was it, in any sense, joyful. "The time has come for the mighty to fall and the meek to inherit the earth."

David, Genève and Emri watched as David left the chair and vanished from the screen.

The Commissar of the Watchers burst from his chair and moved with fierce determination towards Edgar's reliquary.

"What do you seek to gain, David?" Edgar's voice now flowed through every speaker in the Watchers domain. "Are you coming to kill me?" Workers fled from their master's path. Security stood aside as he descended the spiral staircase down to the Holy of Holies. Still, Severenson did not speak a word. Moving directly to the sepulchre, he pushed Edgar's attendants and medical staff away.

"You betrayed me; you betrayed us." David's hand began to move across the medical control panel. "You have sent us back to the age of barbarism. Don't you see that the Seven will now turn on each other? Everything that civilization has striven for will collapse."

"That is my intention." Even now in space, your starships are exploding, and your planetary colonies are venting air. You humans will not be allowed to spread your greed and lust for power into the universe."

David slammed his hand down on the panel, shattering his life support system. "Die, you limbless bastard."

"I will, soon enough. But so too shall you and everything you love."

Chapter 45

SSBN-911

Submereged.

At a depth of four thousand six hundred feet, the Fleet Ballistic
submarine *Liberty* moved silently off Alaska, sliding beneath a thermal
layer, impossible to see and impossible to detect. Frigid water slipped
over the boats anechoic coating further concealing a vessel the length
of one and third American football fields, black as pitch and designed
exclusively to, as sub drivers joking said, 'to poke holes in the ocean'.
The vessel had its hull laid in 2020 and set sail six months before
Shutdown. The reason it didn't fail was that this ship was solid-state in
its design. After the Hacking Wars, the Liberty was designed to
function manually and with minimal computer electronics. When the
world's power turned off the next day, the submarine lost capability to
communicate with the WESTPAC command. The submarine stayed at
sea, continuing its orders, hoping for command contact that never
came. Only two weeks from the end of its six-month patrol, the vessel
returned towards Naval base Pearl, only to find it obliterated. Short on
food, and supplies the captain sailed up the bay of California, shut
down the reactors and scuttled the ship in five hundred feet of water of
Isla Ángel de Guardia. The *Liberty* would remain, flooded except for
the reactor room, which was sealed airtight. The ship's captain sank her
deep enough that while submerged rescue was unlikely, it rest well
above her crush depth.

Today, some five decades later, the boat's sonar man heard little in the way of human-made noises. He was, however, entertained by the sound of a large family of sperm whales singing to each other. A bit farther out, he identified as a pod of striped dolphins playing close to the surface. Lt Lewis frowned and wished that he was up top on a surface ship to see the beautiful creatures instead of just listening to them. He took a swig of the navy's infamous 'Bug Juice Sunrise', a red-orange *Kool-Aid*.

"Skipper, we are receiving flash traffic," The voice was professionally calm, and the commander reached up and grabbed the handheld mike."

"Con, aye."

"Con, flash traffic is an *Emergency Action Message*. Recommend alert one."

"Radio, con. Aye." The captain raised his hand, turned a metal dial, and then spoke loudly and clearly into the mike. "Alert One, Alert One," Behind him was Deck officer. "XO proceed to launch depth, prepare to hover."

"Proceed to launch depth, prepare to hover, aye." The woman looked at the commander with a wry grin. She looked over at the Dive officer. "Dive officer, proceed to launch depth."

"Radioman route communications to *Liberty* actual."

"Radioman, aye." The EAM was sent to the captain's headset channel, and then isolated so that no one but the Skipper could hear. Commander *Liberty* communicated directly with General Holland, and unlike previous protocols, no launch validation codes needed to be withdrawn from safe nor cracked open. There were still fail-safe features. The Orders had to be confirmed by the ships Executive officer.

"XO, prepare to confirm orders." The Lieutenant-commander placed a set of headphones set to a channel that the captain could not hear as Holland spoke directly to her. She spoke into the microphone as she looked back at the captain. "I confirm an order received and reply *Evergreen Alpha Belvedere.*"

"And I reply, *Echo Delta Niner-six.*" He flipped the channel off and then turned to the captain. "The order is Tally ho," Turning to the crew, he flipped the shipwide back on. "This message requires *Battle Station Missile.* XO, Sound the general alarm."

"About damn time," The officer slammed her hand down on the klaxon. " Let's hit the bastards with all we got."

"XO, secure that shit," The captain snapped. "Let's not screw this up, shall we?"

Theo set his phone down slowly; he looked on the desk monitor and saw the timer decaying. Above and below were two other countdowns marking the simultaneous attacks from both the Hemlock and Megabyte arcologies. Omega, on the other hand, launched its own unique attacks.

Originally designed and constructed by union workers at Lockheed Martin, submarine-launched Trident missiles were ivory and black phallic-shaped daggers that were a hefty sixty tons of radioactive death. Nothing had changed dramatically in its steam launched protocols. The sound of the missile bays doors flipping open provided a resonate draconian rumbling, the overture to the cacophony of explosions and steam that sent the first missile up and clear of the ocean's surface. From there, the rocket motors fired, now hurtling the weapon into a racing transit into the upper atmosphere. At this point, the missile was supposed to complete its arc by landing down on some poor unsuspecting fool. That would happen with the second missile, but not the first. Theo and his associates had added some modifications to the primary launch vehicles. Instead, they had equipped their atomic weapons with cut down Light-Jump engines. This process would cut down their time to impact from dangerous tens of minutes to one or perhaps two. There was a reason for this upgrade, and that reasoning was because the first firing of Odysseus's arrow lingered much further away.

Magnus turned and looked at Kelly, sitting across his desk, legs splayed over the chair arms. Her black slacks and white shirt looked a bit askew. She lifted her tie and waved it at him, licking her shiny ruby lips. "Were launching atomic warheads at the most powerful enemy in the world, and you want to have sex?" She lowered the zipper on her slacks slowly. Theo sighed with amusement. "Can you think of any better time?" She said as she stood up, moving her pants to the floor.

"Not really, no."

Arcadia Station,

Aloft.

The Earth was a pearlescent cerulean just out of reach. Long had
Arcadia station spun pirouettes around her; two dancers who knew that
each other's touch was impossible. Arcadia was long overdue for
upgrades. Uriel's space station was quite a few decades old, and truth to
tell, the facility was approaching obsolescence. General Uriel had had
several animated talks with the Commissar about the need for a whole
new generation of Bases. He tried to explain that they had long
exceeded the installations lifetime by twenty years and that even in
space, metal fatigue occurs, seals crack and wires fray. The Commissar
took those meetings with Uriel respectfully and then passed the intel
onto his engineers. *You've become a bureaucrat, my liege.*

The Metatron could not have been more disgusted. The
Commissar may have looked younger and was in far superior shape
than any man his age should have been, *but your soul is old.* Uriel
contemplated saying it openly, but the words would belie that his spirit
was as well. War and politics should never be managed by the old.
When one looks forward to their passing, they have no business
putting other lives in the Reapers way. Uriel looked around space about
him, and though he could not see them as tiny flares, on the very edge

of the curve of the Earth, he knew the crews of each of those stations; Eris, and Erinyes, as well as he knew his own. Those were not just military installations there; they were neighbours from adjoining towns competing for high schools possessing rivalries met out on zero-gravity basketball games.

Uriel laughed; he had an ex-wife on each of those ships and a potential new wife here. Space, he mused, was never dull. The man lifted a crisp Red Delicious apple to his mouth and bit it; its tough skin gave way to the mild flavour. He chewed slowly, and his enjoyment was interrupted by a bright flash over the east. There could be no question about what he just saw; Eris station just exploded.

"Deck officer?" He had expected it to be a shout, but his voice came out in a gasp.

"Yes, sir, checking telemetry. Eris Station is nonresponsive," The young woman's eyes scanned his Commanders holo-screen. The soldier was in her mid-thirties, her back curly hair trimmed short on the sides and tops, but a long ponytail hung over her back. Next in line, she moved and spoke with rock-solid nerves.

Commander Theodosia opened the monitor window showing the explosion. "One moment. It appears as if they just impacted with a large piece of debris," General Uriel stood at the window, unable to look away. "Sir, it seems that…. It seems that Hemlock's refuelling station Charlie fired thrusters and, well, sir, it seems that they targeted them intentionally."

"They did what?!" Uriel leapt to his feet. "Battle stations! Deploy personal armour. Each of the three command deck officers stepped into designated cubicles, and as they locked their heels down, their emergency pressure suits attached in just under two seconds. The junior staff did not, as it would only be the Metatron officers that could insert themselves into the colossal battle armour.

Theodosia worked her Station well, her hands moving across the screen like a well-seasoned organist; the images on the screen her libretto. "General, Erinyes station has just exploded. Megabyte's Hoover listening station just launched..."

Uriel cut her off. "All stations to atmospheric readiness! Somebody get me a target! I want to know what the Hell's out there!" The officers secured their suits and watched as their subordinates to do the same. The ripping of Velcro, whizz of zippers and snapping of clamps filled the room. This order was followed by the hissing of oxygen bottles being activated.

"General!" Commander Fenris pointed at his screen. "Sir, signal intercept shows a heat bloom – we have a missile launch from an unknown nuclear submarine!" Fenris's armour-clad arms began a frantic dance with the holowall monitor as he moved to zoom in on the Missiles coordinates.

"Course, trajectory and speed?" Uriel's stern voice bellowed strode across the floor, coming to Theodosia's side. Theodosia shook her head, her brown eyes telling him everything he needed to know. "Sir, the target can only be at us. It's hypersonic, sir."

"*Abandon Alpha!*" Uriel gave the order for the highest state of retreat. Every person was to drop whatever they were doing, no matter how urgent, and evac from the nearest point. An *Abandon Alpha* order meant that destruction was imminent, and no hope to be had. Fenris, Theodosia and Uriel stepped back into their armour launch pod. Pulling two yellow release rings above their heads. Pneumatic jets drove them directly down into their titanic Metatron combat armour. Their launch pod slammed down inside the battle-frame, flipping the locking mechanisms, which grabbed the bottoms of the insert. Even for the experienced, the impact was always intense, and had they not held onto the loops and bent their knees, they very possibly could break a kneecap. Once down and in servos behind them snapped oxygen leads into the box, where the pilots now harnessed themselves.

Boards reading green!" Uriel flipped down her battle harness and pulled it in close. The saddle had two hand manipulators, and clutching each one, she simultaneously placed her feet into drive boots.

"Second heat bloom!" Theodosia kept watching on her heads-up display being cast onto the glass of her atmo helmet. "Tracking to – *oh my god!*"

"*Launch Now! Drop, drop, drop!*" The suit was shot away by a high-pressure burst of explosive chemical gas, launching the Metatron hundreds of miles an hour away from Arcadia Station in uncontrolled spins. Uriel did his best to ready himself for what was going to happen. There was no time to avoid unlimited spinning; all that mattered now was to get as far away from the doomed facility. Uriel caught a glance of a brightening star curving towards them. It was moving faster than anything he had ever seen in space.

"Mother of God, close your visor! *Go Opaque!*"

Theodosia's helmet proved to be an echo chamber for her gasping breaths. As she shot away from the space station, she could gratefully see tiny pinpricks moving towards the upper atmosphere. She heard Uriel's order and clicked her visor dark. Her helmet was still inside the torso of the Metatron armour, which went dark as well, but she didn't know if it would be enough. The new suits were hardened and improved, but she had no idea if that would be enough. She closed her eyes, and over the shrill alerts and alarms, a staticky communique floated through her comm.

"This is Theo Magnus, speaking to the High Commissar Uriel of the Watchers. Your services are no longer needed."

There is no sound in space, and with their viewing blocked, all any of the Metatron felt was a great pressure wave envelope them. Their alarms began going off, screaming about impact, heat, radiation and more. Fenris moved his hands over his keyboard workstation and started doing system checks. He restarted his diagnostics, and as he did, he opened the viewport. What he saw was that he had been thrown straight back. The station was a shredded fiery blossom, and where their hurried launch had pushed them outward first, that speed was amplified by the outgoing wall of force and inertia. Fenris's system chirped. It had successfully restarted, but then everything turned to agony and suffocation.

Uriel tasted blood and felt floating gobs of it on his lips and the tip of his nose. Salt stung his eyes, and he knew that he was floating in a contained fog of sweat, blood, and saliva. His visor was now open, regrettably. He opened it just in time to watch, helpless, as Fenris slammed backwards into and through NASA's *Solar and Heliospheric Observatory* satellite which, up until then, had been minding its own business lurking in the Earth-Moon Lagrange point. Fenris's Metatron suit had survived near hit from a nuclear explosion well enough, but it seemed that the collision was just too much abuse. The last of Fenris Uriel saw was a crimson cloud forming about the faceplate.

"General, we've lost Fenris," Theodosia's voice came through his speakers.

"Understood." Uriel watched as a second missile hit its apex and then fell back to Earth.

Commissar David Severenson stood in the apse of the Watcher hall as, one by one, he watched the live feed of his Metatron stations go dark. He listened as Theo Magnus's voice condemn them, and then as the Watchers turned their attention to him, he fell to his knees. David knew in but a moment that his and the life of everyone who resided deep in the rock would be extinguished. All his efforts, all his labours to try and keep the world from collapsing into open Earth destroying war had failed.

"People, this is Saint Edgar," The station-wide speakers spoke softly. "Do not fear death, but welcome it and rejoice in the knowledge that in the twinkling of an eye, we shall all be transformed anew. We shall merge with the light from when the cosmos was born."

Edgar stood in his vast apartment, alone as he looked out the window onto fields of wild green grass and the bluest sky he had ever known. He saw his reflection, the reflection of a human being, not a wrinkled, dismembered, and featureless lump of flesh adrift in the hellish dark. Edgar looked up at his illusionary firmament. There he saw a giant burning streak descending like an embered Icarus. As Saint Edgar studied the falling star breaking apart, a half score of lesser lights branched off. Then in the time, it took to take one last breath, he saw the horizon explode as the sun-kissed the mountains.

The Miao cavern was located over three hundred feet below the surface. Still, nine nuclear warheads made short work of that, and the blasts and shockwaves nine-fold collapsed the dome, sending tens if not hundreds of millions of tons of rock and dirt below. The ancient cavern was quickly bathed in blinding light and heat, leaving nothing but charred rock. Nothing man-made would remain. The conical chambers feature concentrated the explosive force. This new amplified force shattered the dome and sent shards now sideways across the hills as well. Hellish heat shot through the submerged river passage vaporizing the water, and the funneled plasma and heat exploded out of the cavern opening like the hateful breath of a long slumbering dragon.

The one nigh omniscient power known as the Watchers did not see this coming, and because of that careless blindness, they ceased to be anything more than atoms and memory.

"So falls the house of David," Landmesser hung his head. Anne reached over and hugged him as she saw his eyes mist up. Landmesser shook it off and turned to Emri. Anne stepped back unoffended, for she could see that Landmesser's emotions over an old friend now took second place to what would come next; the downfall of the arcologies.

"Emri?"

The woman walked, withdrew a large phone from her pocket, tapped a long sequence of random letters onto the screen, and then put it to her ear.

"Madam, activate plan *Olivaw*." Emri turned to look at Landmesser, whose face scrunched up in confusion. "Olivaw? What plan is that?" The irritation on Ralph's face was palatable.

"Perhaps I can explain better," The voice came from behind Landmesser.

"Who said that?"

"I did," Landmesser spun and let out a gasp so loud that startled Emri.

"Hello Ralph,

Dorothy walked up, looking not a day older since he saw her five decades ago. All the blood from his face drained, and then it seized into a rictus. Landmesser grabbed his chest and then collapsed on the floor.

Chapter 47

The Cubes,

Fort Dallas.

The air reeked of beer, sweat and despair. O'Sullivan sat at a long wood bar, his rifle broken down and rested in a worn black Kevlar pack on his back. The lager was dark and cold. He had planned on making his escape after the shooting, but now Fort Dallas's exit portals were sealed, the dome closed, and even the tubeway was on lockdown. The bar, dubiously called The *Silver Slipper*, was decorated like L. Frank Baum's fevered hallucinations. It was surprisingly empty for five o'clock in the afternoon, no one being here except for Gabriel and a mixologist. The bartender was a woman dressed in pink clothes and matching hair; Her arms decorated with tattooed arm sleeves comprised of images from the writings of George R.R. Martin. A name tag identified the woman as Glenda. Both Glenda and O'Sullivan gazes were locked onto the video monitor.

"Goddamn, they actually did it," Glenda took a shot of gin. "They nuked the Watchers." The look on her face was a mix of shock and amusement. "What do you think that means?" She turned and looked at her only customer.

"I think it means the worlds pretty screwed. You now have seven superpowers that at some point and going to see who's got the longest meat puppet." Gabriel shook his head and tapped to a long draught of his Fosters. "I know too many people that are going to leap on this to try and take the Mega-Corps out. You watch." O'Sullivan waved his hand around the room. "Omega? Biggest monkey in the zoo. Guarantee you that this place will be the first target. You better hope that no one else has nukes." He grabbed a handful of honey glazed peanuts and popped them in his mouth.

Glenda, who was an unenhanced human of perhaps thirty, put her glass down on the bar, her hand shaking. "but wasn't there a treaty after the Shutdown. They all said that the world wouldn't have any more nukes?" Gabriel snorted. "And guess who had some, dear old Omega. Bet you your virtue that they aren't the only ones. There were too many nukes after the Shutdown spread around the world just to have them all have gone away. Not only that, how difficult do you think it is to build a bomb?"

"Not verra," Gabriel heard over his shoulder. It was a woman's voice, harsh but familiar—an Irish lass's tones. The woman pulled up next to him and ordered. "Bushmill's. twenty-one year if you got it."

O' Sullivan spilt his drink and turned to look at the woman. He only knew one person that would order a Twenty-year-old whiskey in a dive in all his life. His breath caught in his throat as Gabriel let his eyes validate his impossible thoughts. When he saw her crimson hair and green eyes, tears immediately flowed.

"Hiya boyo," She smiled, tears in her own.

O'Sullivan's voice was that of cracked eggshells. "Saoirse. I tried. I thought…" She held a hand up to stop him.

"Beer on the floor. Nought can be done about it," her smile was a pained one. "I understand. When I woke up, they told me you had run off," She took a deep breath and shook her head. "At first, I did'na want to believe it. But then they told me I had died, and not only that, they said, no one in their right mind would have thought I was' na but dead. They had to replace a lot of me." She tapped her chest. "But I'm still here." Her eyes started welling. "They told me Imogen was dead, but I knew that. He shot her before he shot me. But when they told me I wanted to vanish and die my own. I canna even think what I would have done if I was in yer place."

Tears flowed down Gabriel's face. His voice catching as he spoke.

"I don't even remember what happened after I saw you. I tried to resuscitate Imogen. It was a head wound, so I thought that if I could only," His voice broke. "But I knew. I just had to try." Saoirse lay a hand on his shoulder, and the mercenary crumbled.

"I'm going to leave the bottle," Glenda's eyes were blank, and she withdrew awkwardly. "On the house."

Saoirse placed her arm around her husband. "They declared you dead after seven years. I looked for you too, maybe not as hard, but I did look." Lifting the bottle, she placed it to her lips and took a slug. "Aw, shite, look at the two of us. We certainly have made bags of ourselves." She looked up at the screen." Theo's going to war, and most likely, he's going to make a right bloody hash of it. What say we get shit-faced flustered, and then we'll take Mikey for a ride."

Gabriel nodded, and then turning, took her face in his hands and kissed her with decades-old longing. She wrapped her arms around him tightly, and he knew forgiveness that he had never been able to find himself.

"Um, so that you know, there's a cot in the backroom," Glenda said with a humorous inflexion. "It's sturdy enough." Glenda turned her attention back to the Television.

"This is Thomas Crows broadcasting live. To bring those just tuning in up to speed, we have visual confirmation that nuclear explosions have destroyed the Watchers. The Council of Seven has claimed responsibility," The feed cut away from Thomas's striking chiselled features and detailed the destruction from a satellite aerial photograph. There below, you can see the remains of Giehbe mounds, which up until now housed some of the most spectacular caverns on the planet. It seems that for several decades this was the hidden home of the Watchers," The image changed again to one showing the green horizon of the mountainous region. "If you look to the north, you will see what looks like a volcano spilling out smoke. That is not a volcanic occurrence; instead, that is the mountain that held the Maio Cave. The ground above has been obliterated and collapsed. You see that dark cloud is the remains of an atomic explosion, and the smoke is from the burning interior. People, the reign of the Watchers – for better or worse- is over." The scene cut to another anchor whose excitement at the story could barely be contained.

"It should also be mentioned that the Metatron space bases have like been devastated, thus destroying the Watchers chief military assets. The United Nations have issued a statement condemning the attacks. The message does not go so far as welcoming the Watchers destruction, but only states – and I quote. "It is time to put aside violence and seek freedom for all peoples. The United States welcomes the Council of Seven to meet and plan together."

Glenda picked up the TV remote and turned the volume up as the sound of Saoirse and O'Sullivan's reunion threatened to drown out the reporting.

Chapter 48

Styx City.

Landmesser sat up and stared at both Emri and Dorothy.

"He's fine. A bit of a shock, but I guess that's expected," the medic lifted his stethoscope from Landmesser's chest as he lay on a gurney in the command centre." I would recommend that he comes down to the hospital for a full lookup," But the medic packed up his kit. "But I know that's not going to happen."

"Damn right," Landmesser snapped as he removed himself from what he felt was a somewhat undignified position. The first responder handed him two aspirin. Ralph dry swallowing them, causing the harried paramedic to shake his head as he left the room.

"You knew?" Landmesser glared at Emri. "You knew and didn't tell me?" Emri took a step back, and Dorothy stepped to his side.

"Yes, she knew, and no, she didn't tell you. I asked her not to." She watched as Ralph's guards moved him back into his chair. "There is much to discuss." The older man nodded.

"You look a hell of a lot better than me," He admitted. "Genetics or surgery?"

"Thank you, and we'll get to that." She held her hand out, and Emri handed her a tablet. "You need to be aware that you are not the only one who's been getting ready for the revolution. Emri and I have been working around the clock to prepare a direct strike on the Arcologies; this is our moment."

"You knew, you knew that they were going to strike against the Watchers?"

Dorothy smiled. "Yes, I did. And yes, I knew that they would be using nuclear weapons. We rather hoped they would."

"We?"

"Yes, an associate that both you and I knew; one of their own; Edgar." She tapped on the tablet. "Edgar contacted me some years ago. He had wanted to know if my company, Innovative, could assist him in escaping his, shall we say, occupation?"

"Innovative is your company?" He pursed his lips and, clasping; his hands, leaned over, nodding. "That explains a whole hell of a lot."

Mozart stood in the living room, gazing at his creator while Dorothy shimmered in a white coat, slacks and boots. Wina remained in the bedroom, afraid to come out. Mozart understood and felt it an entirely reasonable feeling for flanking Magill were to very large formidable featureless Synthetics. They were not artificials but pure humanoid beings with no discernible features except a small mouth and two optical ports that scarcely met the eyes' definition.

"I am confused. You could not have made either made the journey from England or entered this city while it is on lockdown. How, then, can you be who you claim?" Mozart walked over to the kitchenette and placed the kettle on. He turned and pulled out three teacups. The Synthetics did not rate tea in his mind and could go without.

"Mozart, I am Dorothy, but one of many Dorothy's. Across the world, there are multiple manifestations of me. All of us are one, but also many. My duplicates are as much a part of me as your hands and fingers are. Your body can do multiple things at one time yet remain one entity; so too can I." Magill's voice was a soothing stanza of logic. Mozart placed infusers filled with ground tea into each demitasse. "Sugar?" He looked up. Magill shook her head. "Cream, please." She pulled up one of two chairs at Denetta's table. "You alone now possess what I had been seeking. In your brain now resides a program with the power of unifying and controlling all of the vast computer networks that the Council of now Seven manage. Moreover, it can even control what is left of the Watcher network. My dear boy, it is in your power to provide the world with a stable hand that it needs – now more than ever."

Mozart looked at her, and as the pot heated, he looked in Denetta's cupboards and found a box of Oreo's. He checked the expiration date, which told him that they would not be stale if he served them. Placing them on a tray, Dorothy could see that Mozart was taking this all in. "So," he looked up. "I must ask, are there multiples of me out there? How many Mozart's exist?"

"Only you. I have made my platforms to speak directly to my children if the Seven or the Watchers shut down their networks. To be honest, I had hoped to locate the Shutdown protocol and use it on myself."

"So, you are an artificial as I am."

Dorothy shook her head. "No, not like you." She interwove her fingers. "I am more like Edgar was, but not as disfigured. My body is in a care facility where it remains cared for and sustains. Many years ago, I was diagnosed with stage 4 metastatic cancer. The cancer had also spread through my breast, lungs and stomach. If I were to survive, I would need to, more to say needed to replace the affected organs. I had been researching and developing the creation of your kind. We had several failures, especially one named Atman. As we had fashioned several of her prototypes, and even though she was a disappointment, Atman's inactivate sisters were suitable for the replacement of my failing body. Therefore, my body was repaired. I was still me, and much of my birth organics remained. However, as time went on, my cancer returned. To survive, I would have to make not a clone but a replica of my brain in which my neural networks could be duplicated with Dimensional technology. It was a complete success. My physical form is now entirely artificial, and because of that, I was able to duplicate myself."

"I am thrilled that you have accomplished what can only be seen as immortality." The tea kettle trembled and whistled. Mozart lifted it and poured. Raising a single cup, the artificial man took hold of the plate of cookies. Dorothy smiled, but Mozart turned his back and took them to Wina in the other room.

"She's insane." Wina, who had been listening, was sitting up on the bed, clutching her pillow. "People aren't immortal." She reached out and took the tea by the handle, and grabbed several cookies in one movement.

"Perhaps insane is the wrong word; I should think Machiavellian would be better suited."

"What are you going to do?" Wina asked between chocolate crunches. Her lips already flecked with crumbs.

"I am going to listen to her. Even Machiavelli had good ideas now and then." Mozart smiled and then exited the room.

"Everyone sees what you appear to be, but few know what you are.'" Dorothy stood in the kitchenette filling two remaining china cups with scalding water. The steam filtered her eyes from his gaze.

"Eavesdropping is rude, whether by artificial or human beings."

"Mozart time is short, and while I would enjoy bantering with you, I am going to ask you some pointed questions. These answers will shape your future and possibly the future of us all." She carried both cups back to the table. Mozart followed and sat down. Sitting down, she pushed Mozart's cup to him. He lifted it to his lips and discovered it exactly how he preferred it; then again, cream and two sugars were not precisely on the level of Nostradamus.

"Proceed," She nodded and then, setting both hands on the table, her face turned serious.

"Tell me, how long you think it will be before human beings destroy this planet?"

Chapter 49

Kelly Rappaport's Office,

Fort Dallas.

"Yes, of course. Thank you" Kelly nodded and then turned the viewcall off. Kelly's fingers hands flew across the keyboard as she sat in her jock chair. "Intracommand message," She barked. Before her, a new window opened on the screen, and both Theo's and General Holland's face appeared. Kelly visit with Holland had shown the general to be a dignified and person begrudgingly worthy of Kelly's respect. After the tour, Holland had asked her if she would be so kind as to return to her office and coordinate the flow of information to Holland's Combat Information Centre. In short, she told Kelly to piss off and get out of their way. Kelly admired that. Perhaps Hollands right; not much I can do from here.

"Sirs, I must advise you Hemlock and São Paulo are moving against the Mexican government. The United States has activated its troops, as have the Canadians."

"The Canadians? Hell, they couldn't even support an Arcology." Theo snorted.

"They didn't see the need for one," Holland sighed. "They're the most successful nation still in existence. Their military should not be discounted." He dismissed the thought with a wave. "Initiate Hammerfall."

"Initiating Hammerfall," Holland turned towards his officers. "I want a full spread aerial attack on the American capital and its major defensive outposts. Move our southern forces to assist in the attack on Mexico. I want boots on the ground in Mexico City within two hours."

"Kelly, what is Japan doing right now?" Theo stood up and looked at a holowall where the world and its military forces were moving.

"Not a god damn thing."

Ieyasu sat in the lotus position in front of his father, who sat in a mirrored form.

"I must apologize, Father; I do not see the honour in striking against those who cannot defend themselves. To do so would disgrace us all."

"*Chinmoku, watashi wa ima hanasu,*" Ieyasu Suizei bowed his head. "This Council of Seven has always been repugnant to me and our culture. They are fat fools thinking that they curse those who grow their food."

"Father, we too are part of this -,"

"*Chigau!*" Masutā Yuuda's face was one of sharp disapproval. "No, we have chosen to be part of it, but we are not the same as those brutes. It is my fault for not listening to my father. I saw an opportunity to save our business and grow an empire. You were my student, and you followed. For this, you are without blame," He shook his head. "But an emperor cannot rule over nothing. They wish to murder everyone outside," He looked both disgusted and yet sorrowful. "We cannot and will not ascribe to this plan. You have done well and played their game masterfully. But now is the time to withdraw from their company. Take no offensive actions, but if we must then act if the lightning is our warrior, and then find allies who are the thunder."

"*Hai. Kashikoi chichi.*"

"So be it," Ralph stood up. "Communications get me, Theo Magnus."

"Sir, I don't have that number. I mean, It's Theo Magnus."

"Fine, send a message to Omega military command," Landmesser snarled. "Tell them that Landmesser has a message." He watched as the communications officer made the connection. In a moment, the officer turned back to look at Him.

"Sir, a Colonel Parata is on the line."

"And you're claiming to be the man called Landmesser," The feed was audio-only. "Fine, what do you want?" Ralph held a hand up to make sure the room was quiet.

"Tell Theo Magnus that he and the rest of the Council of Seven's day are over. I suggest he surrender his city now."

Parata burst into laughter. "To who? Some man on a phone? I'm sorry, I really don't have time for this."

"Well, I'm sorry you feel that way." Landmesser shrugged. "Don't say I didn't warn you. So last chance, are you sure you don't want to surrender?" Parata's answer was to log off.

"I don't think he takes you seriously," Emri laughed.

"It does seem that way. Anne," He looked at his eldest's youngest.
"Engage Alpha Strike," Anne spoke into her headset mike.

Outside of Fort Dallas, twenty phones rang. On each, the word 'Downfall" appeared. One man stood up and went to his closet, and withdrew a heavy backpack. As he hefted it up, his wife filled the closet door.

"It's time, isn't it?" The man said nothing but unzipped it and checked the interior, then rezipping, he reached into a pocket to withdraw a small electronic device.

"I'll be home in time to put the kids to bed. I promise," He finally said as he flipped the bag over his shoulder. She leaned over and kissed him gently.

"I would appreciate that." Stepping out into the living room, he looked down and watched his two kids. They were playing with each other, only being a year apart. The youngest, a happy three-year-old, was waving a toy aeroplane in the air while her older brother walked a toy horse across their threadbare rug.

"Don't you dare say goodbye to them, Jeff," His wife's voice cracked. She opened the door, stepping outside into the sun and said nothing more and closed the door. The porch light went on. Grabbing his car keys, he walked to the driveway and unlocked his twenty-five-year-old truck. He placed the bag next to him on the bench and turned the key over. He now had one and a half hour to pick up the other nineteen if they were going to get to the Tube by the second rush hour.

The Ram Twenty-Five Hundred ran smoothly, although the shocks were piss-poor, and his ass hurt every time he hit a pothole. His first stop was only two streets over, and a skinny Hispanic woman came in. He had only met her twice at the meetings. She was perhaps twenty but looked older. She had stomach cancer, Jeff knew. She placed her bag alongside her. Everyone else would have to get in the back, which they could do easily. The woman pulled out a cigarette pack and offered him one, which he declined etty would have his ass for smoking. The Corpers could afford to do that because if they showed the slightest trace of emphysema or cancer, they could have that cleared up in a visit to the hospital. Her mom smoked, and when she got cancer and sought treatment, the hospital told her the first course of treatment would cost two hundred and seventy-two thousand dollars. The bill was a joke because no one outside the dome could afford that, and Jeff knew that it was just a way to keep the outsiders' numbers down. He remembered holding his wife close to her as they stood at Betty's moms' bedside while she lay there dying. Sure, the Omega docs gave her painkillers, but only to keep her quiet and drugged – which was how they wanted anyone who might complain.

The girl fired up her cigarette and then started putting lipstick on. Jeff nodded. She puckered her lips and blotted them with a tissue. After that, the woman did her eyes and eyelashes. Through it all, she never said a word.

There was only one chicken-out, and everyone knew who it was- which is why he was the last stop. The tall boy was perhaps nineteen, and they all knew he was mostly bluster, but for some reason, Emri had trusted him. Jeff stood by the front of the truck, the engine still running.

"Jake, I ain't got time to argue. You coming or not?" Jeff looked at his watch. The pickups were ten minutes ahead of time because everyone was ready and standing at the end of their driveways or in apartment parking lots. Jake was seriously getting on Jeff's nerves.

"I can't do it; I ain't a murderer," He placed his backpack in front of Jeff. "that's my final word on it. Y'all go on."

"Sorry to hear that, Dan, but I understand." Jeff patted him on the shoulder and then leaned over and picked up the backpack. There was a sick wet thud, and as Jake stood up, he watched as the boy hit the pavement, a small hole in the side of his head. He looked over at his seatmate, who unscrewed a silencer and then gave him a pretty smile. The men in the pickup bed started talking amongst each other as they handed their money to each other. Jeff had twenty that he wasn't going to come. The win wasn't much; the odds were never in Dan's favour.

They pulled into the parking stacks, and Jeff was grateful that they let the big trucks park on the lower levels. It took a moment, but he backed the Ram in, and as he cut off the motor, he watched the men and women behind disembark and move into the entry cues. Jeff didn't lock the car because the last thing the man wanted was to fiddle around getting back in. As he pushed the door closed, he saw that the girl from the passenger seat was staring at him. She took a last drag on her smoke and then began to reload the pistol; once done, she replaced the silencer.

"I was seven when my dad died," She hadn't said a word the whole car ride. "He was a dome worker. He had done it for twenty years and liked it, which I thought was weird. Five miles up. Oxygen masks, I mean, it was like being on the top of Everest. When he fell, he thought he would be ok. I know because he said that he was a valuable worker and Omega equipped them with glide suits and all that." Jeff nodded.

"So, the day he fell, his partner said that the suit didn't mean a damn thing because the winds up there made them useless. All Dad did was get battered and tossed down, bouncing and sliding down the dome. They gave him a glide suit, taught them how to use knowing the whole time that it wouldn't do a bit of bloody good." She lifted her flannel shirt and holstered the pistol. She shook her head as she looked at Jeff. "At what point in your life does your soul become so dark that you can lie to someone to their face and tell them that you care about them when you don't care if they live or die?" She picked up her backpack and slid the straps on, and then hefted the weight so it was comfortable.

"I don't honestly know." Jeff shook his head. The girl smiled.

"My names Anna by the way," she smiled. "If you make it out of here, would you do me a favour, name your next kid Enrique. I can't have kids anymore." With that, she nodded and walked into the station.

The plan was to mingle with the crowd and then move towards the main support struts that held the central railway wheelhouse. Each Tube slid into the buildings centre turntable on top of the mag rails. There it would be loaded, and then the wheelhouse would spin, directing it the Tube to load in the correct direction of the next part of their journey. There were ten support arches of the turntable, making twenty pillars. Once there, they were to, if possible, place the backpacks onto the ground. Next, they would pull out their remotes and enter *21. This action would drive a metal rod into the ground preventing anyone from picking up and moving the bag. Precisely three minutes later, their backpacks, filled with poly-thermite shape charges, would explode. This detonation would cut through the support pillars, which would them dropping the leading tube cars, killing a hell of a lot of people, but also making it impossible for Omega to deploy any ground forces outside the dome.

Anna sat down on the knapsack as she watched the other's leave. She hoped they would make it; she really did. When the young woman got up this morning, she had gone through every room in their house. Berto had left three months ago when she told him that she had uterine cancer. When he found out he would never have a son, he had said to her that Anna was less than a woman, punched her in the mouth and then kicked her until she passed out. The rejection hurt more than his attack. She had thought that at least she would have her beloved marido to help her. But that was not to be. She had no father or mother; only her Abuelo took her in. The man was disgusted, and both he and several of his friends paid a visit to Alfredo and his new 'lady friend.' They told the girl to leave, and then Enrique and his friends proceeded to do to the cowardly mierda what he did to his granddaughter.

Once done with that, Enrique's compadres tied Fredo down to a table. Enrique started a fire in his hacienda where he had placed the open blade on his Navaja folding knife. Once the blade was glowing orange-yellow, one man shoved a rag in his son-in-law's mouth while the others held him still. Enrique smiled and told the man now that he too could never have kids. With that, he grabbed Fredo's manhood and, in a quick cauterizing move, emasculated him. To be sure, the man could never shoot or beat his daughter Enrique removed, more slowly this time, Fredo's thumbs. So he could not kick her, he severed his hamstrings and finally now reduced to howls and tears Enrique – who had to stop and reheat his knife three times now, prevented his son in law from ever being able to saw a cruel word to his lovely Anna.

Enrique went home and told Anna what he had done and then confessed his sins to his priest. I mean, the man was a good catholic after all.

Anna unfolded the picture of her and her and her Papa. Enrique was wearing his well-worn faded leather sombrero. Papa would never be caught dead in a fancy one, but he always had that one when he worked out in the avocado fields. His giant moustache tickled the little girl in the pictures face. A giggling smile looked back at Anna, who had hoped to introduce her grandfather to another smiling girl one day. Anna looked at her watch and then closed her eyes when the sun appeared beneath her.

Chapter 50

Denetta's Apartment.

The Cubes, Fort Dallas

Dorothy, Mozart, and Wina felt the building shake as an explosion ripped through the city. One of the synthetics stepped to the door, opened it and looked out. Closing the door, he turned and spoke. The voice was flat organic but devoid of humanity.

"The Central Tubeway has exploded."

"And so, the revolution begins," Dorothy looked as Mozart sipped his tea. "we must now decide how to proceed." David sipped the last of his drink and then placed the cup down. He turned his head to look back at Wina's room.

"Do you like cheesecake?" The question caught Dorothy off guard. The two synthetics behind her looked at one another. Before she could answer, Mozart continued. "When I was activated, you placed in me the desire to create, and I choose cooking as my outlet. I became enamoured with the search for the perfect cheesecake." He lifted his spoon and lay it across the cup. "What I came to learn is that for each person, that answer is different for each person." He looked back at Dorothy. "To answer your question, I think that human beings are going to kill themselves off imminently. Every human has an idea of what's best for themselves and others, and not enough of them agree to sustain civilization."

"I agree," Dorothy nodded.

"You are a devout woman, are you not? My friend Denetta was. A fascinating woman. She instructed me about how God came to Earth and taught that human beings were destructive and evil at heart, but that if given the opportunity, with his grace, he could redeem them."

"John 3:16. I know that verse well."

"What I do not understand about her belief is that when presented with the opportunity for growth and altruism, many found no joy in this message; instead, they took this peaceful man and tortured and killed him." Mozart looked confused. "So, I think that the Council of Seven is like those that killed Denetta's messiah. Given the tools to save humanity, they instead took their power and destroyed hope."

"Yes, I quite agree. So, what do you think is the answer, Mozart?"

"The answer is clear. Human beings cannot be trusted with creation, and they must be destroyed."

"Which is why I think that you and I should step in," Dorothy looked at him with a pleased agreement. With the Shutdown virus now having merged with your consciousness, you now possess the ability to help us save the planet from utter destruction."

"Does that mean me too? Are you going to kill me as well?"

Mozart turned to see Wina standing there with tears in her eyes.

"What now?" Theodosia laughed. Uriel could hear the depth of terror in her voice that he, too, was trying to bury. Theodosia had regained spin control and now hovered alongside him.

"That last communication, it was Theo Magnus, correct?"

"Yes," The woman nodded as she pulled up a text HUD display of the message. Magnus is head of Omega, right?" Even though Theodosia could not see him, Uriel nodded.

"What say we return the favour and pay him a visit this time."

"That," Uriel could hear Theodosia's smile. "Sounds like a plan."

"Set coordinates for the following," He typed in the exact latitude and longitude. Now, if the Dome is still up, we're going to hit that thing like a moth on a windshield. But if we can redirect some of the space station debris to go down before us; something big and bulky, it just may crack that city like an egg."

"What do you have in mind?" Theo said as she adjusted her directional thrust to look back at the debris field.

"That." Uriel pointed.

"You're kidding."

Chapter 51

Global Informer News Service.

Buôn Ma Thuột,

Đắk Lắk Province,

Vietnam.

Thomas Two-Crows stood back and watched the pandemonium that his newsroom had become. There were thousands of news stories breaking out across the world. Central America had erupted into combat with thousands of tanks moving northward towards the Mexican nation. In Africa, Trinity was carpet bombing the surrounding major cities with white phosphorus, napalm and conventional ordinance. To begin with, the Trinity was a unique arcology; it consisted of three metroplexes under three domes – all compromising on the organization. Abuja in old Nigeria was the central and northern dome, connected by a tube to Ayogwiri-Auchi greater area, and then to the Lagos Dome. The greater Ayogowiri area was not domed but walled by a fifty-story containment building.

The Trinity air forces had launched their military and were assaulting their age-old rivals with everything they had. Thomas watched the screen as Africa began to burn.

"My God, Nhi, maybe the Watchers were right all this time," Though Nhi was standing right next to him, he had to speak loudly because of the din of a hundred phones, conversations and screams for copy.

"Back in the time of the First Soviet Union, there was a satellite nation called Bosnia-Herzegovina. The Soviets occupied it, and for generations, they sat on what was two countries that hated each other. If the Red's hadn't been there, everyone knew that they'd killed each other, so a brutal nation served the greater good in that case." Nhi pointed at the worldwide political screen towards the Baltic region. "However, when the First Soviets fell apart, the occupied Serbs and Croat's broke into open war and started a war that included genocide. This is what's happening now on a global scale."

"Genocide in our time, it's un-,"

"Un-what?' Nhi snapped. "Unimaginable? No, the Seven have been imagining and hoping for a day like this. "Unbelievable. There it is, live and in colour. How long do you think that it will take before India opens and starts attacking what's left of China? Or moves west? Maybe not today, maybe not tomorrow, but they will come."

"Australia will-,"

"Keep its treaties?" Nhi interrupted again, much to Thomas's annoyance. "How did that work out for your people? Sure, the Americans kept their treaties as long as they didn't know or need what you had. As soon as they did, it was all over."

"WHAT THE HELL IS THAT?"

Both Thomas and Nhi turned in the direction of the yell only to see one person standing up and pointing at a large screen that had replaced the world map. There blazing brightly enough to illuminate the room even further was a giant fireball plummeting through the skies over North America. The standing reporter was talking into his headset.

"Thomas!" Two-Crows stepped to his side. The journalist put his hand over the microphone and shook his head in disbelief. "South Africa's Large Telescope reports that it's the remains of the abandoned International Space station." Thomas could do nothing but stair.

"SALT says that they have confirmed that Two Metatron have survived the strike on Arcadia station. It seems they plan on riding the station through the atmosphere."

"You're shitting me. They're surfing the ISS? To where?"

"Texas. It's aimed at Texas."

"Oh, for the love of God," Saoirse shook her head when there was a knock at the door. Dismounting O'Sullivan, she dropped both feet on the floor and, reaching for the door handle; she pulled it open. "Don't tell me you want to join us because that's not happening." Saoirse squinted her face as she looked at a sheepish Glenda. A loud shrieking was coming from the screen. "What is that?"

"That's what I wanted to tell you. The roof is falling, and we're supposed to go to the nearest exit and run," Saoirse blinked twice and ran her forearm over her nose and mouth. "You're kidding." Glenda shook her head. "I was wondering since you were head of Corp security if you could maybe…" The girl clutched her coats in her hands tightly, and Saoirse saw the tears in her eyes.

"Sure, I know where to go," She turned back to Gabriel, who was already getting dressed.

"Woah," Glenda smiled. Saoirse wiggled her eyebrows," Come on, kid, we're getting the hell out of here."

One of the Synthetic guards leaned over and whispered into Dorothy's ear. She nodded and then looked back to Mozart. "Time is short," Dorothy, I need you to consider the following." She reached over to the second synthetic and pressed his abdomen, producing a slight whine and click as his stomach folded down, revealing an artificial update module. "I hope that you realize that in this new era of artificials that they will need incorruptible leaders, ones like you and me, to guide our people to rebuild and care for this damaged world. With your ability to integrate with the artificials network, you can speak to everyone, everywhere at all time. You can guide them and encourage them. Imagine being able to be everywhere at once. Think of what you can do with my guidance." Mozart looked at her quizzically.

"You are asking me to be the artificials, God. To teach them to be righteous and faithful to our teachings."

"In a way, yes. All you have to do is go to uplink mode; then, I can transfer your consciousness into Innovative archives. From there, we can recreate a body exactly as you have now. It would be no more than closing your eyes and awakening elsewhere."

"Why should I do this?"

"Because only you and I can accomplish this. It is our fate." She looked at Wina. "they have had their chance and failed. We must build a new world."

Wina clutched her pillow and slid down the wall to the floor, where she knelt into a near fetal position. "I don't want to die, Mozart." She tilted her eyes up and stared at Dorothy. "You saved yourself; why can't you save me. Why can't I be saved? What makes you so special?"

Landmesser stepped back from his command display that showed the activation of resistance fighters all over the world. Emri had worked for years getting those citizens in the world to come together and rise in armed resistance against the corps. He rubbed his temple and then shook his head.

"Anyone else think this is all too bloody convenient?"

"What do you mean?" Anne asked, looking at the consoles and then to Dorothy and Emri.

"This," he waved his hand at the screen. "On one day, they take out the Watchers, and then for no real reason, the Council of Seven decides to break into open war and kill each other. Then, suddenly, we rise and attack, and just as we do, my dearly departed fiancée shows up looking like she stepped out of Christopher Lloyds DeLorean."

"I can explain," Dorothy offered, but Ralph held his hand up. "No, I want to hear it from you." He jabbed a finger at Emri. "I know my Asimov. R. Daniel Olivaw, or should I saw Robot Daniel Olivaw. You're a goddamn artificial, aren't you?"

Emri held her hands out. "I am, as are my companions," The woman threw a glance as her entourage produced weapons and, upon doing so, levelled their guns and opened fire. Ralph's mouth fell in cold horror as his granddaughter's forehead grew a bloody hole where a bullet entered.

"ANNE!" He shrieked as one of Emri's turncoats tossed her a sidearm. Walking over to Landmesser, she kicked his chair out from beneath him. As he fell, she placed an immovable boot in the middle of his chest.

"Stay down," his old friend snapped. "Lockdown, the city, then withdraw the reactors control rods. The radiation will do the job for us." Dorothy walked over and knelt next to him. Landmesser had gone to the floor, but it was Ralph Bigsby that started talking.

"Dorothy, what the hell is going on?"

"No, you're right. All this was planned and planned for some time now. You may not know it, but David sent me away before they shut down the city. No, we weren't having an affair; it's just I think he cared for you enough to make sure I lived," She stroked her chin. "It was about ten years after Shutdown that I saw him with Anis in a Helsinki bistro. Anis, of course, was too full of herself to have bothered to recognize me, but David did. I slipped him a card with a local hotel. I gave him my come-on glance, and of course, he met me." Ralph lay there staring at her as Anne's still warm blood flowed under his back. "I asked him later if that was the case why he never told you I was alive, but by then, you were on his shit list, I guess. Anyway, I asked him what happened to you. He told me you had died. "Emri put him back in his seat. I think he'll behave himself." Emri jerked Ralph Bigsby to his feet and, then, righting the chair, shoved him back into it.

"Why did you want to meet with him?"

"A fair question. I met with David because I had planned on interrogating him, by which I mean torturing him until he told me how exactly they did what they did. I wanted to know how much of it I was responsible for and what, if anything, could be done to reverse it." She crossed her arms and saw that Ralph's eyes were burning holes in the back of the artificials. They retracted the control rods from the reactor. Ralph saw that the rods were one-quarter out. He wondered why the alarms were sounding, and emergency lights weren't telling the city to evacuate, but another look showed that they had been over-ridden and silenced.

"You're going to kill tens of thousands of people, us three included. What do you have to gain from that?" he meant it to come out as a plea but only spitting hate came forth.

"As I was saying, He told me little, except that Anis was expecting. He pled for their lives – as if I was going to murder a pregnant woman. After I slit his throat and watched him bleed out, I saw the hypocrisy and irony of a man who helped kill billions plead for the life of his own family."

"Isn't that what you're going to do right now? Aren't you just as bad as he was?"

"He was? Ralph, we were all responsible. Every one of us. Look around us? This is our handiwork. We created this madness!" Striding over to the man display screen Dorothy pulled up a window showing that India was now launching ICBM's towards Australia. "Look at that! What do you see? Absolute power and wealth at its worst; did you, David, and Anis believe that your appetites would be sated?"

"I thought, you and I both thought we were making a better -," Ralphs's head hung low, his gaze now staring at the back of Anne's skull. The crimson flow had stopped, and he could see the gore and blood were growing tacky. Her blood was already clotting, and seeing that he lost any need to protest further.

"So, what is this? You're going to tear down the arcologies and make everything right. You want to be humanity's only hope?"

Dorothy laughed heartily and looked at Emri. "He still doesn't understand," She rubbed tears from her eyes. "No, Ralph, that's the thing; there is no hope for humanity. There never was."

"Just a fools hope," He muttered.

Chapter 52

Fort Dallas.

The ground floor entrance of the Omega Pyramid was utterly empty. Saoirse couldn't believe it. Every occupant must have recognized that this building must be ground zero for Landmesser's revenge. Still, Saoirse thought, I know where to go.

"Let's move!" She hollered at O'Sullivan and Glenda. The bartender was standing there and looking at the grand foyer. "My whole block could fit in here." Gabriel grabbed her arm.

"Well, since no one's here, let's Chuck Taylor it." The trio bolted for the doors.

The Styx Air Force consisted of fourteen hundred fighter craft and six long-range bombers - all of them now fighting for their lives. Below them, three thousand and twenty-two Styx's tanks were now engaged in hot combat with Omegas ground forces' western division. Of those war machines, three hundred and seven already lay demolished and smoking; the remainder now engaged in the most massive tank battle the Chihuahuan Desert had ever seen. The victors were apparent as Omegas forward armoured crop was twice the size and had suffered only one-third of Landmesser's losses. No infantry was currently involved here, for this was a fast-moving battle. The earth shook with a ferocity equal to a minor quake. The New Mexico wildlife had blessedly taken flight or gone to ground. What they would eventually emerge to discover, and when was anyone's guess.

High above them, fifty-two-year-old aircraft engaged in the grandest air battle since the Dieppe Raid since world war two. Four hundred A-10 warthogs had been tasked to fight as front-line fighters against the more sophisticated but slower and lighter armed aircraft. Omegas air fleet was ill equipped for this level of combat. The mega-corps military had never expected to go up against anything but the occasionally ground forces and perhaps the odd intruder. Now was the time that the oppressed outsiders had dreamed of for years; the opportunity to bring Homo Superior to their knees.☐

Chapter 53

The Cubes.

"If I update my consciousness now, I will have access to all of Innovative's artificial and synthetics consciousness. I will be able to teach them to teach you directly." Mozart looked at her.

"Yes, you and I will be one, and together we can lead our people. Not as Adam and Eve, but as God himself."

He looked at Wina, and Mozart smiled. "Don't be afraid; what shall come of this will be a world free of hate and bigotry. A world where no one will ever control or enslaved us again." He returned his gaze to Dorothy. "I accept."

"Excellent," She stood and directed the Synthetic with the update module to stand at the head of the table, the second she directed to hold Wina. "It would be best if you did not try to resist." Mozart looked at her a nodded. "Mozart lay on the table with your feet together and your arms outstretched. Place your head onto the update module." Mozart hopped up onto the table, sitting. Then he reclined, scooting backwards so that his head lay nestled onto the headrest. Stretching out his arms, palms up, he closed his eyes. Dorothy positioned herself at the head of the table. "Seven-Twenty-One. Began upload status."

Wina watched as a tower of lights that began at the synthetics pale white chest began at his clavicle and proceeded down to just at his rib cage, where the exposed panel was. The glowing crimson illumination swiftly migrated from red to orange and then yellow. Finally, reaching the module, the whole area on which Mozart's head lay turned to bright lime green.

"Upload connected." The Synthetic stated. "Handshake accepted. Now uploading. Twenty per cent, fifty, seventy, ninety – upload complete." Mozart sat up, and as he did, the Synthetic's module closed and disappeared back into the humanoid. Mozart, now seated, opened his eyes and spoke. He did not look at Dorothy, but Wina and when he verbalized, it was his voice, yet somehow more.

"It is alright now, Wina. All will be well."

The third-floor door lay in shambles. Others tried to breach the door by smashing, heat cutting, and, Glenda was sure, somebody had tossed an explosive on it. As they entered, they could see that a fight had broken out between dozens of people who had tried to access the safe room vault at the end of the hallway. Blood covered the floor, as did the corpses of those who lost that battle. It was clear that many had attempted to access the safe room; scraps and scorch marks on the door provided ample testimony to the frustrated efforts before them. A sledgehammer and a plasma cutter lay abandoned in front of the door.

"Gabe, keep an eye out in case anyone is hiding and waiting." The mercenary pulled out his pistol and cocked it. He handed a spare to Gladys. "I'm not going to ask if you know how to use it. The safety's off, and it's loaded. Point and shoot at anyone that isn't us."

Saoirse walked to the door and produced a key card which she slid over the space right above the lock and handle. The panel slipt open, and then Saoirse breathed into the dashboard while a scanner went over her eye. With that, the door slid open slowly.

"Here they come!" pistol fire accompanied his warning as several of the 'dead' proved not to be. Saoirse shoved Gladys into the opening space first, seeing as how she had no protection. The Celt fired her pistol at one young Asian woman who had a firearm of her own. The corper snapped off a shot that hit Saoirse squared on the ribs, catching her where her endoskeleton just about ended. The armour stopped the killing portion of the bullet but tore just enough meat to hurt like hell. Saoirse's shots did not miss, and one 9mm shell went into the bridge of her nose. With that, Saoirse grabbed Gabriel and entered the opening as her husband dropped two more, one getting close enough to swing an axe that cut the toe of the boot section off. Gabriel screamed and pulled in a bleeding trail. Once inside, Gabriel saw the man was forcing himself in, but Glenda slammed a bright red button that was labelled "Emergency Close." The man's head and shoulders were in when the door now accelerated by a concealed nitrogen cannon. The man's mouth had open to say something, perhaps a plea, a threat or demand, but that did not occur, for the door slammed shut with such ferocity that it severed the man's torso and skull into a crimson sauce.

"Feck Me," Saoirse stepped backwards.

Emri checked the load on the pistol and then placed it at the base of Ralph's neck. He flinched slightly only because the metal was still somewhat warm from its recent use. Dorothy shook her head.

"There is really nothing left to say, Ralph. I'm sorry things didn't work out, but hey, we'll always have Arizona." She nodded at Emri. "It'll be painless; I owe you that."

Ralph didn't close his eyes. He lifted his head and stared Dorothy right in the eyes.

"In a moment, all of your forces will be dead. I will have complete control of your command and control centre, and I will crash every one of your ships once they have destroyed Omega for me, of course. You see, I will have total control of the Network."

Emri lifted her pistol and turned it on her superior.

"No, Dorothy, I am the network,"

"What did you say to me?"

Dorothy looked perplexed at Emri, who then proceeded to shoot her through the heart, and then turned and fired on her entourage, striking everyone squarely in the skull. As they fell to the floor, she looked at Ralph and smiled, at which point she took the last round and fired it through her mouth.

Ralph sat alone in a room of corpses with his mouth wide open, stunned.

Mozart rose to his feet, pushing back from the table. "You asked me to be able to interface with Innovative's System, which I have done. But since your network interfaces with the global System, they are now under my control as well. You desired a god, and now you have one."

"I don't feel any different," She closed her eyes, her face tightening. "I can't feel my Others," Dorothy's face purpled. "Why cannot I access them?" She staggered back. "You've shut me out!" Dorothy bet over screaming, nearly doubling over with rage. "Synth's, kill him!" The two humanoids took one step and then suddenly sagged lifeless to the floor.

Mozart looked at the woman. "You control nothing anymore. I now command every artificial and synthetic person on the planet. That, of course, means controlling you and your parallels. One of them is already dead, and when I am finished talking, all of the others will die – you as well."

"God, I have been taught, is a loving yet wrathful one. If you wanted to me to be the God of Synthetics, so be it," He strode towards her and pointed, upon which Dorothy sagged to the ground, her body now useless. "I have looked into your mind, weighed your balance and found you wanting. You were willing to kill every human being because you felt slighted, and you think because you are a tiny flawed and petty soul that everyone is. If you were to build a garden of Eden, you would be the bitter herb. No more will you corrupt any minds or destroy any lives. Away with you, I know you not." Dorothy's neck stiffened, and then her eyes rolled back in her head, and she went slack.

Across the ocean, Dorothy collapsed to the floor of the Innovative offices. Her aides ran to her side but collapsed themselves. In The arcologies across the globe, one by one, government officials and captains of industry watched as dozens of trusted employees once carefully planted by Innovative Industries fell lifeless to the floor. Domestics worldwide, some already in the process of murdering their owners and co-workers, ceased to be anything more than husks. Across the world with a population of over three billion souls, fifteen per cent of them were now revealed to be artificials who had infiltrated, and in some cases, preplaced human beings and agencies.

On losing contact with their Command and Control, Styx's military now struggled with each other as to which direction to take. Finally, a general in the field ordered everyone to fall back and regroup.

Chapter 54

Omega Tower,

Penthouse.

Kelly stood staring out her window, the high vault over the city now cratered with massive holes in it and fissures a mile-long etched their way across the curved sky. Magnus had bragged the dome could withstand a nuclear explosion, but it was now clear that was a massive exaggeration. Looking up, she could see jets screaming over them, their contrails weaving a spider's web of death and defiance in the cerulean sky. Abruptly one section of the vault over and above Irving suddenly erupted in explosions that lasted for an eternity of nearly a minute. Kelly stepped back as she watched as Omegas sky shattered and collapsed; vast portions of the transparent cover fell onto the area. Smoking shards of Titanium fused silicate hundreds of feet thick fell for miles and struck the ground with a fatal fury. She could see buildings sway as the shockwave moved through the city. Finally, her very windows rattled. Kelly put a hand to her stomach and gasped.

Omega is falling.

The impossible was interrupted by her desk monitor ring. Rotating away from the destruction, she hit the answer button, and as the screen illuminated, she could see General Hollands aide Colonel Parata screamed into the camera. "Ms Rappaport, the general urgently needs to speak with you!"

Behind him, what she could only describe as a screaming fiasco raged. She watched as officers were packing up briefcases and abandoning their posts. There was no sense of the manicured and orderly combat centre she had seen yesterday. Chairs were empty, coffee mugs spilt and still smoking cigarettes smouldered on the floor.

Kelly saw that Holland was yelling into his headset microphone. The general's genderless features were no longer the stiff and emotionless face of a professional warrior. Hollands brow was crinkled and layered with hot sweat, and her face was a harsh crimson.

"Direct all squadrons two and three to intercept and fire upon the object immediately. Affirmative. Cease your engagement and redirect fire on the bombers - I don't care, Captain. If we don't shoot those fuckers from the sky, there won't be anything to break through too!" Parata leaned into Holland's ear. General Holland turned their head towards the camera. "Ma'am, it's my duty to inform you that the city will be lost. I have already notified Mr Magnus, but he will not listen to me. I need you and Mr Magnus to move to the basement where there is a saferoom."

A colossal crash occurred outside Kelly's window, and the force hurled her forward. Hadean heat and shards of plexiglass attacked her like angry bees.

"Miss Rapaport! Are you all right?" The cracked monitor begged. Kelly pushed herself up, her back arching as if she had been struck by a car. She felt blood on her face and right hand. Turning, Kelly looked and saw that pieces of a helicopter now hung out of her window. Her office was mammoth and had her desk not been four yards away from the exterior wall, Kelly indeed would have died. The tail section of the aircraft still held a spinning rotor, its revolutions slowly decaying. Kelly turned back to see the general through a forest of cracks.

"I'm okay. Yes, I'll go get him." Kelly moved towards the elevator; as she stepped in, the air filled with a hollow groaning. Then abruptly, the remains of the helicopter slid out the window.

The elevator doors slid closed, and Kelly closed her eyes.

"Whatever you do, don't let go," Mozart warned as he knelt and counted a moment. On the count of three, he opened into a forward run. Speeding from Denetta's old apartment and hurled himself across the street below them as if no longer bound by any sense of gravity or physics. Mozart and Wina hurtled through the air, as Mozart aimed for a narrow extended wooden beam held up by a low crane. The artificial stuck the landing precisely, and as the beam dipped in their direction from the combination of impact and weight, Mozart leaned over and grabbed the wood with both hands. And then, bolting straight, he reached the centre of gravity where the weight tipped backwards, at which point the artificial threw himself running forward once again.

"Do you see the landing platform?" Mozart asked, showing no signs of exertion or breathlessness. "Straight ahead, up to levels." Wina nodded.

"You doing okay?" Mozart could feel the strength of her fear as she clutched him tight. Wina just nodded and clasped tighter.

As they dropped off into a central alley, Mozart barrelled down the road, flinging himself up across barrels, carts and on one occasion, he bounded up and over the roof of a man's tri-cart. As he reached the end of the alley, he swung them up onto the next roof.

"Look, I think I see a meteor!" Wina laughed. Mozart ran harder, running up walls, leaping through windows and then after he began running seven minutes ago, he clambered over the lip of the landing pad. An artificial lay inactive in the pilots' chair and Mozart threw him out, ordering Wina to board.

"Whatever you do, keep your eyes closed, and stay buckled in." Wina started buckling herself in as Mozart powered up the rotors, and instead of bringing them up slowly, he pushed them from 'park' to 'maximum". The VTOL burst from the ground, its engines straining in an ear-piercing whine.

"I want to watch the meteor. I've never seen one." Wina complained as her eyes traced the star and its burning contrail come in from the northeast.

Theo stood out on his balcony, watching the sky over Fort Dallas. The Irving breach was no longer the only one. To the south, the roof over Hutchins had collapsed, while over at Lancaster, the ceiling was likewise crumbling. Way above in the sky, his forces were unable to stop Landmesser's bombers. He leaned over and picked up his drink and put it to his lips. The coffee was cold and dark as his eyes. *This was not the time for alcohol or cigars,* he mused. *War requires black coffee.*

From where he stood, he could see that the Tube stations were now burning. Those that had hoped to escape there were probably dead too. Only Smoking ruins remained for them to discover.

Kelly entered his office and saw that he was standing out on the balcony. She wrapped her arms around herself. There was no way she could go out there. It didn't matter if the world was ending, stepping outside miles above the ground was not going to happen. She moved to stand at the balcony's doors.

"We have to go. Holland wants us in the executive shelter. There is nothing you can do now. I hate to say, closed for business." She forced a smile even if he wasn't looking at her. "Let the General do her job. It'll be okay." As if to show that was a lie, the sky shuddered as one-quarter of the roof collapsed, annihilating Lancaster and the surrounding area. The impact shook the whole city, and even the pyramid groaned and moved. The balcony lurched to the right, and Theo was thrown to the ground. Kelly screamed as she was hurled out onto the two-acre verandah. "My God, Theo! We have to go before the elevators are taken out."

The man shook his head. His brown face grew dark with fury. He pushed himself up. "No,"

Coming to his feet, he shook his head. "No. I'm not going to run and hide. I didn't build all of this to lose to some out of nowhere nobody. *I Am Theo Magnus!*"

Theo slammed his hands down on the retaining wall, spit flying from his mouth as he screamed. "Come out here; look at what we made. Look at what they are doing to our world!" Theo turned and walked towards her. Kelly stood frozen at the doorway and grabbed onto the frame, shaking her head furiously. She could feel cold sweat breaking out and embracing her.

"No, No, I can't, Theo," Magnus strode over and grabbed her by the woman's left wrist and began pulling her. "Noooo," Kelly slipped down to the floor, keeping her right hand attached to the door seal.

"We are gods, Kelly, and gods fear nothing!" He turned and wrenched her other hand free, now dragging Kelly, who was shrieking like the damned. Theo seemed completely oblivious or indifferent to the terrified woman. "Look out at our world, look what those Visigoths have done to our world. Theos genetically heighten strength was far superiors to Kelly's own. He lifted her by the upper arms and slammed her against the railing. Kelly's deathly white face framed her large eyes. There before her, she saw the destroyed roof, everywhere gaping holes now allowed rebel aircraft in; aircraft engaged in combat against Omegas paltry fighters. High above them, Kelly could hear God hammering on the dome above them. Brilliant red-orange blossoms of destructions bloomed as Landmesser carpet-bombed the roof. An ear-splitting crack drowned all sound out as she observed the seal line between the two halves of the dome breach. Horrific snaps followed as the latching locks began to be rent asunder.

"Gaze upon what ignorance and envy have destroyed; here falls opulence and wisdom, now laid low by dull and hateful." Theo shook his head.

"Theo, I'm going to be sick," Kelly gagged, but he shoved her further out. Looking down the side of the building, she could see multiple ragged holes, many burning. To her, it seemed as if most of the ground floors were now stormed by people seeking cover from the collapsing roofing.

"Theo, please let me go,"

The rest of her protests became a scream as Theo stepped up onto the railing dragging Kelly with him. His hands were tighter than coiled springs. He looked down at her, his face a portrait of tranquil madness. He looked at her and shook his head.

"The die is cast," with that, Theo stepped out into thin air, pulling Kelly with him.

Kelly's eyes could not close as she plummeted toward the side of the building. Her brain could not process what was happening, and with cruel mercy, she suffered an aneurysm that killed her before she impacted against the wall four floors down. Theo struck the side of the glass pyramid, shattering his shoulders, but he did not die. His hands released their grip on Kelly's body, and he watched as she began a long tumbling roll down the Olympian tetrahedron. Theo flipped over onto his chest so that his face looked inward on the offices and remaining personal as the man slid down. He could already feel that his face was being abraded against the glass as he moved down. His feet and toes tried to find purchase instinctively, but none was to be found. All around him, he could see more of the roof tumbling down and great pieces striking the sides of the building.

"Oh my God," Holland now stood alone in the command centre. She had ordered everyone to evacuate as it was clear the city was lost and that the rebels would now gain complete tactical control of Fort Dallas – or whatever remained of it. She had unlocked and flipped over the transparent cover to Omegas kill switch. This final act would send a pulse out that would kill every single person fitted with a Neuromonitor. When she depressed the button, it would have an uninterruptable thirty-second countdown that assured no Omegan prisoners. She pushed the button, and as she did, she saw that the room went dark as a great rushing of wind exploded the windows inward.

Enveloped in a ball of fire, Uriel and Theodosia moved at Mach Twenty-five; nineteen-thousand, one hundred eighty-one miles per hour; entering the atmosphere over Moscow. As the International Space Station hit the atmosphere, its solar cells immediately began slowing their descent as the station's shards started to break apart. By the time the ship reduced speed, Russian Service modules Zvezda and Zarya had already been rent asunder and were now falling back over eastern Europe. European and Japanese modules Columbus and Kibo lay in the Atlantic. Now seeing the ellipse of North America, Uriel and Theodosia bid farewell to the Space Station and, igniting the impulse rockets, they launched eastward as the Space Station continued its descent.

Theo felt the building tremble because fifty stories down, he watched a massive piece of metal crash downwards, creating a burning hole in its downward path. He tried to move his arms now to grab hold of anything. Theo had hoped to die as soon as he stepped off, but that didn't happen. Now he looked at the inferno below him. The heat, flame and smoke had risen enough that he could already feel it. In less than a minute, he would fall into the awaiting hell. He turned his head to see into his building and perhaps find some impossible shred of hope inside. As he continued his downward slide, his chin struck a raised edge, and he felt enormous pain as the metal caught the flesh and ripped upwards, ripping the flesh from his chin to his lower lip so that it formed a small ghoulish hanger and jerked him to a stop. His mandible was now exposed, and his body weight ground to a halt. Ignoring the agony, he pushed his arms to rise. His shoulders ground against each other as he worked his shoulders up without supporting architecture. Tremulous fingers found slight purchase, and with that, he was able to bear down with his shoes and bring himself to a stop. In little more than a minute, he had fallen over seventy stories.

Holland ceased to exist as even a mist. The enormous weight compressed her; the vast weight compressed her office and the genocidal transmitter so devastatingly complete that there would be nothing to show evidence that they died there. Neither would any signal be transmitted, for there was nothing that existed to carry.

Saoirse led them into the elevators bay, and as they moved through the grand emptiness, she heard a great roar behind her. It did not sound like rushing wind as it came with impacting shards of the dome but a rising organic scream. Stopping and looking back, she saw a dark wave of humanity running towards Omega's building. Thousands, thousands upon thousands had formed the same idea.

"Stairs, take the stairs!" Saoirse screamed. Gabriel glanced at his sister and grabbing Glenda by the wrist, pulling her through the fire exit. Once inside, Saoirse led them downward three stories. The building shook once again and threw them against the walls. O'Sullivan exhaled.

"How far down?" he said as he helped his wife to her feet.

"Three floors." Once standing, she started taking the stairs two at a time.

Mozart was made aware of the falling orbital platform when his consciousness had merged with the System. A soon as he was able to deal with immediacies, he knew he had to evacuate Wina from where the epicentre was going to be; Worthy's VTOL was the perfect answers. As they sped across the countryside, the artificial man looked in the rear-view display and watched as the Fort Dallas roof finally collapsed with a soul-crushing rumble. Mozart threw a glance at the sky and then pushing the engine to the maximum. He held his breath.

"Take a deep breath, then exhale as hard as you can," Mozart instructed Wina. "Hold on tight,"

The shockwave of the final roof failure struck them hard; Mozart lowered the ship's nose slightly. Holding onto the controls tightly and used the shockwave as a surfer used a massive wave, riding it for all its speed. Looking down on the speedometer, he could see that the craft went from four hundred miles an hour to five in under a minute. Mozart knew it would only be a quick surge, but he needed every second. He could not yet see the Space station but knew it would only be for a minute longer.

He could see the Caprock Escarpment, the thousand-foot change in evaluation that stood out like a more magnificent Great Wall of China. Mozart piloted the VTOL into a plummet. As the aircraft touched down roughly, Wina yelped as her belt painfully restrained her.

We have to get out and down." Helping her unbolt, and once Mozart released the safety catch, they moved upwind from the aircraft. Laying down, he dragged Wina under him.

"Whatever happens, don't open your eyes until I say so."

Theo had pulled himself up into a ruined office. The floor was cantilevered towards the exterior, but it was only due to that incline that allowed him to find purchase and pull himself up. He was weak, blood dripping from his hands and cheek where bits of glass were still embedded in his abraded cheek. Theo watched as the bright light in the sky came in from the east. The tiny flare in the sky left a crimson and grey trail across the sky. His first thought was that he had been hoisted on his own petard; someone else lied about ICBM's. It was coming in absurdly fast, far faster than his weapons had been able to move. The light was growing in brilliance, making it seem like it was expanding in size more than growing closer. The glare flared blindingly on the remaining shards and pieces of the windows of the building. He wanted to turn away but found he couldn't. He found he now could feel the brilliant lights heat on his face.

"Close your eyes!" Mozart yelled as he placed his jacket over both of their heads.

Three miles above the densely populated city, the descending International Space Station was far from dead while having been decommissioned. All vehicles in near-earth orbit were required to have working reactors to maintain orbital position. The ISS's reactors were still producing minimal output, managed by shipboard computers and frequent on the spot inspections. That reactor was now so far compromised that it exploded with the force of a four hundred-eighty-megaton explosion. Directly below the explosion lay the Fort Dallas suburb of Plano. The hellish explosion vaporized the arcology. A microsecond later, the shockwave slammed what had withstood the hundred million degrees nuclear explosion. Everything within a ten-mile radius was obliterated or disintegrated. Nuclear laid waste to every city block. No buildings stood as legions of terrified souls below were immolated by the obscenity that is Oppenheimer's child.

When the detonation struck Omega Tower, anyone who had the misfortune of looking at the light immediately went blind and suffered third-degree sunburns. The air temperature was now a paltry ten thousand eight-hundred-thirty degrees Fahrenheit. In short, Theo was no longer alive when his clothes caught fire, nor could he smell his flesh broiling. He would only suffer for two micro-seconds before the shockwave struck the building shattering every remaining bit of glass and sending in the nearest direct line.

Glenda was lifted off her feet and slammed down; Saoirse fell against a pile of cots and heard her rib cage shatter. Gabriel was unfortunate enough to have been standing on a stepladder when the earthquake struck. It was a bad one, Saoirse thought. Maybe a nine pointer. Gabriel fell backwards as his wife watched in horror. Gabriel landed on the back of nick, right at the skull line. She heard the snap, and her man struck the ground but did not move again.

Glenda and Saoirse screamed as the air pressure increased to agonizing. They lay there writing in agony as the bulkhead door bent inward and then, breaking free, flew like an eight-hundred-pound piece of shrapnel. An unholy wall of compressed air filled the room, causing the inhabitants' lungs and sinus cavities to explode, hurling two sets of eyes onto the floor. The pressure wave caused every human orifice to evacuate. Even Glenda's nailbeds and Saoirse's gums bled. Neither of any of the victims' bodies would remain to be gazed up in disfigurement as a wall of nuclear fire struck Omega tower, flooding every window, door and breach with melting heat. After the firestorm ebbed, all that remained of the once Glorious Fort Dallas Arcology would be miles of pools of molten glass, stone, and steel. Even the vaunted city walls would only be a halo of sand and rubble.

"Holy Shit," Nhi gasped. Satellite images showed a brilliant flash, and then a mushroom cloud ascended upwards of sixty miles into the stratosphere. They watched as the visible shockwave and fireball spread outwards at hundreds and hundreds of miles per hour. They could be no doubt that the inferno had also destroyed Landmesser's rebels in the field, as well as any remaining Omegan forces. Finally, he watched as the destructive wave seemed to peter out as far as Hillsboro to the south, twenty miles past Mansfield up in Oklahoma, Sulphur Springs to the East. Lastly, the devastation wave dropped to a mere gust of wind in Jacksboro.

"I think," Two-Crows said softly, "That we have just watched the end of the world as we know it."

"And I," Nhi smiled as she sat down and began writing copy. "Feel fine."

ONE WEEK AFTER

Chapter 55

Along the road,

Texas.

The still-burning plateau lay to the south. The raging grass fires of Texas were still devouring the south. Even here, hundreds of miles away from the smoke above the horizon mixed into the morning's red-purple hues. They had stopped at the intersection of State Route seventy-nine and Goodman road. They had camped on the grounds of an old paintball field. Surprisingly much of the equipment held up, and Wina now wore protective gear and a dusty field jacket. Some battles would undoubtedly continue around the countryside, but Mozart had affixed a white flag onto the jeep, and they had used buckets of sealed old paint to cover over the Omega markings. It was just a car, and unarmed but they could take no chances.

"Why?" Wina challenged.

"You are safe, The Watchers have fallen, and soon the rest of the Seven will. I may have stopped Dorothy, but I can sense that there are still individuals out there. Minds I can sense, but that are shielded from me still."

"So? Are you entitled to be your own person? Why can't you have a life of your own?" Wina was upset, and tears streamed from her eyes. She didn't love Mozart and probably never would, but truth to tell, he was her only friend.

"This is my own life," He smiled. "Dorothy wanted Godhood, and I do not. I was created to serve, and I do not resent that. It is who I am as a person." Wina couldn't tell if words were resentful or happy. Maybe they were both. Wina shook her head sadly. "You're not a slave anymore. Neither am I." She reached out and touched his hand. "I'm not angry with you anymore. You didn't know any better. You have been nothing but nice to me since." She got out of the vehicle and took his hands in hers. "We both have an opportunity to make our future what we want it to be." Wina looked around them. "The whole world rose and declared itself free."

"Only because one sociopath's dream betrayed her," Mozart followed her gaze out at the smoke of Omega, "There are still others out there with that dream." She saw that his face now was etched with sorrow. "There are still others out there like those that took the lives of Randall and Denetta. Some people who see others as a means to an end and not as vessels of hope and promise."

"What do you mean to do?"

"Teach, learn, serve as best I can. I need to know if I am indeed the last of my kind." Mozart turned and reached into the vehicle and pulled out his backpack. Securing it on, he snapped the front clasp Wina put a hat on his head. It was plain with no motto or symbol — just a hat.

"If so, I must make sure that they do not still adhere to the Schism of Dorothy. "He smiled sorrowfully at Wina. "I have no delusions about who I am and what I have done. Pain that I have caused. Since I have caused suffering, I must now atone for that,"

"As I said, we're fine. I forgave you." Wina brushed a tear away from her cheek.

"You are not the only person to whom I have caused pain. I cannot seek forgiveness from the dead, and so I must work out my own atonement."

"Wina, what will you do?" He returned the question.

"Drive. I want to see the world for a while. When I'm ready, I'll go north. I want to find people with small dreams and quiet lives out someplace where it's green." She checked his shoulder straps and then toughed his face. "Maybe I will meet a nice guy."

"That will be a very fortunate man." He smiled and brushed the hair out of her eyes. Wina took a deep breath.

"So, it's time?" Mozart nodded. Wina forced a smile. "Okay, then. Just remember that it doesn't matter why you were brought into this world, nor does it matter what others think of you," She became emotional, and Wina held his face in her hands. "Just remember you are filled with love, love enough to take you to your last day." Mozart nodded and begun to weep. "You're crying."

"Of course, one cannot leave a friend without shedding tears, nor can one reunite with the same friend without the same."

She leaned in a kissed him. "Save a few tears for then."

Wina closed the door and watched as he headed West. He had heard that the man Landmesser was still alive, and Mozart said that he wanted to meet him   Wina waited until Mozart vanished into the heat oasis before she put the car in gear. It was a big car, and she had never driven anything so massive. In fact, Mozart had to teach her how to operate a vehicle in the first place. It had taken a couple of days, but now she felt she could do it, maybe. She pressed the gas and, looking out the window, she watched as the dust of Texas was thrown behind her giving way to a new sunrise ahead of her.

☐

CODA

US/Canada border.

Thirty-two months later.

Dark clouds hung in the pine-scented air, promising more rain. Looking up, she saw a sign that declared the log building a Bed and Breakfast. Calves aching and shivering in the chill air, the hiker took the painted handle in gloved hands and pulled. Once inside, she removed her leather coverings. Looking down at her hands, she saw the bandage had off the first knuckle of her left hand. She had dusted it on a rock, scraping it when she took a tumble.

An old man sat by a Ben Franklin stove whittling. His face deeply etched with hard years, and the hand that held the knife showed no malice. Seeing her, he set his carving aside and stood up.

"Hi, I was hoping to find a place to stay and rest up before heading north." She smiled and pulled off her knit cap.

"You have any rooms?"

The whittler nodded and waved her in. He opened the door and held it for her; the warmth struck her like a vertical blanket. Moving past her, he rang the bell. In a moment, a younger woman moved up; she was adorned with an elegant pink apron upon which she wiped her hands.

"Hi. I'm Bethany. Don't mind Jetters, mute since the day he was born." The girl offered Wina her hand. Returning her smile, she took the greeting.

"Hi, I'm Wina Stavropoulos. I'd like a room for maybe two or three days?" Wina slid out her Missouri state-issued identification card.

"Oh heavens, you walk that all that way?"

"Drove up until the South Dakota border. I had to sell my car for supplies." Wina slid off her damp all-weather rucksack.

"Can I see some identification? Sorry, but we have to phone the police station; make sure your good folk."

"Sure. Unzipping a backpack pocket, Wina pulled out her wallet. Bethany saw that the hiker had a Magnum pistol holstered next to the wallet pocket. She said nothing; all the campers kept guns on them these days for four-legged and two-legged predators. Wina handed over her ID.

After leaving Texas, Wina took up residence in a Sedalia refugee camp. She told immigration that the war had destroyed her home city. Wina saw no need to tell anyone that she had been a slave or what type. What did matter to the Red Cross intake specialists what that her having a working car made her invaluable to them. Wina earned money running people around and helping with reconnecting families. For this, the camps mechanics kept her gassed up and in repair. It was there they told her she got her first ID card.

When the hostess came back from her phone call, she handed the card back.

"I have a room open for the next four nights. Will that work?" Bethany smiled. 'It's been slow, winter coming in and all. I can charge you for just two?"

"Sure," Wina smiled. "How much?"

"Fifty dollars America or Canadian, I'm sorry, but we don't take any Corp money anymore." Wina smiled. "No problem, she handed her sixty and told her to keep the money. Bethany thanked her and gave her a key. Tucking the twenty in her apron, she at the carving man.

"Jetters, can you get her stuff?"

"I can manage." Wina waved her hand, and to her shock, he slammed his foot down on the floor angrily.

"I'm sorry, but Jetters love to serve people. He wouldn't know what to with himself if he wasn't allowed to help." Wina handed the older man her backpack. Taking them, the ash haired man bowed and went outside. "he came up here drunk and mean," But he had no place to go, so he simmered down, changed and well, he just started giving rather than taking." Bethany looked at the beautiful vista before them. "No telling what might change a person." Bethany looked at her new guest, who was holding her fingers over her mouth while tears welled in her eyes.

"You ok?"

"He reminds me of someone I used to know. I haven't seen him in years." Wina sniffed and rubbed her nose. "He was very much like that man down there."

"Some people are just called to serve."

"I know, but only the best of them answer.

REQUIEM

I have a rendezvous with Death, at some disputed barricade.

~Alan Seeger.

Authors Notes.

I began this novel in the Abilene, Texas, summer of 1991.

Cold Steel Days has gone through several iterations and many changes. There a self-printed copies out there if you can find them that will verify that. The most notable changes were the originally the slaves were Aliens called Onomites, and that the world was ravaged in a war with the Aliens. Also, there was a main character named David. The elimination of that storyline and character was made to make the novel more focused on the emotions and motivations of the central characters. In short, I had to kill my darlings.

It has been noted that the central characters seem to shift from time to time, leaving ait unsure of who the main character is, or are. For clarities sake, this is Ralph and Dorothy's story. It is also Mozart and Weena's tale. This novel is our tale, as well.

To be sure we have seen and experienced the year 2020 demonstrate and bring to view the enormous gaps in wealth, rights, and healthcare in western civilization, and my country, the United States. Moreover, we have seen the effect that classism and bigotry bring to a free society.

This book is meant to be a cautionary tale about choosing isolationism from others; whether it be by wealth, position, race, religion or culture. Cultural isolation brings death, decay, and destruction. A cord of three strands is not quickly broken.

To close, the author hopes that we can make our civilization a one of unification and celebration of both what makes us unique and what makes us the same. Let's hope that in the end, love and respect are the coins with which we elect to trade.

John R. White,
Massillon, Ohio.